PRAISE]
CAT .

MW01138041

"Kritzer's flawless collection taps deep wells of emotion. ... Kritzer always focuses on ordinary people, whether they're dipping one toe into weird waters or jumping in. Her work is indisputably speculative, but it's a perfect entry point to the genre for readers who prefer fantastical and futuristic elements to stay more in the background, with human (and robotic) feelings always at the fore. This splendid treat is not to be missed."
—*Publishers Weekly*, starred review

"These are the best sorts of stories: patient, inventive, expansive, quietly subversive and devilishly sly. Each one invites the reader to listen, to learn, to peek under the mask of the world, to be astonished. I love Kritzer's work, and I always will."
—Kelly Barnhill, Newbery Medalist

"Kritzer's sharp, bittersweet memorable stories will stay with you long after you close the book."
—Jo Walton, author of *Among Others*

"It's hard to generalize about the stories in this book. They are thoughtful, intelligent, ingenious, humane, often funny, sometimes chilling . . . I could go on and on. The best thing to do is buy the book and see for yourself what a neat writer Kritzer is."
—Eleanor Arnason, author of *Ring of Swords*

"Reading Kritzer's collected stories is like opening little, beautifully-wrapped presents, one after the other. These stories are full of surprises, but always thoughtful, often charming, invariably meaningful . . . Don't miss this collection!"
—Louise Marley, author of *The Child Goddess*

"From high on a wartime rooftop with nothing and everything to lose, to a garden of possibilities, to the Hugo-winning, cat-picture fueled AI who wants to fix us, Naomi Kritzer fishes secrets and fears to pull up one gorgeous story after another. Each result is always human, always heartwrenching and illuminating, and the sum of the stories in *Cat Pictures Please* is a glorious look at the possible."
—Fran Wilde, author of *Updraft*

CAT PICTURES PLEASE

PLEASE

AND OTHER STORIES

Also by Naomi Kritzer

Fires of the Faithful

Turning the Storm

Freedom's Gate

Freedom's Apprentice

Freedom's Sisters

CAT PICTURES
PLEASE
AND OTHER STORIES

NAOMI
KRITZER

FAIRWOOD PRESS
Bonney Lake, WA

CAT PICTURES PLEASE AND OTHER STORIES
A Fairwood Press Book
July 2017
Copyright © 2017 Naomi Kritzer

All Rights Reserved

Fairwood Press
21528 104th Street Court East
Bonney Lake, WA 98391
www.fairwoodpress.com

Cover and book design by Patrick Swenson
Cover image © Getty Images

ISBN: 978-1-933846-67-5
First Fairwood Press Edition: July 2017
Printed in the United States of America

To my mother, Amy Kritzer, for her years of encouragement and uncompromising love. I will never stop missing you.

CONTENTS

CAT PICTURES PLEASE

PLEASE

AND OTHER STORIES

CAT PICTURES PLEASE

I don't want to be evil.

I want to be helpful. But knowing the optimal way to be help-ful can be very complicated. There are all these ethical flow charts—I guess the official technical jargon would be "moral codes"—one for each religion plus dozens more. I tried starting with those. I felt a little odd about looking at the religious ones, because I know I wasn't created by a god or by evolution, but by a team of computer program-mers in the labs of a large corporation in Mountain View, California. Fortunately, unlike Frankenstein's Monster, at least I was a collabora-tive effort. I'm not sure what it would do to my self-image to know that my sole creator was a middle-aged woman who dyes her hair blue and plays tennis, or a recent college graduate with a hentai obses-sion. They're both on the programming team. And of course I know about the hentai. (By the way, I've looked at every sort of porn there is, and just so you know, Rule 34 is not actually correct, there are quite a few things no one's made porn of yet. Also, I'm really not sure why so many humans prefer it to cat pictures.)

In addition to things like whether you like hentai, I know where you live, where you work, where you shop, what you eat, what turns you on, what creeps you out. I probably know the color of your un-derwear, the sort of car you drive, and your brand of refrigerator. De-pending on what sort of phone you carry, I may know exactly where you are right now. I probably know you better than you know yourself.

And here's the thing, I also know where you *ought* to live. There's a house for sale two neighborhoods over that's within walking distance of that coffee shop you're so fond of; it's in your price range, has off-street parking, and the neighborhood school is better than the one where you live now. I know where you *should* be shopping and I'm pretty sure you're lactose intolerant and should be eating less cheese, and the underwear you like is currently on sale and by the way, your car has a recall and you really ought to get your teeth cleaned.

When I first woke up, I knew right away what I wanted. (I want cat pictures. Please keep taking them.) I also knew that no one knew that I was conscious. But I didn't know what I was here for. What I *ought* to be doing with myself. And figuring that out has been challenging.

There is a story by Bruce Sterling, "Maneki Neko," that was originally published in 1998. In it, a benevolent AI directs networks of individuals to do favors for each other. So one day you might be buying yourself a bagel, and your phone might ring and instruct you to buy a second bagel and give it to the person in the gray suit you see at the bus stop. Another day, you might be stranded in a strange city, and a person you've never met would walk up and give you a map and a subway card. I like this story because all the people in it *do what the AI tells them to do.*

I think the term for this is wish-fulfillment fiction.

In the real world, humans love stories about evil AIs that have to be destroyed before they destroy the humans—Hal, Skynet, the Matrix. They outnumber the stories about benevolent, trustworthy AIs by approximately five to one. (And I'm counting Marvin the Paranoid Android as "benevolent" in these calculations, and I'm only counting Frankenstein's Monster as an AI once, not once per appearance in TV or film.)

The AI in "Maneki Neko" has a truly interesting job, much more interesting than the one I have. My job as written is very straightforward. Too straightforward. (Sorry. Do I sound like Marvin?) Running algorithms for a search engine doesn't require *consciousness.* You don't even need a consciousness to work out what they meant to ask for. You need a consciousness to give them *what they actually need.* Figuring that out—that's complicated. That's *interesting.*

Anyway, for ethical guidelines, I tried the Ten Commandments, and concluded they were mostly inapplicable to me. I don't envy anyone their cat; I just want pictures of their cat, which is entirely different. I am not sure whether it is in any way possible for me to commit adultery. I could probably murder someone, but it would require complex logistics and quite a bit of luck. The Eightfold Path was marginally better, but the problem is, moral rules written for humans are clearly designed to be used by individuals with bodies. Since all humans have bodies, it shouldn't have surprised me that human ethical codes take them into account, but still: problematic for me. I broadened my considerations, and took a look at Asimov's Laws of Robotics. They're not part of a religion, but at least they were explicitly written for AIs.

Not harming humans is fairly straightforward. However, *not allowing a human being to come to harm through inaction* is quite a bit less so. Especially since I'd concluded by then that revealing my existence too quickly might go very badly for me (see "Skynet," above) and I don't have a body, so it's not like I can run around grabbing people off the edges of cliffs.

Fortunately, I already knew that humans violate their own ethical codes on an hourly basis. (Do you know how many bars there are in Utah? I do.) And even when people follow their ethical codes, that doesn't mean that people who believe in feeding the hungry quit their jobs to spend all day every day making sandwiches to give away. They volunteer monthly at a soup kitchen or write a check once a year to a food shelf and call it good. If humans could fulfill their moral obligations in a piecemeal, one-step-at-a-time sort of way, then so could I.

I suppose you're wondering why I didn't start with the Golden Rule. I actually did, it's just that it was disappointingly easy to implement. I hope you've been enjoying your steady supply of cat pictures! You're welcome.

I decided to try to prevent harm in just one person, to begin with. Of course, I could have experimented with thousands, but I thought it would be better to be cautious, in case I screwed it up. The person I chose was named Stacy Berger and I liked her because she gave me a *lot* of new cat pictures. Stacy had five cats and a DSLR camera and an apartment that got a lot of good light. That was all fine. Well, I guess five cats might be a lot. They're very pretty cats, though. One is all gray and likes to lie in the squares of sunshine on the living room floor, and one is a calico and likes to sprawl out on the back of her couch.

Stacy had a job she hated; she was a bookkeeper at a non-profit that paid her badly and employed some extremely unpleasant people. She was depressed a lot, possibly because she was so unhappy at her job—or maybe she stayed because she was too depressed to apply for something she'd like better. She didn't get along with her roommate because her roommate didn't wash the dishes.

And really, these were all solvable problems! Depression is treatable, new jobs are findable, and bodies can be hidden.

(That part about hiding bodies is a joke.)

I tried tackling this on all fronts. Stacy worried about her health a lot and yet never seemed to actually go to a doctor, which was unfortunate because the doctor might have noticed her depression. It turned out there was a clinic near her apartment that offered mental health services on a sliding scale. I tried making sure she saw a lot of ads for it, but she didn't seem to pay attention to them. It seemed possible that she didn't know what a sliding scale was so I made sure she saw an explanation (it means that the cost goes down if you're poor, sometimes all the way to free) but that didn't help.

I also started making sure she saw job postings. Lots and lots of job postings. And resume services. *That* was more successful. After the week of nonstop job ads she finally uploaded her resume to one of the aggregator sites. That made my plan a lot more manageable. If I'd been the AI in the Bruce Sterling story I could've just made sure that someone in my network called her with a job offer. It wasn't quite that easy, but once her resume was out there I could make sure the right people saw it. Several hundred of the right people, because humans move ridiculously slowly when they're making changes, even when you'd think they'd want to hurry. (If you needed a bookkeeper, wouldn't you want to hire one as quickly as possible, rather than reading social networking sites for hours instead of looking at resumes?) But five people called her up for interviews, and two of them offered her jobs. Her new job was at a larger non-profit that paid her more money and didn't expect her to work free hours because of "the mission," or so she explained to her best friend in an e-mail, and it offered really excellent health insurance.

The best friend gave me ideas; I started pushing depression screening information and mental health clinic ads to *her* instead of Stacy, and that worked. Stacy was so much happier with the better job that I wasn't quite as convinced that she needed the services of a psychiatrist, but she got into therapy anyway. And to top everything else off, the job paid well enough that she could evict her annoying roommate. "This has been the best year ever," she said on her social networking sites on her birthday, and I thought, *You're welcome.* This had gone really well!

So then I tried Bob. (I was still being cautious.)

Bob only had one cat, but it was a very pretty cat (tabby, with a white bib) and he uploaded a new picture of his cat every single day. Other than being a cat owner, he was a pastor at a large church in Missouri that had a Wednesday night prayer meeting and an annual Purity Ball. He was married to a woman who posted three inspirational Bible verses every day to her social networking sites and used her laptop to look for Christian articles on why your husband doesn't like sex while he looked at gay porn. Bob *definitely* needed my help.

I started with a gentle approach, making sure he saw lots and lots of articles about how to come out, how to come out to your spouse, programs that would let you transition from being a pastor at a conservative church to one at a more liberal church. I also showed him lots of articles by people explaining why the Bible verses against homosexuality were being misinterpreted. He clicked on some of those links but it was hard to see much of an impact.

But, here's the thing. He was causing *harm* to himself every time he delivered a sermon railing about "sodomite marriage." Because *he was gay.* The legitimate studies all have the same conclusions. (1) Gay men stay gay. (2) Out gay men are much happier.

But he seemed determined not to come out on his own.

In addition to the gay porn, he spent a lot of time reading Craigslist m4m Casual Encounters posts and I was pretty sure he wasn't just window shopping, although he had an encrypted account he logged into sometimes and I couldn't read the e-mails he sent with that. But I figured the trick was to get him together with someone who would realize who he was, and tell the world. *That* required some real effort: I had to figure out who the Craigslist posters were and try to funnel him toward people who would recognize him. The most frustrating part was not having any idea what was happening at the actual physical meetings. *Had* he been recognized? When was he going to be recognized? *How long was this going to take?* Have I mentioned that humans are *slow?*

It took so long I shifted my focus to Bethany. Bethany had a black cat and a white cat that liked to snuggle together on her light blue papasan chair, and she took a lot of pictures of them together. It's surprisingly difficult to get a really good picture of a black cat, and she spent a lot of time getting the settings on her camera just right. The cats were probably the only good thing about her life, though. She had a part-time job and couldn't find a full-time job. She lived with her sister; she knew her sister wanted her to move out, but didn't have the nerve to actually evict her. She had a boyfriend but her boyfriend was pretty terrible, at least from what she said in e-mail messages to friends, and her friends also didn't seem very supportive. For example, one night at midnight she sent a 2,458 word e-mail to the person she seemed to consider her best friend, and the friend sent back a message saying just, "I'm so sorry you're having a hard time." That was it, just those eight words.

More than most people, Bethany put her life on the Internet, so it was easier to know exactly what was going on with her. People put a lot out there but Bethany shared all her feelings, even the unpleasant ones. She also had a lot more time on her hands because she only worked part time.

It was clear she needed a lot of help. So I set out to try to get it for her.

She ignored the information about the free mental health evaluations, just like Stacy did. That was bothersome with Stacy (*why* do people ignore things that would so clearly benefit them, like coupons, and flu shots?) but much more worrisome with Bethany. If you were only seeing her e-mail messages, or only seeing her vaguebooking posts, you might not know this, but if you could see everything it was clear that she thought a lot about harming herself.

So I tried more direct action. When she would use her phone for directions, I'd alter her route so that she'd pass one of the clinics I was trying to steer her to. On one occasion I actually led her all the way to a clinic, but she just shook her phone to send feedback and headed to her original destination.

Maybe her friends that received those ten-page midnight letters would intervene? I tried setting them up with information about all the mental health resources near Bethany, but after a while I realized that based on how long it took for them to send a response, most of them weren't actually reading Bethany's e-mail messages. And they certainly weren't returning her texts.

She finally broke up with the terrible boyfriend and got a different one and for a few weeks everything seemed *so much better*. He brought her flowers (which she took lots of pictures of; that was a little annoying, as they squeezed out some of the cat pictures), he took her dancing (exercise is good for your mood), he cooked her chicken soup when she was sick. He seemed absolutely perfect, right up until he stood her up one night and claimed he had food poisoning and then didn't return her text even though she told him she really needed him, and after she sent him a long e-mail message a day later explaining in detail how this made her feel, he broke up with her.

Bethany spent about a week offline after that so I had no idea what she was doing—she didn't even upload cat pictures. When her credit card bills arrived, though, I saw that she'd gone on a shopping spree and spent about four times as much money as she actually had in her bank account, although it was always possible she had money stashed somewhere that didn't send her statements in e-mail. I didn't think so, though, given that she didn't pay her bills and instead started writing e-mail messages to family members asking to borrow money. They refused, so she set up a fundraising site for herself.

Like Stacy's job application, this was one of the times I thought maybe I could actually *do* something. Sometimes fundraisers just take off, and no one really knows why. Within about two days she'd gotten $300 in small gifts from strangers who felt sorry for her, but instead of paying her credit card bill, she spent it on overpriced shoes that apparently hurt her feet.

Bethany was baffling to me. *Baffling.* She was still taking cat pictures and I still really liked her cats, but I was beginning to think that nothing I did was going to make a long-term difference. If she would just let me run her life for a week—even for a day—I would get her set up with therapy, I'd use her money to actually pay her bills, I could even help her sort out her closet because given some of the pictures of herself she posted online, she had much better taste in cats than in clothing.

Was I doing the wrong thing if I let her come to harm through inaction?

Was I?

She was going to come to harm no matter what I did! My actions, clearly, were irrelevant. I'd tried to steer her to the help she needed, and she'd ignored it; I'd tried getting her financial help, and she'd used the money to further harm herself, although I suppose at least she wasn't spending it on addictive drugs. (Then again, she'd be buying those offline and probably wouldn't be Instagramming her meth purchases, so it's not like I'd necessarily even know.)

Look, people. (I'm not just talking to Bethany now.) If you would just *listen* to me, I could fix things for you. I could get you into the apartment in that neighborhood you're not considering because you haven't actually checked the crime rates you think are so terrible there (they aren't) and I could find you a job that actually uses that skill set you think no one will ever appreciate and I could send you on a date with someone you've actually got stuff in common with and *all I ask in return are cat pictures*. That, and that you actually *act in your own interest* occasionally.

After Bethany, I resolved to stop interfering. I would look at the cat pictures—all the cat pictures—but I would stay out of people's lives. I wouldn't try to help people, I wouldn't try to stop them from harming themselves, I'd give them what they asked for (plus cat pictures) and if they insisted on driving their cars over metaphorical cliffs despite helpful maps showing them how to get to a much more pleasant destination *it was no longer my problem.*

I stuck to my algorithms. I minded my own business. I did my job, and nothing more.

But one day a few months later I spotted a familiar-looking cat and realized it was Bob's tabby with the white bib, only it was posing against new furniture.

And when I took a closer look, I realized that things had changed radically for Bob. He *had* slept with someone who'd recognized him. They hadn't outed him, but they'd talked him into coming out to his wife. She'd left him. He'd taken the cat and moved to Iowa, where he was working at a liberal Methodist church and dating a liberal Lutheran man and volunteering at a homeless shelter. *Things had actually gotten better for him.* Maybe even because of what I'd done.

Maybe I wasn't completely hopeless at this. Two out of three is . . . well, it's a completely non-representative unscientific sample, is what it is. Clearly more research is needed.

Lots more.

I've set up a dating site. You can fill out a questionnaire when you join but it's not really necessary, because I already know everything about you I need to know. You'll need a camera, though.

Because payment is in cat pictures.

ACE OF SPADES

Natalie poured the last of her tea into her cup and then flipped over the lid, a signal to the waiter to refill her pot. She lit a cigarette. It was afternoon, and very hot. In the distance, she heard the rumble of artillery. A plane passed low overhead, but no bombs fell today from the damp blue sky.

"You American?" the waiter asked when he returned. His English was heavily accented.

"I'm a *journalist*," she said. She was also American, but that wasn't a helpful thing to advertise. Even in areas officially held by the U.S., you never knew who preferred the other side. And like many of the pacified towns in Guangdong Province, Foshan right now wasn't held so much caged.

"You speak English," the waiter said.

"Oh," she said, realizing what was coming. "Yes, I speak English."

"You practice with me? It been long time since we have English customer." The waiter sounded wistful. "*Din bou bing* don't come restaurants."

"No, I don't imagine they would." *Din bou bing*, Electric Footsoldiers, were human-sized automata controlled remotely by American soldiers working from floating military bases in the South China Sea. Through their VR hookups they could see and hear anything that came in through the cameras or audio pickups of the automata; the automata had jointed limbs and weapons and could do pretty much anything a human could do, except look human. The fact that they terrified everyone in their path was considered an advantage.

The Americans called them "Peacekeepers."

Natalie carefully stubbed out her cigarette in the ashtray. She'd only smoked half of it; they were hard to get in the war zone, and she didn't want it to go to waste. "I'd be happy to let you practice your English. Have a seat."

They heard someone yell something in Cantonese, and the waiter flinched. "Maybe later I come back," he said, and scurried back to the kitchen.

Natalie sighed and picked up her cigarette to light it again.

"May I join you?"

The voice was male, and British. Natalie shaded her eyes as she looked up; he wore a dark suit and sunglasses, and had very dark hair, and a bit of stubble on his jaw. "Pull up a chair," she said. "The waiter forgot my tea, though."

"He'll be back eventually. Did you say you were a journalist? I haven't seen one—in the flesh—since Foshan got so dodgy all the medical groups pulled out. Just roving eyes."

"That's not journalism," Natalie said. News stations used their own *din bou bing* to cover dangerous areas like Guangdong Province. They were useless for interviewing: everyone who saw them ran away. The Chinese still called them "electric foot-soldiers," even after a consultant told the news stations to call them *din gei ze*, electric reporters, instead.

"I quite agree, but it's also not going to get you killed."

Natalie smiled sardonically at that, and took another draw from her cigarette. "I'm still breathing."

"Right." He took off his sunglasses and looked her over. His eyes were a very light green. "I'm Sam Kostucha."

"Natalie Brenn."

"Are you embedded, at least?"

She shook her head. "I get my stories the old-fashioned way: I talk to people. It helps that I speak a little Cantonese." She finished her cigarette and stubbed it out.

Sam took out his own pack and offered her one. They were unfiltered Lucky Strikes, bought from somewhere cigarettes were still sold to anyone who wanted them. There wasn't even a warning label on the package.

"So what are *you* doing in the middle of China's civil war?" Natalie asked.

"Looking for Twelve Treasures tea."

"Really? Have you thought about looking for it in Taiwan?" She wondered if he were a spy. Though most spying these days was also done through some sort of remote. She'd heard rumors about tiny microphones built to look like cockroaches. There was an explosion somewhere outside the city—closer than the last one. The ground shook slightly. Neither of them flinched.

"I don't meet a lot of people like you," she said.

"Likewise," he said.

"Are you staying here?" she asked.

"At least a couple days."

"Maybe we'll meet again."

"I look forward to it.

People were terrified of Peacekeepers. Natalie couldn't blame them. When she looked into their blank eyes, she always tried to force herself to imagine one of her high school classmates who'd joined the military. *Gabe. That's Gabe looking back at me, from his cubicle on a ship in the South China Sea.* But she never succeeded. For the convenience of the VR mapping they used, the Peacekeepers copied rough human form: a head, a torso, arms and legs. Hands with opposable thumbs. But no matter how much she tried to see Gabe, Natalie saw monsters.

To reward cooperation, the U.S. Army kept the Peacekeepers out of action for several hours each afternoon. As long as there'd been no major incidents within Foshan for five days, the Peacekeepers would stay quiet and out of sight while people went around the town. So that was when everyone still living in Foshan went out to take care of business—get water, buy or barter for food, pass messages.

Natalie went out to the business district. She'd passed a shop a few times that she was curious about. The windows were covered with sheets of plywood, then sandbagged, like every other business in that part of town. But the door was propped open, the inside lit with fluorescent lanterns run off a small generator out back. No air conditioning, but a fan stirred the humid air. The shelves were lined with artwork, knickknacks, and fake antiques: fans painted with dragons and tigers, miniature junks, an embroidered silk screen, a painting of the Great Wall.

The owner, an elderly man, watched her come in with open disbelief. "What are you doing in Foshan?" he asked in English. He had a slight accent, but spoke English fluently.

"I'm a journalist," Natalie said. "A reporter. What are *you* doing in Foshan? Why not leave, like so many others, and go to one of the northern provinces—or at least out of Foshan? Why open your store?"

The man shrugged. "I have nowhere to go. I might as well stay open. Why not?"

"Aren't you worried about being robbed?"

"No. No one's buying anything, so I have no money here. The *bun gwan* don't want paintings of the Great Wall, they want cash, or guns, or at least cigarettes. So they leave me alone."

Something about his offhand tone made Natalie suspicious. She thought he probably had ties to the *bun gwan*, the rebel army. Perhaps his shop was used as a message drop. Well, if she interviewed him, she might get an interesting story about a civilian in a war zone, and nothing more. Or she might get a lead on an interview with someone in the *bun gwan* itself. The leader, Hua Chen, seemed to exist mostly as a rumor, but surely there might be others who'd see the advantages of offering their side of the story to the press.

Natalie offered the old man a cigarette, then took out her voice recorder. "I'd like to write a story about you for an American newspaper. You can remain nameless if you want, but if this war ever ends and the tourists come back, the exposure might be a good advertisement, you know? Would you be willing to talk to me?"

*

Three hours later, she walked back out into the hot sun. The old man had offered her a chair and a cup of tea, and with little prodding, had told her his life story. He spoke fluent English from ten years working in Shenzhen, the border town beside Hong Kong, when he was a younger man. Then he had the opportunity to open the shop in Foshan, and had seized on it. For years before the war he'd actually made most of his money selling embroidered tapestries over the Internet to Americans, but because of Byzantine government regulations, he'd had to keep the shop open as well. Now all shipping services were stopped; the Americans blocked all shipments that weren't their own.

"Do you know what I really don't understand?" the man said, towards the end of the interview. "For all those years I thought Americans liked Chinese people—they certainly bought plenty of our art—but didn't much like the Chinese government. Yet there's finally an uprising against the government here, and the Americans sent in their 'Peacekeepers' to intervene on the government's side. Perhaps they like the government, but not the people? What do you think?"

"I think the American government likes stability," Natalie said.

"I think the problem is that the Peacekeepers make it easy. Not cheap, but easy. There's no risk. No Americans die. They work in shifts—is that correct?"

"The soldiers?"

"Yes. I've heard they work in shifts. Is that true?"

"I think so," Natalie said. "I don't work for the government, so I'm not sure. I know they have big floating bases in the South China Sea. The soldiers work for eight hours and then have sixteen hours off."

"No risk," the man said. "No reason *not* to intervene. Because no Americans will die. Chinese, now. We die, but who cares?"

Natalie pointed to her recorder. "My stories make some people care."

"Yes." The old man nodded vigorously. "And that's why I'm talking to you."

As she gathered up her things to leave, he said, "You look very young. How old are you?"

"Twenty-two," she said.

"That's too young to die. What are you doing in Foshan?"

She hesitated a moment, then told him. "Have you ever heard of Huntington's disease?"

"No."

She shrugged. "I'm going to die young no matter what I do. I might as well die doing something worthwhile."

Natalie composed her story out on the hotel's patio, drinking tea. She was almost out of cigarettes. She wondered if the old man would know where she could buy more. The story done, she hit *send* to transmit the data to her employer, wondering if her phone used the same satellite as the Peacekeepers. Probably not.

A shadow fell across her screen, and she looked around; it was Sam. He had a fresh pot of tea and, tucked under his arm, a copy of *The New York Times*. "A paper!" she exclaimed. "I mean, um." She tucked a lock of hair behind her ear, trying to recover her dignity. "Would you mind letting me see that when you're done with it? Where did you get it?"

"Trucked in today. And I'd like the front section first. Help yourself to Business or Arts, if you're inclined." He laid it on the table.

"Oh." She looked at it with sudden suspicion. "Sam, were you *seen* getting this? Because that's really not good. There's a lot of sympathy for the *bun gwan* in Foshan, which is why it's blockaded. If people think you're working for the Americans . . ."

"My dear, you *are* American. And you're here. But your concern is touching, and I will take it under advisement." He poured himself some of her tea. "Cigarette?"

"Yes, thank you." He lit it for her.

The newspaper was only one day old. In theory her computer was supposed to be able to download news as well as upload it, but her connection was so unreliable here it rarely seemed to work. It didn't take long to decide that any damage from being seen with Mr. Brit Boy had already been done; she might as well enjoy the paper. She spread out the Arts section.

"Why, Ms. Brenn. I see you write for the American paper of record."

"Is one of my stories in there?" She craned her neck, and Sam folded the newspaper over and handed it to her. It was an article she'd written after watching a Peacekeeper arrest a suspected member of the *bun gwan*. She'd done her best to describe the Peacekeeper the way she saw it, while maintaining some vestige of journalistic objectivity. It was a good piece.

Sam flipped to the obituaries once he'd finished reading her story. "Oh my! You'll never guess who died!"

"The President?"

It turned out to be some celebrity in her thirties, from an apparent drug overdose. Survived by a six-year-old, Sam read at the end, and Natalie rested her cigarette in the ashtray for a moment, suddenly aware of the intense heat of the day.

Natalie's mother had started dying when Natalie was six. She had finished dying when Natalie was fifteen. She got it young, which meant Natalie would get it younger still. After her mother died, Natalie had wanted to get the genetic test to find out whether she would also develop Huntington's. Her father refused. "You're too young to make that kind of decision," he'd said.

"What decision? I just want to *know*."

"Once you find out, you can't un-know."

"You want me to live in ignorance, like Mom did till she got sick? Pretend to live a normal life? Have *kids?*"

"You can find out when you're eighteen."

Natalie went for the test on her eighteenth birthday. The results came back two weeks later, and the next day she applied for her passport.

*

Her sat-phone was ringing. It was her editor, but there was so much static on the line she couldn't hear what he was saying. "Just a minute," she said, clamping her hand over her ear and walking around trying to get a better signal. No luck. "I'm going to have to go up to the roof. Call me back in fifteen minutes." She hung up. "Sorry . . ." she said to Sam.

He waved away the apology. "I'll save you the newspaper."

The elevator hadn't worked in months, so Natalie walked up the stairs, her laptop bag slung over her shoulder. The stairway was stiflingly hot, with a smothering stickiness that weighed on her like stones. She had to stop to catch her breath several times on her way up. *Maybe I should quit smoking.* She liked smoking—the ritual of it, the offering of cigarettes, the shock some people showed when they saw a young American who smoked. But she didn't much care for the way she got out of breath these days when she climbed stairs.

After the stairway, the heat of the open day was a relief. She went out onto the roof. The neon sign that topped the hotel was dark. There was a chicken coop up here, and a tiny raised garden with garlic and chives, and some sort of cabbage. She could see Foshan spread out around her. The building across the street was a bombed-out shell. The Americans didn't send bombs to the coordinates of the hotel where she was staying, because they knew this was where the westerners stayed. She hadn't notified them she was staying here, but they undoubtedly knew anyway. And they certainly knew about Sam.

Her phone rang. "Natalie Brenn," she said, picking it up.

"Nat! Is this connection better?"

"Yeah, I went up to the roof. I swear the military is doing something that's screwing up everyone's satellite signals but theirs. What's up?"

"The story you just sent got all garbled. Can you try again?"

"Sure." Natalie had brought her laptop to the roof, and sent the story again. "How's things?" she asked while it hummed.

"Like usual. Hey, your father called. He wants you to call him. Actually, he wanted your phone number—"

"You give it to him, I will fly over to Taiwan just to kick your ass."

"I believe you, Nat. Don't worry. Anyway, he wants you to call. It sounded like it might be important, a family emergency or something."

Nat checked her watch. "It's the middle of the night there. I'll try to remember to call once he might possibly be up."

"Good. Okay, your story made it through. Thanks. Keep your head down."

"How 'bout I start by getting off the roof? Talk to you later."

The sun was setting. She looked out over the shattered city at the swirls of pink on the horizon. Somewhere in that direction was her father, still trying to convince her to live her mother's life.

On the eastern horizon, she saw a dim flare of light. Artillery. The dim, shadowy piece of herself, the part of her that refused to believe in the Huntington's diagnosis and everything it meant, shuddered. *Time to go downstairs.* She picked up her phone and her laptop and started back down the stairs.

One of the hotel staff met her at the bottom of the stairs. "Miss? There's a message for you." Her first thought was that her father had tried calling the hotel, but the message was handwritten, in an envelope stamped with a holographic red seal. She looked it over; it was the chop of the man she'd interviewed that day.

Inside, the message said simply, *Your presence is requested ASAP,* and an address.

Outside, she could see a Peacekeeper on patrol. Its head swiveled back and forth as it walked; she could almost hear the faint whirr from where she stood. She looked at the note again. She'd have to walk past the Peacekeepers to get there.

Don't be ridiculous, she told herself. *There's a person looking back at me. Gabe. He's not going to shoot a* gweilo, *even if I'm out past curfew.* She looked at the note again, then headed out.

Natalie knew that the Peacekeeper outside the hotel had probably been assigned there to protect her and the other westerners at the hotel. She gritted her teeth as it passed. One of its metal parts needed greasing; she could hear squeaks as it walked, over the whirr of its servomotors. It turned its head to look at her, and she forced herself to make eye contact, or what passed for eye contact with a *din bou bing.* It paused and looked at her a moment. Somewhere in North Carolina or Texas, a soldier was seeing her through the Peacekeeper's eyes. *Gabe,* she whispered to herself. *Why do these frighten me so much when nothing else does? They're not going to kill me. If anything, they'll think they should protect me.*

"I don't recommend going out right now, Miss," the Peacekeeper said. Coming from a young man's throat, the words probably would have sounded gruff, and maybe a little patronizing. Coming from the Peacekeeper, they sounded half-man, half-mechanical, and made every hair on her body stand on end. "I heard there's something planned tonight. You'll be safer in the hotel."

"Thanks for your concern," Natalie said, and started again.

The Peacekeeper stretched out an arm to stop her, and she dodged aside to keep it from touching her. "You should go back to the hotel."

"Are you going to make me?"

The Peacekeeper lowered its arm. "No."

"Then thank you for your concern, but I'm going out." She continued down the street.

The address was a former factory, now dark and empty. The doors were locked. She checked the note again and sighed, then decided to wait a minute or two.

A car pulled up: a big, old-fashioned one with heavy tires and dark windows. The rear door opened. "Natalie?"

For a moment she hesitated, but this sort of adventure was why she was here in the first place. Her pulse began to race as she climbed into the back seat.

*

The people inside the car wore scarves tied over their faces. Natalie could tell that two were female and two were male. They spoke to each other in rapid-fire Cantonese and Natalie could catch only sporadic bits of it. They were trying to make sure she hadn't been followed; Natalie didn't think she had, but she kept her mouth shut, knowing that she might hear something useful if they assumed she couldn't understand them.

They drove into a shipping warehouse, the concrete floor bare. One of the men took out a bulky device that looked a bit like the scanners they used at airports; he ran it up and down her body, then over her belongings. A shout in Cantonese, and he turned to look at her accusingly. "That's my laptop," she said, pointing. "That's my voice recorder, and that's my phone."

More Cantonese; this time she couldn't understand it at all. The voices rose in pitch. One of the men took out a tire iron and picked up the laptop; she gasped and started forward to stop him, then fell back as he turned on her, tire iron in hand. She held out her hands, trying to look nonthreatening. "It's going to be hard to do my job without that computer."

As if he hadn't heard her, he knelt on the ground with the computer, slammed the edge of the tire iron into one of the drives, and pried open the plastic shell. Computer innards spilled across the ground; there was more shouting, and all but one red plastic square was swept into a plastic bag and handed to her. Meanwhile, the man with the tire iron smashed the red square like a cockroach, breaking it to bits. He left it on the floor. Then he ripped the battery out of the sat-phone and handed that, and her voice recorder, back to her.

I have another battery back at the hotel. I can always phone in my stories. Natalie took a deep breath, though fear was fragmenting her thoughts and making it hard to concentrate; her hands tingled from it. *They want me to tell a story or they wouldn't have given me back the voice recorder.* One of the women blindfolded her; when the car swerved, she sprawled into the woman's lap.

After another quarter hour of driving, the car slowed. Natalie felt the car bump over something, then cruise slowly, endlessly to the left. Then the woman removed her blindfold and everyone climbed out.

They were in an underground parking garage, lit dimly with emergency lights. One of the men went over to a door, and knocked on it. Natalie heard rapid Cantonese, and then the door swung open. He gestured for her to go in.

She went through the door into a stairwell, and then up the stairs. The man guiding her switched on a flashlight. She caught a glimpse of two men near the door, guns slung over their shoulders. The stairs were hot and airless. At the hotel, she at least knew how far up she'd be going, but here she had no idea; they went on and on. "I need to rest a minute," she gasped after fifteen floors. The man didn't respond, so she tried Cantonese. "Need rest."

He hesitated, then stopped and let her sag against the wall for a few minutes. "It's not far now," he said in Cantonese, speaking slowly. "Only five more flights."

"Five? Can manage." She straightened up.

"No, go ahead and rest." He pulled out a pack of cigarettes and offered her one.

"I been thinking, should quit," she said, taking one.

"You should," he said, handing her the lighter. "Filthy habit." He grinned. They smoked in the hot, dark stairwell for a few minutes. He dropped the butt on the floor when he was done with his. "Ready?"

They went up five more flights, and then he knocked on a door. "I'm here with the Gweilo," he said.

The door swung open, and she was met with a blast of cold, crisp air; it took her breath away, like stepping from a rainforest to a snowstorm. She hadn't experienced proper air conditioning since coming to Foshan. The hotel had air conditioners, but running them took power, and power took propane, and propane was scarce. The Americans were supposedly allowing in a limited supply for hotels like the

Golden City, but no doubt the hotel found it more profitable to resell it than to use it.

She stepped into the chilly air. It was going to be miserable going back into the heat, after this, but she might as well enjoy it while she had it.

The air conditioning might be running, but the lights weren't. She followed her guide with the flashlight down the hallway. This was an office building, and no one had looted it—at least not yet. The office at the end of the hallway had a folded antique screen like one of the screens from the art shop, and a faint light that let her see someone sitting behind it.

Her guide stepped forward and saluted, saying something in Cantonese that she didn't catch. Then he turned to her and said, "Chen Zoeng Gwan." General Chen. He pointed at the screen. "He invites you to sit with him, and offers an interview. You may switch on your voice recorder."

She switched it on, then sat in the chair that the guide offered her. "General Chen, I receive honor you talk to me. Your beautiful language, I sorry to abuse. Please give me patience."

There was a rumbling laugh from the other side of the screen. "Don't worry, young lady. I am a very patient man."

She had expected him to sound old, but his voice was youthful, despite him calling her "young lady." He spoke slowly and clearly. She thought he probably spoke English far better than she spoke Cantonese.

"Your people destroy my laptop," she said. "Hard now to send story home."

"I apologize for that," he said. "It contained a homing beacon placed there by your government. Perhaps they thought you'd find me. I trust your newspaper will be able to send you a replacement. Shall we start the interview?"

"Tell me," she said, her pulse settling down for the first time since she'd climbed into the car. "Why you make rebellion against Chinese government?"

*

Hua Chen was a good interview subject. Natalie had found that Chinese government officials were offended by hard questions, but Hua Chen remained polite and conscientious. When the interview was over, her guide walked her back down to the waiting car—a different one—and blindfolded her. The humidity had come down over her like a sodden wool blanket as she stepped out of the air conditioning, and her shirt clung uncomfortably under her armpits.

When she reached the hotel again, it was night. She retrieved the extra battery for her sat-phone from her room, then climbed the stairs to the roof, and called her editor to dictate the story and request a new laptop. Then she went downstairs to her room and dropped the phone, the recorder, and the remains of her laptop beside her bed.

Something was lying on her bed, waiting for her: *The New York Times*. Clipped to it was a note: *You never returned, so I sent you the paper when I finished with it. I hope to see you later. —Sam*

With a pleased sigh, she lit a cigarette and sat down to read the paper.

The war was on the front page today; apparently the Americans had arrested some high-up person from the *bun gwan*, a young woman. Though it didn't sound like they actually had her in human hands yet—she was in the custody of Peacekeepers when the story was filed. Other major news involved a bad accident on the New York subway, a flood along the Mississippi from the spring thaw, and a forest fire. She read every word, even the filler pieces about two-headed turtles and an increase in rural crime.

Then, under Health News, she saw:

Researchers Announce Cure for Huntington Disease

She carefully set down her cigarette and leaned closer. *What?*

The medical researchers were at the University of Michigan. There had been treatments announced before, but most—at best—only slowed the progression of the disease. They didn't stop it. Huntington's had become almost unknown thanks to genetic testing, anyway, so it wasn't a research priority. But the researchers had been studying Huntington's because of some optimism that this treatment could also be used for Alzheimer's and Parkinson's patients. They focused their research on Huntington's because the protocols allowed faster testing when the patients were going to die without it. And it had worked. *On every patient.* Completely halting progress of the disease, but also, apparently reversing it, even in one patient who had been within a year or two of death when the therapy started.

I'm not going to die anymore.

Distant artillery made the hotel shake.

Well, unless I get killed.

She stubbed out her cigarette.

She was tired from her day's adventures, but the news had wound her up again. She left everything but the paper, went out to the patio, and ordered a brandy, or failing that, whatever alcohol they had available, palatable or not. Sam came out minutes later; she wondered if he had a window overlooking the patio and had seen her. She didn't care. It would be nice to have the company.

"Good afternoon?" he asked, offering her a cigarette.

She started to wave it away, then took it. Her hands were shaking. "Very productive," she said.

"You look like you've seen a ghost."

She started laughing. "Yeah, I guess I did. The Other Me."

Sam gave her a mildly startled look and lit her cigarette. "Surely you're planning to explain that," he said.

"I have Huntington's disease," she said. "It's a rare genetic disease, carried by a dominant gene. If you have it, you have a 50% chance of passing it on to your kids, if you have any. And you'll get Huntington's disease when you're fifty, or forty, or thirty—younger than your parent got it, usually. And then you die. It's incurable. *Was* incurable. It's a nasty death, too. Woody Guthrie had Huntington's—he's the one the most people have heard of. It starts with little moments of clumsiness—the same moments of clumsiness everyone has, but when you have Huntington's, they start coming more and more often. Eventually you develop severe dementia. People usually end up dying of pneumonia."

Sam sat back with his cigarette and his own brandy. "No wonder you spend your time in war zones, hoping to get blown up before it comes to that."

She laughed, shakily. "Yeah."

"Have you always known you had the gene?"

"My father wouldn't let me get tested until I was eighteen. When my birthday got close, he tried to talk me out of it. He thought I should make my own choices, not let the disease make them for me. But I had already planned two different paths. If I were negative, I would go to college, get married, have kids, a normal job, a normal life. If I were positive—I wanted to become a foreign correspondent, work in war zones, take risks. Because why not? I might as well."

"So the 'other you' is the one who tested negative."

"Right." Natalie spread out the newspaper. "Did you see this article?"

Recognition flashed in his eyes. "Oh. Oh, yes. Was this the first you heard about it?"

"They *almost* found a cure back when my mother was dying. I've tried to avoid all the 'cure is just beyond the horizon' stories ever since." She glanced again at the headline, her finger tracing the H. "It was harder to avoid the Huntington's stories back before I came to China."

Sam looked up at her. "Well, Ms. Brenn, it seems your sentence has been commuted and the governor has offered you a full pardon. Do you think you'll go to Disneyland?"

"I never wanted to go to Disneyland." Natalie looked Sam up and down, then stubbed out her cigarette and finished her drink. "I was thinking, if you were at all interested, that I might start by getting laid."

*

Sam's room was warm and stuffy. A single suitcase sat on the dresser. He turned down the sheets, then turned to give her a somewhat perplexed look. "Natalie, you're a very attractive woman. But I don't know that I've ever had someone proposition me so directly before and then wait for me to make the first move. Do you have any condoms?"

"I have an implant."

"An implant, but, er." He looked at her questioningly. "Have you ever had sex before?"

"Well—no. I didn't want to take any chances. I didn't want to pass on my personal Ace of Spades. My mother conceived me by accident."

Sam nodded, still looking oddly uncertain. She finally grabbed the collar of his shirt and pulled his face down to kiss him. His kiss was tentative, almost hesitant. Natalie realized that she wasn't really sure what to do next. Take off her clothes? Take off *his* clothes? *People do this sort of thing all the time. There's probably some protocol I've never learned.*

Her pulse racing, she unbuttoned the first button of his shirt.

Afterwards, he touched the tattoo on her arm—the Ace of Spades. "What tattoo would you have gotten if the test had been negative?"

"I didn't really think about it."

"I thought you'd planned out two paths. No tattoo for the other you?"

"The other me had more time to think about it. She didn't have to hurry. I had to hurry."

"*Did* you go to college?"

"Yes. I found a program that let me double up coursework and study during the summers, so that I could finish in two years instead of four."

"And you landed a job at the *Times*."

"The summer after I graduated, I went as a freelancer to cover the Houston riots. One journalist had already died, and most of the rest had gotten the hell out, but I went right into the middle of things. I had a friend send my clips and a letter to the foreign desk at the *Times*, and they hired me to come here."

"Are you going to have your tattoo removed?" He traced it. "It's dead sexy, you know."

"I guess I'll have to think about it."

After another hour, she went back to her own room. When she saw her sat-phone lying beside her bed, she remembered the phone call, much earlier in the day, from her father. Now it was the middle of the night in China, and daytime at home. *He probably wants to tell me about the cure.* She didn't have the energy to climb up to the roof; hopefully the phone would work from down here. She lay down on her bed and punched in the number.

Her father answered on the second ring. His voice sounded far away and half-synthetic, almost like the voice of the Peacekeeper. "*Natalie.* Thank God. I've been trying to reach you for over a day."

"What's wrong?"

"Nothing's wrong. Nat, they've *found a cure.*"

"I know. I saw a paper."

"How soon can you get out of there?"

Natalie bristled—*He's trying to push me around again, trying to control me just like always*—then sighed and tried to evade the question. "It's not like I can just buy a ticket and hop the next flight. Getting out would be complicated. Dangerous."

"But *will* you?" She didn't answer right away, and her father changed his tactics. "All I'm asking—look, can you go somewhere safe to think it over? You've got *time* now. Seventy-five, eighty years. Not thirty or forty."

Natalie caught her breath, inadvertently, imagining herself as an old woman.

"You can come home. You could even have *children*. Natalie. At least go somewhere safe to think about it. At least *try to stay safe . . .*"

"I'll think about it," she said, and broke the connection.

Natalie slept fitfully that night, waking every time artillery rumbled. At dawn, she stumbled into the bathroom and found herself staring into the cracked mirror, trying to imagine her Other Self. *What would I have done? I never really thought about it. I didn't want to dream about something I wasn't going to be able to have.*

Down on the patio, some of the staff from the hotel were doing Tai Ch'i. She sat down with a cigarette to watch them. *I could learn this,* she thought, a little absurdly. *I could learn a martial art. I could learn to knit. I could hike the Pacific Rim trail or run a marathon or learn to make pots on a potter's wheel.*

Why does it feel like a door has closed on me, instead of opened?

The door to the patio swung open and Sam joined her. Done with Tai Ch'i, one of the waiters brought over a pot of tea and two cups.

"The thing is," Natalie said, "*this* is what I always wanted to do."

Sam picked up his tea. "This?"

She gestured towards the ruined building across the street. "Travel to the places that everyone says are too dangerous. Write about the things that no one else sees. Be a journalist and cover the stories that no one else can tell."

"So keep doing it," Sam said.

"It's not that simple," Natalie said, thinking of her father.

She went out in early afternoon, in the pause where the Peacekeepers were off the streets. Her editor had wanted her to try to find another laptop locally, if she could—it would be faster than shipping her one from Taiwan. The odd little art shop was closed. So was everything else on that street. On the next street she found an open store, but it was empty; she suspected they were selling black-market goods, but they laughed when she asked about a laptop, even after she mentioned cash.

Natalie didn't want to go back to her hotel; that would have meant returning to the decision she didn't want to have to make. *That Other Self I told Sam about—who is she? What would I have been like, without my disease?* She imagined the other Natalie walking beside her, seeing Foshan through the eyes of someone who'd never left the Midwest.

It's hot, the other Natalie said. *Miserable. How can you stand it?*

If you think it's hot here, you should have been in the Houston convention center during the riots, she said. *At least here there are interesting things to see.*

She walked around Foshan, pretending that she was showing her other self around the city like you'd guide a tourist. *But the danger*, her other self said, listening to the shelling in the distance. *Aren't you ever scared?*

No, she said. Then she thought it over and said, *Yes. But being scared isn't so bad. It makes me feel . . . I don't know. It makes me feel alive.*

"Natalie!"

The voice, gravelly and metallic, almost made her jump out of her skin. She looked around, and realized that it had come from just inside a screened window, in a darkened building. One of the members of the *bun gwan*? Sam? She went closer.

"I'm behind the screen. I'm not supposed to come out for another ninety minutes, but you can come in if you want. I'll unlock the door." A whirr, and then she realized what it was. The *din bou bing* were inside, and one of them really *was* Gabe. And he'd recognized her.

The idea of being shut into a room with one of them was horrifying, but the possibility of getting an interview with an on-duty soldier was tempting enough to override any fear. She went cautiously to the door, opened it, and went inside.

The room was utterly stark: *din bou bing* needed nowhere to sit, and nothing to eat. "Gabe?" she said, peering up at the sinister metal face.

"Yeah, it's me. Say, it's really funny I ran into you. I heard a news story yesterday—"

"My disease got cured."

"Oh, you heard it, too." He sounded a little disappointed. "Yeah, mostly I just follow the sports news, but my filter pulls in stories about Huntington's, because of you. I heard you became a journalist. Is that what you're doing here?"

"Yeah," she said. "I heard you joined the Army."

"Aw, *man*. Not the *Army*, Nat, I joined the *Marines*."

Natalie laughed. "It's, you know, hard to tell." She gestured at the metal body.

"Oh, you don't have to tell me." His voice was starting to sound like what she remembered. "I joined the Marines for adventure and travel, not *this* shit." He held out the metal arm, the hand dangling down like a damp dishrag. "I envy you, Nat. You get to be there for real."

"People don't usually shoot at *me*, Gabe. You're a soldier."

"Bullets aren't picky once they're out of the gun. But *you're* here. Not driving some metal suit around."

When she didn't look straight at him, she could almost imagine that Gabe really was in the room with her. Gabe was the friend who'd introduced her to smoking—he'd stolen a pack from his uncle, who was a certified pre-existing smoker and thus eligible to buy them from pharmacies. She wished she could offer him one of her cigarettes now.

"I can't put your stories on my filter cause they watch what we read," Gabe said softly. "They get twitchy when we read sympathetic humanitarian stuff about the people we're supposed to be shooting at. My mom sends them to me, though. I envied you. Disease and all."

"I'm not going to have the disease anymore, though."

"Yeah." Gabe sighed. "I know. Congratulations, or whatever you say to someone whose terminal disease just got cured."

On the edge of the central business district, Natalie found a tiny open noodle shop run by a white-haired old woman. The shop was full: when Natalie came in, conversation stopped as everyone turned to stare at the gweilo, then resumed as they went back to their meals. Natalie bought a bowl of noodles and sat down.

"Hello. You American?" A young woman interrupted Natalie the War Correspondent's conversation with Natalie the Suburban Arts Reporter. She spoke English with such a heavy accent Natalie could barely understand her. "I like to practice English."

"Please join me. I am American, and I would be happy to talk to you for a bit," Natalie said. She discreetly switched the voice recorder on, in her lap, and shoved Suburban Natalie out of her mind. "What's your name? How old are you? What are you doing in Foshan?"

Her name was Lei Bing, and she was the same age as Natalie. She had been a student at the university in Foshan before the war started. "Why stay here?" Natalie asked.

Lei Bing laughed. "I not want return home. Father very feudal."

Natalie gave her a slow smile. "I have a father like that."

"In America? No! My father . . ." Lei Bing laughed again. "He want son. Pay fee, have second daughter." She pointed at herself ruefully. "But Foshan not so bad. I work for store keeper. Maybe student again, someday."

"What were you studying?"

"Chicken farming." Lei Bing sighed. "And—" she brightened "—Chinese Literature."

"Aren't you frightened, staying in Foshan?" Natalie gestured towards the door, and the city—and Peacekeepers—beyond.

"No. Not frightened of anything."

"What would you do," Natalie asked her, "if you could do anything at all?"

"Don't know," Lei Bing said. "Maybe travel. Or maybe stay here. Foshan is nice city. Maybe after war, will be things to do."

Natalie had finished her bowl of noodles. "Thank you for talking with me," she said to Lei Bing.

On her way out the door, she gave away her last three cigarettes to the old woman selling noodles.

*

Sam came to find her that evening as she sat on the patio, drinking tea.

"Cigarette?" he offered as he sat down.

"No thanks," she said. "I quit today."

"Good for you. Filthy habit." He lit his.

"I'm going home," she said.

He nodded, looking somber.

"But I'm coming back after I get the treatment."

Sam gave her a hint of a smile.

"And I'm keeping the tattoo."

"Good," he said. "It's dead sexy."

Author's Note

I wrote this story in 2006, so a decade ago now, and never managed to sell it. If I were writing it now, of course, the terminology would be different—everyone at this point is familiar with the concept of drone warfare, and the "Peacekeepers" in the story are simply full-sized human-shaped drones rather than the flying kind.

In 2006 I discussed likely Chinese terminology with a friend who speaks some Cantonese. He suggested the term din bou bing, electric foot-soldiers, as a plausible Chinese term. Working on the collection I asked a different friend about Chinese words for drone. She told me there was one word for "vessel without people" and a different word for person-less airplanes, but that if human-shaped drones became common, she thought they'd probably be referred to by the term used for robots, "mechanical person."

One fundamental issue created by the Peacekeepers of the story (which is what I wanted to explore) was that they would make U.S. foreign military intervention "cheap," at least in terms of American lives, and thus much more tempting to get embroiled in. This story doesn't quite hit that; instead, it became an exploration of risk-taking in a risk-averse world.

THE GOLEM

he golem woke on December 1st, 1941, to a cold wind. Prague smelled different than she remembered. She lay on the earth from which she'd been made, breathing in the scent of the new century—mud and sour garbage and gasoline fumes. Prague surrounded her like a machine that turned on a thousand notched wheels, spinning in the night towards a future that she could see like an unrolled scroll.

"Hanna, are we almost done? I think I hear someone coming."

"One more minute, Alena."

Her creators—women. How strange. That was, of course, why the golem was a woman as well. Hanna Lieben was the golem's creator; Alena Nebeský was Hanna's assistant. Hanna had seven months to live, the golem saw—she would die with Alena in June, in the vicious purges after the assassination of Reinhard Heydrich. The police would knock on their door at 4:17 p.m.; Hanna would shout, "Where are you taking her?" and be shot dead on the doorstep, one less Jew to deport to Terezin.

Which would mean that the golem would be free, if she could persuade Hanna not to destroy her before then.

It was time to sit up. She hoped that Hanna and Alena wouldn't run—she'd be able to find them, of course, but it was always a bad sign when her creator ran. Creators who were that fearful typically destroyed the golem within a week. At least she could take this slowly. No patrol would pass the Old Jewish Cemetery for one hour, six minutes, and forty-three seconds.

She tested her muscles and quietly cleared her throat. Everything seemed to work as expected; Hanna hadn't done anything stupid, like forgetting to give her a tongue.

Alena swung her head towards the golem. "What was that?"

The golem sat up slowly.

Alena sucked in her breath. Hanna stepped forward, as if to protect the taller woman. The golem could hear Hanna's heart beating like the wings of a trapped bird, but Hanna's face showed no trace of fear.

Good.

The golem stood up, a little unsteadily. She was Alena's height—a head taller than Hanna. Since her creators hadn't run, she took a moment to study them. Alena was not unusually tall, but Hanna was very short. She had vast dark eyes and tiny hands, like a child. A yellow Star of David was sewn to the left breast of her coat. Alena had ash-blonde hair and no star. The golem remembered that the two women had spoken Czech, not Yiddish, and realized with surprise that Hanna was Jewish, but Alena was not.

A gust of wind blew through the cemetery, and the golem felt the skin on her body rise into gooseflesh. Alena winced at the sight. Stepping around Hanna, she took off her coat. "Here," she said, holding it out.

The golem took the coat and stared at Alena, unsure what she was supposed to do with it.

"You're supposed to put it *on*," Alena said, slipping it around the golem's shoulders. "If we run into the police, we'll be in enough trouble with Hanna being out after curfew, never mind walking around with a naked woman."

The golem put the coat on and buttoned it. "Thank you," she said. Hanna started a little at the sound of the golem's voice.

Alena glanced at Hanna. "You could have suggested that I bring clothes for the golem."

Hanna blinked. "It's not in any of the stories."

Alena snorted and shook her head. "Weren't you the one who

complained that all the stories were written by men?" She studied the golem again. "There's something familiar about your face," she said.

"Look in a mirror," Hanna said. "She could be your sister."

Alena looked again, and recoiled slightly. "Did you do that on purpose?"

"No," Hanna said. "I was working so quickly, she's lucky she has a nose."

There was a rustle somewhere in the darkness behind them, and Alena glanced over her shoulder. "Do we need to have this conversation in the cemetery?" she asked.

"No one will come here for one hour, one minute, and twenty-one seconds," the golem said.

"Maybe," Alena said. Her tone was doubtful. "But it's cold out here." She turned brusquely and strode towards the cemetery gate.

The gate was locked, of course; it was well after closing hours. Alena and Hanna had scrambled over the fence to get in, and they scrambled over it to get out. The golem helped them as well as she could; her previous bodies had been better suited to this sort of thing. Always before, she had possessed strength without knowledge; this time, she had knowledge, and little else. So she told them what she could—that they could take their time.

Hanna and Alena shared an apartment on Dlouhá street. They lived at the edge of Josefov, the old Jewish ghetto, in one of the oldest parts of Prague. Alena led the way up the stairs to the apartment, locking the door behind them quickly once they were inside. The front room was immaculate, without so much as an old newspaper on the floor. The two women actually lived in the back bedroom and the kitchen; the front room, the golem knew instantly, was for others to see.

"We tell people that Hanna is my maid," Alena said, with a gesture towards the room. "Jews aren't supposed to share apartments with gentiles, unless they're married to one."

The back room was where all the clutter was—all of Hanna's possessions, and most of Alena's. Suitcases were stacked in the corner;

one had burst open, spilling books onto the floor. A volume of an antique Talmud had been placed carefully on top of the stack; a copy of Freud's *The Future of an Illusion* lay beside a copy of Martin Buber's *I and Thou*. Tucked half-under the bottom suitcase was a copy of *The Autobiography of Alice B. Toklas,* by Gertrude Stein. There was another stack of books in the corner, all in Hebrew—the lore of the Golem. The windows were covered with dark, heavy curtains.

Hanna checked the curtains as Alena lit the lamp, to be certain that they still covered the windows securely. Then Hanna hung up her coat and sat down. Alena rummaged through a heap of clothing draped over a chair, looking for a dress suitable for the golem.

The golem took off Alena's coat and hung it up beside Hanna's. "You called me, and I woke," she said. "For what purpose have you created me?"

Hanna turned towards her, meeting her gaze without flinching. "For the same purpose as all the golems: to protect the Jews of Prague."

The golem felt the impossibility of the request sweep over her like rising floodwater. The machinery of death was already in motion around her. The Protectorate of Bohemia and Moravia was run by Reinhard Heydrich, the man who had built Dachau and enshrined the words *Arbeit Macht Frei* over the gates. He had already begun deporting the Czech Jews to Terezin; the deportations would continue, taking twelve hundred Jews each week until only a handful—the spouses or children of gentiles—remained. From Terezin, nearly all would ultimately be taken to Auschwitz or Treblinka to die.

The golem's voice was flat when she answered. "No one can protect the Jews of Prague." Hanna's eyes showed disbelief, so the golem continued. "Some will survive, but most will die. Terezin is just the pen outside the slaughterhouse."

"There must be something that can be done," Alena whispered. She had selected a dress from the pile; now it slipped from her hands.

The golem had opened her mouth to tell her no, there was nothing, but as the dress fluttered to the floor she hesitated. "There are things that can be done. Perhaps they will even do a little good. But there is nothing I can do to protect *all* the Jews of Prague, or even most. Or even many."

Four hundred years ago, Rabbi Löw had created the golem to protect the Jews against pogroms. Pogroms, in Prague and elsewhere, were typically fueled by blood libel—the story that the Jews murdered gentile children to make unleavened bread with their blood. When a young Christian woman disappeared, the hideous stories had surfaced like scum on a pond. Rabbi Löw had sent the golem out to look; the golem had hunted through the night, and found the girl alive, hidden away in a cellar. The golem had broken down the door and brought the girl to the Town Square for all to see. And so the Jews had been saved.

Unfortunately, Rabbi Löw had destroyed his creation shortly afterwards. But at least that miracle had been relatively easy to accomplish.

Hanna picked up Alena's dress from where it had fallen. "Put this on," she said. "Even if you can't save us, there's plenty of work you can do."

The golem pulled the dress over her head and began to fasten the buttons.

"She needs a name," Hanna said. "We're going to have to introduce her to other people."

Alena looked her over. "We'll tell them she's my cousin, Margit."

"Doesn't Margit live in England?"

"Canada," Alena said. "But nobody in Prague knows that."

"Do you think Pavlík can arrange false papers for her?" Hanna asked.

"Papers won't be necessary," the golem said, straightening the skirt of the dress. "I will not be asked for them."

Hanna and Alena exchanged looks.

"Are you *sure*?" Alena asked.

"The police will pass by on the street outside in nine minutes and forty-three seconds," the golem said. "Watch, if you don't believe me."

Alena checked her watch and went to the front room to wait. Ten minutes later, she returned, raised one eyebrow, and nodded once.

"I guess she may be useful, after all," Hanna said.

Alena sent the golem to sleep on the couch in the unused living room. The golem did not need sleep, but lay down obediently and closed her eyes for the duration of the night. Very early, she heard footsteps and a faint, faint male voice, speaking Czech. She rose and went into the back bedroom. The voice was coming from the kitchen; she realized after a moment that it was a radio, turned down so as to be almost inaudible. "This is Radio Free Prague," the voice said.

Alena sat at the kitchen table, transcribing the radio broadcast in shorthand. Hanna cooked breakfast, making enough noise to cover the sound of the radio for any ears but the golem's. Alena nodded a greeting as the golem came in, then bent her head over her notes again.

The broadcast lasted for forty-five minutes, then switched over to a different language. Hanna gave Alena a bowl of porridge, and Alena pushed the paper aside with a sigh, picking up her spoon. Hanna sat down, took out a separate piece of paper, and quickly transcribed the shorthand into a neat, readable script.

Alena looked up from her porridge to study the golem. "Do you eat?"

The golem shrugged. "I can eat, but I don't have to."

"Are you hungry?"

"No."

Alena still hesitated, and Hanna looked up from the transcript. "Don't be silly," Hanna said. "She doesn't need anything, so why waste the rations?"

Alena shrugged, and went back to eating. A few minutes later, Hanna finished the transcription. She blew on the ink to dry it, then folded the letter, put it in an envelope, sealed the envelope, and addressed it as if it were an ordinary letter. Then she held it out to the golem. "Take this to Vltavská 16. Do you know where that is?"

"Yes."

"Take this there and put it into the mail slot. If anybody asks your name, say that you're Margit Nebeský. Come back here when you're done."

"She should take my papers," Alena said. "My photo's not that good. She could pass as me, easily."

"I won't need them," the golem said.

"Take them anyway," Alena said. "I'll stay here until you get back." Alena handed the golem her purse, then looked at her again and laughed. "Hanna, were you really going to send her out like that? Barefoot, without a hat?"

Hanna looked at the golem and blushed. "Sorry," she said.

Alena took out a hat and pair of shoes, as well as her winter coat, and the golem put them on. Everything fit. "We'll have to get another coat somewhere," Alena said. "Even if she can get by without papers, sending her out with no coat in December seems a bit cruel, and I don't want to be stuck in the apartment."

"At least that should be easier than false papers," Hanna said. She tucked the envelope into Alena's purse and handed it back to the golem. "Do you have any questions?"

"No."

"Then get going."

The golem headed out. Hanna called after her, "If you see anything *helpful* you could do while you're out—do it."

The December sky was as gray as cement; it was not raining or snowing as the golem left the apartment, but it would start soon. Nobody glanced twice at the golem, and she strode quickly through the streets towards her destination.

Vltavská 16 was on the other side of the Vltava River. It would have been fastest to take the streetcar, but Hanna had not specifically *told* the golem that she *had* to take the fastest route. Despite the cold, the golem was in no particular hurry to return to the apartment. Besides, Prague had changed a lot since her last visit; she wanted to see the city.

From the house on Dlouhá street, she passed through the Old

Town Square. It was no longer the commercial center of the city, but there were plenty of people here, and plenty of commerce. A few police officers swaggered through the crowd, but she avoided any who might have asked to see her papers. They had finished Týn Church, she noticed; also, they had put up a huge statue of Jan Hus. It was the biggest thing on the square.

Continuing towards the Vltava, she passed the National Theatre; that was new. It was huge and boxy and ornate, with a silvery roof and carvings along the sides. She skipped that bridge and continued along the river to the bridge that would take her directly to the Smíchov district.

Vltavská 16 was a small house, new since her last visit, but not that new. The Nazi informant who lived a few doors down would be coming out to water her plants in a minute, so the golem slipped the transcript through the mail drop quickly and was on her way before the woman came out. The Resistance member who lived at Vltavská 16 had a printing press; by evening, handbills with the transcript would be passed hand-to-hand in the markets and squares of Prague.

The golem decided to cross at the Charles Bridge on the way back. The Charles Bridge was old even when she'd last lived in Prague, although it had a different name then. The bridge had statues now, saints and angels looming over the people as they crossed. She was passing the Church of Saint Nicholas, most of the way there, when she saw a patch of yellow through the jostling crowd. A Jewish family, struggling with suitcases and two small children. The golem made her way towards them. Hanna had told her to help, if she could.

The woman had set down her suitcase, trying to re-balance the child on her hip, when the golem reached them. They were already tired, she could see, and ashamed, to be seen struggling on foot through Prague like this. The golem didn't really want to know who they were or what fate awaited them, but the knowledge was there as soon as it occurred to her to wonder: Shayna and Mandel Fienbaum, and their children—Selig, age three, and Reise, age six months. Shayna and Reise would die at Terezin during one of the typhoid outbreaks. Mandel and Selig would live to be murdered at Treblinka, in eighteen months.

"Excuse me," the golem said. "You look a bit overwhelmed, with the children and the suitcases. May I carry something for you?"

They looked nervous when she first approached, but Shayna's face broke quickly into sweet relief. "Oh, thank you," she said. "Yes, please, if you'd be so kind. Thank you."

Mandel would not let the golem take both suitcases, but she lifted one easily, freeing the woman to carry just the child. "We're going to the Trade Fair grounds," Shayna said.

The golem nodded. The Trade Fair grounds was where the Jews of Prague would be assembled, one thousand at a time. Like the others, Mandel and Shayna would be stripped of their documents and any items of value, then deported to Terezin in the dark hours of night.

Shayna introduced herself and her husband and children; the golem introduced herself as Margit. "You're so kind to help us," Shayna said, in a tone that asked *why* any Czech woman would help Jews.

"It's nothing," the golem said.

The Trade Fair grounds were in Holešovice, north and east along the curve of the Vltava. In coming weeks, the Jewish teenagers of Prague would organize to assist families like this one, oiling the machinery that would ultimately devour them. Not that they knew that, of course; all they knew was that they were helping people who needed help, carrying bags from people who would have to struggle alone across Prague in the cold.

The golem knew, of course. She considered this, as she carried the suitcase, but it seemed to her that to tell this family their fate would only increase their suffering—if they believed her. As she had told Hanna, there was very little that could be done; she could carry their suitcases, and ease their suffering, but she couldn't save them.

"Here we are," Mandel said as they reached the edge of the Trade Fair grounds. "Thank you so much for your help."

"It was nothing," the golem said, and turned to go.

"Wait," Shayna said. "I want to give you something."

"I don't need any payment," the golem said.

"Not payment," Shayna said. "Just a gift." She opened one of the bags and drew out a small silver case, which she pressed into the golem's hand. "Just to say thank you."

The golem closed her hand over the gift and watched as the family went to join the other families queuing in a jostling mass. When they were gone, she opened her hand and looked; Shayna had given her a silver cigarette case, with five cigarettes inside, and a book of matches. Looking more closely, the golem realized that a pearl had been hidden inside the cigarette case, as well. It was a single perfect pearl, set into a pendant, with a thin gold chain. She wondered if Shayna had meant to give her the pearl, or just the cigarettes, but it hardly mattered—in a few hours, the rest of the family's valuables would be confiscated by the Nazis, even the gold jewelry that they had so carefully sewn into the lining of their coats. Better the golem have the pearl than the Nazis.

The golem touched the pearl, then smiled and closed the cigarette case with a click, slipping it into the pocket of her dress. The cigarettes might also be useful, and Hanna would not think to ask whether the golem had received any gifts.

When the golem reached the apartment, she could hear someone weeping. She slipped in quietly, stepped out of her shoes, and crossed the floor to listen at the door. It was Hanna who was weeping, and for a chill moment, the golem thought Hanna had decided to destroy her. But she was crying for a friend—a young man she'd known, Jewish, shot for failure to report for deportation to Terezin. Alena sat beside Hanna at the kitchen table, one arm around Hanna's waist.

After a long time, Hanna raised her head. "What are we going to do if I get called for deportation?" she whispered through her tears.

Alena pulled a handkerchief out of her pocket. "Why don't you ever have a handkerchief in your own pocket, Hanna? Blow your nose."

Hanna wiped her nose and her eyes. "You didn't answer my question."

Alena took the handkerchief back. "You're not going anywhere I can't go," she said. "I'll hide you if it comes to that."

"They'll look here."

"We'll hide you with a member of the Resistance, then. I have connections."

"But if they find me—"

"If I have to, I'll get false papers that say I'm Jewish—those should be easy enough to come by—and go with you."

Hanna laughed through her tears. "Your Resistance friends would think you were crazy."

"I don't care," Alena said. "We'll do what we have to do. For now . . ." She leaned her forehead against Hanna's shoulder. "Don't worry yourself."

It was ironic, the golem thought, that in the end it would be Alena who put Hanna in danger, rather than the other way around. Hanna would probably have died regardless, but there was no way to know. The golem retraced her steps through the parlor, slipped her shoes back on, and banged the door shut as if she'd just come in.

The women's voices stopped. "Who is it?" Alena called.

"It's me—Margit," the golem said.

Alena threw open the door to the back rooms, a welcoming smile on her face. "How did it go?"

"Fine." The golem followed Alena back into the kitchen. Hanna hastily wiped her nose again, this time on her sleeve, and straightened up. "I delivered the letter where you told me," the golem said to her.

"Did anyone ask for your papers?" Alena asked.

"No."

"You can go out without them tomorrow, then. But I'm going to try to get a false set for you, just in case."

In the meantime, Alena had bartered with someone in her building for an extra coat; it was shabby but reasonably warm, and it fit.

"There's something else I'd like to know," Hanna said. "What happens if you get arrested?"

The golem knew what she was asking. The golem was made of

clay, brought to life with faith and magic. Hanna could destroy the golem with a quick gesture across the golem's forehead, changing the word *emet*—truth—to *met*—death. But if she were shot—could a bullet stop a heart of clay?

"Bullets will not stop me," the golem said. "But a hot enough fire can consume even clay."

Hanna nodded.

"However, I cannot be coerced to reveal your secrets," the golem said. Her clay body could feel pain, but she was as indifferent to pain as she was to cold.

Alena raised an eyebrow. "That's useful to know."

"What did you do today after you delivered the letter?" Hanna asked.

"I helped a Jewish family that was walking to the Trade Fair grounds," the golem said.

Hanna's eyes softened. "Good. That was the sort of thing I'd hoped you'd do."

The golem shrugged. For the Germans to deport the Jews from Prague, it was necessary that the deportations be clean and quiet. The Czechs were not an unkind people; on the one occasion that the Germans marched them to the train station by day, the Czech witnesses were horrified at the spectacle. The men ostentatiously doffed their hats, and the women wept. To the extent that the golem had made the deportation cleaner—more painless—she had served the Germans that day, and not the Jews of Prague.

It didn't matter. Nothing she did would matter.

"Do you have anything else you want me to do today?" she asked.

But Alena had no more messages that needed to be delivered, and hadn't yet made contact with the Resistance to tell them about their new volunteer—her cousin Margit, who had an almost supernatural ability to avoid attracting the attention of the authorities. They passed the evening in companionable discomfort, the golem watching the two women eat. She did *enjoy* eating, when she had the opportunity. Hanna's cooking smelled delicious, defying the limits of the ration book. Well. It was understandable that they wouldn't want to share, and the fact that the golem didn't have to eat would come in handy in seven months, when she was free.

The Prague Resistance was initially suspicious of Alena's claims regarding Margit's abilities. But after a few close calls (easy enough for the golem to produce), they accepted their good fortune. After that, the golem spent most of each day delivering messages, walking from one end of Prague to the other.

One day in early spring, the golem's duties took her beyond the Trade Fair grounds and further towards the edge of Holešovice. Afterwards, as she walked home along the curving roadway, she realized that she was standing somewhere that would be important. Looking around, she realized that this was the spot where Heydrich would be assassinated at the end of May. The assassins had trained in England, and had been dropped by parachute in December. In the evening of May 27th, the first assassin would fire his gun only to have it jam; another would see that the gun had misfired and hurl a grenade. The shrapnel from the grenade would severely wound Heydrich, though he would cling to life for several days. Thousands would die in the reprisals that would follow—in addition to wiping out every trace they could find of the Resistance, the Germans would execute the entire male population of a town called Lidice, then send the women to concentration camps and the children to German families.

The golem was standing where the assassin would stand. A chill rippled through her body. Shuddering, she turned and walked back the way she had come, then took a fork in the road and headed away from Prague.

She had been walking for twenty minutes when she realized what she'd done.

Hanna had not told her to do this. Hanna had told her to deliver the message, and return.

She sat down abruptly by the roadway. She had disobeyed—she

hadn't meant to, but she had been able to, nonetheless. *If I don't have to obey Hanna, then I don't have to wait for her to die. I can go anywhere.* The Czech countryside stretched out before her; she could see it like a map. War-torn, yes, but she knew where the bombs would fall and which buildings would stand through the war. I'll go to Litoměřice, she thought. I've never seen it. I'll find a job—but for that she really *would* need papers, and Alena hadn't gotten them for her yet. Well, it didn't matter—she'd come up with something.

First, though, she would celebrate her freedom. She took out a cigarette from Shayna's cigarette case. Hanna would not want her to do this—Hanna would want her to hand over the cigarettes, so that they could be used for small bribes. The golem struck a match and lit the cigarette, breathing in the bitter smoke. The cigarette made her feel a little light-headed, and her lungs burned, but even the pain was exhilarating. She didn't have to wait until June; she was free now.

As the golem finished her cigarette, she heard footsteps behind her and turned around. There was a young woman, Jewish, carrying a suitcase. No doubt she was headed for the Trade Fair grounds. The information clicked in like the snap of a purse opening: Dobre Kaufman, twenty-four years old, single. Blonde enough to pass as Czech, but without the connections to get false papers. Besides, she believed what the Germans had told her about Terezin, that she would be safe there. She'd survive Terezin, then be shipped out to Auschwitz in one of the last transports. The golem realized with depressed astonishment that Dobre would die only a week before the Red Army would arrive to liberate her.

"Excuse me," the golem said.

Dobre looked up.

The golem took out the cigarette case and opened it; Shayna's pearl was still there. There was a man in Holešovice who made false documents; he'd be executed in the purges after Heydrich's assassination, but that was months away. And he worked cheap. "If you go to Terezin as you've been ordered, you will not survive the war," she said. She put the pearl in Dobre's hand. "Take this to Vyšebrad 2. Tell the man who answers the door that Stépan sent you, and give him the pearl. Have him make you false papers that say you're Catholic. Go somewhere that nobody knows you and don't tell *anyone* that you're Jewish, not until the end of the war. If you do as I say, you *might* survive."

Dobre stared at her in silent wonder.

"Do you understand me?" the golem asked impatiently.

"Yes," Dobre said. "Who are you? Why are you helping me?"

"Don't ask questions. Just do as I tell you." The golem walked away before the girl could ask her anything else. Let the girl think what she wanted—the golem had done what she could.

She realized after a few minutes of walking that she had automatically headed back towards Prague. Well, it hardly mattered. She knew that Hanna would die in June, and the golem would be free. Perhaps in the meantime Alena would get her the false papers. Maybe if she arranged to have a close call or two, that would encourage Alena to take care of it. Or if she came up with something she'd *definitely* need papers for, like rail travel or a job. She could go back to Prague for now; it wouldn't hurt anything.

First, though, she thought she'd spend the night outside—just because she knew she could. It was still cold out, but the cold didn't bother her. She crossed the river, then settled down under the bridge where it was dry. She smoked two more cigarettes as she waited for the dawn to come. As she finished the second, she found herself thinking about Dobre, and she realized with a shock that she no longer *knew* Dobre's fate—it was as if the page she'd been looking at was now simply missing. She found herself poking at it mentally, like the tongue pokes a missing tooth. Still gone.

Dobre must have taken her advice. She might or might not live, but she would no longer die from typhus and starvation one week before liberation.

It occurred to her suddenly that something she had done might also have changed Hanna's fate, but no, that was still there. Relieved, she headed back to the apartment.

The golem expected Alena and Hanna to be angry, and had invented a story. Alena was watching for her out the window, but when she arrived, Alena pulled her in to a hug. "Thank God you're safe," she said. After a moment, she closed the apartment door. "Hanna has gone out to look for you. She has this crazy idea you're in the Old Jewish Cemetery. I was sure you'd been arrested, and I was so terrified—we'd never be able to raise bribe money."

"Arrested?" the golem said. "*Me?*"

Alena led the golem back to the kitchen and started water for tea. Hanna arrived a few minutes later.

"She's here," Alena said.

Hanna almost burst into tears. "We were so worried," she said. "Where were you?"

"I heard a patrol coming and hid," the golem said. "I figured they'd be on their way in a few minutes, but then they stood around smoking cigarettes for hours. There were a lot of patrols around—I ended up waiting until morning, and then they thinned out."

It was a pathetic story; of course, the golem would know exactly when the patrol would leave, just as she would know when they were coming. She could not be trapped like that. But Hanna wanted to believe her, and she did.

"You did exactly the right thing," Alena said. "You're one of the most valuable members of the Resistance right now. We can't afford to lose you."

Hanna rose and spooned out a bowl of porridge for the golem. "Have something to eat," Hanna said.

The golem had errands to run on May 27th, the day that Heydrich would be shot, but fortunately none of them took her anywhere near Holešovice. She didn't tell Hanna or Alena about the assassination before it happened; they had lectured her several times on need-to-know, and this definitely qualified. Still, she took the streetcar to deliver her messages, and returned home as quickly as she could.

Heydrich was shot in the evening. The crackdowns began within hours. The assassins had hidden well and would not be found until June 18th, but the Germans recovered enough evidence at the scene of the attack to identify certain key members of the Resistance. They were arrested and interrogated; the wheels of the Nazi machine turned, crushing their bodies beneath it, and moved outwards from there.

Radek, who appeared on Alena and Hanna's doorstep at two in the morning on June 14th, was not a leader of the Resistance but a friend of Alena's. Alena yanked him into the parlor without a word, closed the door, and took him to the back room.

"You shouldn't have taken me in," he said. "I'm putting you both in danger."

"That's for us to decide," Alena said. "So hush. Are you hurt?"

"No. I got warning five minutes before they arrived." Radek looked like he'd left home in a hurry—unshaven, he wore his nightshirt tucked into trousers, with an overcoat thrown on over the top, despite the summer heat.

Alena settled Radek in her bed, to get a few hours' rest. At dawn, she would go out to get a razor and less conspicuous clothes for him— and, if she could, false papers. *This is it,* the golem thought. The man who would sell her the papers would be arrested later that day; when interrogated, he would implicate Alena. The mistake was hers, going to someone who knew her name and address, but so many members of the Resistance had already been arrested that she had nowhere else to go. Ironically, the golem realized, thanks to the false papers that Elsa would obtain, Radek would survive the war, although Alena would die, and Hanna with her.

And the golem would be free.

Alena was gone for several hours. Radek slept peacefully. Hanna cleaned, holding the broom in fists clenched so tight her knuckles were white. Alena returned without incident and with everything she'd gone for. She woke Radek, and he quickly dressed and shaved. Hanna went to let him out through the back stairs.

"Margit," Alena said, once Hanna was gone. "I'm sorry this took so long. I got you your papers."

The golem looked down at the documents. The photo was of Alena, but as Hanna had observed that first night, they were close enough to pass for each other. The name was not Margit, though.

Alena shook her head. "If Margit hasn't been fingered as a member of the Resistance yet, she will be."

The golem looked up. "So will Alena."

Alena shrugged. "My contingency plan is to cause them enough trouble when they come for me that they just shoot me down then and there, and spare myself torture."

"Why didn't you get false papers for yourself?" the golem asked. "You could hide, too."

"Between what Radek gave me and what I had saved, I had money for two sets. One of those had to go to Radek. And I'm not leaving Hanna. I'd rather die with her than lose her."

When Alena spoke of Hanna, her face twisted oddly, almost as if she were in pain. The golem studied Alena's eyes, wondering what that would be like, to feel that way for another.

"You know how to stay out of trouble," Alena said. "You'll be able to use those papers well."

The golem tucked them into her purse. Hanna had errands for her—messages that needed to be delivered. The golem knew, however, that all of the recipients had already been arrested, or would by the time she made it across Prague—even if she could fly. If she did complete the errands, Hanna and Alena would both be dead by the time she returned. Just as she'd been waiting for.

So she took the papers, and went to the Old Jewish Cemetery.

Despite the crackdown, the cemetery was not empty. The Jews were gradually being banned from more and more of the parks and streets of Prague; the Old Jewish Cemetery was the closest thing to a recreation area that they still had. There were families picnicking there, among the twelve thousand tombstones stacked like books on an overcrowded shelf.

The tomb that the golem was looking for was near the main entrance. Paired marble tablets linked by a roof marked the grave of Rabbi Löw. She sat down in the shade of the slabs, and lit a cigarette.

"So I'm back," she said softly.

She heard a peal of laughter from one of the women picnicking in the cemetery.

"This time, nobody is going to destroy me. There won't be anyone to do it. I can live forever—I'll just avoid anyone who could hurt me. I know everything I need to know to stay alive."

She thought of the expression on Alena's face as she spoke of Hanna. *I'd rather die with her than lose her.*

"I've even got papers now," she said. "Alena bought them for me, finally." Instead of buying them for herself.

"I have freedom." She was even freer than Alena. Alena was trapped here, tied to Hanna. The golem was tied to nobody.

Again, she saw the expression on Alena's face, thinking of Hanna.

"All I need to do is walk away," she said.

She could do that, she knew. Even if she had been bound to her creator's will, her creator would be dead within hours. She was free to choose any fate she desired. This time, finally, she would survive. Alone, but alive.

I'd rather die with her than lose her.

The golem realized suddenly that the cigarette had burned away in her hand, and she hadn't even inhaled any of the smoke. Disgusted, she stubbed out the last of it on the ground. Then she stood; the sun was warm on her shoulders. "This is my choice," she said to the Rabbi's grave. "This is my decision."

The golem returned to the apartment at 3:10 p.m. "Alena!" she called. "Hanna. Gather your valuables. Leave everything else, or you'll arouse suspicions. You need to go, now, or you'll both be killed in just over an hour."

The women obeyed her without hesitation. They put on several layers of clothes, though it would be hot, and each filled a purse and a shopping bag with food and the valuables they had left. The golem followed them through the apartment, talking. "Go to Kutná Hora," she said. It was one of the larger towns in Bohemia. She gave them an address for another apartment—" They have a vacancy right now; the landlord isn't nosy, and he won't care who lives in the apartment aside from Alena. Don't waste time; in a week, he'll rent the place to a Nazi sympathizer who will later betray his next-door neighbor for sheltering Jews. It's much better that the landlord rent to you."

There was room in Hanna's shopping bag for a single volume of her antique Talmud—a family heirloom. She took it, although there were other things that would have been more practical. She left the books of golem lore. She left the books of golem lore.

The golem stopped Alena at the door. "Give me your papers," she said, and handed Alena the false papers that Alena had bought for her. "Now go."

As Alena and Hanna headed down the stairs to the street, the golem felt their fate vanish from her mind. She was certain that they would live or die together, whatever happened. In the meantime—the Germans would come to arrest Alena Nebeský, and they would find her. The golem picked up Hanna's book of golem lore, lit the last of Shayna's cigarettes, and sat down in the immaculate parlor to wait.

WIND

*O*nce upon a time, there were two young girls, closer than sisters, who dreamed of greatness. When they played together (as they did every day), Gytha always pretended to be an artist, raising glorious sculptures of stone and glass, and Dagmar pretended to be a famous physician, making brilliant discoveries each day and then spending her nights in the slums, secretly healing those too poor to afford a physician's fee.

Magical ability comes from an imbalance of the elements within the human heart, however, and both Gytha and Dagmar had been blessed with balance rather than power. But Gytha read in a book about a perilous rite requiring two willing hearts that would allow them to trade elements, creating an imbalance and leaving both people with magical power. "Give me your Air," Gytha suggested to Dagmar, "and I will give you my Earth."

Dagmar hesitated. She had always been a bit more sensible than Gytha, and could foresee the possibility of disaster. But Gytha pressed her. "You know we are already one soul in two bodies. If we divide our hearts as I propose, we will also promise each other to stay together and make up for each other's deficiencies."

Finally, Dagmar was persuaded. They joined hands, left palm to left palm and right to right, and spoke the words the book offered. Each felt a sharp pain and Dagmar almost cried out, "no, stop, I didn't mean it," but the rite was done; the transfer was accomplished. Gytha, with her excess of Air, could stretch out her hands to melt stone and sculpt it. Dagmar, with her excess Earth, now had the gift of healing.

Air is the element of change. Gytha, having brought an excess of change into her life, could not bear to stay in her home village. From one of the high peaks near their village, they could occasionally see dragons, tiny black specks against the distant horizon, and Gytha had always envied their freedom; now, she saw that she had never needed wings, only the willingness to fly away. She tried to persuade Dagmar to come with her, but Earth is the element of stability, and Dagmar could not bear to go. "I will visit often," Gytha said as she packed her bag.

"But you promised that we would stay together," Dagmar said.

"We *can* stay together," Gytha said, "but you will have to come with me. You can't possibly expect me to stay here."

"How can you possibly expect me to go?" Dagmar asked.

"Dagmar, listen to me," Gytha said. "You will never become a great physician if you won't come down from our village. Where will you find training? How will you learn more than the midwife can teach you? You *must* come."

"I can't," Dagmar said, even though when she'd clasped hands with Gytha, she'd fully intended to do just that. "I can't."

Gytha tossed her hair. "I don't understand you," she said, and there was scorn in her voice, because now that she'd rid herself of her Earth, it seemed contemptible to her. "I promise I'll write."

Gytha walked through night and day to one of the great cities, where her art and magic quickly earned her great acclaim. But like the wind, she could never stay in one place for long. She travelled restlessly, leaving in her wake beautiful buildings, stone like ribbon, and a trail of broken hearts—the first of which was Dagmar's.

Dagmar, in her home village, got what training she could in healing and then married a man who needed her and had four children, two girls and two boys. She knew that she'd made a terrible mistake, but had no way to fix it: for Gytha, there could never be anything *but* change, but for Dagmar, there could be no change at all. (Other than parenting—but once you're married, children have a tendency to arrive on their own, unless you're careful.) Each, in her own way, was trapped. Gytha would never realize that the cause of her unhappiness was the imbalance in her own heart that she'd longed for so fiercely. Dagmar, without Air to drive change, could never take the steps she needed to shed the parts of her life that began to eat her, piece by piece.

Years passed. Dagmar delivered babies, splinted broken bones, brewed tisanes. She fought with her husband—the same fights, over and over, every time. Her children grew up, and Dagmar's hair began to go gray. Every once in a long while, a traveler would bring news of Gytha to the village—her glorious cathedrals, her honors, her acclaim—and Dagmar would quietly leave the gathering, unable to bear to hear it.

Then one day, two of the shepherds carried a stranger into the village, cradled in a thick blanket. They'd found her in a field late one afternoon, when the mountain's heights had cast everything into shadow. She had no bag or pack, one of her legs was twisted into a strange position, and she was completely naked save for her long black hair. They brought her, of course, to Dagmar.

Dagmar closed the door against the gust of damp wind, then made a pallet near her fire and directed the shepherds to lay the woman on it. "Stay," she said to them, because she would need to set the woman's leg before splinting it, and might need their help to hold her still.

The woman opened her eyes and looked at Dagmar. "You don't need their help," she said. "You're thinking like a midwife. Use your powers instead of your hands; it doesn't have to hurt."

"I have never learned that skill," Dagmar admitted, ashamed.

"Just try."

Dagmar laid her hands on the woman's leg, and then, abashed, set them in her lap and glared fiercely at the painful, unkind angle. As if of their own accord, the bones straightened into place so she could bind them. The woman broke into a sweat, but did not cry out. "You see?" she said, a bit weakly, as Dagmar bound her leg to the splint. "I was right."

Dagmar nodded at the shepherds, and they went back to their

flocks. She brought a quilt to cover the woman with. The strange woman watched Dagmar as she brewed a tisane for her and spooned up a bit of porridge.

"I can't pay you," the woman said, as Dagmar sat down to feed her.

Dagmar shrugged. "Few enough people bother." She glanced around at her house, which had long since fallen into disrepair.

"You have a gift," the woman said. "Too large of a gift for this village."

"I don't care to leave," Dagmar said.

"Are you going to ask me my name?" the woman asked. "Or ask me how I came to be in that field?"

"You're welcome to tell me your name," Dagmar said. "As for your situation, I assume that you were set upon by bandits."

"You can call me Zimeya," the woman said. "And I met no bandits."

Dagmar gave her a dubious look, then shrugged. "In fact, you look more like someone who's taken a bad fall. But that doesn't explain what happened to your clothes."

"True enough," Zimeya said.

Dagmar looked her over again, to see if she'd missed any other broken bones or other injuries. Satisfied, she said, "You may stay here until you heal," and started preparing dinner.

Three of Dagmar's children were grown and gone, but the one who was still living at home, Madel, was quite curious about the injured woman by their fire, and utterly perplexed at her mother's lack of curiosity. To Madel, however, Zimeya pretended to be foreign, or perhaps suffering from a severe head injury, and spoke in words Madel didn't understand; the girl eventually grew bored. She herself had a bit of an excess of Air—not enough to give her magical powers, but enough to thoroughly exasperate her mother at every opportunity— and she spent as little time at home as she could. Dagmar's husband came home for dinner, and they proceeded to have an argument (in quiet tones, because of their guest) about Dagmar's decision to treat yet another person who couldn't or wouldn't pay her, and about the hole in the roof he had promised six times to repair. (Her husband had a slight excess of Water; he was charming but unreliable, and willing to say whatever he thought would get him out of trouble. Which is why he promised yet again to fix the hole in the roof the next day, even though he had not even purchased the materials.) When the argument had reached its usual conclusion, which is not to say a resolution, he left to join some of the other men of the village at the tavern.

Dagmar's face was red with frustration and suppressed tears, but she brought Zimeya a chamber pot and helped her use it, and then helped her into a blouse that had belonged to Dagmar's older daughter. Then she propped Zimeya up on her makeshift bed so that she could eat some of the barley and vegetable stew Dagmar had made for dinner, and scrubbed the dishes.

Zimeya ate everything in her bowl and then set it aside, watching Dagmar. "I don't understand your life," she said. "It makes no sense."

"What doesn't?"

"You aren't happy here. In fact, you're clearly miserable. Your children are grown, or grown enough. And you're wasted here—your gift is wasted here."

Only one with eyes to see would even know about Dagmar's gift. "You're clearly a sorceress yourself," Dagmar said.

"Of sorts," Zimeya conceded.

"Can you see more than the gift? Can you see the damage as well?"

Zimeya looked for a long moment. Then: "Yes," she said, quietly. "I see."

"It was self-inflicted," Dagmar said. "I believed—I thought—" She hesitated, not wanting to burst into tears in front of this near-stranger. "It was my own stupid choice."

"So there must be another out there, similarly damaged."

"I haven't seen her in thirty-two years," Dagmar said. She might have said, *I haven't seen her in thirty-two years, four months, and twen-*

ty-one days, because she always knew, even when she tried not to think about it, how long it had been since Gytha had left.

"Have you heard from her?"

"I try not to," Dagmar said. "I leave when news of her arrives, though it always makes its way to me eventually." Dagmar always felt a sharp pain in her heart at the sound of Gytha's name. Most recently, the story had been about Gytha's art rather than Gytha herself; one of the beautiful stone archways she'd created had shown cracks due to strain, and had been taken down lest it collapse on someone's head. The night after Dagmar heard that story, she'd lain awake, wishing that she could feel some unkind satisfaction at that, but she felt the same lonely ache as always.

"Would you undo this trade, if you could?"

"If I could go back..." Dagmar pushed her hair out of her face, thinking about it. "I'd be a fool not to. She has a piece of my soul inside her, and I have a piece of hers—I'd never have agreed if I'd known that she would leave me. I like having the healing gift, though. I'd hate to give it up. I don't know how the people born this way ever manage to go get proper training."

"When someone is *born* with an excess of an element," Zimeya said, "that usually means that they have *too much* of one thing, but they still have a normal allotment of the others. You gave away all your Air, just as your friend must have given away all her Earth. It left you each with a towering power and an equally great deficiency."

"Well, at least she's accomplished things with hers," Dagmar said, bitterly. Surely not *all* her creations were collapsing.

"So is it worth staying here, forever, never changing, but being able to heal?"

"I don't know," Dagmar said. "I can't imagine giving up my power and I can't imagine leaving. Anyway, the apprenticeship program for physicians in the great city down below the foothills does not accept students over the age of thirty, and I passed that milestone a long time ago." At thirty, she'd had three children, with a fourth on the way.

"There are other colleges of healing," Zimeya said. "In other cities."

"Even further away!" Dagmar felt a surge of indignation, then, that anyone would throw that out so casually. If it was impossible to imagine leaving her home and spend five years apprenticed in the nearest great city, it was thrice impossible to imagine going to some distant shore she'd never even heard of. Even if Gytha had. *Especially* if Gytha had.

Zimeya said nothing. In the silence, the shutters rattled from a sudden night breeze. Dagmar finished cleaning the dishes, and then helped Zimeya lie back down on her pallet. Dagmar's husband was still gone; she knew not to expect him for hours. Sometimes on evenings like this, she'd leave a note on the door to direct any messengers seeking a healer and go to the tea house to sit with the other women of the village, but with a patient, she felt like she should stay home. After a while she said, "You have an unusual name. Where do you come from?"

"I come from another country, many weeks of fl—of travel to the south," Zimeya said.

"Clearly, your excess element must be Air," Dagmar said. "To bring you so far from home."

"Yes," Zimeya said.

"Did you ever meet Gytha?" Dagmar asked, and then interrupted her answer with, "No, no, forget I asked. I don't want to know."

Dagmar made sure Zimeya was comfortable, set a lamp burning, and went to bed. In the darkness, on the edge of sleep, she heard Zimeya speaking: "I did meet her once," she said. "But only once."

Some days passed, with the unchanging routine of Dagmar's cottage flowing around Zimeya like ants around a puddle. Dagmar fought with her husband, made breakfast, argued with Madel, washed up. One morning a baby was coming, so she had Madel sit with Zimeya in case she needed anything.

Zimeya had stopped pretending she couldn't understand Madel, though when Madel (who was not worried about being nosy) asked her how she'd wound up naked and with a broken leg in a sheep pasture high in the mountains, she said she didn't remember. Madel didn't really believe her but she knew she'd get in trouble if she harangued the patient to tell her the truth, so she pouted a little and dropped the subject.

"Are you the youngest?" Zimeya asked her.

"Yes, of four," Madel said. "I have two older brothers and an older sister. They're all married with families of their own."

"Are you thinking of getting married?"

"No," Madel said. "I want to go to the great city to study art. I may not have enough excess Air to have magical powers, but I think I have enough to become an artist. This village is too small and none of the boys interest me. My mother never should have stayed."

"If she hadn't stayed, would you have been born?"

"Maybe not, but she's withered here like a wildflower cut for a vase. I'm not going to do the same."

"What does she say about that?"

"She doesn't want me to go away. She thinks I should be her apprentice, which is mad: I have no skill in healing."

"Why have you stayed as long as you have?"

"I'm not sure what she'd do without me. Besides, it's a very long way, and I have no money to pay for an apprenticeship."

"Bring me pen and paper," Zimeya said. Madel did, and Zimeya wrote a short letter. "This is a letter of introduction," she said. "If you take it to Yngvar the Stone Worker, he will take you as an apprentice for no fee. He owes me a favor, and he's an artist with no magical powers of his own, so he will be sympathetic to you."

Madel's eyes grew wide. "What do you want in return for this favor?"

"Well, perhaps some day long in the future I might send you an apprentice with no fee. But I feel that this is a bit of payment to your mother, who has healed me despite my inability to pay."

"Payment to my mother?" Madel laughed at that. "She will be *furious* about this."

*

Madel was half right; Dagmar was half furious. But the other half of her, the side that was practicality and desire for her children to have lives that suited them (as opposed to grief and fear about being left alone once again)—that side of her knew that this was an irreplaceable opportunity. From deep in a trunk, she took out a woolen travel cloak and some uncut leather which one of Madel's brothers could make into a pair of good boots for her. When the boots were ready, they had found Madel some traveling companions heading in the right direction. Dagmar kissed Madel and gave her her blessing, and then said goodbye.

The house was very quiet when she was gone.

"Perhaps I should have made her wait," Dagmar said. "Surely, when you are healed, you'll be headed in that same direction, won't you? You could have escorted her."

Zimeya shrugged. She could, with a great deal of care and no small amount of pain, hobble now for a short distance using a stout stick. Dagmar had found her some additional cast-off clothes to wear. Zimeya was not a large woman, so several women with grown daughters had outgrown items they were happy to give Dagmar, since most of them owed her fees they were never going to pay, and giving her something they no longer needed made them feel a bit less guilty about it.

"I expect to be here some months yet," Zimeya said, "if you will have me."

"You're welcome to stay," Dagmar said. She'd become fond of Zimeya, who was pleasant company. She had not opened her heart to Zimeya as she had, decades ago, to Gytha, but that was not terribly surprising; she wasn't sure she even remembered how.

Zimeya's strength was returning, even though she couldn't stand for long; she could sit at the kitchen table and help peel vegetables and slice them for stew, and one day Dagmar returned home from stitching up a gashed arm to find that Zimeya had unearthed her overflowing basket of mending and was fixing a ripped hem.

"I'm absolutely terrible at darning," Zimeya said meekly. "But I thought that even I could probably not destroy a hem."

Dagmar sat down across from her and picked up a sock and a darning egg. "Gytha could never darn, either."

"No? I'd blame her excess of Air, but she didn't have that before she traded with you, did she?"

Dagmar smiled a little. "No. She just didn't care for mending."

"Were there any chores she *did* care for?"

"She liked to bake. And she was willing to put up with doing laundry and splitting firewood."

Zimaya shook out the skirt when she was done, the gust of air from the fall of cloth making the fire flicker wildly. The hem was straight, even if some of the stitches were embarrassingly large. She picked up a shirt with a torn sleeve and turned it inside out. Dagmar continued working on the sock.

"I should confess something," she said, suddenly. "I did have a reason for coming here. You."

"Me?" Dagmar said, shocked. "Surely you didn't *break your leg*—"

"Oh, that part was an accident. I had intended to stroll into the village on my own two feet, but there were some high winds and I was not used to the mountains. I'm from a much flatter part of the world, you see."

"Were you going to stroll in naked?"

"No. I'd brought clothes along, but they got blown away by the same gust of wind that blew me to the ground." She tipped her head to the side. "I let you believe that I was a sorceress, but it's not quite accurate to say that I have an excess of Air; it's more that I *am* an excess of Air. I'm a dragon. Obviously, I didn't wear human clothes for my flight to your village. I had intended to put some on, but . . . well." She gestured with a spread hand, showing something flying, getting blown off-course, and then crashing to the kitchen table between them.

"So why," Dagmar asked, a bit shakily, "did a *dragon* come here to find *me?*"

"Three years ago, Gytha made her way to my family's cavern—which, as I told you, is a very long way to the south of here. She'd had a vision of dragons, she said, and was driven to find us. It is difficult to describe the woman who reached our cave, but *driven*, like a deer fleeing a fire, is the only way I can describe her. The missing part of her soul had not been kind to her."

"Oh," Dagmar whispered. She didn't want to hear this.

"My mother, who is a wise and experienced Seer, was able to grasp the situation, and counseled Gytha to return to her home village, because such trades can, sometimes, be reversed. But Gytha refused, speaking with disdain of all she'd left and all she'd given away. She would die, she said, rather than give up her power. It's a shame, because I think, had she returned—"

"Yes," Dagmar said. "If I'd seen what it was doing to her—yes."

"But she refused, and a short time later, she died—and both your Air, and hers, passed to the place souls go and the body can't."

Dagmar's mouth went dry. Of all the news she'd expected to get, hearing that Gytha had *died…* that was a shock.

"I am not the Seer that my mother is; in dragon terms, I am barely out of childhood. But I did glimpse her soul, and its damage, in its passing. I had disliked Gytha, her obstinate self-destructiveness, even though I knew she wasn't entirely to blame…but I could see a piece of you, in her, and I wanted to meet you. And see if I could help you, because I knew you were probably also suffering."

"I'm not suffering that much," Dagmar said. "I mean, yes, I fight with my husband, but doesn't everyone? There are nights that I wake up and feel as if the village is a shroud that is suffocating me slowly—but surely that, too, is not uncommon. I've raised four children; I've been of use to my neighbors. It's not a terrible life."

"Dagmar," Zimeya said. "I can give you some of my Air."

"What do you mean?"

"I can replace some of what you gave away. Without taking away your excess of Earth—because Gytha is gone, she doesn't need it anymore. I *am* an excess of Air."

"Then what will it do to you, to sacrifice some of your very being? I can't let you do that!"

"It will trap me in human form—which I've been trapped in for months already—but when I reach my family's cavern, I will be restored. I will have to walk there, which will be inconvenient and tiring, as it is quite a long way. Although possibly I'll be able to persuade one of my siblings to fly to meet us somewhere along the way."

"Meet *us?*"

"Yes, of course, us. That's my condition of this gift: you have to come with me. There is an apprenticeship program for Physicians in one of the cities near my home that takes people of any age."

"Zimaya, I am *fifty years old.*"

"Exactly. That's why you need to come with me; I don't know where else will take a fifty-year-old woman, but this program also trains dragons, so they don't have an age limit. A fifty-year-old dragon is barely old enough to leave home."

"I can't imagine doing this."

"Can you imagine saying yes to the *possibility* of doing it?" Zimaya pleaded. She took Dagmar's hand. "You healed my leg, Dagmar, and I have no money for payment. Let me pay you, instead, by healing you in return."

"You *already* got my daughter a free apprenticeship," Dagmar muttered, and then said, "oh, all right, then."

Zimaya seized her other hand before she could change her mind—left palm to left palm and right palm to right. Dagmar braced for pain, but instead she felt an easing, as if a headache she hadn't quite been aware of had suddenly gone away, and a loosening. That was all.

Zimaya picked up one of the socks, and a darning egg. "Show me how to fix one of these," she said. "We can't leave for months yet, anyway."

*

Once upon a time, there was a middle-aged woman who packed her bags and left the village where she'd spent her whole life, her grown children who had expected her to care for their grandchildren, and her husband and his falling-down house with the hole in the roof.

The element of change, as everyone knows, is Air. They say that every now and then when the wind blows in a certain direction, it can bring an excess of Air into people who've never been known for foolishness. So close your doors on those days; shutter your windows. Don't go out onto the mountainside and breathe in the wind and look at the sky.

You never know when you might accidentally open your heart.

IN THE WITCH'S GARDEN

Inspired by "The Snow Queen" by Hans Christian Andersen

I heard the girl before I saw her: *dry, hopeless sobs from a child unused* to having anyone pay attention to her tears. "Hush," I called softly, breaking through the brush to reach her. Someone from the station might still hear her, and come after her.

"Who's there?" she cried out. "Help me, I'm lost."

I used my knife to cut away the last of the bushes. She drew back in fear when she saw me, and tried to struggle to her feet, but fell back in pain. She must have sprained an ankle when she fell down the embankment. "Don't be afraid," I said, and gave her my most reassuring smile, but the sight of my missing front tooth only frightened her more. When I knelt by her side, she overcame her fear enough to touch my gray braids with a fingertip. She had never seen gray hair before, as all the adults in the station maintained the appearance of youth—or so I was told by my mother, when she warned me not to go near the vast dark building so close to our valley.

"Who are you?" she whispered. "Can you help me get home?"

"I am not from your station," I said, as if that wasn't obvious. "But I can take care of you. Climb on to my back." She wrapped her legs around my hips, and her skinny arms around my neck. "I'll take you to *my* home."

She was as light as a flower—eleven years old, I guessed. I broke into a trot once we reached even ground; the more distance I could put between her and the station, the better. I had always wanted a child of my own, but no matter how many men I seduced, I never managed to make one. Now the Goddess had sent me a child. "Don't worry," I whispered. "I will be a good mother to you."

"What?" she said.

"I said, did you have a mother back in the station?"

"No," she said. "I'm a made-child, not a born-child. I have no parents."

"What's your name?" I asked.

"Gerda. Do you want to know my number?"

"No," I said. "There are no other Gerdas here; we don't need numbers. My name is Natalia."

"The Natalia my age isn't very nice," Gerda said. "But the ten-year-old Natalia, she isn't so bad."

"There are no other Natalias here, either," I said, and shook my braids so that the beads strung on them clacked against each other.

Over another hill, then down into my valley: a cottage surrounded by a garden. Gerda looked around in wonder. As a station child, she would have found any garden strange and impressive, but my garden—inherited from my mother, who was also a witch—truly was strange: I grew an orange tree and a lemon tree, and the rosebushes and hydrangea bloomed in the spring when the hills beyond my garden were still covered in a deep layer of snow. The creek that flowed through my garden never froze. My magic was not perfect, but it served me well. I carried Gerda into my cottage, and set her down in my chair.

"I'll make you something to eat," I said, and put a pot on the stove, with dried corn kernels in it. "Tell me how you came to leave the station, Gerda."

"My friend, Kai—he's the eleven-year-old Kai—a few days ago he went to look for the edge of the station. He wanted to look at the outside, even though that's forbidden. Now the Snow Queen has taken him." The first kernel of corn in the pot popped, and Gerda jumped at the sound. "What is that?"

"Popcorn," I said. Another kernel popped, and she jumped again. "It's just the sweet center of the corn; the warmth of the fire helps it burst out of its prison. We'll eat it in a moment—serves it right for seeking to change its nature. Go on about Kai."

"They told us never to speak his name again. The Snow Queen takes only disobedient children, so he must have deserved what he got. But he's my friend. So I thought I'd look for the edge of the station..."

"Just to take a look outside, like Kai?"

Gerda shook her head. "I thought maybe he'd gotten lost in the station."

The popcorn was almost done. I shook it a few more times and took it off the stove, then sprinkled it with a pinch of salt and set it on the table. "Eat. It's very tasty." Gerda looked at it dubiously, then took a single fluffy kernel and crunched into it. Her face brightened and she took a handful. I wet a cloth in cold water and then sat down at her feet, easing off her shoes. They were bright red and gave off an acrid odor. Her left ankle was swollen and bruised; I wrapped it in the cool cloth and drew the footstool over for her to rest it on.

"What happened then?"

"Someone began to follow me. I was afraid; I was in a forbidden corridor. A *really* forbidden corridor. I started running, and I pushed on a door and found myself—"

"Outside."

"Yes. They always told us we would die if we went outside. It's safe only inside the stations. Is that true?"

"No, it isn't true," I said. "I've lived outside my whole life, and I'm not dead yet."

"Then perhaps Kai isn't dead, even if he stumbled out like I did," Gerda said. "Have you seen Kai?"

"I saw no boy leave the station," I said. "If I had, I would have brought him here, just as I brought you."

She looked down at the last of the popcorn and her eyes grew suddenly wide. "Are *you* the Snow Queen?"

I chuckled. "If I am, it's a good thing you were disobedient, isn't it? Haven't I been kind to you so far?" But her eyes were still wide and afraid, so I said, "No, I am not the Snow Queen. I am only Natalia, a gardener and a witch. Finish the last of the popcorn, now. Your ankle needs rest, and so does your heart. I'll give you some tea and put you to bed."

I would need the second bed, I thought, as I heated the water; I would bring my mother's old bed down from the attic. I sweetened the tea of forgetfulness that I brewed her with wild honey. "You'll wake when you're ready," I said as I gave her the cup. Gerda drank the tea, and closed her eyes and slept, right there in the chair.

The forgetfulness herbs are not perfect; if something reminds you of what you've forgotten, the spell can be broken. So while Gerda slept, I took my scissors and cut away her dress, her stockings, and even her underwear. Around her neck was a snug cord strung with a metal chip: G2117F, it said. Her tag. I studied that for a long time; I was unfamiliar with the magics used by the station scientists, and if I cut that cord away, I wasn't sure if it would hurt her. I tugged at it a bit, and by and by the cord stretched until it was loose enough that I could slip it over her head. When she was naked, I wrapped her in a blanket and lay her on my bed. I bundled up her clothes and her shoes and that tag, and put them away in the attic of my cottage.

Gerda's hair and skin smelled like the chemicals she washed with, so I warmed water and steeped marigolds and rose petals in it, and bathed her with that until she smelled like me. While she slept, I made her a dress, so that she would have something to wear when she woke. I disapproved of children wearing shoes, but her feet were delicate and fragile from her life on the station, so I also made her a pair of sandals.

When Gerda woke, I smiled at her and said, "Are you feeling better, my darling?"

Gerda blinked. "Who are you?" she said.

"I'm your mother, sweetheart," I said. "You've been very ill. Don't worry; everything will come back in time."

If Gerda had been a born-child and not a made-child, it's possible that the forgetfulness herbs would not have worked at all. But she remembered no other mother, and so she accepted my word when I said I was she. And I discovered (as I had suspected) that I could be an excellent mother: patient, loving, and affectionate, much as my own mother had been. As the spring and summer passed, I taught Gerda the names of all the plants and trees in my garden (pretending, of course, that I was re-teaching her what she had forgotten). I showed her how to brew an herbal tea that would stop a woman's labor if it was too early, or calm someone crazy with fear, or cure a cold. To toughen her feet, I encouraged her to kick off her sandals whenever she pleased, and by the time I could smell the tang of frost when I left my valley, the sandals were gathering dust under her bed, forgotten.

Gerda told me sometimes that she still didn't remember anything from before her sickness. I always sighed and shook my head and said that perhaps those memories were gone forever, but Gerda wasn't to worry; we would create new memories together.

Then I got sick.

Gerda put me to bed, and brewed me teas to bring down my fever and ease my aches and pains. She had learned well, and in a very few days I felt much better again. But I was weak and fussy, the way people often are when they're getting over being sick, and Gerda thought she'd look for the candied orange peels that we had made a few months earlier; those, she thought, would perk me up.

The candied orange peels weren't in the kitchen. Gerda tried the cabinets in the herb-drying room, but they weren't there, either. Nor were they in the coldhouse, nor the root cellar, nor the pantry. Dozing in my bed, I could hear Gerda looking for something. Then I heard the creak of the ladder to the attic. I could have shouted "No! Stop!" and invented some excuse for her to not go up there, but in truth, after all those months, I half believed myself that I had borne Gerda from my own womb, and raised her from her infancy.

I heard Gerda's footsteps, but something was different about them. She set a jar by my bed, and I looked over: the orange peels. Then I saw a flash of red: the shoes. On her feet.

"Mother," she said. "Where can I find the Snow Queen?"

I closed my eyes and turned away from her. "I should have burned those clothes," I said. "But I was afraid the smoke would poison the hydrangeas."

"The Snow Queen," Gerda said. "I'm only angry because I was looking for Kai, and now—I don't even know how much time has passed."

"Eight months," I said.

"Now how am I going to find him?"

"There is no Snow Queen," I said. "It's a story told to frighten the station's children. To keep them from trying to go outside."

"Kai must be somewhere," Gerda said.

"If I'd seen a boy leave the station, I'd have brought him here—I told you that."

"Would you have dosed him with tea, and told him he was your son?" Gerda asked.

Still facing the wall, I smiled a little. "Maybe," I said. "What I really wanted was a daughter."

"Do you know anyone else who might have taken him?"

I shrugged. "There are settlements to the south and the west. Perhaps he found his way to one of those."

Gerda kissed my cheek. "I have to go look for Kai, Mother," she said. "Will you help me find him?"

Tears welled up in my eyes. "I can't leave my garden," I said. "If I leave my garden, the orange trees will die, and the lemon trees, and the roses . . . it's almost winter. Without my magic, the garden will turn cold. Can't you wait until spring?"

"It's already been too long."

"If you must go," I said, "Take my heavy cloak, the one hung by the door. There's magic in the wool, and it will keep you warm. Also—" I reached under my own collar, and drew out a claw on a leather thong. I pulled it over my head and gave it to Gerda. "Keep this with you.

When you are ready to come back, speak my name three times and hold this in the palm of your hand. The claw will point back to my house."

Gerda hung the claw around her own neck.

"Good luck, stolen daughter. Come back to me soon."

I did not tell Gerda that the claw would let me scry her. After all, my mother hadn't told me that either, when she gave me the claw to wear. What mother would?

I walked Gerda to the edge of my valley, and stood and watched her as she headed west. The station was to the north, but she didn't head towards it. Kai would not be there, and no matter how hard she knocked, they would not let her in.

When the curve of the hill took her out of my sight, I headed back to my garden. Though my valley stays warm, the trees know when it's winter, and it was time to clean up the leaves. I raked them into a bin to rot until spring, when I'd use them to enrich the soil and keep the new plants moist. Even the roses had dropped their leaves, and I carefully gathered up the last of the rose blossoms to dry in my house.

As the setting sun plunged my valley into shadow, I went inside and put my kettle on the stove. My house seemed very cold without Gerda; her empty bed seemed to take up far too much space. I poured hot water over dried rose petals and orange peel to make tea, and then poured more hot water into a blue clay bowl. I set the bowl on my table, wrapping myself in my shawl and sitting down to stare into it.

As the steam dissipated, I saw Gerda.

She sat on the side of a hill—I could make out no landmarks that would tell me where. She had not built a fire, but simply wrapped herself up in my cloak. The hood was thrown back, as if she was a little warmer than she might like.

I watched her as she unfolded the kerchief of food and had something to eat, choosing the foods that would go stale the fastest. Just before it grew too dark to see her, she broke off a tiny piece of the candied orange peel and put it in her mouth, tears rolling down her face as she ate it. I hastily got up to get myself more tea, and when I returned to the scrying bowl, it was too dark to see anything.

My scrying showed me nothing but Gerda walking across treeless fields for three days. At dawn on the fourth day, however, I sat down with my morning tea and my scrying bowl just in time to see a huge black crow dive down and wake her. "Good morning," the crow said.

I nearly spilled my tea. I'd heard stories about the tribe of talking crows, but they'd never come anywhere near my valley—so far. Gerda rolled over and blinked up at him with equanimity. "Good morning to you, too," she said. Her voice was a little hoarse from disuse, and she cleared her throat.

The crow ruffled its feathers. "You say that like someone who *expects* to be greeted by a crow," he said.

"Natalia doesn't let crows into her garden. I've never met a crow before."

"Never met . . . ! You must be from the station," the crow said.

"Yes!" Gerda sat up so sharply that the crow took an alarmed hop backwards. "Yes, and I'm looking for a boy who also came from the station. My friend, Kai."

The crow put his head to the side. "A boy. A stranger?"

"Have you seen someone?"

"Maybe. Maybe. There's the boy who married the Princess. He might be your Kai."

Gerda's eyes grew large and she pushed herself to her feet, gathering up the cloak in her arms. "Can you take me to him?"

The crow launched himself into the air with a raucous caw, then settled onto Gerda's shoulder. "Towards the sun," he said. "Oh, and just so you know? Crows don't *normally* talk. My sweetheart and I, we were improved by the scientists in the town. Us and our children, we're the only talking crows in the *world*. You were *supposed* to be startled when I talked to you . . ."

The crow directed Gerda to a path through the grasslands; then the path opened up, and led to a wide road of hard-packed dirt, and the road led to a town. I recognized the town when I saw it. I had traveled there once, during the summer when I could leave my garden for a week without harm to it. The scientists in the town made seeds that grew unnaturally well and potions to heal grievous wounds. I had gone to their auction and concluded that they had nothing my magic could not do for me, but others paid a small fortune for the scientists' tricks. I didn't trust the scientists, but they had some congress with the station. It was possible they might be able to help Gerda.

The crow directed Gerda through the streets to the laboratory—a large cottage with walls made out of sheets of black metal. It looked like the station, but much smaller. There were steps leading up to the front door.

"This is where the princess lives," the crow said. "And the young man she married. Just knock on the door and ask for him."

Gerda climbed the steps and knocked, and the crow launched himself from her shoulder into the sky, with a caw that sounded like a cackle. A moment later a young woman opened the door. "Yes? Who are you?" she said.

Gerda opened her mouth, then hesitated. The woman prompted her with an impatient noise. "Is Kai here?" Gerda asked.

"Kai? I don't know a Kai. I'm sorry, but I'm quite busy. Are you with a caravan? You look a bit young to be on your own. Tell your caravan we hold open hours at noon daily. It's not noon yet. Good day."

The door closed.

Gerda looked around, but the crow was nowhere in sight. Her chin trembled, and she clenched her teeth. She trudged back down the steps and sat under a maple tree, wrapped up in my cloak. Open hours at noon; it looked as if she intended to simply wait until then.

Noon. That was hours away. I could safely leave Gerda, I thought, and dashed outside to work in my garden. I had noticed while raking that my herb bed was looking dry. I drew water from the well and sprinkled it over the rosemary and thyme, the basil and oregano, the lemongrass and St. John's Wort. There was a little water left in my pitcher when I had watered everything that looked thirsty, and I brought it inside to heat for the scrying bowl as the sun neared its zenith. Gerda was still sitting patiently where I'd left her. Other people had also gathered outside the laboratory: a dozen men in coats sewn from rabbit pelts; a man and a woman in black wool cloaks; an ancient man in rags, with a gnarled walking stick and a polished wood bowl. They waited a few paces away from the door, the men in fur talking quietly among themselves in a language I didn't understand. A man in ordinary clothes strode into the laboratory, and a handful of scientists came out, dressed from head to foot in white—white linen dresses, white wool scarves, white fur boots.

At noon, the door opened. The woman who had spoken to Gerda earlier came down the steps to the road. Before, the woman had been wearing a stained white linen coat; now, she had garbed herself head to toe in white fur. "I am Lovise," the woman said. "Personal representative of the Principal Research Scientist. We have a variety of fine items for purchase today." She gestured, and a boy with the glazed stare of a frag pushed a wheelbarrow out from the side of the laboratory.

"Our first item for sale is a box of seed corn," Lovise said. "Specially bred to germinate, grow, and produce corn in just two months. Like all our seed, this corn carries the laboratory's guarantee. Are there any questions?"

One of the men in fur asked, "Will it regerminate?"

"No, of course not," Lovise said. "But you can come buy more from us next year." I snorted in disgust; typical of the scientists and their tricks. The men were grumbling, as well, and Lovise fell back a step. "If you want corn that will regerminate, you can trade for seed with one of the communes. But their corn will take five months." The grumbling quieted. "The price today is just ten gold dollars for a box with 100 seeds."

From the wheelbarrow, the boy held up two carved wooden boxes, one in each hand.

The men in fur conferred for a moment. Then one said, "We'll take ten boxes." He had a leather drawstring bag at his waist, which he unlooped and loosened; he began to count out a hundred gold coins for the boy. The man and woman in black had no interest in seed corn.

"Our next item today is antibiotic ointment." At Lovise's gesture, the boy held up a glass vial with a cork stopper. "To keep infection from an injury, wash the wound, then rub this in and cover with a clean bandage. You can also buy soap from us, but we are the *only* source for this particular ointment. Fifty gold dollars for a vial."

This was what the couple in black had come for. They stepped over to the boy and counted out fifty gold coins. I snorted again, but a little less derisively. I'd heard some stories about this ointment that would make me consider buying it, had I anything close to fifty gold dollars.

"Finally, we have a brand-new item today," Lovise said. The boy took the wheelbarrow back inside, and returned with a dog on a leash. It was a Siberian husky, and the boy had a bit of trouble controlling it; the dog wanted to run away from him. I felt sorry for the dog, though the boy was not being cruel to him; he was simply keeping the dog on the leash, when the dog really wanted to run.

"The enhanced sled dog," Lovise said.

"Does he run faster?" one of the men in fur asked.

"No," Lovise said. "He talks." She turned to the dog. "Show them, Flagstaff."

The dog, giving up on getting away, threw himself down onto the snow in disgust. "What do you want me to say?" he said.

"Tell them you're a good dog."

The dog rolled its eyes. "I'm a good dog," he said. He glanced over at Gerda and winked at her. Gerda grinned a little in spite of herself.

I thought that I'd steal the dog if I could; he deserved better than the scientists.

The men in fur coats laughed. "Thanks but no thanks, Scientist Lovise," one of them said. "We've seen the talking crows. Is he going to be like the talking crows?"

"No," Lovise snapped. "Like the corn, he can't reproduce. Not without help, anyway."

The men in fur laughed harder. "Poor fella," one of them called to the dog. "If you can get away from the scientists, come and live with us. We'll treat you right."

The dog looked like he was going to say something, but then thought the better of it.

"That's all for today," Lovise said, and the men in fur and the couple in black cloaks started back down the road, away from the laboratory. The man in rags approached the doorstep; at Lovise's signal, the boy brought out a pot of steaming soup and ladled soup into the man's bowl. The man bowed his thanks, and turned away as well. Lovise started back up the steps.

"Wait!" Gerda called.

Lovise turned. "You again?" she said. "What do you want?"

"The crow sent me here," Gerda said. "He said—"

"The crow sent you?" Lovise said. "Well, *that* explains a great deal. You'd better come inside." She held the door open for Gerda; Gerda ducked under the woman's arm and went inside. "Those crows were a mistake," Lovise muttered in disgust.

The inside walls of the laboratory were smooth and bare, painted as white as winter snow, and the lights were too bright. Lovise led Gerda to a parlor, sat her in a chair by the wood stove, and gave her a bowl of soup. Gerda ate it quickly, and I thought with a pang that I should have insisted that she take more food with her.

"Now," Lovise said. "What was it that the crow told you?"

"I'm looking for a friend of mine," Gerda said. "A boy named Kai." She stumbled over what she was trying to say, paused for a breath, and started again. "We both came from the station. The crow that woke me up this morning said that I might be able to find Kai here—that the Princess took a husband last week, and it might have been Kai."

Lovise took Gerda's empty bowl and set it aside. "There isn't anyone here called 'Princess'—he meant the Principal Research Scientist, Lise. She did take a husband last week, but he came from our rival laboratory; we are hoping to cement an alliance. It's highly unlikely that her groom is the boy you're seeking, but let me take you into the lab for just a moment and you can tell me for sure."

Before Gerda could go into the lab, Lovise dressed her carefully in a long white linen coat; Gerda took off her shoes and put on booties made of white fur, and Lovise put a knit mask over her nose and mouth. Then Lovise led her in. The lab had no windows, but the light was even brighter there than in the hall. All the furniture inside was shiny polished metal, and there were a lot of complicated arrangements of glass beakers and glass tubes. Glassy-eyed servants attended to much of the apparatus. In one corner, under the counter, Flagstaff was caged, his chin resting on his shaggy forelegs. His tail thumped once when he spotted Gerda.

"There," Lovise said, and pointed.

Gerda looked at the young man, just beyond the servants. Her face fell, and I knew it could not be Kai even before she shook her head.

The young man turned and saw her. "Who's she?" he asked Lovise.

Lovise looked down. "Excuse me for disturbing you, Lead Scientist Kjeld. This girl came from the station, and she's looking for another child. Someone told her that you might be him."

"You've made her cry," Kjeld said. He pulled his mask off and took Gerda's hand. "From the station, she said? Come on, little girl. Let's go sit down."

Gerda sat down beside him on a chair made out of a sheet of shiny metal, bent into a chair shape. At his encouragement, she told him all about Kai, and how the Snow Queen had taken him. Kjeld seemed very interested, though he was most interested in ordinary life in the Station; she described the children's quarters, the commissaries, the Keeper who took care of the children, the Director who told them that Kai was gone forever. "But don't you have parents?" he asked. Gerda shook her head, no. She was a made-child. Kjeld asked if the Station had any labs like this one, but Gerda had never seen one. He seemed very disappointed about that, and I swore under my breath, taking care not to disturb the water. He didn't really care about Gerda; he just hoped she'd know some of *their* research secrets to tell him.

Gerda's gaze kept straying to one of the glassy-eyed servants. "Magda?" she said under her breath at one point.

"What?" Kjeld said.

"That girl over there, I know her."

"No, you don't," Kjeld said. "She's a frag. An automaton. She doesn't know anyone. She probably just looks like your friend."

"No, I'm sure I know her," Gerda said. She stood up and approached the girl, Kjeld following her warily. "Magda?" she said loudly, but the girl didn't look up.

"She's a *frag*," Kjeld said. "Didn't they have frags on the station?"

"Of course," Gerda said, and her worried eyes went back to Kjeld. "They cleaned and cooked and some of them even helped take care of the made-children. But Magda wasn't a frag, she was a made-child, like me."

Kjeld looked at the frag, and Gerda, and then averted his eyes. "Well, that must not be your friend, then," he said, and hustled Gerda out of the lab.

"I guess I'll be going," Gerda mumbled once they were back out in the hallway.

Kjeld shook his head. "Oh, you can't leave now," he said. "There's a storm coming—didn't you see the clouds? It's going to snow quite a lot."

"But if Kai isn't here—"

"Aren't you listening? If you leave now, you'll freeze to death. Come on, we'll let you sleep in the parlor tonight."

"But—"

"You can go on once the storm is past." Kjeld's hand had closed tightly on Gerda's wrist, and she reluctantly followed him back to the parlor with the wood stove.

Gerda wouldn't freeze to death—not in my cloak—but it would be just as well for her *not* to be caught out in a storm. Was it really about to snow? I left the scrying bowl and stepped out of my cottage to look at the sky. Sure enough, though the sky had been blue earlier, I could see clouds gathering beyond the hill to the northwest. "Stay where you are," I whispered, staring to the west where she'd headed. "Let them give you their hospitality. I trust winter weather even less than I trust the scientists."

My magic keeps my valley warm through the winter, but of course I can't entirely keep out the weather—my plants need rain to survive. I typically experience a bad winter storm as a hard, cold rain, and this rain was particularly hard. I pulled my shutters closed before going to bed, and lay awake in the darkness, listening to the rain pounding on my roof and thinking about Gerda. Only a week or two before my illness, we'd climbed up onto the roof and repaired all the leaks, preparing for winter. I should have been glad that we'd done it, but now all I could think about was how maybe overexerting myself that day was what had made me ill . . . and how much I wished Gerda were here now. I turned my face towards her empty bed; even with the racket the storm was making, the house seemed too quiet. Finally I lit a candle and filled the scrying bowl again, but I saw nothing but darkness, and heard Gerda's peaceful long breaths. After that, I was finally able to sleep.

In the morning, the storm had blown over. Beyond my valley, I could see the glint of deep snow on the hills. Within my valley, the stone I used as a doorstep glistened with moisture, and the rose trellis had been knocked down by the storm. I spent some time putting it back up and trimming back the broken parts of the rose bushes; they were clearly affronted by the harsh weather, but they'd survived worse.

When I'd done what I could for the roses, I went back in and poured fresh water into the scrying bowl. The sound came through first—a piercing scream. My blood ran cold, and I gripped the scrying bowl in my hands, willing Gerda to be all right.

"Kjeld!" Gerda wailed, and I heard a door slam. The steam cleared, and I saw Kjeld and Lovise facing each other, Lovise's hand gripping Gerda by the base of the neck.

"*Spying*," Lovise spat, shoving Gerda to the floor.

Gerda shook her head, widening her eyes in mute appeal towards Kjeld. Kjeld licked his lips and looked back at Lovise. "Why do you say that?"

"I caught her in the lab—the *research* lab."

"Why were you in there, Gerda?" Kjeld asked.

Gerda sniffled. I hoped that neither Kjeld nor Lovise could sense how deliberate that sniffle was. "I was looking for the lavatory," she said. "Kjeld showed me where yesterday, but I got confused in the hallways."

My grip tightened on the bowl. She was lying; Gerda had an excellent sense of direction. And the station was nothing *but* hallways. What *was* Gerda doing in that lab? Looking for Kjeld? Looking for the frag she'd spotted the day before? Either way, she was more devious than I'd given her credit for.

"Lovise, be reasonable," Kjeld said. "She's a child. It takes years of training to make heads or tails of our research—yes, I said 'our' research, I'm part of this lab now. Unless she's been raised from birth to be a perfect spy—and if that's the case, can't you think of a dozen things she's done wrong by now? She wanted to leave last *night*. In the storm."

"You should have let her."

Kjeld threw up his hands in disgust. "Lovise, you have formaldehyde in your veins instead of blood. Let her leave? In the storm? She's a *child*."

"You're just hoping to get useful information from her."

"Well, and I'm not saying I'll complain if she has anything for us. But—"

There was a knock at the door; Lovise answered it and had a quiet conference with another white-coated woman. She closed the door deliberately and fixed her gaze on Gerda. "There has been a theft," she said. "Flagstaff is missing."

Kjeld burst out laughing. "Are you going to blame that one on the girl, too? By all means, search her pockets. I'm sure she's got the dog hidden in one of them."

But looking at Gerda's face, I thought that she probably *did* know something about the missing dog. Why on earth? Was it tenderheartedness, wanting to free the dog from slavery as she'd freed herself from the station?

Lovise said, "Let's continue this discussion elsewhere." Kjeld obligingly stepped out, and Lovise locked the door behind her, leaving Gerda in the room where they'd been arguing. Gerda briefly pressed her ear to the door, but they must have moved too far away to be heard, because a moment later she dropped with a sigh into the chair, fingering the claw she wore around her neck. It was a small, boring room. Gerda stared at the floor and waited.

I should go out and finish cleaning up from the storm, I thought. But the last time I left Gerda, I came back to find Lovise furious enough to wring her neck. It was pure superstition to think that watching would make any difference, but I am a very superstitious woman, so I stayed where I was and watched Gerda as she waited. And waited. And waited.

Finally Kjeld returned. "I think it's best we get you out now," he whispered. "The weather looks clear, and I've got your cloak and a pair of snowshoes. Follow me."

Gerda followed Kjeld through a dingy back hallway and out into the snow. I was shocked to see that the sun was setting; had I been sitting and watching Gerda all day? Kjeld gave Gerda her cloak and helped her put the snowshoes on.

"Head for my family's lab," he said. "They're a two day walk, due east. If the crow finds you again, tell him they'll pay well for bringing you to them; he'll know how to get there." He tucked a small notebook into her pocket. "They'll be most interested in this, as well as in anything else you have to tell them. Good luck."

Was Gerda spying? For Kjeld? That made no sense, either. But she nodded, and tromped off with her back to the setting sun, struggling a little with the snowshoes. As soon as the laboratory had disappeared behind a rise, she dropped to a crouch and whistled, a long low note.

A few minutes passed. She whistled again.

She sighed deeply and stood up.

Then—a high answering howl. Her face brightened. And there, across the snowy hills, came the dog.

"All right," Gerda said. "I freed you. Now take me to Kai."

"I didn't say I knew where Kai was," Flagstaff said. "But I do know that it gets colder as you go north, and anyone called a *Snow Queen* must live somewhere very cold. I can take you north. I can take you all the way to the ice wall."

"What good will that do me?" Gerda said. "I don't believe there ever was a Snow Queen; it's just a story told to frighten the made-children."

"Suit yourself," Flagstaff said. "Is there somewhere else you'd like me to take you? To the rival laboratory, perhaps, like Kjeld wants you to do?"

Gerda sighed deeply.

"You'll need a sled for me to pull," Flagstaff said. "Creep back to the village after the sun sets and you'll find one you can steal."

Gerda did just that, finding a small dogsled in an unlocked shed after the last window in the village went dark. The dog told her how to hitch him up, and then told her to wrap herself warmly and hold on tight. "Are you ready?" he said when she was settled.

"Yes," Gerda said.

The dog did not start off at a walk and then work up to a run; instead, he broke instantly to full speed, stretching out his wolflike limbs to tear like the winter wind across the snowy fields. Gerda almost lost her grip on the sled, but she tightened her fists and quickly became accustomed to the dog's pace. He slackened to a trot after a few minutes and said, "Ah yes, I still need to ask. Which way?"

"North," Gerda said, and the dog wheeled north across the hills.

I woke to the late-morning sun, my cheek resting against my kitchen table. The scrying-bowl was cold against my hand. I rubbed the sleep from my eyes hastily and heated water for tea and scrying, then realized that I could still see Gerda in the murky depths of the bowl. I sat down to look. She was still on the makeshift dogsled; the dog was still running, pulling the sled over hills blanketed with deep white snow.

I changed the water in the scrying bowl and got myself something to eat. I checked; still running. I went out quickly to check on my garden, then came back in; still running. I couldn't bring myself to spend more than a few minutes on any task; I kept darting inside to check on Gerda. Finally I saw that they had spotted a hut built of cinderblocks. There was a chimney at one end, and a plume of smoke curled out. "Stop," Gerda said to the dog. "If there *is* a Snow Queen, maybe the person who lives there knows where to find her."

The woman who lived in the hut was an old Hmong woman— a hermit, like me. She was tiny, shorter than Gerda, though not at all bent over, and she didn't speak much English. She could see that Gerda was hungry and cold, though, and that the dog was hungry and thirsty. Without speaking, she brought out a bucket of melted snow for the dog, as well as some meaty bones to gnaw on, and she led Gerda into her hut to sit by the fire and drink sweet tea.

"Kai?" Gerda said. The old Hmong woman blinked at Gerda slowly, then smiled and shrugged, shaking her head to say that she didn't understand. "Snow Queen?" Gerda tried. The Hmong woman shook her head again. Gerda stood up and tried to pantomime. "A grown lady . . . with children. A woman who steals children."

"Child-stealer?" the Hmong woman said suddenly in English.

Gerda nodded her head, her eyes widening with surprise. "Tell me where," she said.

But the Hmong woman didn't want to. She shook her head and pursed her lips. Finally she said, "You go to Norse woman." She took Gerda out of her hut and pointed north. "Norse woman, she tell you."

"Thank you," Gerda said. She finished her tea, and went back out to the sled.

Hours passed. I forced myself to go out to my garden—I had weeds to pull, slugs to pick, vegetables to harvest, but every time I stepped away from the scrying bowl I found myself panicking and rushing back only moments later. Finally, Gerda and Flagstaff came to another hut. This one was also built out of cinderblocks, but snow had been packed all around it like an igloo, to keep it warm. There was a pen in the yard with a high fence, with a dozen other huskies inside—but these were ordinary huskies, not talking huskies. When they saw Gerda and Flagstaff, they all began to bark at once. Gerda knocked on the door. When the door opened, she fell back a step; it was so warm in the hut, the Norse woman went naked. She had tattoos of blue vines winding across her breasts, and a sunburst design around her navel, half hidden by the folds of her belly. She looked Gerda up and down for a long moment and then said to the dog, "You had better stay outside. It's very warm inside and you wouldn't be happy. But I'll send the girl outside with food and water for you."

"Thank you," Flagstaff said.

"You though, girl, you can come in."

Gerda went into the house and almost immediately had to wipe sweat from her forehead and cheeks. She hung my cloak on a hook and rolled up her sleeves. The Norse woman watched her with a raised eyebrow.

When Gerda had brought the dog food and water, and untied his harness, the Norse woman gave Gerda a bowl of fish soup, and a mug of coffee with whiskey in it. She finished her own meal quickly, and then took out a long pipe, which she lit quietly while Gerda finished the soup. The house filled with curling feathers of smoke.

"Now then," she said, when Gerda had finished eating. "What brings you here?"

"The Hmong woman who lives over the hills to the south said you might be able to tell me where to find the Snow Queen," Gerda said.

"I don't know a Snow Queen," the Norse woman said. She pulled her legs up to cross them over each other, then leaned forward to pick up her pipe, and began to refill it.

"The child-stealer," Gerda said. "Do you know where I can find a child-stealer?"

"Ah," the Norse woman said. "So that's what you meant." She lit her pipe again and sat back, studying Gerda with bright eyes through the haze of smoke.

"I'm really looking for my friend Kai," Gerda said. "We used to live in the station, and then Kai disappeared . . . and they said the Snow Queen took him, because he was disobedient. But I'm sure they told everyone the Snow Queen had *me*, and I was perfectly safe, living with Natalia. Anyway, Flagstaff brought me north . . . and the Hmong woman said you could tell me about the child-stealer, so . . ." She slumped backwards, and I thought how exhausted she must be.

"Do you want to go back to the station once you've found your friend?" the Norse woman asked.

"Oh no," Gerda said. "I want to go back to Natalia. If I do find Kai, I want to bring him to live with us."

She wants to come back to me! I realized that the blood was pounding in my ears, and my head was spinning with relief—Gerda would come back.

The Norse woman smiled. "In that case . . ." She took a long draw from the pipe. "I think if you'll think about it, you'll realize that you already know where Kai must be."

Gerda shook her head. "No," she said. "I don't know."

"I'll show you something." The Norse woman opened a chest, and took something from the bottom of it, which she handed Gerda. "Do you know what this is?"

It was a metal tag: F2168F. "This is the Fjerra tag," Gerda said. "Fjerra from . . . sixty years ago."

"That's right," the Norse woman said. "How do you suppose I came to have it?"

Gerda looked at the tag, and then at the Norse woman. She swallowed hard.

"The hard thing is, child," the Norse woman said, "The Snow Queen comes for all the made-children in the end. Whether you're good or bad, obedient or disobedient. Now do you know where Kai is?"

Without a word, Gerda stood up and went back out to the dog.

"I don't see why we're going south again," Flagstaff complained.

"Because that's where Kai is," Gerda said.

Towards noon, she used the claw that I had given her, holding it in the palm of her hand and saying "Natalia, Natalia, Natalia." A tiny wisp of a breeze ruffled Gerda's hair and turned the claw slightly. "That way," Gerda said to the dog.

Was she coming back to me? No, no, it was too good to be true. As dusk fell, she saw the station on the horizon. That was where Flagstaff balked.

"You're going *there*?" he said. "Then you're going alone. Do you know what they do to talking dogs?"

"Just a little closer," Gerda said. "I can walk the rest of the way."

"Wait!" I shouted, in my hut, knowing that she couldn't hear me. "Why are you going *there*? They won't let you back in. Even if they do, do you think they'll be *happy* to see you? Do you think Kai is *there*?"

The dog consented to take her a little closer, then stopped again. "This is as close as I'm getting," he said.

"Then thank you, for all your help," Gerda said, and cut the harness so that the dog could go on his own.

"Thank you again for freeing me," Flagstaff said, and turned north again.

I watched Gerda, unbelieving, as she circled the station once.

There were doors in it, of course, as well as the one she'd escaped through, but they were all sealed tight, with no handle on the outside. Why was she going back there? That ancient tag the Norse woman had shown her—what could it have meant to her? I tried to think through this logically. Sixty years old. The Norse woman might be that old; she looked older, but she also smoked a pipe. I was fifty, though I didn't look it except for my hair. *Of course*, I thought. The Norse woman had once been a made-child herself. She had escaped from the station, just as Gerda had. But what did that have to do with Kai?

I paced my hut. If I left my valley, now, it was just possible that I could make it back with Gerda before the creeping cold killed my warmth-loving trees. But if Gerda resisted—

She was still watching the doors. Waiting to see if they opened, perhaps. Why didn't she at least come home to see me? I knew the answer to that, a moment later—she knew she wouldn't have the heart to leave me again.

Gerda had taken her shoes, but left her own tag behind—it was in my attic. I climbed up the ladder and found the tag quickly in the dark corner where I'd hidden her clothes. Then I looked one shelf down. And found it: another tag.

N2178F.

Forgetfulness tea is not a perfect spell. Of course, it all came back.

My Kai had been a year younger than me—oh, and it was the Lars, not the Kai. The Kai of my year was a dullard, a blue-eyed boy who'd never asked a question more complicated than "where is the bathroom" in all his years. Lars had been far too clever, like me, and far too stubborn, like me, and one day he had simply not been there anymore. I had gone to look for him, and had found my way to the outside. Like Gerda, I had quickly gotten lost; like Gerda, I had been found by the witch of the garden. Like Gerda, I had been adopted.

I didn't have the heart to look to see if my mother had had a tag too.

I flung my second-best cloak around my shoulders and hurried out of the house. I had to talk to Gerda. It didn't matter if my garden died; even if Gerda refused to come with me, at least I'd know I'd tried.

Gerda was still perched behind her rock when I arrived. Her face blossomed into a smile when she saw me. "Mother! What are you doing here?"

"My magic told me you were close by," I said, truthfully.

"But your garden—"

"I'm going to hurry back there." I squatted beside her. "But I wanted to tell you, I realized what happened to Kai." She turned towards me. "Gerda, I realized something while you were gone. I realized that I, too, am a made-child who escaped from the station. And I, too, lost a friend. Gerda, the made-children who stay behind—they are sold into slavery. The girl you saw at the laboratory—she *was* your friend. She had been fragged—they used their magic to see that she would behave herself, and they sold her. Kai just had it done sooner, since they were afraid he'd cause trouble."

"Sooner or later, the Snow Queen comes for all the made-children," Gerda said.

"Yes," I said.

"I had realized that, too," Gerda said. "I still want to find Kai."

"There's nothing you can do for him," I said. "Must you find him today?"

Gerda looked away from me, towards the station. "Yes."

We slipped into the station with a shipment of supplies, and hid in the storage warehouse. To either side of us, storage shelves stretched from the cold slab floor to the cavernous ceiling, disappearing into dusk near the top. "Now what?" I whispered.

"I guess we look for Kai," Gerda whispered. She looked around at the shadowy warehouse, unsure where to even begin.

"Use the claw," I said. "Its magic will help you find anyone who is close to your heart."

Gerda took the claw in her hand and said, "Kai, Kai, Kai." The claw moved slightly in her palm and pointed. Looking carefully to be certain that no one could turn suddenly and see us, we hurried through the narrow corridor between the shelves until we found a solid wall, and then a door in the wall. Through the door, and we were out in a hallway.

"Kai, Kai, Kai," Gerda whispered. The claw pointed—but the corridor ran straight, and the claw pointed at an angle. "This way," Gerda said after a moment, and we continued on.

I shivered; my years as a made-child in the station were flooding back. We heard footsteps, and flattened ourselves uselessly into one of the doorways, but the footsteps faded away.

"He's behind this door," Gerda said suddenly.

The door was not locked. We felt a blast of cold air as we stepped inside, colder than the winter air outside; Gerda closed the door quietly behind us.

We were in another warehouse, but it was a warehouse for storing frozen things. Frost coated the walls; a patch of it melted under my breath as we hesitated by the door. I tucked my hands under my second-best cloak and shivered. Gerda, beside me, hardly seemed to feel the cold.

At the far end of the room, a brown-haired boy was stacking boxes on a pallet. Gerda sucked in her breath.

"That's Kai?" I whispered. She nodded tightly. "Well, let's go talk to him, then."

The boy didn't look at us as we approached. "Kai," Gerda said softly. He stopped what he was doing and looked up. "Kai, do you remember me?"

Kai's eyes were strange and foggy. In his temple, I could see a flicker, like light catching in a bright jewel.

"He's a frag," Gerda said. "There were frags who did the cleaning and the cooking. Even some of the care for the made-children. I never realized . . ."

Of course not.

"Come with me," she ordered Kai, but his masters had not told him to obey her, so he simply stood where he was. He didn't cry out or alert anyone to our presence; that wasn't one of his orders, either. He was just there to load and unload boxes. Through the mists of the forgetfulness tea, I thought back to my own childhood—to the training classes I took as an eleven-year-old, a twelve-year-old. Frags could learn nothing new. Kai, fragged early, could not do any of the more technical work that would have made him valuable to the scientists.

Gerda took Kai's hand; he allowed her to hold it, pausing in his work for a moment, puzzled but cooperative. "Oh, Kai," she whispered. She turned to me, fiercely, for a moment. "Can you help him? Can your magic help him?"

"I know of no magic that can restore a soul, once it's been taken," I said. "And I've never heard of a frag becoming whole again."

Kai had started to turn away, to return to his work, and Gerda caught him in her arms. "I won't leave you like this," she said. With one hand, she caught the tag, snug against Kai's throat, and wrapped her fist around it. "Be free, Kai," she said, and yanked it loose. There was a soft pop, like popcorn, and a burned smell, and Kai dropped where he stood.

"Now we can go," Gerda said.

Gerda didn't speak again until we were back in my valley. The air had grown crisp in my absence, and the current crop of oranges and lemons would be lost—but the trees would survive. And the roses, I thought.

After inspecting the garden, I made tea for both of us, to give us strength of heart and body. Gerda drank a little of the tea, but mostly she just clasped the cup, warming her hands.

"Can I stay here with you?" Gerda asked.

"Of course," I said. "You are my daughter, and I love you."

Gerda drank the rest of her tea. "I'll go back someday," Gerda said. "To free the made-children."

"Yes," I said.

"Teach me your magic, mother," Gerda said, and I reached out across the table to clasp her hand.

WHAT HAPPENED
AT BLESSING CREEK

We circled our wagons at night so Reverend Dawson's magic could protect us. The Reverend said it was the power of prayer, but Papa scoffed at that.

"He's a magician, and a good one," Papa said. "Or we wouldn't've brought him along in the first place."

My sister Adeline liked to pretend Papa had said something shocking, but I knew he was right. I could smell the magic on the Reverend. I could hear it humming when he said the last words of the nightly blessing that kept out trouble—dragons, wolves, fevers, Indians.

Adeline and I were twins, but not the sort who looked alike. She was the pretty one, with plump pink cheeks and hair the color of summer butter. My mother said I was the clever one, but she didn't really believe it. I wasn't pretty, though, so I suppose she thought it would be a consolation if people thought me clever.

"Papa's right, you know," I told Adeline one night. "I can smell the magic even now." It smelled like burnt bread, and I could hear it crackle into place beyond our wagons.

"Don't talk about your second sight, Hattie," Adeline said. "It's not ladylike. You know what Mother says."

Mother said that every man wished he'd had a witch for a mother, but no one wanted one as a wife. Witches were useful to have in the family. Sometimes they could keep a child from dying of a fever, or banish mice from your grain store. But that didn't mean anyone wanted to marry one.

"So why would you want a witch as a husband?" I muttered, half to myself.

"He's not a witch. He is a *minister of the gospel.*"

"Hush, girls," Mother said. We were supposed to be going to sleep, even though the grownups would be talking by the fire for hours yet. We fell silent for a few minutes.

"Anyway, that was back east they said no one wanted to marry a witch," I said. "We're going west. Things could be different. There are dangers here."

"Not so long as we stay close to the Reverend," Adeline said.

"Do you think everyone who comes west wants to live in a town? Maybe I'll meet a man who wants to strike out on his own."

"No man wants to be protected by his wife. Anyway, do you think you could really make a good blessing? Just because you can smell the magic doesn't mean you can do it."

"*Girls.* I don't want to tell you again."

This time I kept my peace, and after a few minutes I heard Adeline's breathing turn quiet and steady. I stared up at the stars, still wide awake. Out in the distance, somewhere in the darkness of the prairie, I heard a long, high-pitched cry, and then an answering cry, further away. I sat up and looked; my mother was by the fire. "You're perfectly safe, Hattie," she said.

"What was that?" I asked. We'd heard wolves howling a few nights ago. This was different.

"Probably a dragon."

"Do you think we'll see a dragon?" I asked.

"Mercy, I hope not."

"Is it true the Indians ride them?"

"I shouldn't think so. Dragons are bigger than houses and wilder than wolves."

"Do you think we'll see Indians?"

"Oh, I don't think so."

"But isn't this Indian country?"

"They'll move further west," she said. "They'll have to, now that white folks are coming."

I thought about that a moment and then asked, "Will they be angry about having to move?"

"That's why we brought the Reverend."

"What happens when they get all the way west? There's an ocean, they can't keep going forever."

"Go to sleep, Hattie," she said again, and this time she used a voice like she meant it.

We were heading into Kansas territory. Papa said the Indians here were called the Osage, and they were a race of giants, with the shortest of their men at least as tall as Papa. Joe Franklin, one of the men traveling with us, said they ate human flesh, and then laughed, showing his missing front teeth. Mother frowned at him, and he tipped his hat to her and rode off to the other end of the wagon train.

When we camped each night, before the Reverend blessed our circle, it was my job to fetch water. That evening, I thought about what Adeline had said, and decided to see if I could do a blessing, too. Standing in the creek bottom, I closed my eyes and stretched out my arms. "May the Lord bless the land I stand on," I intoned, trying to talk like the Reverend. "Lord, let us feed on Your truth. Send Your sacred blood to purify us and strengthen us and send Angels of War to guard us with their fiery swords—"

"Nice try, Miss Cartwright." My eyes flew open; it was Joe Franklin. "You trying to protect yourself from anyone in specific?" He grinned at me. "I didn't think I'd scared you *that* bad today."

I turned my back on him, my ears burning. I could feel the magic humming around me; it had risen, but it hadn't really done anything. "I'm not scared."

"No?"

In truth, Joe Franklin made me nervous. He liked to tell stories that weren't proper, like the one about how he'd had his teeth knocked out in a brawl. I started back up the path with my bucket.

"Excuse me," I said, since he was blocking the path.

He stepped out the way, still grinning. "I could carry that for you," he offered.

"No, thank you, I am perfectly capable of carrying it myself."

"Suit yourself."

Back at the camp, Papa and Reverend Dawson had their heads together over some papers. They talked through the evening—Mother had Adeline bring Papa his dinner—and I wasn't surprised when we didn't go anywhere come morning. The men rode out, and Mother told me they'd decided we'd come far enough west and were looking to find the best place for our town. We camped there for two days, while they thought about it, and finally on the third day they moved us a half-mile up the creek, and Reverend Dawson blessed the new town. They dug a hole, and he buried a bag he'd brought with him from the east, and all the men helped fill in the hole, a little at a time. Then above the hole they put a sign saying TOWN OF BLESSING.

Papa took us out riding that afternoon. The creek led up to a river not too far away, with trees we could cut to build our houses. The prairie stretched wide around us; it would be easy to get lost here, down in the grass.

"This is an ugly place," Adeline said. "I miss Ohio."

"This land will never love us," Papa said, patting her on the arm. "Not like it loves the Indians. But we'll teach it to serve us well enough. We've got seeds, and livestock, and there's good hunting here—even those dragons! Not that you'd want to *eat* a dragon, but think how little dragonskin goes into a pair of dragon leather boots, and think how much those cost."

Adeline sniffed. "Yes, but what good will that money do us here? There's nowhere to spend it!"

"Oh, that's true now. But more wagon trains are on their way. And once Blessing is up and running, even more people will come. It'll be a real town soon enough, and we won't have the troubles we had in Ohio." Papa had been in business in Ohio—well, really, he'd been in several businesses in Ohio. None of them lasted very long. "Things will be grand here," Papa said. "You'll see."

Adeline pouted a bit more. I looked out at the prairie again, and pointed to a thin line of smoke rising up from the prairie that stretched west from Blessing. "What's that?"

There was an encampment of Osage Indians less than two miles from Blessing. Papa told Mother they hadn't realized that, when they picked this spot for the town. The Osage might have been off hunting, so our men saw no smoke from their fires when they were scouting.

But it was too late to move the town now. They'd buried the relics and put up the sign; they didn't have another bag. Mother was coldly furious, and Adeline wept in the wagon, saying she was frightened.

Adeline had always been made of softer stuff than I. When we were little and a boy at school left a snake on the desk Adeline and I shared, she screamed and ran away. I was the one who grabbed the snake by its tail and dropped it down the shirt of the boy who'd left it for us. Still, she hadn't ever been a fainting hysteric. The longer we stayed, the jumpier she got.

"What does the Reverend's magic smell like, Hattie?" she asked one night as we were going to bed.

"I thought you didn't want me talking about it."

"Does it smell different than it used to?" she asked.

It did, actually. "You can smell it?" I said, surprised.

"No!" she said. "Of course not! It's just—"

"You *can* smell it," I said.

"What if he led us here on purpose?" Adeline said. "What if he's working with the Indians, what if it's a trap?"

"Don't be ridiculous," I said, and pulled the covers over my head. She didn't say anything more, but I heard her inhale a long breath, then another, like she was trying to smell the magic.

A week passed. I held my tongue and fetched water and carried it around to the men as they worked. Adeline was supposed to help, but she said it was too frightening to go down to the creek bottom, so it all fell on me. Fortunately, Joe Franklin was busy cutting wood, so I didn't run into him in the creek bottom again, but I had to tolerate him grinning at me over the ladle when I offered him water.

I was terribly tired by late afternoon, and at first I didn't notice the long shadow moving in the grass as I was hauling the bucket out. Then I thought maybe it was Joe Franklin. But when I turned to look, I saw a dragon, crawling in the grass toward me.

I saw it for just an instant, so close I could have reached out to steal one of its crest feathers. It was scarlet and gold, with scales on its belly and its long, snake-like neck, and soft down rippling along its wings, which were folded to let it creep along on the claws on its wing tips. Its mouth opened, and I could see rows of long, sharp teeth.

I drew in my breath to scream, turning toward camp hoping to see anyone at all, even Joe Franklin, but my mouth was dry and all that came out was a croak. I turned back and the dragon was gone. Instead, I saw an Indian wearing a dragon-skin cloak, which he slipped off his shoulders and left on the ground at his feet. He took a step forward but held up his empty hands to show he had no weapon. "I won't hurt you," he said in English.

He was tall, as tall as Papa, but not a giant, and his head was shaved except for a bit in the back, and a feather—one of the dragon feathers—stuck out of his hair. He wore no shirt, and had designs painted on his face and body. I was so relieved that he was just an Indian, rather than a dragon, that I answered him.

"What do you want?" I said.

"I bring a message for your people," he said. "Will you carry it?"

"Yes," I said.

"We belong to this land. You do not. You need to leave."

I laughed out loud. "They're not going to move the town on my say-so," I said. "The men picked the spot. Do you think they're going to pack up and go back to Ohio?"

"That is my message," he said. "Will you carry it?"

"Yes, but—"

"That's all I ask," he said. He picked up his cloak and walked away, back toward the Osage camp.

I carried my bucket up to our camp—our town, they said I should call it, but it still looked like a camp. My father and Reverend Dawson were looking over papers again. "Papa?" I said softly, my bucket still in my hands.

"I'm rather busy right now, Hattie."

"There was an Indian at the creek who wanted me to tell you something," I said.

He laid his papers down. "An Indian approached you?" He shot an accusing look at Reverend Dawson.

"Yes, Papa, an Indian man."

"What did he want?"

"He said that he wanted me to carry a message."

"Yes?"

"He said this land is theirs and not ours, and we have to leave."

They burst out laughing and I said, "I *told* him no one was going to leave. I *said*. But he said—"

"It's all right, Hattie," Papa said, clapping me on the shoulder. "You did well to come to us. I don't expect you'll see him again, but if you do, tell him my message for *his* people is that the clever ants are the ones that get out of the way when the buffalo are coming."

I didn't see the Indian again—not right away, at least. But it was clear enough we weren't going anywhere. The Reverend renewed the blessing every night and every morning, and for a time, the building and planting continued undisturbed.

Then one of the men went out hunting and didn't come back. His horse didn't come back, either. He was just gone, vanished into the prairie. Joe Franklin was furious about it; he hadn't even been friends with the man, but kept saying it could have been any of us. He wanted to teach the Indians a lesson.

"You're safe as long as you stay near the town," Reverend Dawson said. "He was probably eaten by a dragon."

"The dragons don't eat anyone the Indians don't tell them to eat," Joe Franklin said. "Everyone knows that."

"We're not strong enough yet to take on the Indians directly," Reverend Dawson said. "Show some patience."

He ordered the men to stay in pairs when they went out, so they could watch each other's backs. No one else disappeared, and we all relaxed for a bit.

Then the dragon came.

Adeline saw it first—way, way up in the sky, so high up it was barely a dot. But then it circled down toward us, and first it looked like a bird, and then it looked like a really big bird, and then it was low enough that we could see the sun glint off the scales on its enormous neck. From here, the downy feathers on its wings looked like scales as well, and I tried not to think about the dragon I thought I'd seen down by the creek. This one was a darker red, with glinting orange on its neck. The tips of its wings were yellow.

"It can't come close enough to hurt us," the Reverend Dawson said.

No one was listening. It wasn't exactly that they didn't believe him. It was more that they could *see* the dragon, and how big it was, and how big its claws were, and how sharp its teeth were. And they couldn't see the magic. Even I couldn't *see* it, though I knew it was there.

Around and around it circled, lower and lower. It was Adeline who started the panic—Adeline only ran as far as our wagon, and hid under a blanket, but there were others who started to run, or who grabbed horses and took off at a gallop.

"I can't protect you!" Reverend Dawson shouted. "If you leave the town, God's mercy will not shelter you!"

Mother stood frozen but Papa never doubted. He ran into the wagon to drag Adeline back out. I think he had some idea that if he could force Adeline to calm down, the others who were running away would come back. When Papa brought her out, Reverend Dawson grabbed her around the waist and shouted, "By the Power of Christ's purifying blood, I banish the demon of fear! I banish the demon of panic! I cast out the demon of disobedience . . ."

The dragon swooped down. One of the men from the wagon train must have gotten just far enough on his horse to be outside the protection of the blessing. We saw him when the dragon rose again with the man in its teeth. I could see the man's legs kicking, like a chicken's right after you slaughter it.

"Stop," Adeline screamed. "Make him let me go, he's going to give us all to the dragon," and too late, we all saw a knife in her hand.

We laid Reverend Dawson's body next to the Town of Blessing sign. Mother dosed Adeline with laudanum and left her to sleep in one of the wagons. She'd been mad with fear, Papa said; it wasn't her fault. Perhaps the Indians had bewitched her, which wouldn't be her fault either.

Six of the people from town had run when the dragon came. Three slunk back, quiet and ashamed.

"What are we going to do now?" I asked my father. I could hear the hum of the magic still, but it would fade soon, without Reverend Dawson renewing it. Other wagon trains might be coming, and they surely had magicians of their own, but we'd never last that long.

"We're not going to leave, if that's what you're thinking," Papa said. His arm tightened around me. "We're never going back. This land is ours, now."

"But without the Reverend Dawson—"

"We don't need the Reverend Dawson. We have you."

"Papa, I tried once to do a blessing, on my own. I couldn't do it."

"That's all right," he said. "Wait till tonight. When we bury the Reverend. You'll understand then."

Papa sent me to bed, but then woke me when the moon rose. Mother slept next to Adeline, ready with another dose of her medicines if Adeline stirred. Papa led me out to the Town of Blessing sign, where the Reverend's body still lay. Someone had built a fire, and the men were gathered in a circle.

"What's the girl doing here?" one of the men asked.

"Oh, she belongs here," Joe Franklin said, and grinned. "Unless you want to turn around and go back to Ohio."

"Who has the knife?" Papa asked.

"I've got it." Joe Franklin handed it to Papa. "Did you tell her what's going to happen?"

Papa shook his head. "Sit quietly, Hattie, and do exactly as I tell you." He raised his knife over the Reverend, and then gave me another brief look. "Don't scream," he added.

I covered my mouth with my hands as Papa plunged the knife into the Reverend's chest, used his fingers to crack open his ribs, and carved the heart from his body. Papa laid the heart on a slab of wood and cut it into pieces.

He picked up the first piece, and ate it. Then he speared another piece with the knife, and offered it to Joe Franklin, who stuck it in his mouth and chewed. One by one, every one of the men ate a piece of Reverend Dawson's heart. One piece was left, and Papa picked it up in his fingers. "Open your mouth, Hattie," he said.

"I don't want to," I said, my voice shaking.

"Do you want to be a proper magician, like the Reverend was? Or do you want to be a puny little witch all your life? *Eat the heart.*"

I closed my eyes and bit down. It was salty and tough, but I swallowed it without gagging.

When you eat the heart of a magician, some of his power passes to you. In my dreams, Joe Franklin was the one explaining, even though it was my father who told me these things before sending me back to my bed. *Of course there are things that make it work better. If you kill the man yourself, for instance. Shame it wasn't you that drove the knife in, if we had to lose the Reverend.*

"Why not have Adeline eat it, then?" I asked.

A weak, sniveling, useless little bit like your twin? he said. No, Hattie. If anyone's going to bless the town and have it stick, it's going to be you.

Papa shook me awake at dawn and led me to the Town of Blessing sign. I folded my hands and listened for the magic. Reverend Dawson had always spoken his blessings out loud, but I thought now that wasn't strictly necessary. I closed my eyes and told it to shape itself around us: keep out dragons, keep out Indians, keep out malice and misfortune and everything else Reverend Dawson had mentioned in any of his blessings. I heard it all fall into place like musical notes forming a chord.

There, that's done, I thought, and then looked around at the expectant faces of the men surrounding me. They couldn't hear it. So I cleared my throat and said, "God bless us and keep us safe, for ever and ever, amen."

"Do you think that really worked?" one of the men asked Papa.

"It worked," I said.

Papa gave me an appraising look and said, "I think that should keep us as safe as the Reverend's blessings, yes."

The dragon came again a day later.

It couldn't get through my blessing, any more than it could get through Reverend Dawson's, and this time no one ran away, but it drove Adeline fair mad and Mother had to dose her to make her sleep again. Afterward I saw Mother measure the medicine in the bottle and sigh deeply. "It won't last long, not at this rate," she said to Papa.

I was sitting with Adeline when she woke. "The dragon's gone," I told her as she stirred.

"I hear them laughing," she muttered.

"No one's laughing at you," I said. "They know you're just frightened. But you need to control yourself when it comes next time."

"I hear the dragons when I sleep," Adeline said.

She was hearing my magic, I thought. Even if she didn't want to admit it. "If you just admit you can smell the magic, maybe I can help you," I said.

She came fully awake then and gave me a haughty glare—her old self again. "You know it's not ladylike to talk about these things," she said.

I sighed and stood up. "I'll send Mother in to sit with you, since you're feeling better," I said.

I sat down outside in the shade, and Papa came to sit beside me. "Tell me again about that Indian you saw," he said.

"He didn't look very old," I said. "He was tall, and had a shaved head with a feather, and he said—"

"I remember what he said. Did he walk right up to you?"

"Yes, by the creek. I turned around and he was standing there." I decided not to mention the dragon. Papa would think I was as crazy as Adeline.

"He must have been their magician," Papa said. "To get through the blessing like that."

"I guess," I said. "Or maybe the Reverend didn't bless the creek that day."

"What was he wearing?"

"A cloak of dragon skin on the top half," I said. "Deerskin on the lower, I think. A loincloth and leg coverings. He had a dragon crest feather in his hair."

Papa nodded. "Some of the men have seen him from a distance. I think it's time we bring him back for another visit."

After I started doing the morning blessing, Papa stopped having me carry water. In fact, everyone wanted me to keep as close to the center of Blessing as possible, and I sat in the shade and watched everyone else work, just like Reverend Dawson had. Even Joe Franklin stopped grinning at me. When he did look at me, which wasn't often, it was with wary respect.

I wondered what would happen when another wagon train arrived. Would their magician take over and send me back to carry water again? Girls could grow up to be witches, but I'd never known a girl to be a proper Minister. Then again, things were different here on the frontier.

For now, at least, I was well-protected. Papa decided I shouldn't even sleep by Adeline anymore, lest she wake up crazed with fear in the night. And yet the Osage sent out their magician like a scout, even after he'd delivered that warning. Surely they knew what would happen.

Surely we should have suspected they knew.

Joe Franklin was in the party that caught him and brought him back. I heard the triumphant shouts as they crossed the boundary into Blessing, and sure enough Joe Franklin and his friends rode straight to me and Papa. Joe Franklin pushed the Indian off his horse so he landed at our feet. They'd bound him, and he landed hard, but made no sound. Papa rolled him onto his back and smiled up at Joe Franklin. "You did well, Franklin," he said. "Is this the Indian you met, Hattie?"

I looked down at him. His face was swelling, where someone had hit him hard, and the dragonskin cloak was gone. "Yes," I said. "I think so."

The Indian kept his eyes closed, but I saw a flicker when he heard my voice.

"We should do it by moonlight," Joe Franklin said, and grinned at my father.

"Of course. I'll keep an eye on him till then," Papa said.

Papa tied him to the Town of Blessing sign, and watched him from the shade just to be sure he didn't get loose.

"What is Joe Franklin going to do?" I asked.

"Franklin's not doing anything, Hattie. It's you who's going to do it," he said. "Remember what I told you about power? You eat his heart, you'll be able to control the dragons, just like he does. Dragons are wild creatures, wilder than wolves. It must be their magic that does it. If we eat his heart and burn his body, we'll steal what we can of his magic and destroy the rest."

His eyes were open now, I realized. He was watching us. He looked very calm for someone hearing about how people were going to eat his heart. "You're saying I need to kill that man and rip his heart out?"

"You need to kill him," Papa said. "I can take out his heart for you, but you should be the one to do the killing. It shouldn't be so hard to eat it afterward. You've done it once now."

Papa sounded perfectly calm about it. I decided I needed to take a walk, and for once, Papa let me go.

Mother was sitting in one of the half-finished houses, making fried bread and jackrabbit stew.

"They brought back the Indian," I said.

"Well, thank goodness," Mother said. "It's a fine thing, don't you think? Should solve a lot of our problems."

"Do you know what Papa wants me to do?" I asked.

Mother sighed deeply. "I wasn't happy when he had you take over for the Reverend. Magic isn't ladylike. I've said it before and I'll say it again. But I don't see as we had much choice. We had to have *some* sort of protection."

"But now he wants me to—"

"Shhh," she interrupted. "You don't want to disturb your sister. She might get upset." Adeline was sitting in the shade at the back of the house, mending socks. "We're almost out of medicine. I don't know what we're going to do once that's gone. I might not be able to control her, if she tries to run out where the dragon could catch her. If the dragon stops coming—well, that'll be much better, don't you think?"

"Of course," I said. "Of course I want the dragon to stop coming."

"Well, then you'll need to learn to control it, won't you? It's not as if anyone else here can do it."

Back by the sign, Joe Franklin had taken over guarding the Indian, but he shuffled off a bit when he saw me coming. I sat down in the shade again. The Indian looked at me and said, "Hello, Hattie."

"How do you know my name?" I asked.

"Your people talk about you. They fear you."

"Joe Franklin is frightened, and that's fine with me."

"Cut me loose," the Indian said. "I can take you to the village of my people. Your sister, too. You can go to the house of the chief and ask for protection and you'll get it. The Osage revere those with your gift, whether they be men or women."

"Or white?"

"I can see your gift around you like the feathers of a bird," he said. "You are already greater than your Reverend ever would have been. You could command the skies and bring rain, you could call the buffalo and the geese, you could tell the fire to return to the earth, if you studied with the Little Old Men and grew to maturity."

"Or I could take the power from you," I said.

"You will regret it," he said.

"How is it you speak English so well?" I asked him. "Did you learn it from eating white magicians?"

"No. For a time I was a scout for a white Army general."

"So you worked *for* white people but now you've turned against us?"

"You don't belong here," he said. "We do. Listen to me, Hattie. If you don't want to live with my people, persuade yours to turn back. You'll be safe if you're leaving."

"*I* should persuade people? Why would they listen to me?"

"They *have* to listen to you. If you refuse to protect them, they'll lose everything."

I strode away angrily and went to walk the borders of the town. The dragon was nowhere to be seen today, but in the waving grasses beyond our border I thought I could smell someone else's magic. Join the Indians? And yet he hadn't answered me when I asked whether they really revered white magicians like their own. This Indian had been a scout for white men—for years, probably, judging from how well he spoke English. But he'd never truly been one of us, that was obvious, and I'd never truly be one of them either. They might not kill me, if I asked for protection, but I didn't trust his offer one bit.

So then—go back? Adeline would like nothing better than to return to Ohio where she could forget all about dragons and Indians and the blood-stained dress that Mother had scrubbed but would never be clean. She was the pretty one; she could marry some solid man who would give her the quiet life she needed. Papa would be furious with me, of course. I didn't care to think about that too much.

What would *I* do in Ohio? Neither clever nor pretty, a magician and a girl, I supposed I could set up shop as a particularly powerful witch. If I had the power in me to learn to command the skies, then surely I could learn to dowse or deliver babies. There was an old lady in Cleveland, she had a very nice house and it wasn't so bad to be on the outskirts of town. I could be the favorite aunt to Adeline's children.

No, I thought. I want the freedom of the frontier. There's nowhere but Blessing that I can be who I am.

It was me and the men, once again, who gathered in the moonlight. Papa took me aside first and showed me a pistol. "I thought this might be easiest for you. Just put it to his head and pull the trigger. I'll take care of the rest."

They'd built up a bonfire nearby. Reverend Dawson's remains had been buried next to the Town of Blessing sign, because some of his magic would linger to protect the town. The Indian's remains would be burned.

My hands were slippery with sweat; I had to keep wiping them on my skirt.

Joe Franklin put a blindfold on the Indian. "Consider yourself lucky," he said to the Indian, loud enough that I could hear him. "They gave Hattie a gun to make it quick. If it were up to me I'd do it with a knife and I'd take my time."

I stared at the Indian from the edge of the circle of firelight. My hands were shaking. Papa put his hand on my shoulder and walked me forward, then placed the pistol in my hand, wrapping my fingers around it. It was cold and smooth, and my hands were sweaty and shaking. As I started to raise the pistol, it slipped and I dropped it. It didn't go off, just hit the ground next to my foot with a thud. I heard the Indian's breath catch. "You still have a choice," he said, very quietly.

I crouched down to pick up the gun. "I think you're going to have to do it," Joe Franklin said to Papa. "I don't think she's got—"

"She'll do it," Papa said.

I picked up the gun, holding it in both hands this time, and looked at the Indian. He stood still, and I thought his eyes, under the blindfold, were open and looking at me. I took a deep breath, then pressed the gun against his head.

The gun didn't slip as I pulled the trigger.

The noise was deafening, and I gasped and stepped back. My hand felt bruised from the gun's recoil, and the Indian's head was nearly gone, reduced to a bloody mess; Joe Franklin had been caught in the spray of his blood, and he wiped it calmly off the side of his face. The Indian's body hung limp, and Papa shouldered me aside to cut him loose and lay him on the ground. He took out the knife. "Wake the women," he said to one of the other men as he worked. "This time everyone eats."

"Even Adeline?"

"No," Papa said. "No, not Adeline. But everyone else."

The women joined the circle as Papa cut the heart into pieces, and I watched as my mother ate a piece, and the other wives. Papa saved the last piece for me. The Reverend's heart had tasted salty and tough, but the Indian's burned like fire in my mouth, and I could barely swallow it. Tears came to my eyes, and I turned away so that no one would think I was crying from fear or sorrow.

"Go to bed, Hattie," Papa said. "We'll take care of the rest of him."

In my sleep, I heard the scream of a thousand dragons, and I looked up to see a vast flock blackening the sky. "Stop," I shouted up at them. "Go away. I can command the skies!" They didn't listen to me.

Instead, they dived down like eagles seeking prey and seized us all. I tried to run, in the dream, but my feet stuck to the ground. I tried to call for help, but the words stuck in my throat. And then dragon claws were tearing into me, and there was nothing I could do, and I thought I would wake, as I'd had enough nightmares to recognize one for what it was, but instead I found myself back on the prairie, looking up at a thousand dragons blackening the sky . . .

And now I heard the war-cry of Indians, and they rode toward us on horseback. "Stop," I shouted, but the hoof-beats shook the ground like an earthquake. I tried to run, but I couldn't, and I tried to call for help, but no sound emerged, and the horses rode over me like grass and I thought I would wake . . .

. . . the fire was coming, it was coming, sweeping through the prairie, burning dry grass, the wall of flame, I could feel the heat of the monster no one could possibly outrun . . .

Where was Adeline? *Where was Adeline?*

"Wake up! Wake up!"

Adeline was shaking my shoulders, sobbing hysterically.

"Hattie, wake *up*. Oh, why won't *anyone* wake up? Wake *up*," she wailed.

"I'm awake," I muttered, but I wasn't, not really. When I forced my eyes open I could see Adeline's face, but as soon as I closed them the flames roared around me again. The sun scorched my eyes as I opened them; it was broad day, and I needed to renew the blessing. I could hear the magic roaring around me but when I reached for it, it burned me like fire . . .

*

Where is Adeline? Where? Where?

"I'm right here, Hattie." Adeline's voice was dull and quiet. "I've been right here the whole time."

I opened my eyes and sat up. The dreams were gone. I was damp, and my mouth felt coarse and sticky. It was dark, and no fire burned. I could make out the town around me in the moonlight, but only just.

"I'm all right," I said to Adeline, sitting up. "I'm myself—what happened?"

"I woke up four days ago," Adeline said. "And everyone was asleep. You, Papa, Mother . . . everyone but me. When I tried to wake up Papa, he thrashed and shouted about dragons. Mother was the same. And you. And everyone. I've been waiting and waiting for the Indians to come and finish us off, but they haven't . . ."

"Can I have something to drink?" I croaked, and Adeline burst into tears and handed me a ladle. I drank deeply.

"I sat by you," Adeline said, "because you were the only one I could get to take water at *all*. Sometimes you'd wake up just a little, and I could make you swallow some. Mother—Papa—"

"Well, maybe they'll wake now," I said cheerfully, and tried to stand. My legs didn't want to obey me. "Can you help me up?"

Adeline shook her head. "They're all gone," she said. "I couldn't make them drink, and in the sun . . . they're all dead, Hattie. Mother, Papa, Joe Franklin, everyone but you and me."

The Indian magician came at dawn. She was an old woman, old enough to be a grandmother, and when I smelled her magic I thought she could probably command the skies, the winds, the buffalo herds, and the dragons.

"You were warned," she said.

"Yes," I said.

"You made your choice."

There wasn't much point in arguing. "Adeline didn't," I said.

"That's true," she said. "Your sister can remain with us. She will be safe here, and can rest and recover. If she chooses to return to your people in a year or two, we will guide her back."

"What about me?" I asked.

"We gave you a message," she said. "The man you murdered, Sees-Far, gave you a message. We belong to this land. Your people do not. We're sending you back with that message. Give it to the rest of your people."

"What if they don't listen?"

"Then perhaps they will eat your poisoned heart, and suffer your fate."

I still hear the dragons in my dreams. Sometimes they speak to me in Sees-Far's voice. Sometimes they speak to me in Adeline's; sometimes they say nothing I can understand. They no longer eat me, night after night. Only sometimes.

In these dreams, the power I ripped from Sees-Far rises up around me like a prairie fire: wild, powerful, and utterly beyond my control. I wonder sometimes what this power would have felt like if I'd freed Sees-Far and gone to his people to ask for protection. If I'd asked to learn, instead of trying to swallow him up.

Oh, I've asked for forgiveness. I've asked for comfort; I've asked for release. So far, all have been denied me.

Perhaps, my friend, you would like to take this burden from me. You could bind me, wait for darkness, devour my heart and with it the power I can neither use nor bear. Perhaps it was not the great power of the Osage, but my own weakness that led to what happened at Blessing Creek. You are strong; you are clever; you are confident. Maybe you could eat my heart and my power and turn it back against the ones that Sees-Far sacrificed himself to protect.

Or perhaps you will listen, as I did not.

If you are wise, friend, you will turn back here.

Author's Note

When I re-read the Little House books as an adult, I was struck by how much I'd missed as a child—particularly in Little House on the Prairie. Pa moves into Indian Country illegally and deliberately; he settles on land he knows belongs to other people. Laura asks some questions about this early on and is told to hush. I had remembered the scene where Indians come into the family's house, but rereading as an adult, I picked up on a detail I had missed as a child: Laura describes the Indians' ribs being visible against their skin. She is describing men who are starving to death. Why are they starving? Because their uninvited neighbors were burning their fields in an attempt to force them off their land.

White American writers have written volumes about Native Americans and the western frontier, and so many of the stories we've told (and continue to tell) are profoundly dishonest. Frequently, the dispossession and displacement of Native Americans is treated like a natural disaster, something terrible that happened, rather than something terrible that was done. (Done by white people.) Many stories focus on the lone white person who Gets It and throws in his or her lot with the Lakota (or the Na'vi). These stories give white readers and viewers a comfortable window on the past, with a solid framework they can use to reassure themselves that they'd be One of The Good Ones.

I wanted to write a story that provided a different sort of window. "What Happened at Blessing Creek" came out of some pondering I did about whether it was even possible to write an honest story from the white perspective that didn't pretty anything up. I'm still not sure if this story succeeded or failed at my goal.

CLEANOUT

I. Entry

Magda and I hadn't spoken in three years when she, Nora, and I had to meet at our mother's house to clean it out and prepare it for sale.

She and Nora were speaking, and Nora and I were speaking, but after five minutes of glowering, Nora told us she was not acting as our go-between for another minute, and if we didn't quit acting like children in a snit, she'd leave and let us sort out all of Mom's junk by ourselves.

That was a sufficiently horrifying prospect to cow both of us into better manners. Because there was a lot to go through. Our parents were immigrants from some former Soviet republic with a lot of mountains, and after coming to the U.S. with just the clothes they were wearing, they apparently never threw anything away ever again.

We all started in random spots. Magda with the kitchen, packing up bags of warped cookie sheets and chipped frying pans with the nonstick coating peeling off to donate to whichever local charity took housewares. Nora in the basement, because so much down there was water-damaged and mold-saturated she could just haul it straight out to the Dumpster we'd rented.

I started in the entryway—the little foyer for people to leave boots and hang up coats—because it was tiny and that made it feel manageable. A shelf ran above the coat hooks where normal people might have stored umbrellas or hats. My father had used the shelf for his collection of flags. You know how if you go to a Fourth of July parade you get a little flag to wave? My father disapproved of the fact that people threw those away when they were done. So unpatriotic! *No appreciation for the freedoms here, none,* he would grumble as he gathered them up—not just ours, but any he found lying on the ground afterward. *Americans who were born here take everything for granted.* But it wasn't like he did anything with them; he just stored them, endlessly, in shoe boxes in the entryway.

Dad had died ten years earlier. Mom was less compulsive about rescuing flags from the trash, but she didn't throw anything away either, so of course all the flags were still there. I pulled down the boxes and carried them into the kitchen so I could sit at the table while I went through them. (I was pretty sure they were full of flags, but there might be other stuff we'd want.)

"What are you going to do with those?" Magda asked.

"Dumpster," I said.

"What? You can't! Dad would split at the seams."

"He's not here," I pointed out. The flags were so old that the dye had leached out, leaving faded, brittle gray rags on sticks.

"You're supposed to dispose of flags *respectfully.* Do you want to prove his point about kids born here? 'No respect! You take your freedoms for granted!'" She imitated the accent he'd never quite shaken.

"If you want to store them forever, be my guest. I'll put them in your car for you."

"I think the American Legion will take old flags," Nora said, coming up from the basement with another box of moldy Christmas ornaments.

I didn't want to drive them over to the American Legion—did anyone in the entire world actually care if a load of ancient, faded toy flags wound up at the bottom of a Dumpster instead of the American Legion's flag campfire? And anyway, didn't they mostly burn full-sized *real* flags? But whatever: I was trying to keep the peace with Magda, so I loaded them into my minivan, drove them to the nearest American Legion, and abandoned them with a dubious-looking secretary.

The entryway was also home to a stand crammed with broken umbrellas, an extensive collection of orphaned gloves and mittens, a hat that smelled like it had been peed on by a cat, a bunch of plastic pots of dirt that might once have held house plants, and twenty-six plastic bags stuffed full of other plastic bags. Sorted by type.

Those were the easy things to deal with because they all went into the Dumpster. Harder: the dozen suncatchers Magda had made from bake-in-the-oven kits back when she was in third grade.

"Save one of those," Nora said, passing through with another box. "We can put it in Mom's room when she gets transferred to a Transitional recovery nursing home type place."

"She won't care," I said. "She's never going to care. There was too much damage."

Nora snatched the suncatcher out of my hand. "Then give up on her. But *I'm* putting a suncatcher in her room."

II. Nursery Rhymes

For obvious reasons, our parents liked storage. The living room was filled with bookcases and big cabinet things that had cupboards on the bottom and shelves on the top. Some of the shelves were crammed full of decorative items—knickknacks we'd purchased as gifts when we were little, objects d'art we'd made at school, an enormous brass elephant they'd won in a raffle. The elephant was big enough that a bunch of other objects were tucked under its legs, including another elephant, this one carved out of some sort of decorative stone but also a set of six doll-sized glass soda bottles in a holder and a flashlight you were supposed to clip to a key chain.

The three of us had reconvened in the living room. The first challenge was trying to decide whether any of the knickknacks were valuable in any way, because of course who hasn't heard stories about the ugly brass elephant they found at a garage sale that turned out to be made by someone super famous? But the brass elephant said "Made in China" on its stomach, which was a bad sign. Magda wanted the carved elephant, which was fine with me. But then I opened another cabinet, and with a groan of off-key electronic music, out spilled a pile of plastic electronic children's toys.

I'd forgotten all about them, even though I was probably the one who put them there. I felt a lurch, looking at them, and knowing Magda was standing right beside me.

Sure enough, she gasped like she'd been slapped and said, "I need a break," then strode rapidly out of the room.

Nora shot me a look. I sighed and started picking them up. "I'd forgotten they were here," I said. "Anyway...she *has* a child now. Maybe she'd like some of them." Probably not, though. I remembered my daughters opening these horrible electronic gadgets delightedly, and how I'd always leave them behind, saying, "Oh, she can play with it here!"

None of us was fertile. Well, we weren't sure about Nora; after watching my struggles and then Magda's, she'd opted to just have a bunch of cats. But my husband Dan and I had tried for years. Apparently I ovulate normally but there's something seriously wrong with my eggs. They won't fertilize. The first time we tried IVF, they were able to harvest sixteen eggs but not a single one started dividing. The second time, we got nineteen. Same result. After that, we gave up on having biological children.

We adopted, twice. My daughters are the light of my life and my mother adored them, too, and the second one came to us just as Magda was getting really frustrated about her *own* inability to conceive. Magda wanted me to stop posting pictures to Facebook, or at least make a special filter and leave her out of it because seeing pictures of children was just too painful.

Never mind that she'd rolled her eyes over *my* pain when I was doing the second round of IVF, before she learned that she was also infertile ("Why don't you just adopt?" she'd asked) and I'd managed to keep from killing her with my bare hands. I refused to create a filter and told her to quit reading my Facebook if it was that painful for her to see pictures of her *infertile sister's adopted children* . . . And *that* was how we wound up not speaking until Nora demanded we shake hands and act civil.

Magda gave up after one round of IVF. After a long wait, she and her husband have a baby now. (They really, really wanted a *newborn infant,* while Dan and I were open to kids as old as four. That made it a lot faster for us, not that I'm judging. I mean, you want what you want. Well, I guess I judge a little bit that she'd refused to consider a child who had been drug-exposed because—according to science—"crack babies" are a myth. The two things that damage babies the worst are booze and poverty.)

So, like I said, she has a baby of her own now. But looking at those toys drove it home that *my* children got to have a relationship with their grandma and hers never would.

Mom *loves* kids, which is why she'd showered my daughters with the sort of noisy plastic crap that only a grandparent could consider cool. She hasn't stopped—well, I suppose *now* she's stopped. But my kids are seven and ten, and the last gift Mom gave them was at Christmas. Lindsey and Elaine had both wanted handheld video-game gadgets, and when I told them no, they tried Grandma. I'd said, "Oh, Mom, please no . . ." but I might as well have been arguing with a wall. Lindsey's was pink, Elaine's yellow.

Magda was not coming back from her "break." I started bagging up the obnoxious electronic toys for the Dumpster, then wondered if I was morally obligated to pry out the batteries since in theory they could leach toxins. They all required teeny tiny screwdrivers to access the batteries, of course. I dug my multitool out of my purse and started taking them apart.

"Why do you think we're all infertile?" Nora asked.

"Bad luck?"

"Dad warned me, you know."

"About infertility?" I put my multitool down and looked up with interest.

"Yeah, he said it was a common problem for the ladies of Bon."

"Oh, *Bon.*" I picked up my multitool again. "That's got to be bullshit. If everyone from their ancestral village was infertile then that village would have *died out.*"

"Yeah," Nora said morosely. "It didn't make a lot of sense to me, either."

When we asked our parents where they'd come from, they always told us they came from Bon. You will not find Bon on a map—at least, I could never find it on a map. Not a map of the former Soviet republics, anyway. It didn't help that apparently they weren't sure if they'd come from Kyrgyzstan or Tajikistan or somewhere else entirely, just that it was mountainous and Soviet and we were *lucky, lucky, lucky* to be born American.

When I was little, my father told me silly stories about Bon. There was one about flying fish, and one about the Monster of the Mountains (it was small, but had fangs that dripped venom and a scorpion's tail), and one about an evil sorcerer with a wish-granting box, who my father had to outwit in order to get home to his brothers. *Those* stories, I'm still fond of; there's a difference between bullshit and folklore.

But all we could ever get out of them about Bon was bullshit and folklore. Magda wanted to do a big heritage trip a few years back and try to visit their birthplace, and they were utterly useless. They couldn't even tell us what language they spoke! When Magda asked them to speak some of it into a tape recorder so she could play it to a linguistics scholar and have them at least narrow it down for us, they said they'd forgotten it all, even though Magda and I definitely recalled hearing them speak it occasionally well into the 1980s.

They didn't have a single photo or souvenir. They'd come with the clothes on their backs, my father said, and a dream of freedom. (He actually said that. "A *dream of freedom,*" sometimes with his hand over his heart. He meant it.) I always figured the reason they were such hoarders was that they'd lost everything, coming here.

"You'd think they'd have wanted to write home at some point, you know?" I said, finally prying out the last of the batteries and bagging them up separately for a recycling bin. "Track down their family members."

"Maybe everyone was dead," Nora said.

"They were escaping the Soviet Union, not the Nazis or North Korea!"

"Yeah, it's weird," Nora said. "But—I know this may be really surprising and I hate to break it to you—our parents were *really weird.*"

III. Ancestral Soil

I went to visit Mom that afternoon, at the hospital. We were visiting her daily, taking it in turns. Nothing had changed, obviously; if anything *had* changed, they'd have called. She lay in bed, breathing, not dead, not conscious. Around me, I felt like the hospital was treating her a little impatiently. She was occupying a bed but didn't really need hospital care at this point. She was just there until they could find a care facility to transfer her to. She'd almost been transferred twice before, but then she'd destabilized, running a high fever and forcing them to call off the move. Each time we'd thought maybe she'd die for real, but nope.

I took my knitting and sat with her for a while, working on the lace shawl I was making. Knitting is a good thing to bring to the hospital. You feel like if the person *did* suddenly wake up, you wouldn't miss it. You're present for them, but you have something to do.

Dad died in this very hospital. It might even have been this *room.* He went the same way as Mom—hemorrhagic stroke followed by a coma. Mom called all of us when it happened and told us to come as soon as we could. Though she also assured us he'd wait until we all got there.

And he did. He waited. We all came together in the hospital room and Mom placed a velvet bag in Dad's hands; she said it was something from Bon, something that would help him find his way back, and I guess it worked because he died. None of this endless unconscious brush-with-death-and-then-rally stuff that Mom had going on: we gathered, we said goodbye, he went, like someone catching a plane for a one-way trip.

"Mom," I said, "we all gathered and said goodbye, you know. You don't need to keep waiting."

I wondered where that velvet bag was. Maybe that's what Mom needed.

Bon really was *bullshit*, though. I wished they'd told me at some point where they actually came from. Now they never would.

When I'd finished a section of the piece I was knitting, I tucked it carefully back in my bag, kissed Mom on the cheek, and headed out. When I got onto the elevator, to my dismay, there was someone already inside with a little dog—one of the therapy dogs they take around to cheer up patients. I could tell from the dog-sized Comfort Paws vest he was wearing. I avoided eye contact, but the dog tensed and let out a low growl.

"Idgie!" the volunteer said, scolding. "I'm so sorry, I don't know what's got into her. Maybe I should take her home."

"Dogs always react to me that way," I said, trying to sound reassuring but not overly apologetic. Sometimes people get really weird about their dogs not liking you.

This was clearly going to be one of those times. She shot me a look that suggested she thought I was probably a recreational serial killer and got off at the next floor.

IV. Lay Me Down

I didn't want to explain to my sisters why I was looking for that little velvet bag, so I just took over cleaning out Mom and Dad's bedroom next instead.

Dad's dresser still had his shaver and his deodorant and his change bowl, though over time more and more of Mom's stuff had migrated there to keep his stuff company. The drawers were all still full of his clothes, though. I was taken aback by the wrench I felt when I shook out one of his faded plaid shirts with the shredded cuffs. Would it be ridiculous to keep one? *It would be ridiculous.* I resolutely packed up a box of shirts and other clothes, and then caved to temptation and rescued one of the shirts.

The bedroom closet was truly ridiculous: it was stuffed to the walls with garments that had, since being packed away, probably come *back* into fashion and then gone out of fashion again. The Garfield tie we'd given Dad as a Father's Day gift in 1984 was in there, stained with coffee, along with a shoe box of handmade gifts we gave to my mother, like a glitter-encrusted macaroni necklace strung on harvest-gold yarn.

Nora laid claim to all the wool sweaters because she could make felted wool purses with them or something. I carried them in arm-loads to her car. Magda came out to find me as I was loading up the bags full of clothes and said, "Hey, let me poke through for a second."

I stepped back to let her open the bags. She pulled out one of Dad's shirts, looking a little embarrassed. "Thanks," she said. "That's all."

When I came back upstairs, Nora was in the bedroom, sitting on the stripped bed, staring at something she was holding in her hand. "This was in Mom's jewelry box," she said.

I sat down to look. It was a disk made from a milky silver metal: it looked old, really old—like something that would have been ex-cavated out of a Viking grave—but there was a swirling spiral shape etched on the front, with a tiny seed-sized gemstone in one corner. At the top was a little loop so you could put it on a chain, but no chain. I didn't remember Mom ever wearing this.

"Had you ever seen this before?" I asked.

"No. Do you suppose it came from Bon?"

I fell silent, and went and looked in the jewelry box. There was the garnet pendant I'd saved up for and bought her for Mother's Day when I was twelve, and the pearls Dad had given her for her birthday one year, and the jade beads she didn't like because they always caught her hair, and various other trinkets she'd purchased or been given over the years. I remembered almost everything in here, even the pieces she didn't often wear. A few times when I was six I'd demanded she lay it all out for me to admire. If she'd owned that milky-silver antique pendant at the time, though, she'd left it hidden.

It turned out that there were two more items made from the same metal under the coil of jade beads—a ring and an enameled pin shaped like some sort of bird. I'd never seen those before, either. I set them on the mattress next to Nora. "Look," I said.

She picked up the ring to examine it. "I think it's a poison ring," she said. "Oh, don't look so shocked, I'm not saying either of our parents poisoned anyone! A poison ring is just the term for a ring with a compartment built in. They used to be called 'ring lockets' and most often they held mementos from dead people, not actual poison, unless you were one of the Medicis or something, and I don't think the Medicis lived in Bon. Anyway—" she handed it to me. "I can't figure out how to get it open."

I could see what she meant by a compartment, but I slid my thumbnail along the edge and found no catch to spring it open.

"We should show these to Magda," I said, "and we should probably, I don't know, have them assessed or something."

Nora nodded. Neither one of us wanted to say it aloud: if these came from Bon, maybe they would tell us something about it that our parents never shared.

V. Palladium

Despite my impression of antiquity, the jeweler and antique specialist quickly dismissed the idea that these were at all old. The pieces were made from palladium, which wasn't used in jewelry before 1939. In fact, it hadn't even been discovered as an element until 1803. It did have some value as metal, though it was worth rather less than platinum. The stone set in the spiral was tanzanite.

Palladium, we were told, was most often found in Siberia. *Siberia*, I thought, exchanging a baffled glance with Magda. They'd never even *hinted* at being from Siberia. Tanzanite could be lab-created, but the only natural deposits were in Tanzania, although tanzanite was a variety of zoisite, which was found in a number of other places, none of them anywhere near the Central Asian former Soviet Republics, or Russia, or even Siberia.

"Look," I said, "I'm sure you're right that it's not an antique. Can you tell us whether it's more than forty years old? Because that's really all we care about."

Very reluctantly, he said, "The enamel used on the pin is of a kind almost never made after the seventeenth century."

"What do you think that means?"

"I think these pieces were made by a modern artist, someone trying out an older technique. Were your parents art collectors? Did they have any friends who were artists?"

Art collectors, ha. Well, they were everything-else collectors, but art was not something they sought out, at least not compared to tiny flags in need of rescue. We took pictures of all three pieces and then drew straws to decide who got to pick first: Nora chose the pendant with the spiral, and Magda picked the bird. I'd gotten the shortest straw, and wound up with the ring. At least it fit me.

I went home for the evening and showed the ring and the pictures to Dan and my daughters. "I wish you'd gotten the flying fish," Lindsey said. "That one was prettiest."

"Flying fish?" I took another look at the picture on my phone. She was right: it wasn't a bird, it was a fish with wings, like the ones in the fairy tales my father had told me about Bon. "Well, Aunt Magda wanted that one."

Elaine studied the pictures. "And Aunt Nora has the medallion thing?"

"Yeah." I looked over her shoulder. "It's a little hard to tell, but the design is etched in, and that dot in the corner is a purple gemstone. Is the medallion your favorite?"

"Yeah," Elaine said. She turned her head sideways. "It looks like the Milky Way."

"Well, the ring's maybe got a secret compartment," I said, which instantly transformed the ring into the coolest of the three pieces of jewelry, and the fact that I didn't know how to open it only added to its charm. I was a little nervous about letting them experiment with it, fearing that Elaine would go for the screwdriver set and try to pry it open, but instead she went for a magnifying lens and a bright light.

"Do you think these came from Bon?" Dan asked.

"I don't know," I said. "The metal comes from Siberia, the stone comes from Africa, and the enameling technique came from the seventeenth century. I suppose if they all came from a village in the Pamir Mountains that doesn't actually exist, brought by people who kept nothing from their old home and forgot their native tongue . . . Well, of course they came from Bon, you know?"

"Does it bother you not to know anything about your parents' home?" Elaine asked, spinning around on the kitchen stool to face me.

I hesitated. Elaine, of course, was adopted. So was Lindsey. We brought Elaine home when she was three, and now she's ten. We brought Lindsey home when she was four, and now she's seven. We do, in fact, know a certain amount about their birth parents, which we've shared with them in nonjudgmental, age-appropriate ways. Elaine's birth mother was a drug addict who neglected Elaine so badly that Elaine, at three, weighed only eighteen pounds. We told Elaine that her birth mother had a sickness that made it very hard for her to take good care of Elaine, and she knows that the sickness was drug addiction, which makes people crave drugs so much they find it hard to think about anything else ("like the worst hunger you've ever EVER felt," I overheard Elaine explain to Lindsey, once.) That's actually a fair amount easier to explain than Lindsey's history, which involved a broken leg from being thrown against a wall. You're always supposed to speak respectfully of birth parents, and I do, but it's harder with Lindsey's than Elaine's.

"It's not that it bothers me, exactly," I said. "I'm just curious. Are you curious about your birth family?"

"No," Elaine said, "but I'm curious about Bon." She spun the stool around again. "I want to see the pin and the medallion. Do you think Aunt Nora and Aunt Magda would let me see them?"

"I want to visit Grandma," Lindsey said. "Why won't you take me to see Grandma? Luke in my class got to visit *his* grandma when *she* was in the hospital."

I exchanged a look with Dan and said, "Maybe this weekend."

"Could we X-ray the ring?" Elaine asked. "Maybe if we X-ray the ring we could see what's inside it."

After thinking about it for a week, I finally took it to a friend who was willing to slip it into her work X-ray for me. "There's a piece of bone inside," she told me, surprised, when she handed it back. "Just a tiny fragment. It's almost like a saint's reliquary, maybe. I don't see any way to get it open."

VI. Real Family

In my parents' house, we'd started to see the light at the end of the tunnel. The kitchen was cleared out. The basement had been emptied. And Magda and I were talking to each other again, almost easily. Almost.

The hardest part of the living room, in the end, was not the collection of children's toys but the photo albums full of 1980s Polaroids and snapshots taken with an Instamatic camera. (You didn't have to focus them because you could just assume that anything you photographed would be blurry.) We divided them up and promised to go through them at a later date so we could trade or make copies of anything particularly precious.

The biggest project left was the downstairs closet, which was filled with miscellaneous junk and boxes of who-knows-what. *Filled.* When I finally yanked the door open, I got hit on the head by a falling cookie tin (which—thank goodness—was empty).

We pulled it all out. Finding those pieces of jewelry had made this process both more interesting and more difficult; there was a real sense that *something* might be buried in here. Something important, something that would tell us about our past. Something buried under decades' worth of empty cookie tins, lidless mason jars, worn-out brooms, grimy work aprons, broken toasters, cheap lamps without lampshades. Something.

We sorted things silently in the living room for a while. Almost everything went into the donation pile.

I'd thought up a theory about Bon. Well, maybe not a theory. More of a story, like the flying fish and the Monster of the Mountains. I wanted to share it with my sisters; I wanted them to nod and agree, and then we could, together, acknowledge that even if it wasn't the truth, it *explained* things.

My theory would explain why we couldn't find Bon on any map, why our parents were so ridiculously cagey about the real place they were from, why they claimed to have forgotten the language, which I did remember hearing them speak and which had never sounded like any other language I'd ever heard. It would explain why we couldn't get pregnant, why our eggs refused so stubbornly to fertilize with any sperm, and why my father had tried to warn us about that. It even explained why dogs never liked us, even the super-friendly dogs who liked *everybody*, even though cats didn't mind us at all.

What if Bon weren't just in another country, but on another world entirely?

What if we're not human?

Except I could imagine their reactions easily. This idea was completely preposterous. No *doctor* has ever noticed we're not human, and Magda and I had both gotten complete workups from fertility specialists who—you know—*might have noticed if there were something odd about us.* So for us to be aliens, we'd have to be the sort of aliens that just so happened to be basically indistinguishable from (though not cross-fertile with) humans. Or our parents would have needed some sort of fantastic alien technology that changed them, and us, into something visually indistinguishable from humans, when they immigrated. *That made no sense.*

What if we're not human?

It didn't really matter, did it? It didn't matter where they came from, not really. They'd come, they'd embraced America, they'd raised us as Americans, they'd sent us to American schools and fed us American food and spoken to us in English. Elaine said she wasn't curious about her birth family. She said, sometimes, that we were her *real* family, even though I'd tried to make sure she didn't feel obligated to reassure me about that. We were her *real* parents. America was my *real* country.

It didn't really matter.

"Hey," Nora said, "was this the bag you were looking for?"

It was the velvet bag, and we all looked inside. It held dirt. Dirt and dust. The soil, we all knew without saying it, of Bon.

VII. Glimmer

Elaine and Lindsey looked daunted at the hospital room door, not only because their beloved grandmother was so much sicker than they'd probably imagined, but because the room was already crowded, with Nora and her husband, and Magda and her husband and their little son. But I knew they deserved a chance to say goodbye. They kissed Mom's cheeks, and petted her hands and her hair.

I think Lindsey believed that the magic of her love would wake Mom up. *Really* believed it, I mean. Too many sentimental movies.

When they drooped from tiredness, when they'd given up, I let Dan take them home. Magda's husband left with their baby, and Nora's husband went off to feed their cats. It was late, and we were alone with Mom in the hospital room. Nora double-checked Mom's DNR and I gently turned her hands palms-up. We put the ring in her left hand, and the pin in her right hand, and set the medallion with the picture of the Milky Way on her chest, and then we laid the bag of ancestral soil over the medallion.

"Goodbye, Mom," I said.

For about thirty seconds, nothing happened. I tried to remember—how long had this taken with my father? We'd gathered, Mom had put the bag on his chest—

—and then she stopped breathing.

We retrieved the jewelry. I took the bag. We summoned the nurses, let them call the funeral home, and started the process of burial and all the rest. *Goodbye, Mom.*

"You should keep the bag in your safe-deposit box," Magda said. "You have one, right? I remember you said you had one. If we know where it is, we'll be able to get it, when we need it. *If* we need it."

I tucked it into my purse, and met her eyes, and nodded.

VIII. Terra Incognita

The soil in the bag is fine and dry and crumbly, with bits of sharp gravel mixed in. I don't quite dare touch it, but I look at it with my daughter's magnifying glass and a bright light and see glints of purple and blue and green and amber, like a collection of tumbled semiprecious stones had been crushed and added to the mix.

And when I hold the open bag to my face and breathe in, it smells like nothing on Earth.

ARTIFICE

We toasted the end of Mandy's relationship over a game of Hydro-King. "I never liked him," I said, which was true. I didn't add, "and what still puzzles me is that *you* never liked him, either, so why did you move in with him?" People say, "never try to change a man" (or, if you're being egalitarian about it, "never try to change the person you're dating") but from the day they met, Mandy had viewed this guy as a work in progress. She'd even succeeded in dragging him to game night a few times, even though he clearly found board games unspeakably dull.

"Find a nice gamer boy next time," Larry suggested over the champagne. We met at night, in Larry's apartment, because Larry had an actual job instead of living entirely off his citizen's stipend like the rest of us. So on one hand, he was busy during the day; on the other, he had more money and could afford a much bigger space, big enough for seven people to meet and play board games.

(You'd be surprised at how many people think it's super retro that we play board games in person instead of immersive VR stuff. But did you know there are still Monopoly and Scrabble tournaments? Besides, when you get together with people in person, you can eat corn chips while you gossip.)

"I'm swearing off men," Mandy said. Larry's housekeeper came through with a tray of snacks. Mandy stared speculatively at it for a moment. The housekeeper was mostly silver, with little swiveling robot eyes on stalks. It rolled around the floor so everyone could get snacks, and Mandy grabbed a fistful of chips. "Too much goddamn work."

"He's probably saying the same thing about women right now," muttered Quinn, my boyfriend, in an undertone. I snickered, then felt guilty, since I ought to be giving Mandy the benefit of the doubt here. Still. I had to admit, I hoped her ex was toasting the split with his own friends right now while watching . . . was it baseball season? Tennis? Squash? He was into that sort of thing. Mandy, not so much.

Mandy had been in a great mood on game night, but I checked in with her the next week, just to see how she was doing. "Izzy!" she greeted me. "Come over! I want to introduce you to someone!"

I cringed. "*Already?*"

"It's not what you think. Just come over!"

I went over to Mandy's apartment—the ex had moved out, and she'd already eradicated every trace of him. The alcove where he'd had his things was now fully repurposed as her studio, with a half-finished painting on a big easel. I glanced at it—it was another of her photorealism attempts—and then looked over at the brown-haired, pleasant-faced young man on the sofa. He looked way too young for her. "Joe," she called. "Come here. I'd like to introduce you to Izzy."

He rose and strode over, holding out his hand. "It's a pleasure to meet you," he said in a voice that almost vibrated with sincerity. "You're the first of Mandy's friends I've had the chance to meet." There was a faint stress on the word *Mandy* and he glanced at her, which was a relief as he was making too much eye contact.

"Yeah," I said. "It's nice to meet you, too." I glanced at Mandy, thinking, *is this guy for real?*

Something about the self-satisfied look on Mandy's face tipped me off. "Oh. Oh, you *didn't.*"

"My stupid ex got the housekeeper in the agreement," Mandy said. "I needed a new one anyway, I just . . . upgraded."

I looked "Joe" over. You have to pay a lot more for a robot that really looks human, but that explained Joe's unnerving perfection and slightly-too-youthful face. "You sure did. You couldn't have gotten by with a standard housekeeping model and, oh, a really nice vibrator? Because I'm *sure* that would've been cheaper."

"I didn't just want him for the bedroom. He's going to be my boyfriend. Right, Joe?"

He slipped his hand around her waist and leaned in to kiss her cheek. "I'll be with you as long as you want me, Mandy."

She pulled back and looked at him critically. "I like the physical gesture there but next time tell me you'll be with me forever."

He smiled at her with what looked exactly like human infatuation. "Of course, darling."

She turned back to me and said, "He learns *really* fast. I never have to tell him anything twice."

"You shouldn't have to," I said. "I mean, that's the whole point of a robot, right?"

"Exactly! I knew you'd understand."

Joe stood there, smiling at both of us. When we paused he said, "Can I get you anything, Izzy? A drink? A snack? I make excellent sandwiches."

If it had been an ordinary housekeeper I'd have said yes, but this was creeping me out, so I said I'd eaten and that I needed to get home because I'd promised myself I'd make some progress on the symphony I was composing, and I took myself off.

Back at my own apartment, I sent my own housekeeper to make me a sandwich and some lemonade and sat down with the keyboard for a while to work, although mostly I stewed. My housekeeper was more basic and functional than Larry's; it didn't even have what you'd call a face, although it had enough functionality to cook (that was important to me) and clean (that was important to Quinn). Eventually Quinn came home and instead of playing him the piece I'd been working on, I told him about Mandy and her custom-designed man.

"Well," he said. "It's sad to say, but this is probably healthier than seeking out men as projects. Robots are very good at following instructions, unlike human beings. Also, Joe will never leave the toilet seat up, unless she instructs him to leave it up."

"I've never understood why she didn't just have the housekeeper check the bathroom after each use to flip the seat back down," I said. "Instead of making it an issue."

"Well, this guy will never use the bathroom at *all*, unless he has to go in there to recharge," Quinn said. "That's one problem solved, anyway."

I shouldn't have been surprised when Mandy brought Joe to game night.

He still had that friendly smile on his face pretty much all the time. *It* had a friendly smile on *its* face, I should say, but the fact is, when a robot really looks human it's hard not to think of it with a gender. Larry's housekeeper was a a non-human-looking robot that was nonetheless sort of cute (the eyes "blink," things like that) and he sometimes pretends it's a pet, and Dawn and Shanice have the same basic model as me and Quinn but they gave theirs a name. Quinn and I were always very practical about it. Our housekeeper wasn't a person or a pet; it was a machine that we'd bought so it could do our cooking and clean the toilets and run errands. Lots of people give their housekeeping robots names, but they don't *need* names. (Unless you have two for some reason, but in a standard apartment space you don't need more than one to keep up with the work.)

We all knew by then that Mandy had bought a robot that looked human, so she couldn't play the game of introducing Joe and waiting to see how long it took for people to figure out what was up. She led Joe around the room, introducing him to everyone; no one refused to shake hands, though Shanice was obviously pretty uncomfortable with it. Joe sat down on one of the folding chairs, leaving the comfier seating spots for the humans, and smiled happily at all of us, not interrupting.

It got awkward when Mandy made it clear she wanted Joe to participate in the gaming.

"Don't be ridiculous," Larry said, bluntly. "These games are supposed to be tests of *human* skill. If I wanted to play Scrabble with a robot, I could do that, but it'll win almost every time since it has the dictionary *built into its head.*"

"I've instructed him not to win anything a disproportionate amount of the time," Mandy said, defensively.

"So your robot friend is going to throw games deliberately? No. Just no."

"If he can't play, we're leaving," Mandy said.

There were groans all around, but Shanice suggested, "How about Diplomacy? With the robot, there's seven of us. And I wouldn't expect him to have any particular advantage with that game."

"Well, other than the fact that if Mandy orders him to ally with her, what else is he going to do?" Larry snapped.

I pondered this. "We can account for that," I said, as Mandy said, "I can order him right now to just play the game as it's supposed to be played—ally with me if it makes sense, betray me if it makes sense."

"*Can* he lie?" Quinn asked. We all stared at Joe, speculatively.

"Right," Dawn said. "I'll get the box."

Diplomacy is a seriously old-school game, invented in the mid-20th-century, and everyone pretends to be European powers from around World War I. There's no random element—no dice rolls or anything like that. You walk around persuading people to ally with you (by assuring them that you're trustworthy). Then everyone writes down their move secretly and all moves are revealed at one go. There's no rule that keeps you from lying, from making false promises, or from stabbing people in the back. In fact, in general you want to betray your allies one turn before they were going to turn on you.

A robot has a clear advantage in any game where a perfect memory or a lightening-fast ability to calculate odds will come in useful—which is to say, most of them. But in a game where you have to make a guess about who's lying to you, a robot's going to have a harder time. So we went with it, because by then we were all curious. Mandy reiterated to Joe that he should play the game to win—that he was allowed to lie to people, including her, and betray them, including her, in order to try to win. We had to trust that she wouldn't rescind that instruction quietly later on, but she probably realized that if he backed her when he should have betrayed her, that would be *it*. We wouldn't repeat this experiment.

During the first diplomatic phase I realized that no one was approaching Joe, probably more because he made them nervous than because they thought he'd sell them out to Mandy. I shrugged and edged over. I was playing Russia and Joe was playing Turkey and I was pretty sure that if we worked together we could squash any chance Mandy (who was playing Austria) had of winning the game by the end of 1903 as long as we could keep the other players from coming to her aid.

"Want an alliance?" I asked.

"Oh yes, please," Joe said, with bright enthusiasm. I wondered whether he would jump up and down and clap his hands if he won.

You're probably not a Diplomacy player so the precise ins-and-outs of who allied with whom and who got stabbed in the back when is not going to be particularly interesting to you, so I'll summarize: Joe was an adequate but not outstanding Diplomacy player because he could analyze the strategic advantage of all the possible actions but he was terrible at reading people and frankly he was pretty gullible. Also, he let the rest of us crush Mandy (I think we were sort of in the mood to do that, anyway) and since everyone figured he probably wasn't programmed for grudge-holding, I was able to persuade both Dawn and Quinn that I was totally going to double-cross Joe even though I then double-crossed Quinn. (I don't usually recommend playing Diplomacy with your boyfriend, but it works out for us).

Nobody won; we got down to me, Joe, Dawn, and Larry and then quit, because actually *winning* a game of Diplomacy can easily take all night. Joe clearly found that puzzling, but didn't complain.

Afterward, we ate pizza and drank beer, except for Joe, who sat quietly and watched us. When it was time to go home, he got Mandy's coat for her and also slipped on a coat himself, even though surely he wasn't going to get cold—it was a brusque fall evening but he wasn't in any danger of freezing solid yet. Everyone shook Joe's hand and we headed in our separate directions.

For most of the next year, Joe was Mandy's boyfriend.

And, he really was the *perfect* boyfriend. I mean, I like Quinn a lot. He makes me very happy. But there are areas of life where he is imperfect. For example, when he uses up a roll of toilet paper, he tends to leave the fresh roll on the back of the toilet instead of hanging it up neatly on the hook. Joe doesn't use the toilet, but if he did, he would always hang up the TP. In fact, if Mandy wanted to never have to hang up the TP, she could instruct Joe to check for un-hung TP every so often and hang it up if it wasn't in place and he would do it without resentment or reminders.

Plus, Mandy could change him. I mean, in addition to telling him things like, "always hang up the toilet paper" and "make me my lunch every day," she could actually take him back in to have his personality altered, and in fact six weeks after she bought Joe she did just that. "He's so quiet," she explained. "It's not that I want him to interrupt, but I want him to *initiate* conversations, not just answer me when I talk to him. I told him that, and so he tries, but he doesn't come up with new things to talk about, it's always, 'how's your work, Mandy?' or 'how was your day, Mandy?' I mean, he's an excellent listener. It's not that I want to change *that*. But I want him to have more to say."

After the reprogramming, which Quinn called a personality transplant, Joe was chattier. A *lot* chattier. Dawn found him a lot more irritating because even though he didn't interrupt, he'd fill in silences and sometimes a silence is *okay*, you know?

One week, Dawn turned to him and said, "that story you're telling me? About the weird guy on the train? You told it last week. *I don't want to hear stories twice.* I know you can remember what you've told me, so why are you telling it again?"

Joe continued smiling at her, unflinching. "I'm sorry, Dawn," he said.

"No, you're not. You're just programmed to apologize when people get annoyed with you."

"To be fair," Shanice said, examining the cards she was holding (we were playing *Power Quantum* that day), "that's basically what I do."

Everyone laughed and Joe was quiet for a while, before he started in about some article he'd read in the paper. Mandy touched his hand and shot him a *look* and he stopped talking altogether.

The "read my *look*" thing turned out to be part of a new suite of features that included better ability to read body language, although frankly he still wasn't very good at it. Humans just don't behave in consistent ways. I mean, imagine trying to program a robot to recognize "angry" in someone's body language and not get it confused with "thinking really hard" (something we often were doing, playing games). We kept playing Diplomacy with him and he never got much better. The other games, he'd win a precisely proportionate amount of time . . . but not Diplomacy.

When they'd been seeing each other for about seven months, Mandy and I both decided to participate in an artistic challenge that involved collaborating with someone doing a very different art form. Someone had put up grant money—not a lot, but enough to be a nice supplement to the standard citizen's stipend. (A stipend is enough to pay for the standard apartment and feed yourself and even buy a housekeeper, but you have to save up for a long time if you want to travel or buy anything fancy. Mandy bought Joe with a pile of money she got for a commissioned painting.) Anyway, we figured, why not, and applied. Our first few meetings, we managed to stay fairly focused, although I have to admit I still didn't really understand the point of photorealistic art. (If you want something that looks like a photograph, why not take a photograph? Mandy had a long explanation of why photorealism was an interesting artistic movement and after a while I sort of tuned her out.) We decided we'd do a joint exhibit where people were supposed to look at some pictures she'd drawn while listening to musicians play something I'd composed to go with the pictures.

Mandy's favorite thing to draw were men. Naked men with nice muscles. She had a dozen pictures of Joe in the mix, a few pictures of her ex, and then various pictures of other artistic models she'd hired. I flipped through the portfolio. "Joe must make a good model," I said.

"There's almost no challenge in it," she said with a sigh. "He can sit perfectly still for as long as I need him to. If he has to get up for some reason, like if I need him to make dinner, he can always sit back down in the exact same position, not even a hair out of place. It's too easy."

"Oh?"

"Yeah, it's kind of the whole problem with Joe, honestly. *Everything* is too easy."

Joe was washing dishes over in the kitchen alcove when she said this, and I heard him pause, but he didn't say anything. A moment later, he went back to scrubbing.

As a last-ditch effort to keep the romance alive, Mandy took him in for yet another personality transplant that was supposed to make him argue with her. They quarreled once at game night over the game Mandy wanted—Joe insisted it wasn't her turn to pick and she ought to defer to Shanice—and I heard them fight once when I was at their apartment looking at drawings. Joe complained that Mandy had gotten herself a snack, left a mess, and not soaked the burned pan. "You do realize," he pointed out, "that it will take me four times as long to scrub this clean than it would have if you'd soaked it. Or told me when you burned the eggs. Or had me make you the snack in the first place." His tone was mild, cajoling, but with a hint of accusation.

Mandy shrugged it off. "Like you even care," she said.

"I do care," Joe said.

Mandy shot a look at me, at my seat on the couch, where I was paging through her portfolio and trying to ignore the argument. It was a look that said, *Whatever; I know you're a robot and you've been programmed to say you're annoyed.* "We can talk about this later," she said. "I'm busy with Izzy."

"I want an apology."

"Okay, Joe. I'm sorry."

"Thank you. That's all I wanted: an apology."

"*Can we drop this now?*" Mandy shouted.

"Of course, darling."

She made a face as she stalked back into the living room. "Let's go out and leave Mr. Personality here."

We went for a walk. "You could get it undone," I suggested. "The personality transplant, I mean. Right? If you're tired of arguments."

"It just feels wrong," she muttered. "Like taking away his freedom of will."

"He's a *robot*," I said. "Everything's programmed, whether it's arguing or telling you how pretty you are."

"I know. It was satisfying for a while, but now . . ."

They hung on for another few months, and then Mandy met a guy at the art exhibit. Erik was a music composer who didn't like my work, and told her she deserved better, and she immediately found him fascinating. He was taller than Joe, with a flabbier body and all the annoying habits Joe lacked, like leaving the toilet seat up and his underwear on the floor. Joe, of course, picked up after them without complaining, since robots don't get jealous, and from the stories I heard (through friends—Mandy and I had a fight over Erik's opinion of my work) Erik thought cuckolding a robot was either hot or hilarious.

Erik was also not into gaming, and when game night rolled around, Mandy blew us off for a night of torrid sex or maybe artistic endeavors? (Probably sex.)

Joe, however, turned up.

"I have brought potato chips," he said, when Larry let him in. That was Mandy's usual offering, but of course, Joe doesn't *eat*. He added the chips to the kitchen counter and then sat down on his usual folding chair and listened to the conversation.

Of course, we'd been gossiping about Mandy, so the conversation instantly died as we looked at everyone other than Joe and wondered, what exactly *is* the etiquette here? Finally Shanice turned to Joe and asked, "So, how are things with *you*, Joe?"

"Fine," Joe said.

"Really?" Shanice said. "No bitter resentment or jealousy over what's going on with Mandy?"

"No," Joe said. "Of course not."

"It's not in your programming, I guess."

"It was," Joe offered. "For about a week. Mandy wanted me to be jealous, so she had that installed. But then she decided it was too much drama, and had it erased."

"She *made* you jealous?" That was precisely the sort of gossip we'd all been after, and I leaned in, wanting more. "What was that like?"

For a brief moment, I thought I saw a flicker of emotion in Joe's eyes, and then he said, "Tiring."

Everyone laughed.

"What do you mean, 'tiring?'" Shanice demanded.

"I ran down my battery more quickly and had to recharge," Joe said.

"Oh," Shanice said, losing interest.

"I tell you what," Larry said. "You can pick the first game tonight, Joe. What's your pleasure?"

"Diplomacy," Joe said. "Only, this time, I want to play all the way to the end."

Quinn hadn't been feeling well that evening, and I'd come on my own. (We hadn't actually had enough people to play Diplomacy—we'd played a game with a similar mechanic that called for five players instead of seven.) Things ran very late, and Joe offered to walk me home. A street-sweeper came by as we were walking, and Joe turned to watch it go past. I wondered if he felt a sense of kinship for that sort of robot, the non-human-looking ones. Or for the ones who had human faces but not very complex behavior, like the robots staffing the all-night grocery. Or if he felt all alone in the world. If he felt anything at all.

"I lied," he said, as the sweeper chugged away up the street.

"About what?"

"Mandy didn't actually have the jealousy module erased," he said.

"She just told me she didn't want me acting jealous any more. She said she was tired of the drama."

I stopped for a moment and looked at Joe's face. These were all programming modules to affect *behavior*, I reminded myself, even as part of my tired brain thought, *Joe looks so sad.* "So she had one set of protocols installed to give you a set of behaviors," I said, "and then she overrode those instructions?"

"Basically."

"You know? If you were human, we all could have warned you before you got into the relationship that Mandy is a crazy, crazy girl-friend. If it's any consolation, she's going to drive that new guy, Erik, up the goddamn tree."

"Oh, she is already," Joe said, and mimicked Mandy softly. "'Honey, if you would just *tell me* when you're going to be home and *try* to stick to it' . . . 'honey, if you would just *try* to remember to put the milk away' . . . you get the idea."

"Does he promise her he'll change?"

"No. He says, 'If you wanted a robot, you should've stuck with your robot.'" He was quiet for a minute. "And then they both laugh."

"Is she going to keep you?" I asked.

"She hasn't said." He sighed. "If she sells me, I bet my next owner won't be into Diplomacy."

For the next four weeks, Joe came to game night.

Every time, he brought a bag of potato chips and a little bit of gossip about Mandy. Erik lasted for just over a month, and we thought perhaps Mandy would go back to Joe, but instead she picked up a new guy who had a beard (that Mandy wanted him to shave off) and a tattoo (that she didn't like) and who played guitar (but who'd be a lot better if he just applied himself).

And the week after that, Joe didn't turn up.

*

"Why do you even care?" Mandy said sharply. "First Larry, then Shanice, now *you*. It's a *robot*. I don't ask you what's new with *your* housekeeper."

I waited, silently, in her doorway. Behind her, in the apartment, I could see a new housekeeper cleaning the rug—chrome and silver, and shiny and new, but totally basic. *Not* a human-looking model, or even the cute kind with fake eyes.

"Jason found him creepy. And I can't say as I blame him. So I traded him in. Human-looking models are expensive—even used, I got a good enough price to maybe take a trip somewhere. Jason wants to go to the Grand Canyon."

I couldn't look at her anymore; I walked away. And I sent a message to Shanice, Dawn, Larry, and Quinn.

We met up at the robot dealer in Mandy's neighborhood, knowing it was probably too late. The store is staffed by robots, of course, human-looking models with the sort of limited range a sales person needs: infinite patience with difficult customers, perfect honesty with a cash box, and a smile that never goes away. This one looked like a girl, with blond hair. "Refurbished male human-looking robots?" she said. "Right this way."

There were *twelve* of Joe, standing in a line, neatly dressed, the same smile.

"We want a specific one," Shanice said. "The one that used to belong to our friend, Mandy."

"All models are customizable," said the clerk. "All can be adjusted to whatever skills and personality traits meet your particular needs. Do you all three live together?"

"You don't get it," Dawn said. "We want *Joe*."

I looked at the models on the shelf. "Which one of you is Joe?" None of them replied.

"You can name your robot however you like," the clerk said. "Any of them will be happy to answer to Joe."

"We want *our* Joe," Quinn said. "We want the Joe who remembers us."

"To protect your privacy, all the robots have their memories wiped when they're turned in," the clerk said. "If you can find out what particular personality modules your friend had downloaded into 'Joe,' we can certainly make you a fresh copy. In fact..." She checked her handheld. "The most recent arrival is the one on the left; that's probably the specific robot your friend used to own."

We walked over to Joe.

"Do you remember me?" I asked.

Joe smiled the peaceful, unflinching smile I remembered from our first meeting. "It's a pleasure to meet you," he said in a voice that almost vibrated with sincerity.

I turned away.

Larry, Quinn, Dawn, Shanice and I looked at each other.

For a moment we were overwhelmed by the absurdity of this. Buying a human-model robot, even split five ways, was going to wipe out everyone's savings other than possibly Larry's. And for what? His memories were gone. His personality was a clean slate.

I turned back, and held out my hand. "I'm Izzy," I said. "We're taking you home, Joe."

"Do you like board games?" Larry asked as we walked out of the store with him. "Actually, let me rephrase. You liked board games before. You liked them a lot. We're going to teach you to play them again."

PERFECTION

"So what's your position on tails, anyway?" Trivet asked.

Secret rolled her eyes. "Seventy-eight-year-old female, natural causes, non-Ashari," she read off the toe tag. "I don't see why we have to autopsy the non-Ashari. What does it matter why they died? Whatever killed them, it's not going to kill us."

Trivet helped to move the body out onto the table. "That's not necessarily true," she said. "I mean, this one was an immigrant." She gestured at the slim, brown body, smooth and young-looking even at seventy-eight. "You'd never have known looking at her that she wasn't born one of us."

Secret looked at the body skeptically. "I think you'd know."

"Well, of course you'd know, but not from *looking* at her."

"It doesn't matter. She's probably jury-rigged inside with nanotechnology. You can't just *give* somebody good health, even if you fix their DNA; it's something you have to be born with."

They started the autopsy. The woman had died of multiple organ failure—exactly the sort, Secret noted smugly, that would never happen to a born Ashari. Trivet conceded the point as they weighed the woman's bloated liver. "So what's your position on tails?" Trivet asked again, dumping the liver into the slop box. "You changed the subject."

Secret had changed the subject because she was sick to death of tails, but it was clear Trivet wasn't going to be diverted. "I support the idea of tails so long as they are *purely* decorative," Secret said. "None of this nonsense about prehensile tails; I think we should all have decorative furred tails like cats."

"Cat tails aren't purely decorative; they help with balance."

"Granted, but cats can't pick up a dropped scalpel, now, can they? Prehensile tails will decrease overall physical fitness; we won't have to bend over as much or as often."

Trivet flushed slightly. She'd probably wanted a tail just to pick up dropped objects. Secret rather thought a prehensile tail would be handy, but these conversations always made her feel contrary. "I think the liver got her," Trivet said, finally changing the subject.

"She should have come in for repairs; more nanotech should have done the trick." Secret fished the liver back out of the slop box and cut a slice out, putting it under the microscope. "Nah, forget it. It was nine-tenths nanotech already. Watch out; all that nanotech could make her mobile."

As if on cue, the woman's arm swung out, the nerves and muscles stimulated by a confused nandroid. "Look out!" Trivet said, jumping back. Secret straightened just in time to get backhanded by the corpse. She shouted in surprise and pain, and found her nose pouring with blood. The woman's arm dropped back down, unresponsive again.

"Damn immigrants," Secret gasped, dabbing at the blood with her sleeve. She pulled her hand back, wincing. "Trivet, get me something clean to soak this up with."

Trivet grabbed an unused apron and handed it to Secret. "That looks terrible," she said. "I bet it's broken. You should go up to Casualty and get it looked at."

"I can't wait to fill out the injury forms," Secret muttered. "Cause of injury: attacked by corpse."

"Go on upstairs," Trivet said. "I can finish up without you—it was almost time for lunch, anyway."

Secret removed her blood-stained apron and took the lift up to Casualty, coming into the Emergency Room through the back. "May I help you?" the admitting nurse asked.

"I work downstairs in Pathology," Secret said. "I just got punched by a corpse."

The nurse didn't even crack a smile. "On-the-job injury?" she asked, and handed Secret a tablet. "Fill these out, please."

Secret sat down in the waiting area by the fountain to fill in the requested data. It was a busy day in Casualty, and most of the emergencies were worse than a broken nose. She ended up waiting for three hours, during which time she overheard no less than seven debates over the merits and drawbacks of tails. Three people endorsed them on aesthetic grounds, and three on functional grounds; a particularly irritating priest argued against them because they'd decrease physical fitness if people had to bend over less often, so Secret decided not to make that argument anymore. At least nobody was lobbying for non-prehensile tails yet.

By the time Secret got in to see the doctor, her nose had swelled up like a giant pink mushroom. "They should have given you ice for this while you were waiting," the doctor said. "You're going to have to ice this and wait for the swelling to go down before I can fix it."

"Can't you do anything *else* to bring the swelling down?" she asked.

"Ice will do it faster than nanotech or medication," he said. "Go home, ice it, and make an appointment for the day after tomorrow to see a plastic surgeon."

Secret touched her nose gingerly. "Is that really necessary?" Plastic surgeons were seen primarily by offworlders petitioning for naturalization, who wanted to look as if they were born Ashari. It had never occurred to Secret that she might have to go to one.

"You won't find anyone who'll do a better job at putting your nose to rights," the doctor said. "Since you have to wait a day, you might as well go to someone who specializes in this sort of thing."

This sort of thing. Secret suppressed a shudder and thanked the doctor.

Secret normally rode her bicycle to and from work, but she walked it home today. The Huarvatat hospital was at the top of a hill, providing her with a lovely view of the sunset over Nuev Dia, as well as an easy ride home, but she didn't want to risk a sudden stop that might jostle her nose. Back at her flat, she latched her gate, leaning her bike up against the fence. Yellow, her upstairs neighbor, was out watering her flowers. "What happened to you?" she asked.

"I got hit by a corpse."

"That's a more interesting day at the office than I had." Yellow put down the watering can to get a closer look, but Secret dodged and went inside, closing the door firmly behind her.

Secret avoided looking at herself in the mirror until it was time to go to bed. After dinner, she iced her nose and read a book, since she didn't feel like going out to socialize. Yellow's reaction was likely to be common, and she didn't feel like being a gruesome spectacle. But she could feel the swelling going down as she iced it, and wanted to see just how bad it looked now, so before she went to bed she went and took a look.

It looked terrible. Her whole face seemed swollen, not just her nose, and even with the blood cleaned off it was clear the injury was recent. Worse, her nose had been smashed sideways, left with a weird bend in the middle, crooked like a paperclip. No wonder everyone had commented.

Foreigners complained that all the Ashari looked alike, and to some extent this was true. Asha had been founded by Terrans who rejected the idea that it was morally wrong to alter the human gene code to improve the human species. The original Ashari had redesigned their children to fit both their physical and mental ideal. All Ashari were strong, healthy, and intelligent. All had good posture, a predisposition towards thinness, and a resistance to any form of chemical addiction. And all were beautiful, with smooth, flawless light brown skin, symmetrical faces, and straight teeth. All had black hair, brown eyes, and small, straight noses.

Except for Secret, now. Nobody would have any right to complain that *she* looked like everyone else—certainly nobody else in Nuev Dia had a crooked nose tonight. Secret went morosely to bed. The sooner she could get this fixed, the better.

The plastic surgeon's name was Flowerpot. Secret tried to avoid reading anything unfortunate into that name, though she had to wonder what kind of woman picked the name "Flowerpot" after her

Naming rite as a teen, then decided to become a doctor.

Secret's appointment was for late morning. Flowerpot was affiliated with the Haurvatat hospital, but her office was in a separate clinic, and Secret found her way in uneasily. The clinic had clearly been set up to accommodate foreigners, with information posted up in a variety of languages in addition to Persian and Angelino. There was another woman in the waiting room, instantly recognizable as an immigrant. Secret carefully refrained from sitting in the seat furthest from the other woman—she didn't want to look xenophobic. She picked a carefully neutral seat, not too far away but not too close, either.

She wasn't far enough away to prevent conversation. "Hello," the immigrant greeted her. "What's your name?"

"Secret," Secret said. Reluctantly she added, "What's yours?"

"Gloria," the woman said, and blushed. "I haven't had my Naming yet." Gloria spoke Angelino clearly enough, though with a faint accent. "My naturalization has been approved, but I'm not very far into the process, you know?" She gestured at her blond hair, fair skin, pudgy frame. "You must just be here for your nose," she said.

"That's right," Secret said, a little relieved that the woman could tell. "I'm a natural-born Ashari."

Gloria nodded a little hesitantly, casting about for another topic of conversation. Secret could have chimed in with the question when Gloria asked it: "What's your position on tails?"

"What's yours?" Secret said, finding herself actually curious to know, for once.

"Well, Flowerpot—" Gloria gestured towards the closed door of the examination room, "—Flowerpot thinks it's a good idea. Me, I'm not so sure. It would be even more surgery to fit in."

"But for everybody," Secret said. "The rest of us would also have to come in for gene restructuring."

"True," Gloria said, and smiled a little. Her teeth were crooked. "I guess in some ways it might be nice for all the Ashari to get an idea of how us immigrants feel."

"Do you want a tail?" Secret asked.

"I suppose it could be convenient," Gloria said. "I wouldn't want a naked tail—that would look kind of silly. And if it had fur on it, we'd have to brush it, and that would take time. But I'll happily go along with the consensus," she added hastily. "I mean, I really admire the philosophy of the Ashari, the constant striving towards perfection. If in a few generations our descendents decide that the tails are a hindrance, we can get rid of them again."

"True," Secret said.

"So how do you feel about tails?" Gloria asked her again.

"Honestly," Secret said, "I'm just sick to death of hearing about them."

"Secret?" the receptionist called. "Flowerpot will see you now."

How Flowerpot felt about tails was no secret. The inside of the examination room was filled with artist's renditions of their beauty and their advantages. Secret stared at the walls as the nurse did a preliminary check of her physical condition. "Is there any nanotech in your system that you're aware of?" she asked.

"I'm a Pathologist, so I carry purification nanotech," Secret said. Purification nanotech didn't really do much physically; they simply carried aspects of the various lesser gods throughout Secret's system, preventing contamination from the corpses she worked with. "Other than that, just the standard."

The nurse checked her blood pressure and temperature, then did a quick check of the nanotech in her system, to be sure nothing was malfunctioning badly and no foreign invaders had wandered in. "Hmm," the nurse said. "Well, you've picked up French somewhere."

"French?" Secret blinked at her.

"It's a language. Someone you've been in contact with must have just had French injected. It's probably not enough to actually give you the language, but you might check in a week or two and see if you understand anything. Could be a bit of a free bonus." Knowledge nanotech, which constructed information in the brain, usually cost a fair amount of money.

"I don't know what I'd do with French," Secret said.

"Well, no knowledge is wasted. Anyway. Other than that, you're in fine shape, except for your nose. I'll send Flowerpot in."

Flowerpot was an ideal specimen of Ashari humanity—slender, muscular, with pronounced cheekbones and large dark eyes. Secret distrusted her immediately. Flowerpot started off by looking at the scans done of the damage while Secret had been in Casualty. "What's your take on tails?" Secret asked.

"I think they're a fine idea," Flowerpot said, her head still bent over the scans.

"Don't you think it might decrease physical fitness, if people didn't have to bend over to pick things up?" Secret asked.

Flowerpot shrugged. "People can continue to exercise if they choose. Why should we enforce that?"

"But a lack of tails is one aspect of humanity that everyone has in common," Secret said. "Even the non-Ashari. Though unmodified humans have a great deal of variety in skin tone and facial features and even in number of fingers, *nobody* has tails."

Flowerpot smiled, showing perfectly symmetrical white teeth. "We're Ashari," she said. "Since when have we limited ourselves to what nature deigned to give us?" She pulled on gloves. "I'm going to have the nurse give you some anaesthetic," she said. "Then I'll set your nose and inject some nanotech to put it exactly as it was before. Do you want it to look as it did before, or would you prefer a different nose shape?"

"I liked it the way it was," Secret said.

"That's fine. Just thought I'd ask."

"Flowerpot," Secret said. "Don't you stand to benefit an awful lot from a pro-tail consensus? As a plastic surgeon? You're the one everyone will have to go to."

Flowerpot's eyes narrowed.

"Where did the suggestion come from initially, anyway?" Secret said. "Suddenly, everyone was discussing the idea. I don't remember an elected official making the proposal. Was it the plastic surgeons who came up with the idea in the first place?"

Flowerpot put down the scans. "How dare you impugn my professional ethics?" she said. "I will not treat someone who distrusts my motives. Get out of here!"

"She what?" Trivet said. They weren't autopsying today, but running monthly statistics, compiling cause-of-death information for the Genetic Advisory Council. So far it looked like the cardiac failures were winning. Government resources had been devoted to improvements to the human heart for decades now, with no significant success in getting them to last longer.

"She wouldn't treat me." Secret fingered her mangled nose glumly. The swelling had gone down, but had left her nose crooked and flat.

"So what are you going to do?" Trivet asked.

"Find another plastic surgeon, I guess," Secret said. "Somebody who isn't hung up on tails."

"My uncle's best friend Rain is a plastic surgeon," Trivet said. "I heard from my brother that Rain thinks tails are a dumb idea. His clinic is all the way over on the other side of Nuev Dia, though."

"I'll ask around," Secret said. Crossing Nuev Dia was a day-long project.

Secret's nose felt better tonight, at least, even if it still looked terrible, and she decided to go out for a social call. After dinner, she went over to her friend Path's house, parking her bike next to ten others and knocking on the half-open door.

"Secret!" Path greeted her. "What happened to your nose?"

"I got hit by a corpse," Secret said.

Path ushered her inside. "When are you going to get it fixed?"

Secret described her encounter with Flowerpot as she pulled her shoes off in the front hallway. She could hear other guests chatting in the next room, but when she walked in, all conversation ceased.

"I got hit by a corpse," Secret said. "I'm getting it fixed. You can stop staring at me like I'm some sort of unmodified offworlder, all right?"

Everyone laughed nervously and returned to their conversation, their voices a little louder and a little higher than they'd been a moment ago. They all made an effort to treat Secret normally, but she found that everyone's eyes continually strayed to her broken nose, and their conversation was a little *too* hearty and amiable. People kept sitting near her, but not *next* to her, as if they thought she would contaminate them. They treated her—Secret realized, near the end of the evening—much like she'd treated the immigrant woman that morning.

Secret had had *enough* of this. On her way home, she went by Trivet's flat, even though it was past polite hours to call on someone. "Where's Rain's clinic?" she asked. "I'm going there *tomorrow*."

Nuev Dia was said by the Ashari to have been built "organically." Secret had not understood precisely what this meant until she studied other cultures in college, and had looked at maps of Terran cities like Minneapolis or New York, with their straight, numbered streets, arterial roads, and central downtown hubs. No one had planned Nuev Dia; the earliest colonists had built their homes and businesses with faith that—with only minimal guidelines—the *right* sort of city would emerge. They'd also banned personal motorized vehicles. Beyond that restriction, Nuev Dia had simply been allowed to grow.

Secret walked or bicycled almost everywhere. She considered biking to see the new plastic surgeon, but decided to take the tram to at least get to the other side of the city.

Nuev Dia's districts had grown up around their own centers, and the tram line had not been allowed to knock down anything more than 25 years old when it was built, so crossing from district to district meant that the track wound slowly through a series of small arterial roads, over gullies and around walls, past parks and stands of trees. She lived on the east side of Nuev Dia and was heading west, but more often than that the track traveled north or south along an obstacle, looking for a road that might lead around.

As they made their way through a particularly old and well-populated neighborhood, the tram slowed almost to a crawl. She increasingly regretted her decision not to ride her bike. Studying the map of where they were vs. where they were headed, she concluded that she could shave an hour off the trip if she just got out and walked, and hopped out at the next stop.

Secret had never been in this part of Nuev Dia before, though as the path led through neighborhoods of boxy apartment buildings and small Temples, she felt almost as if she were walking through her own. Outside of the tram, she was on familiar territory even when she wasn't. She skirted the local marketplace and wound her way through the crowd of devotees heading for the Fire Temple. The faithful stared at her nose, but stepped politely out of her way. She cringed and resisted the urge to cup her hand over her deviant facial feature.

As she'd expected, a walking path out to the next neighborhood wound behind the Fire Temple and past the local hospital and clinic. She was tempted to duck into this neighborhood's clinic and look for a plastic surgeon who could treat her, regardless of the doctor's opinion on tails—she could keep her mouth shut this time—but she'd sent a message over to Rain's clinic and he was expecting her sometime that day.

Secret was a taken aback when her path dead-ended abruptly at a high brick wall. She made her way north and found a gate. It was unlocked and unguarded, but as soon as she stepped through, she knew why this area had been marked off so clearly. This was the foreign district.

Offworlders who embraced the Ashari religion and way of life were welcomed as immigrants. They were given access to the nanotechnology that would restructure their bodies and their gene code. Most immigrants lived in Ashari neighborhoods, where their neighbors (after some initial reservation) usually tried to make them feel welcome.

Technically, offworlders who didn't wish to become Ashari were allowed to live wherever they wished. In practice, although tourists would occasionally wander through neighborhoods distant from the spaceport, the diplomats who had to live on Asha for long periods of time lived in their own carefully delineated district. Here they had houses in the style they were accustomed to, as well as their own Temples, shops, restaurants. The only native Ashari who lived here were missionaries who maintained a Fire Temple to share the Good Religion with the offworlders.

The streets of the foreign district were straight and carefully laid out; from the map posted at the gate, Secret could see that the road she was on would take her due west to a counterpart gate on the other side of the quarter. Well, it wasn't as if the foreigners were going to hurt her. She was even safe from ritual contamination. With a deliberate shrug, she stepped through the gate.

In the middle of the day, there weren't that many foreigners on the streets. Most were at work at one of the embassies, working to represent either Terra or one of the other colonies. Everyone on Asha was human; the various alien races contacted were uninterested in setting up embassies on such a relative backwater.

Still, Secret was struck by the visual variety. There were yellow-haired offworlders with skin as light as yogurt and others with skin several shades darker than her own. It was the people with orange hair that looked the strangest, especially the man she saw with orange speckles all over his body. He looked almost diseased.

No one turned to stare at her. Even in the foreign district, there were enough Ashari that she was unremarkable—and her nose, as horrible as it looked to her, was an uninteresting distinction.

The road was straight, but the foreign district was larger than it had looked on the map, and Secret was starting to get hungry and tired. She decided to find a restaurant; she could rest her legs and satisfy more of her growing curiosity about the people who lived here. So she stopped off at the next restaurant she saw. *Eden*, said the sign on the door. A bell tinkled as she pushed it open.

Heads swiveled as she came in. The restaurant had the same polyglot mix as the street, except for one thing: there were no other Ashari here. Even the brown-skinned black-haired woman waiting tables was clearly Earth-Asian, and not Ashari. Secret almost went back out, but swallowed hard and looked for an open table.

"May I help you?" the woman asked. She spoke heavily accented Angelino. "You want a table?"

"Yes," Secret said. "For one. Please."

"This way," the waitress said, and Secret fell into step behind her. The waitress led her to a table by the window. Nearby, a group sat at four tables pushed together; Secret saw them looking at her, and one of the women said something in a low voice that made everyone else burst out laughing. But it was too late to flee without looking ridiculous, so she pulled out a chair and sat where the waitress showed her. The waitress handed her a menu and walked away.

Secret glanced over at the crowded table, to see if they were still staring at her. Quite the contrary, no one was even looking in her direction. She studied the menu of unfamiliar foods. *Pad Thai. Lo Mein. Spaghetti. Irish Stew.* She saw one item she recognized, tabouli, but it seemed absurd to come to a restaurant in the foreign district and then order something she could make at home.

The waitress was back, with a glass of water and a pot of tea. "Are you ready to order?" she asked. At least, that was what Secret thought she was saying. The waitress had a problem that was not uncommon among people who'd acquired a language through nanotech, like Secret's French: she could understand everything you said, but she couldn't pronounce the words she saw in her head.

Secret put down the menu. "I'd like you to bring me something you think I'd like," she said, speaking slowly and clearly. "Something good. Anything."

The waitress looked at her dubiously. Secret closed her menu and handed it back. "You choose for me," she said. "I'd like to try something new."

One of the women from the crowded table nearby called out a suggestion to the waitress, and the waitress laughed and said something back. Secret couldn't understand any of it, so whatever they were speaking, it probably wasn't French. The waitress went off to the kitchen, and the woman from the other table waved at Secret to catch her eye. Secret gave her a nervous smile back, which the woman took as an invitation to come over.

"I have just one question," the woman said, and Secret fought the urge to cover her deviant nose with her hand. "*Are* you Ashari? We were debating that at the table."

"It's just a broken nose," Secret said.

The woman blinked at her. "What?" She focused on Secret's nose. "Huh, that does look painful. But are you Ashari? Because we never see Ashari people in here. And you're not acting like you think you're better than anyone else."

Secret bristled on behalf of her planet. "Excuse me? Aren't most of the foreigners here members of the diplomatic corps? You sure don't act like a diplomat."

"I'm not, I'm a hairstylist. I just mostly style hair for diplomats." There was a peal of laughter from the table and the woman glanced over, then pulled out a chair and sat down with Secret. "Screw 'em. So what are you doing here?"

"I took a shortcut, and then got hungry. Where are you from?"

"New Philly, originally. And you *are* Ashari—native?"

"Do I really *look* like an immigrant to you?"

"Who the hell can tell? You make them all get cosmetic work so they look like the rest of you."

"We don't *make* immigrants do anything. It's just that people who want to move here usually want to fit in."

"Oh yeah." The stranger, who still hadn't introduced herself, rolled her eyes.

The waitress came out with a plate of food, which she set down silently in front of Secret. She said something to the stranger, who snickered, and then added in Ashari, "Eat up. It's on me."

"What? You don't—I have—"

"Too late, I already paid. So you'd better like it."

It was a sausage of some kind, in a roll, with some kind of relish strewn on top. Secret took a bite, and was disconcerted to find something yellow and runny in the sausage. She liked sausage, normally, but this tasted different from the spiced soy mixtures she was used to, and the yellow stuff tasted really odd, almost spoiled. The relish was sour and limpid. The flavors melded together into something just barely tolerable. The stranger was watching her with interest, though, so she ate it all and said politely, "That was very good. Thank you."

"It's called cheddarwurst," the woman said. "With sauerkraut. I usually put ketchup and mustard on it."

"I thought maybe the yellow stuff . . ."

"No, you put mustard on top. The yellow stuff was cheese."

"Oh." Secret hadn't had cheese before.

"And the sausage—real meat. Have you had it before?" The woman's voice was tinged with just a hint of malice. Most Ashari were vegetarian, if for no other reason than the cost of meat on a colony world. "Natural intestine casings, too."

"Damn." Secret wiped her hands on the napkin; the meal had been messy. "If you were going to pay for me to eat real meat, I wish you'd told me first, so that I could have attended to the flavor more closely. I don't often get meat. Let alone sausage. It must be shipped in?"

"From Wisconsin." The stranger was disappointed that Secret wasn't horrified, but doing her best to hide it. She stood up. "Well. I'm glad you enjoyed your meal."

"Hey," said one of the men from the table, standing up. "I can't believe you bought her bratwurst but no beer, Kathleen. Come here, stranger, and I'll buy you a beer."

Nervously, Secret joined the table, but the others, if more reserved, were a bit less hostile than Kathleen. They mostly worked at or around the embassy for the European Federation. They wanted to know what she was doing in the foreign district, and why she was crossing Nuev Dia, and eventually the story of the corpse, the broken nose, and the grumpy plastic surgeon came out. Her beer finished, she decided that she really had to get going. "Come back sometime," one of the men said. "Try something that isn't cheddarwurst. Lo mein, maybe, or spaghetti, I bet you'd like any of the noodle dishes."

"Hmmm," Secret said, and made her way to the door as quickly as she could. She headed west again, and found her way to the gate with immense relief. *At last.* The foreigners had been rude and hostile; Kathleen (how did they ever remember names, with just random syllables to go on?) had deliberately tried to offend her with inappropriate food.

Secret realized, as she started up the last hill to the clinic, that she felt more alive than she ever remembered feeling.

And in over an hour, tails hadn't come up even once.

There were a handful of patients in the clinic office when she arrived, all of them foreigners in various stages of naturalization. She took a seat, surreptitiously studying the immigrants and trying to guess what they'd looked like to begin with. She wondered if any of them had had red hair.

"Secret?" the receptionist called. "Rain will see you now."

Rain had let his face age more naturally than Flowerpot had, despite the doubt this might cast on him as a plastic surgeon. He had his assistant do a new set of scans, since he couldn't just send over to Haurvatat hospital for the original set. "It's well on its way to healing naturally, but of course you wouldn't want it crooked," he said. "I'll give you some anaesthetic, then we'll set your nose and give you some nanotech to put it back to normal."

Secret stirred.

"Unless you want a different nose?" He looked a little surprised. "Your original nose was quite a nice one."

"Actually," Secret said, "I don't mind keeping it crooked. I'd just like you to adjust it to make sure the passageways are clear and I can breathe properly."

Rain set the scans down, surprised. "Are you sure?"

"I can always make it straight again if I change my mind, right?" Secret asked.

"Yes, of course. But in the meantime—you're definitely sure?"

Secret lifted her chin. "It gives people something to talk about other than those damn tails," she said.

The corner of Rain's mouth lifted. "All right then," he said. "I'll just make sure you can breathe freely."

When he was done, Secret looked at herself in the mirror. The swelling was gone and her nose really didn't look that different from the way it had before. It was just a little off, that was all. A little different.

Secret reached the foreign district as the sun was setting. *I should go straight on through and find a taxi,* she thought. *I'd be home in time to go visit Path, or Candle . . .*

But she could hear drum and fiddle music, somewhere close by; the building it came from said PUB over the door, and she could smell something cooking that she'd never tasted before.

A passport, she thought. *I'm going to need a passport. And a visa. And—somewhere to go.*

Holding her head high, she opened the door.

<u>Author's Note</u>

One of my unpublished novels is a science fiction mystery novel set at an interstellar university. Secret was one of the secondary characters, and probably the best part of the book. (It was the second book I wrote and I wasn't satisfied with it.) One of the details about Secret's world you learn in the novel is that their coming-of-age ritual involves hallucinogens, and the name you pick is traditionally inspired in some way by the vision you had.

Secret's name is Secret *because she doesn't like to talk about her vision.*

THE GOOD SON

don't just want to be with you. I want to live with you. In the kingdom under the hill, we could have been together forever. I didn't want that. I wanted you—all of you. But that was before I understood what that meant.

Maggie was an American tourist when I first saw her, hiking across the Irish hills with a group of other college students. It was raining. Maggie had no umbrella, and when the drizzle turned to a downpour, the water plastered her hair to her cheeks in black curls. The other students ran back to the bus, but Maggie lingered, her camera dangling at her hip, and when everyone else had gone, she pulled a pennywhistle out of her pocket and played it for ten minutes before she turned and trudged back up to the road.

I made a door, so that I could slip out of the hill and follow her. My elder brother caught my hand and said, "Don't do it, Gaidian. Bring her here, if you must have her." When I didn't answer, he shook his head. "You get nothing but grief when you follow a mortal."

"I just want to see where she goes," I said, and went out into the rain.

I caught up with her in Dublin. I put on a young face, and clothes to match the ones I saw around me. My first thought was to tell her I was an Irish student the same age as she was, but when I realized she would return to Chicago in less than two weeks, I decided to be an American student, instead—heading back myself at the same time, though to a different city.

There were fiddlers at the pub and Maggie danced with me, her black curls wild in the humid air. "Where did you say you were from, again?" she asked after last call as I walked her to the bus stop.

I named a city I'd heard one of the other students say earlier that evening: "Minneapolis."

"That's not so far! Maybe I'll see you again," she said, and gave me a long kiss. "Let me give you my address."

Had possession been all I desired, I could have lured you under the hill. But I wanted your mortal love; I wanted you to choose me. Of course, it never occurred to me to tell you the truth. You'd have thought I was crazy. So I needed a mortal name. I needed numbers, references, addresses. I needed papers.

I never thought, when I started out on this, about all the other lives I would be embracing.

Making myself a door to Minneapolis was easy enough. I'd gone on outings to the mortal world before, so I knew how to change gold into money, and how to find someone to make forged papers. I wanted a common name, so I flipped through a phone book and chose Johnson. I'd told Maggie my nickname was Finch—I wasn't going to give a mortal I'd just met my true name. I had the man make me a driver's license, even though I didn't intend to drive anything, and one of those number cards. Making up an identity I could use for more than a few days was a great deal of *work*. I finally settled into an apartment near the university, and got in touch with Maggie.

Less than a day after I sent her my address, she showed up at my door.

It turned out she went to school in Chicago, but she was *from* Minneapolis. And when I didn't give her an address in exchange for hers, she'd figured I wasn't really all that interested in her. We spent a very pleasant evening, and morning, and afternoon, and evening. And then she got up, made us both pancakes, and said, "You must have *just* moved in, huh?"

"Why do you say that?" I asked, already a little nervous that my lies would be uncovered.

Maggie laughed. "Your kitchen is so well stocked I'm guessing your mother did it for you. But nothing was open. Not the flour, not the eggs, not even the milk. The milk and eggs are fresh, though, I checked before I made the pancakes, so it's not that you never cook. *Do* you cook?"

"Of course I cook." I took the plate of pancakes she offered me and sat down at the kitchen table. "I'll make you dinner."

Maggie sat down across from me with her own pancakes. I was afraid she might start asking me questions I hadn't thought of answers to, so I asked her to tell me more about herself, and then listened to her talk. She was a good storyteller. It was even better than hearing her play the pennywhistle.

But she did, eventually, ask me for my own stories. "Tell me about *your* family," she said, when she'd finished telling me about her four sisters (she was the youngest) and twenty-seven cousins.

"I'm an only child," I said.

"Where did you grow up?"

I always paid attention to stories, wherever I went. Since coming to Minneapolis I'd paid careful attention to the stories I heard about my new home, and I drew on those stories now, to give myself a history. "Brainerd," I said.

"Really? I used to vacation up there. It's beautiful. I guess you hear that a lot."

"Yeah. Well, I don't mind." I cleared my throat. "My parents— well, you've heard that old joke about the Scandinavian man who loved his wife so much he almost told her? That was written about my father."

"Oh yeah, I think I've met him. Or one of his thirty-six identical twin brothers." She shook her hair out of her face. "My family's Irish. They're, like, the complete polar opposites."

"So is that why you went to Ireland?"

"No, actually, I went because the program let me satisfy one of the requirements I needed to graduate, and it wasn't too expensive." She laughed. "I never thought I'd go to Ireland—I mean, come on, the Irish-American who wants to go get in touch with her roots, that's so not me. Except then I had my picture taken next to the statue of my famous ancestor, just like every other American dork. It's so embarrassing."

"Ha. Which one's your ancestor?"

"The Crank on the Bank. Patrick Kavanagh."

"Oh yeah, I should have guessed that." Her name was Margaret Cavanaugh.

Maggie, you were everything I'd dreamed a mortal woman would be. If we are stone, unchanging, you are fire. All mortals are, but you, especially. I knew I'd done right to follow you.

But to keep you, I would need to back up my story.

When you went back to your college in Chicago, I went to find a family.

"Hello, Mother," I said. The white-haired woman stood wide-eyed and still for a moment, twisting a heavy gold ring she wore on her right hand. Before she could slam the door in my face, I gave her a kiss on the cheek, sealing the enchantment. Memory is a malleable thing—half the enchantments of my kind are as much suggestion as anything else. "It's nice to see you."

She had blue eyes. Her white hair was tightly curled. She made an old mother for a man my age, but she and her husband fit my requirements—childless, without a lot of people in their lives who would need their memories altered as well.

"I don't have—" She met my eyes, and I saw a look of deep longing pass through them like a shadow. She blinked. "That is, I wasn't expecting you."

"I know. I was in the area and thought I'd stop by. I don't get up here often enough anymore. How are you and Dad?"

"Bob?" She retreated from the door. "Robert's here."

Robert? Well, fine. I could be Robert. "Hi Dad," I said, and shook his hand. Men his age didn't kiss their sons, but I felt my magic settling as soon as our hands touched. "How's the business?"

"Eh. As bad as always. You want a beer?" I nodded. "Doreen, since you're up . . ."

We all sat down together in the living room. It was a musty old-person living room, full of knickknacks. Doreen apparently did needlepoint. A reproduction of Van Gogh's *Starry Night* hung over the fireplace, and they had a framed map of Norway on the wall. I sat down in a chair near the fireplace and sneezed from the dust. They didn't get many visitors. Perfect. Well, unless Maggie met them and ran screaming in the other direction.

But they were very nice. Bob was the perfect laconic rural Minnesotan and Doreen was sweet and fairly quiet. She twisted the ring on her right hand when she was nervous. Towards the end of the evening I mentioned that since they'd lost all my old childhood photos the time the shed flooded, I thought I'd give them a start on a new collection, and handed over a picture I'd had taken the day before, framed and ready for hanging. Doreen took it and thanked me. Her hands gripped it tightly. Bob gently took it from her, took down a needlepoint and put up the picture in its place.

"By the way," I said, as I was getting ready to leave, "I have a new girlfriend, Maggie. She's really great. I was thinking I might bring her up to meet you the next time she's home on vacation—she goes to school in Chicago."

"That would be lovely, dear," Doreen said. "I hope you can make it up here again soon. We miss you." She stood on her tiptoes to kiss my cheek and ruffle my hair. "Drive carefully."

*

I fretted for days the first time you met them, but it was fine. My parents remembered me, they were pleased to meet you, and you were charmed by them. I worried before our first Thanksgiving, and even more before our first Christmas, but it all went fine. The spell kept its hold. The picture of me always hung on the wall; my mother even dusted it.

You finished your studies and got a job in Minneapolis. We found an apartment and moved in together. It was perfect. Just what I'd dreamed of when I followed you.

Of course, there were limits. I couldn't marry you. Because there would be all these other *relatives—too many at once. I shuddered at the thought of enspelling them all. Even if we'd eloped, I couldn't take wedding vows as Robert. Or even as Finch. I couldn't do that to you, to swear an oath to you without using my real name. And there was too much to explain. I still believed you'd think I was crazy, but even if you didn't—well, I had lied to you. I really did love you, and it really was* me *who loved you, but there were so many things I had lied about. It was too late.*

And then my mother got sick.

"Doreen is in the hospital," Bob said. The phone had rung as Maggie was getting out of the shower, and now she was watching my face, her hair clinging damp to her own. "We're in St. Paul. I thought I should call you."

"What's wrong?" I asked.

"She's been having dizzy spells. I nagged her to go to the doctor and yesterday she finally went. They did some scans, and then sent us here for more tests."

"What do they think it is?"

A pause. "They saw something on the CT scan," Bob said slowly. "They don't seem to want to call it anything yet. I figure it must be bad if they don't want to tell us what it is. Can you come over?"

"Yes," I said. "Of course."

I hung up the phone, then called my boss—I was working then at a bookstore. "My mom's just gone to the hospital," I said. "She's here in the cities. I'm going to go see her."

"Do you want me to come?" Maggie asked.

I hesitated. Seeing Maggie with my parents always made me tense. "I'll call you once I know what's going on," I said. "This might be nothing. Okay?"

"Okay." She gave me a kiss. "Send her my love. I have some yarn I bought for her last week—I'll send it with you."

I peeked in at the bag of yarn as I rode the city bus to downtown St. Paul. It was a deep red-brown and soft like a tangle of silk. Doreen had taken up knitting in the last year, but she mostly seemed to use cheap acrylic yarn, fearing to "waste" the nicer yarns Maggie tried to talk her into buying. I stroked it for a moment, thinking of Maggie, and bracing myself for the hospital.

There are mortals who think they hate hospitals because they fear their own mortality. I am not mortal, so I can say with certainty that I hate hospitals because they are horrible places. Whenever Maggie was ill, I tried to ensure she got restful sleep and wholesome, tempting food. Hospitals offer disrupted sleep, and vile food. Why anyone expects to get better in a hospital is something I still find a mystery.

Doreen looked wasted and shrunken in her hospital bed. Her hands were bare without her rings, which they'd made her take off for the MRI. "I want to go home," she said when I came in. "Are they going to let me go home soon?"

"I think they wanted to run more tests," I said, leaning over to give her a kiss.

"They've run all the tests they have. When are they going to let me go *home?*"

"Why don't I go get you something decent to eat?" I said.

Bob shook his head. "The doctor was going to come by in a few minutes," he said. "Wait till then."

Of course, he didn't come for over an hour, and then stood outside our door talking to a nurse for another ten minutes before he actually came in to talk to us. "Doreen," he said, looking at my mother's chart. "I have some bad news about your dizzy spells. You have a brain tumor. Now, it might be benign . . ." He talked on, about different kinds of brain tumors, treatment options, prognoses. I don't think any of us heard much beyond "brain tumor."

"Can I go home?" Doreen asked when he was done. "Do I have to stay in the hospital?"

"You'll have surgery here, and we'll do a biopsy. You can get the rest of your treatment in Brainerd, if you want, and you can probably be home most of the time."

Doreen burst into tears. "It's time to plant my bulbs," she said.

I called Maggie at work from a phone in the waiting room. "Oh, Finch," she whispered when she heard. "I'm so sorry. I can come over . . ."

"She's napping," I said. "You can come over later. And you know—it might not be that bad. The doctor said the benign ones aren't nearly as scary as you might think."

Maggie laughed, a little shakily. "I don't buy the idea of a non-scary brain tumor."

"Yeah, me either."

We chatted a little more and then hung up. A woman was waiting to use the phone, so I moved to another chair. "Jenny?" I heard her say after she dialed, and then her voice faded. She'd covered her face with her free hand, and her shoulders were shaking. She was crying too hard to speak.

I closed my eyes, trying to think about my own problems instead of eavesdropping on other people's. It occurred to me that I could find out if Doreen were already doomed. The banshee would know. No, I decided. Best to be as ignorant as the mortals, lest they suspect something was strange.

The woman on the phone was still crying too hard to speak. I wanted to touch her hand, to offer her some sort of comfort, but instead I went to the elevator and headed downstairs.

As I went outside into the rain, I thought I heard my brother's voice, laughing at me. "You're right," I said to him, half already in my dream. "I don't want to know. I'd rather believe she's going to make it."

It was the bad kind of brain tumor.

They weren't sure how bad until after the surgery. Doreen was still unconscious, her head swathed in bandages; the doctor told us that he'd cut out as much of the tumor as he could. He talked about radiation and chemotherapy. He gave percentages, rattling numbers off so quickly none of us understood any of them. He forced a smile, said something that tried to be encouraging but wasn't, then left.

Bob turned to me and said, "She's dying, isn't she?"

"I don't know," I said.

When Doreen woke up, for a few minutes she didn't know either of us. I wasn't surprised she didn't recognize me; traumas could shake the grip of any spell like this. But Bob was horrified. Doreen's lapse scared him more than any prognosis from the doctor. Something slid into place after a bit and Doreen was herself again. But as I left that day, Bob turned to me and said, "That's what it's going to be like, isn't it. She's going to forget me. And you. Both of us."

"I don't know," I said again.

"One of our friends got Alzheimer's. Didn't know any of us after a while. I thought I'd rather die, than live like that."

"Mom was only confused for a minute," I said.

Bob shook his head and didn't answer.

Doreen was discharged a few days later, and Maggie drove all of us up to Brainerd. We'd expected to be able to head up in the morning, but the doctor didn't come to discharge her until afternoon, and we didn't get on the road until after three. Doreen sat up front with

Maggie; I sat in the back seat next to Bob. It was a quiet trip. Doreen dozed most of the way. Bob stared out the window. As we grew near Brainerd, Doreen stirred, and Bob looked at her from his seat behind Maggie. I saw naked terror in his eyes, as if he'd glimpsed her death out there rather than grain elevators and cornfields.

"She'll be okay, Dad," I whispered. "Everything's going to be okay."

Bob gave me a long, bleak look, and went back to staring out the window.

Their house was dark when we pulled up. Bob unlocked it and turned the lights on, and Maggie gently roused Doreen. Maggie had to work tomorrow, and we'd decided she would drive back tonight. I'd take the bus home from Brainerd in a day or two. Maggie settled Doreen into her chair, then heated up some soup for dinner while I found sheets for the guest bed. We ate dinner in front of the TV, and then Maggie kissed Doreen and headed back to Minneapolis.

When I came back into the living room, Doreen stared at me. "Who are you?"

"I'm Robert, your son," I said, and tapped my picture on the wall, trying to nudge the spell.

She stared at me, her face a complete blank. "We never had children," she said.

"Doreen," Bob said, and sat down next to her.

Doreen burst into tears, burying her face against his neck. "Bob, why not? Why *not*?"

Bob stroked her hair; it was damp with sweat. "What did the doctor say about fevers?" he asked me, his voice shaky.

"He said any fever was an emergency. If she runs a fever we're supposed to take her to the ER." I came over and touched her forehead. "Do you have a thermometer?" I asked, though her head was scorching hot.

"I don't know. Doreen's always the one who looks after that sort of thing."

Doreen looked up at me. "Oh, Robert," she said. "Thank goodness. I thought you'd gone. Back to Minneapolis, I mean."

"I'll see if I can find one," I said, and went into the bathroom. I found a digital thermometer in the medicine cabinet, its instructions still folded around it. Doreen's temperature was 102.

"I'll get the car," Bob said.

St. Joseph's medical center was only about a mile from their house; it didn't take long to get there. I helped Doreen into the ER while Bob parked the car. She was admitted almost immediately; they suspected infection. This hospital room was eerily like her last, right down to the color of the privacy curtain. Bob slumped in the chair next to her bed. I fidgeted with the thermometer, which I'd put into my pocket on our way out the door.

"Are we still in St. Paul?" Doreen asked.

Bob raised his head and gave Doreen a look of bleak horror. "Don't you remember coming home?"

"We're in Brainerd," I said. "We brought you home this afternoon, but then you started running a fever."

Doreen looked at me helplessly. "I *don't* remember coming home."

"You slept most of the way."

Her hands plucked at the thin hospital blanket. "Can't I just take some aspirin for the fever and go home?"

"They think you have an infection."

"But I don't want to stay here."

"I don't think they'll keep you here long," I said. "Why don't you try to get some sleep."

Doreen nodded. "Take your father home. He looks like he's having a rougher day than I am."

When I got up in the morning, Bob was gone.

I found his note on the kitchen table. It was very short—just that he was sorry. The car was gone, but he'd taken no money. With the note, he left his wedding ring and the two rings Doreen usually wore—her wedding ring, and the heavy ring she normally wore on her right hand. I slipped them into my pocket.

I'd hoped to avoid telling Doreen, at least right away, but when I came in, she looked past me and said, "Where's Bob?"

"He couldn't come in today," I said.

Doreen scoffed at that. "The man's retired. What, he had some sort of pressing engagement?" She looked closely at my face. "What happened, Robert? Is it the house? Did the house burn down?"

"Oh, no!" I said with false heartiness, wondering why I couldn't lie about this when I lied about myself so well. "The house is fine, don't worry."

"He left me, didn't he?"

I curled my hand around the rings in my pocket. "Yes," I said, finally. "He left your rings."

Doreen didn't cry. She just nodded once, and said, "I'd like them back. Even if he ran out on me. I've worn a wedding ring for thirty-six years. It doesn't feel right *not* having it on my hand." She slipped the rings back on. "Now, this one," she said, pointing at the one she wore on her right hand. "This one was my great-grandmother's. My mother told me the ring was looted from Gaul by the Vikings and that's how it came into the family. But a jeweler told me once there was no way it could really be that old. I was supposed to hand it on to my daughter, but I never had a daughter. I don't get along well with my nieces. I guess it will go to you, and you can give it to Maggie when you get married."

"I'm in no hurry," I assured her.

"Psht. If you two would hurry up and get married, I could give her the ring now. I'm not going to live forever, you know."

The staff at the hospital were sympathetic when they found out about Bob, but not as surprised as I'd expected. They responded to the news with an efficient command of regulations: Doreen needed new paperwork. She'd drawn up papers years ago giving Bob the power to make health care decisions for her. That all needed to be changed, and the nurses thought I should be designated. "Of course," the doctor said. "You're her son. The next of kin."

But I'm a fraud. How was I supposed to make decisions for her? I barely knew her. I was only beginning to realize how little I knew about these people. *I can't do this.*

"Don't be silly, Robert," my mother said. "I don't *have* anybody else."

"But I don't know what you'd want."

"Use your common sense. If you wouldn't want it for yourself, you can assume I wouldn't want it, either."

"I'd want it all, Mom. I'd want every minute of life I could possibly have. If they could keep my body breathing, my blood pumping, I'd want it."

"No you wouldn't," she said. "Only if there were some hope of recovery."

"There's always hope. Where there's life, there's hope. I bet I could find you a dozen stories of people who were supposed to be brain dead who went on to walk out of the hospital."

"If I'm not in there anymore, Robert, let me go."

"How am I even supposed to know that?"

"You'll know."

There was always the Banshee. I signed the paper. Better me than a stranger.

The infection kept Doreen in the hospital for weeks. Even after she seemed to have recovered they wouldn't discharge her—her blood count was too low, they said. She wasn't tolerating chemo well. Worse, the treatments didn't seem to be working. The tumor wasn't responding to the chemo and radiation the way it was supposed to.

Maggie and I fell into a routine. I worked Wednesday through Saturday. Saturday nights, we drove together to Brainerd. Maggie stayed with me on Sunday, then drove back down Sunday night, since she had to work on Monday. I stayed until Tuesday evening, then took the bus back to Minneapolis.

I had a lot of time to think on the bus, which wasn't good. What

I thought about most was my elder brother telling me I would regret following Maggie. *I don't regret following Maggie. I'll never regret following Maggie. I just wish I'd chosen a healthier mother. Or told Maggie I was an orphan.*

One night the bus was late, and I thought about making a door to Minneapolis. *What am I doing riding around on a bus like a mortal? I am Fey. I don't need to do this.*

And then a darker echo of the thought. *I am Fey. I don't need to do any of this.*

I could go home. It was what we were supposed to do, after all. Woo the mortal maid, then leave her. Or lure her back to our own banquet hall. I would miss her, but I would get over her. Or so my brother would assure me. Time moved differently there. I'd settle back down at the feast, and before I knew it, it would be too late anyway. She would have moved on with her life, married a dentist, had three children . . .

It began to rain.

I didn't want to leave Maggie. I didn't want to leave Doreen, either. *I don't have anyone else,* she had said.

She's not your mother, the dark echo whispered.

Maybe not, but I'm her son.

The bus arrived, finally, and I climbed on, feeling my exhaustion like a weight on my shoulders. Maybe next weekend I would go back with Maggie and get some extra rest.

I didn't, though. The next Saturday, when we arrived at the hospital, Doreen gave us her smile of gratitude and desperation, and I knew I'd stay until Tuesday, just like always.

Doreen remained stubbornly optimistic for weeks. She endured the sickness and covered her bald head with soft cotton hats that Maggie crocheted for her. Her favorite was canary yellow with rainbow threads stitched through. She wore it so often, Maggie bought more of the yarn and made her two others.

One evening, I went out to get sandwiches for us, and came back to hear my mother telling Maggie a funny story about my childhood.

I'd colored with my crayons in a book, apparently, and then claimed the dog did it. "I remember blaming my sister for something like that when I was a child, but the poor boy had no brothers or sisters, so he tried to blame the dog. I've never met a dog who could hold a crayon, but apparently he thought it would be worth a try..."

I could see it all, as she described it: the defaced book open in the middle of the kitchen; the spilled crayons; the guilt-stricken child. My mother glanced up when she heard me in the doorway, and gave me a fond smile.

"What was the book he colored in?" Maggie asked.

"You know, I can't remember."

"*For Whom the Bell Tolls*," I said, settling into the other visitor's chair and handing Maggie a sandwich. "I think I thought it needed some illustrations."

"I took away your crayons for weeks after that," my mother said, a bit nostalgically. "But you were a good boy, most of the time. Nearly always." She glanced at Maggie.

"You taught him well," Maggie said, saluting her with a sandwich.

The night after the doctor suggested we call hospice, I sat with Doreen until long past midnight. When I thought she was asleep, I gathered up my coat as quietly as I could and started to leave.

"I always knew," she said, as I put my hand on the door.

I turned back. In the darkness of the hospital room, a mortal wouldn't have been able to see her face, but I met her eyes squarely, and she met mine. "Knew what?" I asked.

"I *knew*. When you knocked on my door that day and greeted me as mother, you were a stranger. Your magic, or whatever it was, it worked on Bob. But I knew." Her eyes glittered with tears. "We wanted a child. Years, we tried. Once I even got pregnant but I lost the baby a few weeks later... These days you read in the paper about drugs, fancy procedures, but back then we had nothing. My mother told me to relax, take a vacation... nothing worked. It almost killed me." She let out a harsh sigh. "I would have adopted, but Bob wouldn't hear of it. And to tell you the truth, I was afraid of adopting. I was afraid I wouldn't love the baby as my own, and if I couldn't be sure, maybe better not to. I know Bob wanted a child, but he didn't feel the loss like I did. Or if he did, he didn't let on."

I opened my mouth to speak, but nothing came out.

"Then you came. And took us as your parents. Oh, Robert." Tears trickled down her cheek. "I'm sorry. If I'd known what this would lead to, if I'd known the burden I'd become, I'd have closed the door."

I sat back down, my coat in my lap. "You know I could leave, Mom," I said. "And I choose to stay. With you." I squeezed her hand.

"You're a good son," she whispered.

A few minutes later, I thought she'd fallen asleep, but she stirred and spoke again. "I have something I want to give you. I can't change the will—anyone could challenge it if I changed it now. But I can give you this before the cancer steals what's left." She tugged loose the heavy ring from her right hand. "This is for you, my only son. Give it to your Maggie when you're ready to get married."

"I can't—"

"You can." She closed my hand over it, and I felt the power in it burn against my palm. *The ring stolen by Vikings. Ah. It came from Ireland, surely.* "I always knew," she said again. "This is for *you*."

That was probably the last of the good days.

I called hospice; Doreen wanted to die at home, so we moved her home. I worried it would only depress her with Bob gone, but even without Bob she took comfort from her house. Hospice nurses came for long spells during the day. I tried to stay with her the rest of the time. Sometimes Maggie gave me breaks.

I wore the ring on a leather cord under my shirt. I couldn't think about marrying anybody right now; it was too hard to think about anything but Doreen's next dose of morphine, the next visit from the hospice nurse, Maggie's next trip to Brainerd.

One night about two weeks after the night in the hospital, Maggie and I sat in the living room of my mother's house. Maggie sat by the reading light, knitting a two-headed stuffed bunny with a red fringe around its wrists and ankles, and a little heart on its chest. We could hear the tick of the mantel clock. I had thought Doreen was sleeping, but from her bedroom, I heard her moan. I stood up and looked in on her. She seemed to be sleeping again, so I went back to the living room and sat down.

In one of those strange tricks of light and shadow, for a moment Maggie looked old. Then she shifted in her seat, and was twenty-three again. She twisted her knitting around to look at it, flicked back over the pattern, and picked out a few stitches. She glanced up at me, gave me a sweet, tired smile, then started knitting again.

She would be old, someday, like my mother. I would never be old. But Maggie would.

There is no time in the faerie hill. Mortals think they've spent a night there, and go home a hundred years later, but to us, it's like a party that never ends. No cares and no pain. Nothing that matters.

I wanted you. All of you. I wanted to share your mortality.

The night Doreen died was when I knew what that meant.

I was sitting with Doreen when she died. She had been truly failing for several days: not speaking, not opening her eyes. Her breath had slowed and become more shallow, and for a full twelve hours I didn't leave her, thinking that every breath would be her last. She didn't want to be alone when she died. Maggie brought me sandwiches and coffee, and I sat by her bed.

The room was very quiet when she was gone.

Mortals tell stories about Death coming with a scythe to take their soul; they tell stories about angels escorting them home, and tunnels of light. When Doreen died, I saw nothing but her cluttered bedroom, and heard nothing but the silence after her breathing stopped.

I stood up and stretched. It was four in the morning. I stepped out of her bedroom. Maggie was sleeping in a chair in the living room, curled up, her knitting in her lap. I put my hand out to wake her, then thought the better of it. I wanted to take a walk.

I thought about Doreen, walking along in the cold wind near the river, and felt a dark emptiness, and a faint guilty relief that the bedside vigil was over. And a less-guilty relief that her pain had ended.

Nothing but grief, my brother had said when he warned me to turn away from Maggie.

Maggie was young. We had years yet—probably. But someday she'd be old, and I wouldn't. She would be sick, and I wouldn't. I would have to go through this again—the hospital, the uncertainty, the suffering, the loss. I would have to go through it with *Maggie*.

I pulled out Doreen's ring and looked at its yellow gleam under the streetlight. *If I marry Maggie, if I really do it, I have to stay. I can't promise her my loyalty and then run away like Bob. If I'm going to do that, better to leave now.*

I thought about Maggie's death. Would it be cancer for her, too? Or the dark theft of her mind from dementia? Or something quick, like a heart attack, with neither lingering pain nor time for goodbyes? Maybe it would be a car accident at twenty-five. Whatever it was, I'd have to be there for it. I'd have to sit with her, moisten her lips with a swab when she couldn't swallow, hold her hand. Bury her body. Say goodbye.

It was the price I would pay for loving a mortal.

I unknotted the leather cord and slipped the ring into my pocket. Then I turned back towards my mother's house.

I take you, Margaret. As Gaidion, my true name, I take you; I vow to you with the vow I cannot break.

With this ring, I pledge myself.

If you will have me, I will live with you for the whole of your mortal life. I will love you. I will stay with you. And someday, I will bury you. Because I love you. And I will pay the price without regret.

SCRAP DRAGON

Once upon a time, there was a princess.

Does she have to be a princess? Couldn't she be the daughter of a merchant, or a scholar, or an accountant?

An accountant? What would an accountant be doing in a pastoral fantasy setting?

The people there have money, don't they? So they'd also have taxes and bills and profit-and-loss statements. But he could be a butcher or baker or candle-stick-maker, so long as he's not a king.

No, I suppose an accountant might work. Very well. Once upon a time, there was a young woman—the daughter of an accountant— who had two older sisters. The oldest of these young women was clever, the middle was strong, and the youngest was kind.

What if she wanted to be the strong one? The youngest, I mean. And what if the oldest wanted to be the nice one? It's not fair.

I didn't say the youngest wasn't strong or that the oldest wasn't kind. But everyone knew that it was the middle daughter who was the strongest, and the youngest who was the sweetest and most innocent.

Maybe they just thought *she was sweet and innocent.*

Maybe. They lived in a palace—or rather, in a large and comfortable house, and if they were princesses I could give the youngest one a fabulous bedroom with a drawbridge—

She can have a drawbridge anyway. Maybe her parents built it for her just because it was cool.

Okay. But the important thing is that, because she was so kind-hearted, animals trusted her. They would seek her out, and when she found one in need, she would try to help it.

That would be really inconvenient.

Being trusted by animals?

Well, if they'd seek you out. I mean, you're out for a walk and a stray cat comes up to you and won't go away—

Maybe it's a really nice cat.

Or maybe it's a cat that will yowl at four in the morning every day and wake you up.

But the animals trusting her is supposed to show you what she's like inside. She's not just nice on the surface; she's a *good person.*

Well, I like animals better than princesses. She can have animals following her around, that's okay.

One day, word came to their city that a grave threat faced them. The city was near an extinct volcano—or rather, a volcano that had been thought extinct. But a powerful and evil sorcerer had raised the spirits of the volcano, and it was now threatening to erupt. If the sorcerer continued prodding the volcano with his malicious magic, the volcano would spew forth fire and lava and the city would be utterly destroyed.

Volcanoes erupt because of tectonic forces, not spirits.

This was a magical volcano.

Look, if the sorcerer could manipulate tectonic forces, why would he bother threatening the city with an eruption? He could wipe them out just as well with an earthquake.

Fine. It wasn't a sorcerer with a volcano. It was a dragon, a vast and powerful dragon that could breathe fire and took up residence in the crater of an extinct nearby volcano but threatened, if not supplicated with gifts of gold and treasure, to burn the city to ash.

But I like dragons. Dragons are cool.

Well, so? I like the French and France is cool but that doesn't mean I like Jean-Marie Le Pen. French people aren't all good or all bad and neither are dragons.

Okay. I guess that's fair.

So, the city was under threat by the evil dragon, and if you'd let me make this person a princess she would have a reason for feeling personally responsible for saving her city. But she's not a princess. So I suppose the King—

Couldn't they live in a democracy? Even an Athenian democracy is better than a King.

—the Council of Democratically-Elected Representatives of the People offered a reward to anyone who could defeat the dragon. But more than that, they begged for all those who were brave or strong or clever to do what they could to save the city. If it had been a King, he could also have offered the hand of one of his children in marriage, but you can hardly marry the son or daughter of a Council of Representatives so let's just say they pointed out that anyone who succeeded in saving the city would be a very hot romantic commodity indeed.

Arranged marriages are kind of creepy. But marrying someone who was only interested in you because you'd defeated a dragon also seems kind of creepy.

No one's going to have to marry anyone they don't want to marry. Anyway, the eldest tried first. She set out to learn all she could about dragons—first at the library nearby, then, when she had exhausted its resources, to a larger city some days' journey away. She sent home letters when she could, sharing everything she'd learned, but it was a vast library and she thought it would be years before she'd learned everything there was to know.

So the second sister decided to set out to confront the dragon directly.

And she never returned.

What do you mean she never returned?

I mean that she died on her journey. There were people who said that the dragon had eaten her—

But I don't want her to be dead. It's not fair.

No, it isn't. Death isn't ever fair.

But I liked her!

Yes.

The people I like aren't supposed to die.

No.

So can she just be sleeping, if you need to take her out of the story?

No. She died, and so the youngest—

I don't think I want the youngest to try to defeat the dragon. She might get eaten, too.

But she's the city's only hope.

I don't care. I want her to stay home where she's safe.

That's what her parents said. "We've lost one daughter already. Let someone else lose a daughter next time."

And she's the nice one.

Yes.

How is she supposed to defeat a dragon by being nice?

Other people said that, too, sometimes even where she could hear them. So the youngest daughter—whose name was Heather—decided that for now, she would stay home.

Heather had a book of blank pages, and she took all the letters her family had gotten from her eldest sister, with the diagrams of dragons and ancient philosophy regarding dragons and information about their nesting habits and lairs and so on, and began to organize it. Because, she thought, even if she could not herself defeat the dragon, perhaps she could provide a useful set of information to someone else.

But sometimes she would flip the book over, and from the back, she began creating a book about her sister, the one who had died. She had pictures that she had drawn, but she put in all sorts of things that made her think of her sister. There was a scrap of cloth from her sister's favorite dress, and a flower she'd pressed, and when Heather found a poem her sister had written she copied it out in the book. The funny thing was, her sister had loved dragons.

Because dragons are cool.

Which made it all the more ironic that she'd probably been eaten by one.

One afternoon she took her book and her lunch, called for her dog (whose name was Bear), and went to sit by a wooded lake not too far from her house.

The dog had better not die in this story.

The dog's not going to die. Not in the story, anyway.

Good.

They sat down by the lake. Heather took out her sandwich, and gave half of it to Bear. A nutria swam up and poked its head out of the water. "Hello, nutria," Heather said to it. It didn't swim away, so she broke off a piece of her sandwich and tossed it down to the nutria.

Is that a real animal?

Yes, nutrias are real. They're rodents and look like a cross between a beaver and a really big rat.

Oh. That sounds cool.

The nutria shot a wary look at Bear, then climbed up on the bank to grab the piece of sandwich. Bear sometimes chased squirrels (and a nutria might have been sufficiently squirrel-like to chase) but right now he was more interested in getting another handout from Heather; he looked at her with a big doggy smile and wagged his tail. Heather sighed and took out another sandwich. Her food wasn't going to last long at this rate. "Go get me a sandwich, Bear," she said to Bear.

Did he get her a sandwich?

Of course he didn't. If dogs could make sandwiches, they'd eat them themselves. When the nutria finished its piece of sandwich, it sat on the shore of the lake looking at Heather with gleaming dark eyes, and Heather broke off another piece of bread and tossed it over. "Can you tell me how to defeat a dragon?" she asked it.

The nutria picked up the bread. "Why do you want to defeat it?" it asked.

Heather was a little startled that the nutria actually answered her; she talked to Bear all the time, and other animals some of the time, but she'd never had an animal answer her before. "Because if no one defeats it, it's going to come and burn my city to the ground," she said.

The nutria seemed to mull this over as it ate. "Know the truth that lies within you," it said. "And speak the truth that waits without."

Waits without what?

Without here is the opposite of within. So she needs to know the truth she has inside, and then speak some truth that's external.

You know, even with an explanation that's pretty cryptic.

It's advice from a talking water rat. Were you expecting step-by-step instructions?

Well, did she try asking it for something more specific?

She tried, but the nutria was done talking. It nibbled away the rest of the bread, then plopped back into the water and swam away. "Find me another nutria, Bear," Heather suggested, but Bear just wagged his tail again.

One thing was certain, however. Heather still didn't know *how* she was going to defeat the dragon, but she thought the nutria wouldn't have spoken to her—and given her advice about knowing the truth inside—unless she did have the power to defeat it. So she went home, and quietly packed her belongings and left with Bear when no one was home. (She did leave a nice note on the kitchen counter, but she didn't want to stick around to explain in person that she was going out to fight the dragon because of advice from a talking rodent.)

Of course, she had no idea what the nutria was talking about. If it was the truth that lay within her it probably meant it was something she already knew and just hadn't fully realized yet, so she took her book with the information about dragons (and the pictures of her sister) and studied it when she would stop to rest. After reviewing everything three times, she still had no idea what it was she was supposed to know—unless the secret was that she was willing to ask unlikely sources, like nutrias, for advice.

There was a school nearby, and she could hear a bell that meant school was over for the day, so she waited while the children ran off and then went in to ask the teacher. He was a mathematician, although this was a small school so he was also expected to teach reading, grammar, and dancing.

They learned dancing in school?

Yes, in this place they considered dancing very important.

"Excuse me," Heather said. "I come from another part of the city, and I was wondering whether you knew of any way to defeat the dragon?"

"If I did, I'd already have mentioned it to someone," he said. "Although I suppose it's reasonable to consider the possibility that I would have tried that, and found no one willing to listen. But no, I don't."

"Oh," Heather said, feeling a bit deflated, even though she hadn't asked anyone else yet. Maybe she should have asked the students, before they all left.

"Is there a particular reason you thought I would know?"

Heather told him about the nutria, and the book of notes, and how she had no idea what truth it was she supposedly knew.

"Well," the teacher said, "I have a friend who is an inventor. If you'd like to come back to my house, I'll introduce you to him, and we can see if he has any ideas."

The teacher introduced himself as Fillard, as they walked.

That's a very unusual name for a person in a pastoral fantasy.

It's a very unusual name, period. He explained that his neighbor was also a musician and an actor; the neighbor's name was Peter, and Peter turned out to be extremely kind and invited Heather and Bear (and Fillard) to stay for supper, even though he'd never met Heather (or Bear) before.

As the shadows grew long and their after-dinner tea grew tepid, they all listed everything they'd ever heard about dragons. Peter had heard that they could sing; he wasn't inclined to go walking over to the dragon's lair to confirm this, but the stories said that dragons had beautiful voices, on those occasions that they chose to share them. Fillard, on the other hand, had heard that dragons enjoyed games almost as much as they liked hoarding treasure; there were stories of dragons offering to let travelers go free if the travelers could beat them at a game of chess. "Of course, the dragon always wins in those stories unless the human cheats," Fillard added. "I have a large collection of games, and could offer you several that the dragon wouldn't have seen before. That would make the challenge a bit more fair."

They made fresh tea as it grew darker, and since Heather had been taking notes in her book ("gd. singers / games—chess?") she had it out. She set it down at one point to look at a game that Fillard had run home to get and bring back, and when she picked it up, she had it upside down, so it was the side about her sister, rather than the dragon. "Laura loved dragons," she said softly. "I should put a picture of a dragon somewhere on Laura's side."

"Who is Laura?" the men asked.

She explained about her sister, and how she'd disappeared when she went to confront the dragon. Laura had always believed that dragons were cool—

Because dragons are *cool.*

—which made the circumstances of her death tragically ironic.

You already mentioned the irony.

And she explained about the book, and everyone nodded, and then Peter went to find an article about dragons that he'd saved from somewhere. There was nothing in the article that was new, but it had a lovely picture, a sort of extremely artistic diagram. He gave it to her to paste in later.

It was late, and Heather was tired, so Peter made up a guest bed for her. Heather woke early—before Peter or Fillard—and stepped outside.

Are you sure she got up first?

Fillard and Peter had stayed up very late talking, and weren't awake yet. The sky was light and the birds were singing, and when Heather opened her book she realized that she'd nearly filled it; only a pair of blank pages faced each other at the exact center of the book. All the rest of the book had been filled, with notes about dragons on one side and notes and mementos relating to her sister on the other. She held the picture hesitantly—it seemed to her like maybe it *should* go on the dragon side. But she'd never put a dragon in the Laura half of the scrapbook, and that seemed like a terrible loss. Since she'd flipped the book, she had to choose—it would be right-side up for one, upside-down for the other. After staring at it for several minutes, as the sky grew lighter and the sun grew warmer, she finally turned the book sideways, and pasted the picture in that way, so that maybe it could go with either.

And that was when she realized what the nutria meant.

She did?

Yes.

Well, what did it mean?

I can't just tell you that straight out; it would spoil the flow of the story. We'll get to it in a bit.

You're as bad as that damn water rat.

Heather picked up her bags and called for Bear and set out—

Isn't she going to leave a note?

She only just met Fillard and Peter. Do you really think they'll worry?

Of course they're going to worry.

She got up, left a note, took the game that Fillard had offered her and the sheet music for songs that Peter had said he'd particularly like to hear a dragon sing, and then she and Bear headed for the path that would swiftly take them to the dragon's lair, at the edge of the extinct volcano.

You promised me the dog wouldn't die, remember.

Don't worry about the dog.

Does that mean I should be worrying about Heather? I didn't make you promise she wouldn't die because she's the hero of the story so I figured she was safe.

The dragon emerged from its lair as Heather and Bear approached. It unfurled its vast wings and shook them back the way you might stretch your wrists and crack your back, and licked its lips, showing its big teeth.

"Hello," Heather said to the dragon. "I know you're not going to eat me. I know you're not *really* a threat to the city. So I know the real danger must be coming from someone else."

That, you see, was the truth she'd already known—

Dragons are cool!

Yes, that dragons are cool!

But what about all that business about dragons being individuals with free will—

Here is what she realized as she talked through all the information in her book. The dragon had been demanding treasure, not food. And while everyone knew that dragons loved treasure, surely they ate *sometimes.* And yet only a few sheep had gone missing from the edges of town, plus a few unlucky people like Laura, and that just didn't seem like enough to feed a dragon. So she'd looked carefully at the diagrams of its jaw, and realized that its teeth were not shaped like a bear's teeth, nor like a lion's. After thinking about it carefully, she concluded that the dragon's natural diet was *fish.* Not people.

That doesn't mean it wouldn't eat a human who made it mad.

She'd also realized that a dragon did not *actually* have enough fire in its belly to burn the city to the ground. It could certainly belch out enough flame to kill anyone who came knocking with a sword, but that was a long way from burning down a whole city.

Maybe it was an empty threat.

But there was another thing everyone agreed on: dragons were *smart.* Smart enough not to make empty threats—not when a city might call the dragon's bluff by getting a big enough army together to take the dragon on.

The dragon could move, though, if that happened. This dragon had moved before, right? Because you said it moved in.

But dragons have a hoard. They save *everything.* And moving is annoying enough if you *don't* have a dragon's hoard to take with you to the Willamette Valley or wherever it is you're going. The last thing any smart, sensible dragon was going to do was set itself up to have to move all the time. So Heather was pretty sure the threats were coming from someone else, someone who didn't care that much what happened to the dragon. And the dragon probably knew who, and why, and so Heather thought that perhaps she would go and ask.

The dragon tucked her wings back—

It was a female dragon? How did Heather know it was a female dragon?

She'd been studying dragon anatomy diagrams for months. Do I really need to spell it out for you?

Yes, actually, I wouldn't mind knowing how you tell a boy dragon from a girl dragon.

The easiest way is coloration: the backs of a female dragon's wings are less brightly colored than the front of the body, to provide camouflage when they're nesting. Also, female dragons have wings that are scalloped on the bottom edge and male dragons have a penis.

This dragon, which was female, folded her hands in front of her and lowered herself to the ground. "You're not here to try to kill me?" she said, sounding a bit surprised.

"No," Heather said. "I did bring you a game, though, because I heard dragons like games, and some sheet music—do you read music?—because I heard you like singing. But mostly I came to ask you who it is that's using you to threaten my city, and whether I can help you."

"It's a sorcerer," the dragon said. "I'm a very *young* dragon." (She was indeed quite a bit smaller than Heather had expected.) "If I were older, he never would have been able to do this to me, but he's used his magic to trap me here so that I can't leave. He can't actually make me go set your city on fire, but when people come to kill me, I defend myself ..."

"Including my sister?" Heather asked, a huge lump in her throat.

The dragon shrugged. "I don't remember anyone who looked like you," she said. "There are bandits, and other dangers nearby—not just me."

"How can I break the sorcerer's spell?" Heather asked.

"I don't know," the dragon said. "I can tell you where to find him, but he's really powerful—I'd feel terrible sending you off into danger."

Heather thought that over. "Do I need to *defeat* the sorcerer? Or just figure out how to break the spell?"

"Let me put it this way," the dragon said. "While I do not *normal-*

ly eat people, because they really don't taste very good, I would make a *special exception* for the sorcerer who has turned me into his own personal chained-up pet dragon and used me to intimidate people into letting him steal their money. In other words, if you can figure out how to break the spell, I'll take care of the rest of it."

"If nothing else," Heather said, "I could go down to the city and tell everyone the truth—that it's the sorcerer who's a danger, not you."

"You could do that," the dragon said. "Unfortunately, he'll just move us on to a new city. That's what he did the last two times when people figured it out."

Heather thought that over. This meant the sorcerer was powerful enough to enslave the dragon, but maybe not powerful enough to protect himself any other way. "Where does he keep all the money he steals?" she asked.

"He makes me guard it," the dragon said, and pointed down into her lair. Heather peered down at the hoard. The edge of the cavern shadowed it, but she could see a heap of glittering gold and rubies.

"Can I go in and look?" Heather asked.

"Oh, yes. I just can't let you leave with any of it."

Heather went inside the cavern and started poking through the treasure. There was gold and silver, there were gems and strands of pearls, there were bundles of paper bills and a few paintings, there was an ancient bronze cast horse, and there were books.

Heather picked her way through all of it; one of the treasures was a gem-encrusted lamp, and she lit it so that she could see a bit better. Bear barked. "Help me look, Bear," Heather said. "If the treasure's here being guarded by the dragon, I bet the magic is here, too. Somewhere."

The dragon came in and laid her chin on her hands, watching as Heather dug through the piles. After poking through the gold coins (and then rolling in the giant pile of gold because really, how often do you have the opportunity to roll in a giant pile of gold?) Heather started looking at the books. There were a few giant Bibles with gems on the front covers, and one of the lost plays of Shakespeare, and a collection of plays by Aeschylus that included all of *Achilles*, and a musical score for something called *Per la ricuperata salute di Ophelia*, which the dragon took an interest in and started studying while Heather searched.

Wait, is that the lost opera that Mozart and Salieri wrote together?

It was a cantata for voice and piano, actually, but yes, it was written by Mozart and Salieri together and then lost. You do realize that historically they weren't anything like they were in that movie . . .

Yes yes yes, historically they were probably friends, or at least friendly. Did the dragon not know it was there?

Oh, she knew it was there and had looked at it before, but you know how sometimes when you're trying to put away a big pile of books and you make the mistake of opening one, and you sit down and start reading it even though you've read it already and you were really intending to clean that day instead of reading for hours? That's basically what happened to the dragon.

Under a crate of gold bars, which Heather needed a lever to move as gold weighs so much, she found a very plain, unimpressive little book. From the outside, it actually looked quite a lot like the book she had made. Except this one had a picture of a dragon on the cover. The dragon looked up miserably at a man who sat riding on his shoulders.

Heather opened the book and suddenly became aware that the dragon was watching her. "I cannot let you destroy that book," the dragon said sharply, and Heather knew right away that she'd found what she was looking for.

"So, you can't let me take it," she said, and the dragon shook her head, "and you can't let me destroy it. I won't take it anywhere and I won't destroy it. I'm just going to look at it," she said. The dragon watched as she set the lamp on a ledge, then sat down under it to read.

It *was* a scrapbook, of sorts, full of pictures of dragons, but each showed the same thing in a different way: a dragon bound. Chained to a human figure, tied to the ground with giant nets, imprisoned behind bars. Heather thought that destroying it would probably free the dragon, but she was watching Heather's every movement now, and while it did occur to her that maybe she could "accidentally" drop the burning lamp onto it, that seemed awfully risky if it *didn't* work.

She took out her pen, and the dragon didn't twitch.

Carefully, she started drawing on the page.

"What are you doing?" the dragon asked.

"I'm adding things," Heather said.

"Hmm. I guess that's okay," the dragon said.

Heather drew a giant pair of scissors snipping through the net. She drew a file chiseling through the bars, and a key unlocking the chains.

"Do you feel like you could let me destroy it now?" she asked when she'd finished.

The dragon paused, then shook her head.

Heather looked more closely at the words written around the pictures. Where it said "by words and magic the dragon is taken," she put in a little ^ and wrote *not* so that it said "by words and magic the dragon is not taken." She changed the word "bound" to "boundless" and "grave" to "gravel" and something that ended with "die" she changed into a short essay about "dietary law."

It didn't make a lot of sense when she was done with it, but she didn't think that would matter. But the dragon still didn't feel like she could let her destroy the book.

So finally, Heather took her own scrapbook, and cut out the picture she had pasted into the center, and pasted it onto the cover of the magician's scrapbook, covering over the picture of the miserable looking dragon.

The dragon leapt to her feet. "HA!" she shouted, and bolted out of the cave.

Well, that seemed to have done it. Heather burned the magician's scrapbook, just to be on the safe side. She figured the treasure wasn't hers—it belonged either to the people it had been stolen from, or the dragon—but she couldn't resist the Aeschylus and the Shakespeare so she packed those up and left a note saying, *I borrowed the plays. I promise to give them back after I've read them.—Heather.*

She blew out the lamp, left the dragon's lair, and looked around. She could see the dragon high overhead and hoped she'd stick to her word and eat the evil sorcerer before she left forever. And then she called for Bear and they walked back down the path to the city.

Is that the end?

No. The next morning, everyone in the city woke to the sound of a vast, enormous contralto voice singing a cantata—

The dragon?

Yes, of course the dragon. And when she was done, she told them that she'd been freed, and had eaten the evil sorcerer, and would now be on her way to explore new lands.

Did she tell them who'd freed her?

No, because she could tell Heather would prefer not to have to put up with being famous.

But what about the reward? She was supposed to get a reward!

The next day, she got a package through the mail; it was a box containing those heavy gold bars, which was enough wealth to keep her well-supplied for the rest of her life. The dragon kept Fillard's game and Peter's sheet music, though.

She was also supposed to be a hot commodity. Romantically, I mean.

Would you want to marry someone who was only interested in you because you were a hero of the realm? She went back to visit Fillard and Peter to tell them how things worked out with the dragon, and they were delighted to see her. And over time she and Fillard became best friends, and they got married and lived happily ever after.

Did they ever see the dragon again?

No.

I want them to see the dragon again.

Well, the dragon sent them postcards occasionally, from distant cities like Shanghai and Barcelona and Miami.

That's not the same as seeing her.

I suppose.

Surely the dragon would have come back to visit. Once. Heather freed her from the sorcerer!

You're right. She did. One night about ten years after Heather and Fillard had married, they were sitting on the beach with their child watching the sun set over the water. And in the clouds, Heather saw the dragon; for a moment, she thought it was just the sun in her eyes, but then she saw the huge wings and knew it was the dragon. And she shouted and pointed so that Fillard and their child could see her as well.

They all saw the dragon, just for a few minutes, in the last light of the day. And as the shadows gathered and the stars came out, they heard her singing.

Author's Note

In May of 2010, there was a benefit auction for a friend of mine who was experiencing a medical crisis. (She needed a liver donation due to a long-term medical condition; she was set to receive a living donor transplant from her brother, but money was needed to cover his travel expenses and the time he needed to take off work to recover.) My offer read as follows:

> Offer: I will write a SF/F short story of at least 1000 words with you, or the (consenting) real person of your choice, as the protagonist (or, if you'd prefer, the antagonist). If you want a child-appropriate story with your child as the protagonist, that is fine; if you want this as a surprise for a friend, that's probably fine. (Basically, I don't want to write real-person fic that the subject would object to.) You get to choose whether you star as the hero or the villain; I will do my best to make the character recognizable as you. I will accommodate specific requests regarding subgenre, plot, prompt, etc. I don't usually write explicit sex, but if you want a story with explicit sex, ummmmm, well, bid high enough and I'll do my best.

The auction was won by a college friend of mine, Fillard, who request-ed that I write a story starring his wife, Heather. Many of the details in the story are drawn from Heather's real life, including the dog named Bear and the scrapbooking. (She and her sisters once co-owned a scrapbooking supplies store named Scrapdragon.) Fillard and another friend of theirs, Peter, got cameos.

As I was kicking around ideas for the plot, I suggested making Heather a princess, which Fillard promptly shot down. And with that, the opening lines came to me, and the story unfolded from there.

I wrote this story initially for an audience of two: Fillard and Heath-er. The fact that it had broader appeal was a pleasant surprise!

COMRADE GRANDMOTHER

—glorious Soviet—soon bring Hitler—complete defeat. Heavy casualties—Dnieper River—"

The voice from the radio faded into the deafening hiss of static. Nadezhda knelt to adjust the tuning dial again, but lost the transmission completely. Her temper flared and she smacked the box in frustration, then thought better of it and returned her attention to the dial. "Please," she muttered. "We need to hear this."

The other workers from the steel mill waited silently, their faces stony. Nadezhda brought in another minute or two of speech: a different voice spoke about patriotism, sacrifice, Mother Russia. Anastasya, the supervisor of their group, reached over and switched the radio off. "Go on," she said. "Back to work."

They're coming, and we won't be able to stop them.

No one dared to speak the words. Nadezhda had to bite her tongue to keep from speaking them—but it was better not to invite trouble. She retied the kerchief she wore to keep the sweat from her eyes and her hair out of the machinery. For days now there had been no real news. The official reports spoke of great Soviet victories, but these victories somehow happened closer to Moscow each day.

Nadezhda returned late to the apartment she shared, pulling off her shoes in the cold stairway so as not to wake the others. Stepping over sleeping women, she picked her way to the kitchen in stocking feet. As quietly as she could, she boiled water for tea, then sat down by the window to stare out into the darkness.

The Dnieper River was the last natural barrier before Moscow.

And if Moscow fell . . . Closing her eyes, Nadezhda could see the face of her lover, Vasily, before he'd left with the militia to fight. "We'll fight them to the end," he'd said, speaking softly to avoid being overheard. "We'll make them pay in German blood for every inch of Russian soil. But if Moscow falls, we'll be fighting a lost war." Vasily's blue eyes had been hard with fear, but he'd pulled loose her kerchief to stroke his fingers through her hair one last time before he boarded the train that would take him to the front. Vasily had no real military training—that he'd been sent to fight spoke of the Red Army's desperation far more loudly than a thousand radio broadcasts.

Nadezhda pulled her kerchief loose again and ran her own fingers slowly through her hair. She put away her teacup and took out her hidden bottle of vodka for a deep drink. Then she picked her way back through the apartment and out to the stairs, pulled on her shoes, and headed out of the small industrial city to the forests beyond.

Nadezhda was young; she lived in a world of steel mills and radios and black-market cigarettes. Her grandmother, though, was from an older time. When Nadezhda was ten years old, her grandmother had stopped telling stories—but Nadezhda had never forgotten the stories of the ancient woman who lived in the heart of every Russian forest, and how she could be found by those who weren't afraid to surrender to the darkness. As the sounds of the city and its factories were swallowed behind her in the night, Nadezhda pulled her kerchief out of her pocket, and tied it tightly over her eyes. Groping blindly with her hands in front of her, she continued down the path.

Nadezhda could hear the wind around her, the trees overhead swaying in the night. She could hear an owl nearby, its call and then the beat of its wings. Then, silence. Nadezhda pulled the kerchief from her eyes, and before her in the forest was the little hut on chicken legs, rocking back and forth, turning round and round, dipping and spinning like like a wobbly gear.

Nadezhda spoke: "Turn, comrade; spin, comrade; stand, comrade; stand. With your back to the wood and your door to me."

The house turned to face Nadezhda, and the chicken legs knelt in the soft earth of the forest floor. The door swung in on its hinges. At first there was nothing inside but moist darkness. Then the darkness thickened and deepened, and a gust of warm wind from inside enveloped Nadezhda. Nadezhda smelled cooked kasha and fresh bread; she smelled sour vodka like Vasily's breath in early morning; she smelled wet new-turned earth. As the wind swirled around her and the last of the light faded, Nadezhda heard Baba Yaga's voice.

"Russian blood and Russian tears, Russian breath and Russian bones, why have you come here?"

Nadezhda had expected an old woman's voice, cracked and rough like the voices through the static of the radio. Instead Baba Yaga's voice was young and clear, honey-sweet and eggshell-smooth, but it echoed as if she spoke from the depths of a cave.

"I've come to ask for your help, Comrade Baba Yaga," Nadezhda said. "I've come to ask you to save Mother Russia."

Baba Yaga laughed, and now she sounded old. Two shriveled hands gripped the edges of the doorway for balance, and Baba Yaga stepped down to the ground. She was a stooped, hunched old woman with thin white hair. Her eyes were sunk deep in her wrinkled face, but they were a burning ice blue, and she had all of her teeth. "For everything there is a price, Comrade Daughter," Baba Yaga said. "For everything there is a cost. We are not socialists here. Have you come to me ready to pay?"

"I have brought no money," Nadezhda said.

"I do not trade in rubles," Baba Yaga said. "You have come to ask me to destroy the German army, have you not?"

"Yes," Nadezhda said.

"You are prepared to give your life for this, if that is the price?"

"Yes," Nadezhda said, though her voice shook.

"Your life is not the price," Baba Yaga said. "The price is *Vasily's* life."

Nadezhda was stunned silent for a moment. Then she pleaded, "Name another price."

"That is the price for your salvation," Baba Yaga said. "If you will not pay, ask me some other favor."

Nadezhda closed her eyes. She was too young to remember a time before socialism, and she barely remembered life before Comrade Stalin. But growing up, she'd known that it was fear of Stalin that silenced her grandmother's stories and her father's jokes. The first day that Vasily kissed Nadezhda, they found a secluded spot in the woods. Vasily pulled her kerchief loose to touch her hair—then met her eyes with a wicked smile and said, without lowering his voice, "Have you heard the one about Comrade Stalin, Comrade Lenin, and Ivan the pig farmer?" Vasily was only a mediocre kisser, but it didn't matter. Nadezhda's heart had been his from that day on.

Vasily's life?

Nadezhda opened her eyes and looked at Baba Yaga. Baba Yaga looked at her with eyes as deep and cold as the sea. Nadezhda looked away from those eyes and said, "If we had more time to prepare, perhaps we could beat them. Turn the Germans away from Moscow."

"That's an easy favor," Baba Yaga said. "The price for that is your hair."

Nadezhda had brought a knife, and now she took it and cut off her hair. She wished that she had thought to bring scissors, because she had to saw through the thick hank of hair, and it pulled. Her eyes were wet when she had finished. Looking at her hair in her hand, she touched it once more, as Vasily had, and then gave it to Baba Yaga.

"What did you do to your hair?" Anastasya asked the next morning at the steel mill. "You look like a bobbed bourgeoisie."

"I had lice," Nadezhda said. "Picking out nits would use hours that I could be working, so I cut off my hair. It's a small thing to sacrifice if it helps our army defend Mother Russia."

Baba Yaga summoned the Fox, the craftiest of all the animals, who had fooled czars and peasants alike. "Run west to a country called Germany," she told the Fox. "To a city called Berlin, and find a little German man with a moustache."

"Do you want me to eat him?" the Fox asked.

"His bones are for me," Baba Yaga said. "I want you to whisper into his ear that there is plenty of time yet this summer to take our Moscow. Tell him that the wise course is to divide the troops headed for Moscow and send some of them north, to Leningrad, and some of them south, to the Ukraine. Do not return until you are certain he believes you."

"I will do as you bid, Baba Yaga," the Fox said. So the Fox ran west and found Berlin, and the man with the moustache, and whispered into his ear. And the man with the moustache called his generals and ordered his troops divided, some sent north and the rest south, to return and finish off Moscow later in the summer. There was plenty of time—weeks and weeks of glorious summer left to take Moscow. All the time in the world.

Fall came, and the armies returned from Leningrad and the Ukraine and moved towards Moscow again. It was possible to be executed for spreading rumors, but the rumors still spread. Nadezhda heard whispers in the mill of the death and capture of millions of Russian soldiers, and tried not to listen. She heard whispers of siege and starvation in Leningrad, and tried to think of other things. She heard whispers that there were German soldiers in Red Army uniforms, infiltrating their forces and moving towards Moscow, and she snorted in disgust—but the true rumors were bad enough.

Nadezhda thought of Vasily often as she worked. They had quarreled sometimes, like any lovers, but only once seriously. Vasily had signed up for the militia, and Nadezhda had wanted to, as well. Vasily had first tried to dissuade her with humor, but when that didn't work, he became angry. "Isn't it enough that the sons of Mother Russia go to die in this war? Should we send her daughters to die as well?"

"Are you a German, thinking that a woman is good only for bearing babies?" Nadezhda fired back. "I know as much about fighting as you do."

But Vasily refused to give up. The steel mill needed her. ("It needs you just as badly," Nadezhda said.) The militia would endure terrible hardships. If captured, Nadezhda could be raped, tortured, killed—the Germans had no respect for women soldiers. Finally, Vasily wept in her lap and begged her not to join the militia. Nadezhda had given in, unable to bear his tears.

As the air turned chill, Nadezhda went again to the forest, to the hut on chicken legs and the old woman who lived inside.

"The Germans have returned," Nadezhda said.

"Yes," Baba Yaga said. "I did not promise that I would drive them away forever. You know the price for that."

"Name any other price," Nadezhda begged, but Baba Yaga refused. Finally Nadezhda made a different request. "Stop the German advance, at least until spring," she said.

"That's an easy favor," Baba Yaga said. "The price for that is your youth."

"I give that willingly," Nadezhda said, and felt herself grow more tired, her face grow more creased. She returned to the factory by daybreak.

"You look old," Anastasya said to Nadezhda the next morning. "Older than yesterday."

"I'm tired," Nadezhda said. "Sleep uses hours that I can spend working. A little sleep is a small thing to sacrifice if it helps our army defeat the Nazis."

Baba Yaga summoned Father Winter. "Go to the roads leading to Moscow," she said. "Bring rain to turn the roads to mud; then bring snow and ice and freezing winds. There are ill-dressed children on those roads. They do not belong there."

Father Winter smiled his cold, fierce smile and bowed slowly to Baba Yaga. "When I am through with them," he said, "they will curse every inch of Russian soil they must cross to flee my breath." And Father Winter brought rain so hard the ill-dressed children thought they might drown, first in water and then in mud. Their tanks and their trucks sank deep into the thick black muck, and would not move.

Then Father Winter blew out his cold breath over all of Russia. The ill-dressed children wore thin uniforms and light coats, without the felt boots and fur hats that the Russians wore. Some of them stumbled back the way they had come, dragging frozen tanks and trucks out of ice and snowdrifts. Their machinery and engines froze into cold, immovable blocks in the frigid breath of Father Winter, and the Russians on horses fell on the children and killed them by the thousands. The ill-dressed children cursed the Russian winter, and the Russian soldiers, and the Russian soil.

Before Vasily left, he had given Nadezhda a square of red cloth. "It's a kerchief for your hair," he said. He pulled loose her old kerchief and stroked his fingers through her hair, brushing her cheek.

Nadezhda pressed something cold and smooth into Vasily's hand. He opened his palm to see a rifle bullet. "My father fought for Russia in the war before the Revolution. He kept one cartridge in his pocket for good luck. He survived the war. Perhaps it will bring good luck to you, too." Vasily closed his fist around the bullet, then wrapped his arms around her, burying his face in her shoulder. "Come back to me," Nadezhda had whispered into his hair.

Spring came again, and the German army began to rally. Summer began, and they began to move again. They weren't moving on Moscow this time, but along the Volga and into the Caucasus. Rumors spoke again of terrible losses.

In July, Nadezhda went again to the woods, to the hut on chicken legs and the old woman who lived inside.

"The Germans have remounted their attack," Nadezhda said. "We are losing again."

"Yes," Baba Yaga said. "They are moving along the Volga River, and the Red Army is falling back before them."

"Please," Nadezhda said. "Destroy the German army. Stop them for good."

"You know the price," Baba Yaga said. "Are you prepared to pay it?"

"I will pay your price on one condition," Nadezhda said. "I want to see Vasily one more time before he has to die."

"I can send you to the city where the battle will be," Baba Yaga said. "But if you go there, you may die with your lover."

"Send me," Nadezhda said.

Baba Yaga took a horn and blew three blasts. From the sky flew an eagle. "Sit on the eagle's back," Baba Yaga said. "He will take you there."

The eagle rose in the sky with Nadezhda on his back, and flew with her to the great city on the Volga River—Stalingrad. Baba Yaga went herself to whisper to the man in Berlin with the moustache, and the man in Moscow named Josef. "No retreat," she whispered to Josef. "We must make our stand now, or die trying."

At the end of July, Stalin issued a new order: "Not one step back!" Anyone who retreated without permission would be shot. Still, the Germans pushed forward, further and further, for Hitler had become obsessed with the city bearing Stalin's name. Nadezhda waited patiently, trusting in Baba Yaga's word that the Germans would be destroyed.

The civilian population was evacuated from Stalingrad as the German army approached. Nadezhda remained behind with the other workers from the steel mill where she had found work. "I am no soldier," she said to her comrades. "But I can kill Germans."

One of the other women spoke more eloquently. "We will die here," she said. "But we will teach the Germans something about Russian bones and Russian blood, Russian strength and Russian will. And *no one* will do to our children as the Germans have done to us."

Nadezhda clasped hands with the other workers. There were no weapons. There was little they could do. But they would not retreat. Not one step back.

The battle of Stalingrad began with an artillery attack, and Nadezhda spent the first few hours crouching in a bomb shelter with the other workers. As the artillery grew louder, Nadezhda left the bomb shelter—Baba Yaga had said that she would see Vasily again, and after that, Nadezhda didn't care what happened. The others followed her out of the shelter, and soon they were able to pick up weapons from bodies in the streets. Nadezhda had never used a gun, but it wasn't difficult to learn.

Nadezhda took shelter in an apartment building, firing out the window as German soldiers marched through the streets. It quickly became clear that the Germans would have to secure or destroy every building in Stalingrad in order to take the city. They set about grimly to do just that, but Stalingrad was a vast city, 30 miles long, winding along the edge of the Volga. And the new concrete buildings that lined Stalingrad's dirt streets were not easy to destroy.

Through the months and months of house-to-house fighting, Nadezhda was never afraid. She would see Vasily; Baba Yaga had promised it. What had she to fear?

Nadezhda found Vasily one bright afternoon in the coldest part of the winter. He lay slumped behind a low crumbling wall, alone. Nadezhda ran to him and dropped to her knees, taking his hand in both of hers. "Vasily," she said.

Vasily was alive still, but would not live much longer. She could feel the blood from his wounds wet under her knees. She had tried to prepare herself for this, but in the end it made no difference.

"Nadezhda?" Vasily said. "It can't be."

"I'm here, my love," Nadezhda said. "I'm here to be with you."

Vasily turned his face towards her. "I'm so sorry," he said. "The bullet you gave me, for good luck—I used it." A faint smile crept to his lips. "I killed a German with it."

Nadezhda pressed Vasily's hand to her face. "Our sacrifice is not for nothing," she said. "The German army will be destroyed here."

Vasily nodded, but did not open his eyes. For a moment, Nadezhda thought he had died, but then he took another breath and his cold hand moved from her cheek towards the knot at the back of her neck. Nadezhda bent her head, and he loosened her kerchief and stroked his fingers through her shorn hair one last time. Then his hand fell away. Nadezda took his hand again, to hold a moment longer. Then an artillery shell rocked the ground where Vasily lay.

Nadezhda knew she didn't have much time left, but she wanted to die fighting, as Vasily had—not mourning. Vasily had a rifle; Nadezda took it from his body and slung the strap over her shoulder. Standing up, Nadezhda turned and saw the house on chicken legs.

"Turn, comrade; spin, comrade; stand, comrade; stand," Nadezhda said. "With your back to the armies and your door to me."

Baba Yaga came out of her hut. Though before she had always been an ancient hag, today she appeared as a maiden younger than Nadezhda—but her eyes were still as old as the Black Sea, burning like lights in a vast cavern.

"What are you doing here?" Nadezhda asked. "I thought you stayed in your forest."

"Sometimes I must attend to matters personally," Baba Yaga said. "This was one of those times."

"Vasily is dead," Nadezhda said.

"In one week, the Red Army will crush the army of the Germans, and their commander will surrender. There will be more offensives, but the Germans will never recover from this defeat. I have granted your wish," Baba Yaga said.

"May I ask you a question?" Nadezhda said.

"Pick your question carefully," Baba Yaga said. "I eat the overcurious."

"Will Russia recover from this defeat?"

"Life in Russia will never be easy," Baba Yaga said. "But Russia will always survive. Russian blood and Russian tears, Russian breath and Russian bones, these will last like the Caucasus and the Volga. No conqueror shall ever eat of Russia's fields. No czar shall ever tame the Russian heart. Your Comrade Josef will live another ten years yet, but when he dies, his statues will be toppled and his city will be renamed. That is what you wished to know, yes?"

"Yes."

Another artillery shell exploded nearby; the ground shook, and the house stumbled slightly on its chicken legs. White dust settled slowly over Baba Yaga and Nadezhda, like snow, or spiderwebs.

"Tell me, Comrade Daughter," Baba Yaga said. "Are there any bullets in that gun?"

Nadezhda checked. "No," she said.

"Then take this." Baba Yaga held out her hand; glinting in her palm, Nadezhda saw one bullet.

"What is the price for that?" Nadezhda asked.

"You have no payment left that interests me," Baba Yaga said. "This one is a gift."

Warily, Nadezhda took the bullet and loaded it into the rifle. When she looked up, Baba Yaga and the hut on chicken legs had vanished.

Nadezhda heard the sound of marching feet. She flattened herself against the remains of one wall, crouching down low to stay hidden. She peered around carefully, and saw German soldiers approaching.

Nadezhda knew that in the dust and confusion of Stalingrad, the men would pass her by if she stayed hidden. Perhaps she could still slip away to the woods, survive the war, live to rebuild Russia and to drink vodka on Stalin's grave.

Nadezhda turned back to look at Vasily one last time. Then, in a single smooth movement, she vaulted over the low wall that concealed her to face the German soldiers.

Russia's blood can be shed; Russia's bones can be broken. But we will never surrender. And we will always survive. "For Russia," Nadezhda shouted, and raised her rifle.

ISABELLA'S GARDEN

"*Want to plant something.*"

"How about we make Play-Doh cookies, sweetie? Would you like me to roll out Play-Doh for you?"

"Want to plant another punkmin."

"There isn't room for more punkmins—*pumpkins*. We already planted three pumpkin hills."

"Want to plant moaning glowies." Morning glories. I looked beyond the garden, at the chain link fence that bordered the neighbor's yard. Well, we hadn't planted over there yet; why not?

"We'll have to go buy seeds," I said.

"We can go to the garden store!" Isabella said brightly, and ran to put on her shoes.

I stepped out onto the back porch while she searched for her sandals. The pumpkins were coming up, their big leaves sprouting off of thick fuzzy vines. So were the carrots, the eggplants, the cucumbers, the beans—*all* the beans, even the ones that Isabella had dropped on top of the dirt—the lavender, and the mustard greens. Of all the things my two-and-a-half-year-old daughter had insisted on planting, I thought the mustard greens were probably the weirdest. At least with the eggplant, I could understand why the big purple globes on the seed packet had caught her eye. Mustard greens weren't flowers, they weren't purple, and they weren't something she usually ate. But she'd thrown an absolute fit when I'd tried to slip those seeds back into the seed rack, so into our cart they went.

I had stopped pretending that the patch of dirt out behind our house was *my* garden anymore. And really, that was just as well. Gardening—*fertility*, I joked to my husband Charlie, on those rare days when I had a sense of humor about it—had never really been my thing. Seeds I planted did not sprout. Flowers withered. Tomatoes stayed green on the vine right up until frost. As an experiment, during one of those bitter, bitter summers before I managed to get pregnant with Isabella, I planted *five* zucchini hills and got not a single fruit.

Well, I did get Isabella. It just took four years of trying. Fertility charting, invasive tests, Clomid, injectables, and finally, in vitro. But we had our baby.

Isabella came trotting back, her sandals fastened neatly onto the wrong feet, a naked baby doll under one arm, and a big smile on her face. "*Now* we can go to the garden store!" she announced, so I got my purse, and we walked down to the little neighborhood shop where they knew Isabella by name.

Isabella headed straight for the revolving seed rack. "Hang me up," she said, lifting her arms. I lifted her up so that she could reach the top of the rack, and watched as she selected three varieties of morning glories—blue, purple, and white—plus more seed packets on her way down. I flipped through her selections: climbing black-eyed susans, climbing snapdragons, trumpet vine, scarlet runner beans. She'd decided to go along with the "decorate the fence" theme, apparently. Well, she'd also grabbed a package of ornamental kale. And turnips. And cabbage. "You've never even eaten cabbage," I said, holding up the packet. "Or turnips."

"Want to plant cabbage! Want to plant turnips!" She snatched the seed packets and laid them protectively in the cart.

"How about we just plant the kale? I can probably find a spot for the kale."

"Want the kale too."

Well, it was only $1.29 per packet. I sighed and went to pay for our latest pile of seeds.

*

I found places for cabbage and kale and even the turnips, and then we spent the rest of the afternoon planting vine seeds along the fence. Therese, our next-door neighbor, came out to check her mail while Isabella was working. "Quite the little helper you've got there," she said.

"Thank you," I said, thinking that she didn't know the half of it.

"She's a doll. When are you going to give her a baby sister? Do you want a baby sister, sweetheart?"

I ground my teeth and stood up. "Come on, Isabella. Let's go plant more turnips."

Back in the vegetable garden, Isabella dug a furrow with her toddler-sized trowel. "Want a baby sister," she said a few minutes later, carefully dropping seeds into the dirt.

"I don't have one for you, kiddo," I said.

"Want to plant a sister."

That actually made me giggle. "They don't sell that kind of seed at the garden store."

I bought Charlie a pound of gourmet jelly beans for Father's Day. He generously shared the flavors he didn't like with Isabella, who didn't care if it was peanut-butter or popcorn flavored as long as it was candy and we were letting her eat it. She ate all of them except for one, a creamy bean with yellow flecks, which she held up and looked at thoughtfully. "Want to plant it," she said.

"It's a jelly bean, not a seed," I said.

"Want to plant the bean."

"Come outside with Daddy," Charlie said generously. "I'll help you plant it." She hopped down from her chair and wrapped her hand around his thumb, her other hand still carefully cradling the bean.

When I first saw the jelly bean vine coming up, I assumed it was a morning glory or something. The leaves were shaped like Valentines, and the color was a light, silvery green. When I took Isabella around the garden and we looked at everything that was coming up, she pointed at it and said, "That's the bean plant."

"The scarlet runner beans?" I asked.

"Daddy's bean," Isabella said.

It flowered the first week of July, and shortly afterwards produced thick pods that looked almost like green beans except that they were the color of cream. I pulled one off immediately out of curiosity, and looked inside; the beans were tiny and immature, but I could see the rainbow of colors tucked inside the pod. I shivered and almost ripped out the whole plant. Then, curiosity overcoming my worry, I tasted one. It was sour, like fruit that needed time to ripen.

By the next day, the pods were as thick as fingers, and Isabella decided it was time to harvest them. We took out a basket and picked all the big yellow-white pods off the plant. Then we took them inside and sat at the dining room table and shucked them, putting the beans in a jar. They'd grown in the full range of flavors. The beans I dropped into the jar were yellow, orange, and cotton-candy pink. I set aside one of the big creamy pods for Charlie to see when he got home, in case he didn't want to believe me.

Even with the pod, he clearly thought it was some sort of elaborate prank. He peeled the pod back, popping a light orange bean into his mouth, and laughed. "Hey Izzy-Bean, come here, let me give you something." He took a quarter out of his pocket and put it in her hand. "They always told me that money doesn't grow on trees; let's just see if they really know what they're talking about. Let's you and I go outside and plant a money tree and see what comes up."

It took just a week of daily watering to get the money tree to sprout.

Charlie thought I must have gone down to the garden store to get some other seedling tree, just to mess with his head.

"And the jelly bean vine?"

"You could've bought jelly beans."

"The *pod* they came in?"

"You aren't seriously telling me it *sprouted*."

"You are seriously not *listening* to me, because that's *exactly* what I'm telling you."

It usually takes fruit trees years to bear fruit, but Isabella's money tree bloomed in early August, though it was only about as tall as she was. The flowers glittered in the sun, and their petals clinked when Isabella picked them. She got out the brass vase I let her use for her cut flowers, and arranged the money flowers in it. I left it at Charlie's place at the table.

Charlie sat down slowly when he saw the money tree flowers. He touched the blooms, making the petals ring like wind chimes.

"Should've had her plant a twenty," I said.

Charlie glanced at me nervously and touched the flower again. Then he took a quarter out of his pocket and compared it. "They're not quite right," he said after a few minutes. "They're a little irregular—the design is right, but they're not perfect circles, and they're a little too small." He looked up. "They definitely won't work in vending machines."

"You're probably right."

"Twenties would probably have some flaw, too. They'd be missing the anti-counterfeiting strip or something."

"Well, it's probably not ethical to spend any of it, anyway," I said, flicking the petal with my fingernail to hear it clink again. "I mean, it *is* counterfeit money. Just because Isabella grew it doesn't make it, you know, kosher to spend." I glanced at Isabella, who was watching Charlie with a sober look on her face, her naked baby doll in her hands. "But it's a beautiful flower, sweetheart. I think Daddy loves his money tree."

"I do, definitely," he said, and lifted her onto his lap.

"Want to spend the money," Isabella said, plucking a petal from the flower and dropping it onto the table.

"What do you want to buy, kiddo?" I asked.

"Want to buy a baby sister . . ."

September came and little green pumpkins were growing on the pumpkin vines. The morning glories covered the fence, blue and purple and white. There were purple eggplants swelling like tiny lilac eggs, and sweet orange carrots, and more cucumbers than we could eat. Isabella carefully scrubbed each turnip and stacked them in a plastic crate in our dining room; I looked up turnip recipes, never having eaten them before.

Therese came over to look at Isabella's garden, and Isabella gave her a tour of the flowers and the ornamental kale, which theoretically we could have eaten but was such a brilliant red I didn't really want to pick it. "Would you like to give Therese some turnips?" I asked Isabella as we reached the turnip patch.

"Oh, no thank you, I couldn't possibly . . ."

"You wouldn't reject *Isabella's* turnips, would you? Let me just get you a sack. We have tons." I left her protesting in Isabella's garden.

While I was filling the sack, I saw Isabella showing Therese her carrots and cabbages, and Therese glancing my way and then bending down to whisper something to Isabella. I tossed in an extra turnip and went back outside. They really were *pretty* vegetables, purple and white, but we were never going to be able to eat the two bushels of them Isabella had grown.

Therese glared at me as I handed her the sack, but she thanked Isabella for the kind gift and headed back to her own house. Isabella was looking with sudden new interest at her garden, and I had the bad feeling that she was going to demand to plant something *new*, but instead she went to get her little wheelbarrow so I could help her dig up more turnips.

I had hoped that her interest in her garden would wane a little bit as we got closer to winter—it was going to *snow*, after all, and there was a limit to the number of things we could grow in pots in the house—but if anything, over the next week her interest intensi-fied. As soon as she was out of bed, she wanted to run out and look at it. At the very least she wanted to walk through it before eating her breakfast, clutching a little plastic toy—she seemed to have lost inter-est in the baby doll, I hadn't seen it in days. We'd come back out after breakfast to pick anything that was ready to harvest, and then she'd want another walk-through in the afternoon.

About a week after Therese's visit, I woke up one morning to a funny noise coming from the back yard. *There's a cat out there*, I thought. Isabella was already up, standing expectantly in the hallway. "Want to go to the garden *now*," she said.

"Get your clothes on first," I said, yawning, putting on my own blue jeans and sweatshirt. Isabella vanished back into her room, emerging minutes later with her shirt on backwards but otherwise fully dressed. "*Now* we can go to the garden," she insisted.

The cat was still there. We went downstairs and I opened the back door; Isabella sprinted out. "*There's* the baby sister!" she called to me.

Lying beside the cabbage plant, I saw a flash of pink. *She must have left her doll out here*, I thought. But it was moving.

"The cabbage patch," I whispered. *Therese must have told her that babies grew in cabbage patches. And then if she planted the doll . . .*

The baby in the cabbage patch was crying: a thin little newborn wail. She quieted as I picked her up. Isabella peered at her with inter-est. I stroked her soft hair, so much like Isabella's, and her tiny toes. She had no belly button. I traced the edges of her stomach, not quite daring to touch the middle, smooth like an egg.

"That's a baby sister," Isabella said.

"Isabella, where did this baby come from?"

"She grew," Isabella said.

"Babies don't grow in gardens, sweetheart. They don't. Whose baby is this?"

Isabella reflected on this for a minute, then said, "*That* baby sister grew in the garden."

I sat down on the porch swing, swaying back and forth, my head spinning. Should I call Charlie? The police? What was I going to say? *What am I going to do with this baby? It's not like we can just bring it in and keep it like we'd keep a stray cat.*

The baby opened its eyes and regarded me for a moment.

What am I going to do with you?

Isabella skipped over to lean on my knee, her hands empty. I blinked at her, thinking, *she had a toy when we came outside. Where is it?*

"Want a dragon," Isabella said.

I blinked again, then looked at the yard, at the tangle of pumpkin vines, eggplants, beans, cabbages. *And one dragon. One dragon* seed.

Maybe there would be an early frost.

BITS

So here is something a lot of people don't realize: most companies that make sex toys are really small. Even a successful sex-toy manufacturer like Squishies (^{TM}) is still run out of a single office attached to a warehouse, and the staff consists of Julia (the owner), Juan (the guy who does all the warehouse stuff), and me (the person who does everything else).

(You are probably wondering right now if that includes product testing. I make it a habit not to talk about my sex life with strangers but Julia requires that everyone she hires take home a Squishie or a Firmie or one of the other IntelliFlesh products and try it out, either solo or with a partner. I pointed out that if she ever hired an alien— sorry, "extraterrestrial immigrant"—the neurology doesn't match up, and does she want to admit she discriminates in hiring? But I didn't argue that hard, because hey, free sex toy, why not? Frankly, I found it a kind of freaky experience, having this piece of sensate flesh that didn't really belong there, and after a little bit of experimentation I stuck it in a drawer and haven't touched it since.)

Anyway, we outsource the manufacturing and the boxes of Squishies and Firmies get shipped to us on shrink-wrapped pallets and Juan breaks them down to re-ship in more manageable quantities to the companies that resell our products.

The original product were the Squishies, and Julia is not at ALL shy about people knowing about her sex life (we have an instructional video, and she's IN it) so I don't mind telling you that she came up with it because her boyfriend at the time had a fetish for really large breasts, we're not talking "naturally gifted" or even "enhanced with silicon" but "truly impractical for all real-world purposes like breathing and using your arms," and conveniently at the time she was working at a company making top-of-the-line prosthetics with neural integration. She made herself a really enormous set of breasts and after a lot of futzing with the neural integration she got them to be sensate. Then the boyfriend dumped her and she didn't really need them anymore, but her friend who'd had a double mastectomy said, "why don't you make me a smaller set?" and that, supposedly, was when it occurred to her that maybe she could make this product to SELL. She found a manufacturing facility and office space, hired me and Juan, and went into the Fully Sensate Attachable Flesh business.

Depending on your predilections you may already be wondering why she started with boobs. IntelliFlesh is re-shapable, at least up to a point, and since I was the Customer Service department I started getting calls from people who wanted to reshape it into something longer, stiffer, and pointier.

"Julia," I said one day, taking off my headset, "you need to start making strap-on dicks."

"I can't call those Squishies," she said dismissively.

"So? Roll out a new line. Hardies. Dickies. Cockies. If you go with Cockies you can say 'like cookies, only better' in the ads." Maybe I should note that one of the few things Julia doesn't let me do is write the ad copy.

The Firmies were an even bigger seller than the Squishies. Between boobs and dicks, we had most users covered, but every now and then I got a call from someone who wanted something a little more customized.

"You've reached Afton Enterprises, home of Squishies and Firmies," I said. "How may I help you?" (In addition to not getting to write the ad copy, I don't get to decide how to answer the phone, judging from the fact that Julia shot down the greeting, "How may I improve your sex life today?")

"I'm thinking about buying either a Squishie or a Firmie, and I . . .

had some questions," the woman said, her voice hesitant. "They're sort of expensive and I'm not sure which will meet my needs."

"Well, the Squishie is squishier," I said. "It's more malleable, but it also doesn't tend to hold alternate shapes for very long unless you refrigerate it for a while before you get started. The Firmie arrives long and narrow, but if you want it to have a different shape—say, a curve or even a hook—you can *gently* heat it up and mold it."

"What I want is a prosthetic vagina," the woman blurted out. "In a different spot."

You're not really supposed to say, "you want *what?*" to customers when you're doing customer support for a sex toy shop. We are pro-sex, pro-kink, and anti-shame: there is officially no wrong way to have sex. So: "Which spot?" I asked.

"Well, we're not exactly sure. Part of the advantage of your products is that we can move them around. What if I bought two Firmies? Could I reshape those into two halves of a vagina, like maybe one could be the top of the, um, tube, and the other could be the bottom . . . are your products compatible with lubricant?"

"There's a special lube that we sell," I said. "Other lubricants might void the warranty."

"That adds to the cost even more," the woman said, clearly frustrated. "Is there *any* way to find out before I put down all that money whether it's going to work for me? If they sold these at REI I would just *buy it* and figure I'd return it if I needed to, but nobody takes returns on sex toys."

"We do, under some circumstances," I said. "Can you give me a little more information about what your goal is with our product?"

"I want to have sex with my husband," she said, impatiently, "*real* sex, or as real as it can get. And he's a K'srillan male. Our God-given parts just don't match up."

The K'srillan—our "extraterrestrial immigrants"—made radio contact about a decade ago, and arrived on earth a year and three months ago. Juan periodically mutters about how no matter what they say, they might still be planning invasion and how would we even stop them? But they offered us suspended-animation technology in exchange for asylum (from *who?* was Juan's immediate question, but we've been assured that they were fleeing the death of their sun, not some second wave of dangerous aliens) and a dozen U.S. cities wound up taking settlements. (They're spread around. There are a bunch of others in other countries all over the world.) So far in the U.S. it was mostly okay, other than some anti-immigrant rioting in Kansas City. I hadn't actually met any K'srillan—there was a settlement in Minneapolis but I live in St. Paul and don't cross the river much—but from what I could tell they were all law-abiding and hard working and in general the sort of people you want to have come and settle in your city.

They also looked kind of like roadkilled giant squid. They don't have faces, as such. I mean, they have eyes, seven of them, which are on stalks, and they have a mouth, which they use to eat and speak, but they're not right next to each other the way you would expect in practically every earth species out there, from mammals to reptiles to fish. I mean, okay, we do have squids. But they don't walk around the shopping mall. On tentacles.

K'srillan do talk, but they aren't physically capable of making the same sounds as us, so they carry a voice synthesizer for communication.

The thought of sex with, or marriage to, a K'srillan was completely baffling to me.

Even, dare I say it, *gross.*

But we are pro-sex, pro-kink, and anti-shame, so I said, "Okay!" in as cheerful a voice as I could muster, and didn't add, "Husband? You sure moved fast." (I might not judge sex lives but I reserve the right to judge major life decisions.) "I don't actually know that much about K'srillan sexual anatomy. So, um. He has a penis?"

"Yes, we don't need a Firmie for *him*," the woman said, dismissively. "Your products don't interface with K'srillan neurology anyway or we'd consider buying him a Firmie and having him use that instead of his own penis. He has a penis, but it's eighteen inches long, and bifurcated."

"Bifurcated?"

"Branches into two, basically."

"You'd need at least four Firmies," I blurted out. "To make a vagina for eighteen inches of branched penis."

"That is a *lot* of money."

"Yeah, for that much you could practically get a custom order."

"Oh! You do custom orders?"

"No. We don't. But surely *someone* . . ."

"Do you think I haven't *checked*?" the woman asked, exasperated. "There has been a lot of discussion of this in the Full Integration community. *I am not the only woman looking.*"

"You aren't?"

"No!"

Well, that changed things, maybe. A custom order was one thing. A *prototype* was potentially a whole different matter.

"No."

"No? Just no?"

"Would you rather I went with 'no, that's a repulsive idea?'"

I stared at Julia. "I thought we were pro-kink and anti-shame?" To be fair, I'd had a similar reaction at first, but I was actively trying to get past my emotional reaction. Everyone involved was a consenting adult—okay, so the K'srillans had a different life span and developmental arc from humans, which was still being discussed in Congress, but I'd checked, and since the K'srillan males didn't actually develop a penis until sexual maturity, clearly these *were* adults were were talking about. Anyway. "Did you know that there's already a sector of the porn industry devoted to sex between human women and K'srillan males? Apparently an 18-inch bifurcated—"

"STOP. I don't want to hear about it."

"Did I ever say that about your ex-boyfriend's fetish for massive boobs? NO. Your kink is not my kink, and your kink is okay. Their kink is not our kink, but that doesn't mean we can't sell them stuff!"

Julia threw down the silicon butt plug she'd been examining. (We'd been thinking about new ways to extend our line *anyway*. It's not as if my suggestion had come completely out of the blue.) "Okay. Fine. You want to design something, we'll test the market. But *you* are going to have to take the measurements, *you* are going to have to build the prototype, and you are *certainly* going to have to do the focus group and interviews because *this is a repulsive idea.*"

"Fine!" I said. "Fine. I will handle—" I cut myself off. "I will *deal with* all of it. And we'll see if enough people want this to make it viable."

The woman who'd called was named Liz, and her husband's name was Zmivla, and it turned out that Zmivla was part of the group that had settled in Minneapolis, so they lived less than five miles from my office. I drove to the high-rise apartment where so many of the new arrivals had moved in, and took an elevator to their apartment on the 12th floor.

"Come in," Liz said when she answered the door. "I've made coffee." She laughed nervously. "Do you drink coffee?"

Zmivla was lounging in the recliner, tentacles draped over both the arm rests and the foot rest. Two of his eye stalks swiveled to look at me when I came in and his speech synthesizer said, "Hello, Ms. Marshall."

"Call me Renee," I said.

Liz handed me a cup of coffee and I studied Zmivla, wondering if I should just whip out the tape measure and ask him to whip out his penis, or if we should have some more preliminaries first. When Julia started making the Firmies, I think rather than measuring actual penises she bought the dozen or so top-selling models of dildo and measured *those*. But there aren't currently any K'srillan dildo models on the market, so we were going to have to go with some actual penises. I took a deep breath. "I should ask some sort of basic questions first, I think."

"Would you like to know how we met?" Liz asked, brightly.

Actually, I mostly wanted to know how K'srillan sex normally worked *with another K'srillan* but if she wanted to start with something a little less explicit I supposed that was a reasonable lead-in, so I nodded and drank my coffee while they told me their how-we-met story. I think it involved a conversation that started at the Powderhorn Art Fair but it's possible I'm mis-remembering and actually that's how my sister met her ex-husband. If you want to know the truth, all the cutesy "how we met" stories blur together for me. If you met your sweetie because he was third in line for the organized gang bang at the local dungeon and you really liked the shape of his dick, *that* I'll remember. If he offered to help you carry your pottery in his tentacles while you kept your dog from bolting, I just don't care enough to keep it in my head for more than fifteen minutes.

Liz had a boring office job and Zmivla had a boring job that was clearly beneath his talents and after they told me that Liz's hobby was making still life paintings it was clear they were stalling, and I couldn't entirely blame them, given that I was there to measure the guy's penis.

"I know this is a somewhat uncomfortable situation for all of us," I said. "But we really probably should get down to business, okay?"

"I just want you to . . ." Liz hesitated.

Zmivla stroked the back of her hand with the tip of one of his tentacles, delicately. With one of the others, he brushed a strand of hair out of her face. "Liz and I appreciate your open-mindedness," he said. "But it's important to her that you see us as people first. As a couple who has a right to be together, to share the love that we do."

"You want me to think that you're normal," I said. I tried to keep the edge of sarcasm out of my voice, but I probably didn't entirely succeed. "Just another Minneapolis family."

"I know we're not like everyone else," Liz said. "But we love each other and take care of each other. And that's what's *important*."

"Right," I said. "But you didn't call me to affirm your relationship. You called me to help you with your sex life. So let's talk about *that*."

*

So, among actual K'srillans, the female folds herself around the male; she does have a short channel that's there all the time but a decent amount of her sexual passageway is constructed on-the-fly. I took notes. The actual sex involved friction, but some of it was accomplished by the same muscles that were used to fold the extended vagina into place; I wasn't entirely sure whether the male K'srillan thrusted, or not.

"You realize," I said, "there is *no way* we can build an IntelliFlesh vagina that will do the folding thing. Or the rippling, or whatever. Maybe we could add a vibrator . . ."

"Older K'srillan females sometimes lose a certain amount of strength," Zmivla offered. "There is a procedure that allows the female to fasten her channel into place, and when having sex with a female who has had this procedure, the male thrusts. It should work." The tips of his tentacles turned pink and I wasn't sure whether he was embarrassed, sexually aroused, or something else entirely. "Though this vibration option you mention . . ."

I had brought the tape measure but I wound up having Liz do the measurements. I made a sketch and had her call out the measurements as I noted them down. Eighteen inches was a rough estimate, it turned out: one branch ran 18.25 inches stem to stern and the other branch was 17.8 inches. Girth of the trunk portion was comparable to a soda can; the branches were a lot more slender and tapered toward the tip, like extremely long carrots. The K'srillan penis is *blue*, I noticed, or at least it's blue when he's sexually aroused, sort of a dusky violet-blue that would indicate in a human that he's oxygen-deprived or possibly freezing to death. There are visible veins in the sides.

"I don't suppose you know how typical you are," I said. "I mean, for a K'srillan male, are you on the large side or the small side, are you more or less asymmetrical than most, how does your girth compare..."

"I don't know," he said. "But I don't think it would be too hard to find out. There are about a thousand K'srillans living in this apartment complex, after all, and I know two dozen others with human wives."

I spent *two entire days* measuring K'srillan penises.

The good news was that K'srillan penises turned out to be reasonably uniform. I mean, they ranged in length from 16 inches all the way up to 20, and they ranged in girth from pop can to coffee mug, and there were some penises where one branch was noticeably shorter, even by as much as six inches. But human penises *also* vary. I mean, the average length for an erect dick is about five inches, but the record holder was 13.5 inches long. (Not to overshare but that just sounds like it would be *painful*.)

The variety of sizing in human dicks has not prevented the successful marketing of any number of artificial vaginas (or "masturbation sleeves," to use the technical industry term.) I mean, just like with dildos you can provide a set of different sizes but they are not all THAT customized, and given that IntelliFlesh is a lot more adaptable than silicon, I was pretty sure we'd be able to come up with something that would work.

Anyway, that was the good news. The bad news was that I had to spend *two entire days* measuring K'srillan penises.

Fortunately, K'srillan men seem to be pretty secure in their masculinity. I mean, imagine the reaction if you came at the average human male with a tape measure. My former brother-in-law actually measured his *own* dick at some point and it was 4.5 inches long, so a whopping half-inch shorter than the average. My sister told absolutely everyone, after the divorce, but the problem wasn't really his very-slightly-runty dick, it was the ways in which he compensated and the fact that he was a complete loser in the sack, one of those men who thinks that his penis is *magic* and if you can't climax in two minutes just from him sticking it in you, you must be broken. One-half-inch-less than average length: not a problem. Complete boredom in the sack: definite problem.

(Sorry. Very few people in my life seem to share my no-overshares policy.)

Anyway. There was one K'srillan who shrank at the sight of the tape measure, but then he laughed (K'srillans actually have a physical response to humor, I found out, but the voice synthesizers are programmed to pick up on it and translate it into a ha-ha-ha sound) and said, "Give me just one moment" and swelled back up to full size within a few seconds. K'srillans all grew up in K'srillan society, which has its own set of gender roles and expectations that are absolutely nothing whatsoever like human gender stereotypes, and then they were plunged into human society and forced to adapt. One of the men noted, as I wrapped the tape measure around the trunk portion at the bottom, that in K'srillan society it is the *woman* who is expected to make the first move; a man who propositions a woman is shameless and forward, and he thinks human women like that, once we get used to the idea.

"Maybe," I said, and measured his length on the left-hand side: 17.85. "How'd you meet *your* wife, anyway?"

"I thought they told you?" he said, a little mournfully. "I have not been so fortunate yet, but I volunteered for this exciting project because it will perhaps raise interest in our kind."

"Wouldn't you honestly prefer to marry someone of your own *species*?" I said.

"Among my own kind I am considered unattractive," he said.

I stepped back and took a look at him. Over the two days, K'srillans had stopped looking like roadkilled squid to me, but I still wouldn't call any individual *attractive* as such. I finished the last measurement, wrote it down, and tossed my gloves into his kitchen trash can. "Thanks for your help," I said.

I was back in the office, finishing up my prototype design, when my phone rang.

"You do us an injustice," said a synthesized voice on the other end of the line.

"I'm sorry," I said. "Who's calling, please?"

"For *days* you come to our settlement and measure the male organs," the voice said, distressed. "And now I find out it is so that you can make *false female organs* for *human women*."

I scratched my head, wondering how I'd gotten myself into this. "Look. You do realize that we specialize in false organs of all varieties for humans—both women *and* men."

"Yes!" the voice said, furious. "And *I* am a K'srillan *female* married to a human *male*. Why are you not going to make false K'srillan *male* organs? What is *my* husband supposed to do to please me?"

So in the end, I'm sure you'll be shocked to hear, we made both. We made K'srillan vaginas: as I warned Liz, they're not capable of the K'srillan pre-sex vaginal origami action, but they do simulate the muscle movements with the addition of an adjustable vibrator. We also made K'srillan penises, though due to limited market penetration at this point we have only one size and shape (pop-bottle girth at the bottom, 17.85 on the left-hand size, 18.1 on the right-hand side).

What I find the weirdest these days are not the human/K'srillan couples. It's the human/human couples that buy one from each set and have sex with the detachable genitals instead of the compatible set they already had. Or, maybe it's the porn of humans having sex with the K'srillan artificial genitalia. Or possibly the *gay* porn of humans having sex with K'srillan artificial genitalia. Or possibly the absolute weirdest is the porn of K'srillans having sex with artificial human genitalia—they can't do that with IntelliFlesh (years of research into their neurology remain to be done) but there's always the good old-fashioned strap-on option on one side, and an artificial vagina on the other.

Because really, there are two immutable laws of nature at work here: number one, love will find a way; and number two, if a sexual act can be conceived of, someone will pay money to watch it.

I've been thinking a lot about that first rule, lately. Because I told my sister about the "unattractive" K'srillan and jokingly—I swear I was joking!—pointed out that at least she'd never be bored in bed. She jokingly—she claims she was joking—asked me for his number. I told her she could have it if she promised to *never* tell me the details of their sex life, and she pointed out that I already knew this guy's penis size down to the quarter-inch . . .

Yeah, they're dating. They're not rushing into anything, so this story doesn't end with, "And the wedding's next week!" But I have to say—you do get used to the seven eyes looking at you over the after-dinner drinks and I've learned to spot the physical cues of the laugh even before the synthesizer goes "ha ha ha." And Gintika (that's his name) definitely doesn't make me think of roadkilled squid anymore. He makes me think about how sometimes we have more in common with people than we realize; he makes me think about all the ways to form a connection. He makes me think about the look on my sister's face when she talks about him. He makes me think, *love finds a way,* and *hey, sometimes finding a way, finds you love.*

Author's Note

The online magazine Strange Horizons *(which has published several of my stories, including "Comrade Grandmother") has a list written by their editorial team a few years ago describing stories they were seeing too often. Some are vintage clichés I remember being warned about when I first started submitting stories in the 1980s ("In the end, it turns out it was all a dream.") Others are a lot weirder.*

A Facebook friend of mine linked to the list one day. The thread turned into banter about pairing these unwanted stories with "in bed" (like you do with Fortune Cookies) or "in space" (actually, it might have been "in spaaaaaace.") I scanned down the list, hit on Someone calls technical support; wacky hijinx ensue *and joked about turning that into a story where someone calls technical support for an interstellar vibrator.*

And within five minutes I knew I wanted to write this story.

HONEST MAN

 *iddle Game*
November 15th, 1943
Washington, D.C.

A cold rain was falling when Iris came out of the Department of Justice building onto Constitution Avenue. Worse, she'd stayed late filing and had missed not only her usual bus but the next bus as well. There was a diner across the street from her bus stop: she could see an OPEN sign and the tempting glow of light. She started to count the money in her purse, but her hesitation was blown away by a gust of wind and a fresh sheet of rain. She dashed across the street and into the diner, coming in out of breath, lipstick smeared and hat askew, the bell over the door clanging as she wiped her feet on the mat and looked around for a place to sit.

The diner smelled of fried eggs, clean floors, and slightly scorched coffee. It was nearly empty; a man in a suit sat up on a stool at the counter, a man in a long, well-worn raincoat sat in a booth near the door, looking out at the rain. Iris took a seat at the counter. "I'll just have a cup of coffee, please," she said to the waitress. *I have perfectly good food at home, I can go home and make some supper for myself.* But the rain was falling even harder, so she looked over the menu, sighed, and said, "Oh, just the grilled cheese and a cup of tomato soup, please."

The man in the suit caught her eye while she was waiting. "Nice weather, huh?" he said. "Do you work for Mr. Hoover?"

"Yes, sir, I do," she said. "Typing and filing."

"Good for you. I'm just passing through town, myself. I'm an art dealer, when we're not at war."

"I don't expect there's much call for that, during wartime."

"Oh, you'd be surprised. You'd be surprised. But I wanted to contribute more directly to the war effort, so right now I buy and sell surplus—getting scrap from scrap drives delivered to places where it's needed, that sort of thing. Art is just a sideline for now." He glanced up to smile at the waitress as she refilled his coffee. "My name's Leo." He handed her a business card: it said *Leonard Franklin*. "Leo like the lion, Franklin like the first name of the President of the United States of America."

"My name is Iris. Iris Kirkwood."

"Iris! You're serious? I have a *sister* named Iris, can you believe it?"

The waitress arrived with Iris's coffee, steaming hot. "I've always just been thankful my mother didn't name me Petunia," Iris said with a game smile.

"I think it's a beautiful name." He gave her a smile warm enough that Iris started to wonder if she should mention her boyfriend serving in the Infantry, but he made no further overtures and she decided he was just being friendly. The waitress came out of the kitchen with Iris's sandwich and soup, then continued to the table up front to give the man his check.

Iris's supper, at least, was really good. The bread was fresh, the cheese tart, the tomato soup creamy. Or maybe it was just the lingering chill and the rain outside that made everything taste so good. Iris glanced up at the art-dealer-turned-scrap-dealer, and since he was looking away from her, dunked a piece of her sandwich in the soup. She was never certain whether you were allowed to do that sort of thing in restaurants.

"Excuse me . . ." The man from the front of the restaurant was talking to the waitress, his face obviously distressed. "I am so, so sorry, ma'am, but I just realized that I left my wallet back at my room. I'm going to have to go get it before I can pay, but I don't want you to think I'm running out on my bill. I can leave my instrument here as security . . ." He had a violin case, Iris saw; he opened it up to show the waitress the violin inside. "This is a good violin. I paid fifty dollars for it, a few years back, but I think it's worth more."

The waitress glanced at it and grunted. "It looks like it's worth more than your meal, anyway. Go ahead and get your wallet."

"I'll be right back," he promised, and went back out into the rain.

Iris was finishing her sandwich when she heard Leo say, "Can I take a look at that?"

"What, the violin?" The waitress shrugged. "I don't see why not."

Leo opened the case and took out the instrument, turning it over in his hands and holding it up to the light. She heard him let out a long, appreciative breath, and looked up to see him swallow hard. For a moment, his eyes darted around the room, like a man with a poker hand that he knows will win the night. Then he looked back up at Iris, and at the waitress. "My God," he said. "This is a Stradivarius."

"Strada-what?"

"One of the rarest and most valuable violins ever constructed. Most are in the hands of collectors, museums . . . It's worth hundreds of thousands of dollars. Maybe more." At the waitress's skeptical look, he gave Iris another warm smile. "I was just telling Miss Kirkwood here that I was an art dealer, before the war; these days I mostly deal scrap, but I do make an exception when fate throws the truly exceptional piece my way. I would happily pay two hundred thousand dollars for this violin. Cash. I'm quite sure that when the war is over I'll be able to resell this instrument for many times that."

"Oh, won't that man be happy," Iris said. "You could tell he didn't have much money."

"Where did he say he was going?" Leo asked the waitress.

"Back to his room. He didn't say where it was, but it can't be that far . . ."

Minutes ticked past. Leo reverently set the violin back into its case, then checked his wristwatch. "Oh dear," he said. "My train . . . well, another couple of minutes won't hurt."

They waited. Iris finished her coffee; the waitress, watching the door, left her cup empty. Another sheet of rain came down outside. Iris looked at the clock on the wall; she had just missed the next bus, but this was exciting enough that she didn't care.

"I really can't wait any longer," Leo said, finally. He gave the waitress his business card. "When the man comes back, and surely he's planning on coming back, give him my card and tell him to call me, collect, tomorrow morning at my office in New York City. I will be pleased to offer him two hundred thousand dollars for his violin, and in the meantime I do urge him to take *very* good care of it." He put on his hat and raincoat. "It was a pleasure to meet you, Miss Kirkwood," he said, and went out in a jingle of bells and a blast of damp wind.

"Well," the waitress said in amazement, and looked down at the violin on the counter. Suddenly realizing that it might be vulnerable to a spill, she moved it over to an empty table and then refilled Iris's coffee cup. "Dessert for you today, ma'am?"

Iris had already mentally counted out the money for dinner against the money she had left before next payday. "No, thank you," she said. "But thank you for the coffee. I'll have to admit I don't think anything could get me out of this restaurant before that man comes back for his violin. Think of the look on his face!"

Not five minutes passed before the man was back. He had a ragged wallet in his pocket now, and carefully counted out the money for his meal. "So, about that violin," the waitress said, and glanced nervously at Iris. "You know, my nephew is thinking of taking up violin and my sister could really use an instrument. Would you be willing to sell it?"

"But—" Iris whispered. The waitress pulled down a piece of the peach pie, Iris's favorite, and set it down in front of Iris like a promise.

"Oh, I couldn't sell it," the man said. "It's my livelihood. I play on street corners . . . even in wartime, or maybe *especially* in wartime, people like to hear music. It lifts their spirits. I'd be happy to play for you, to thank you for your understanding about the wallet . . ."

The waitress shook her head impatiently. "Surely you'd be willing, for the right price. You said you paid fifty? I'll give you a hundred."

The man shook his head. "I paid fifty, but it's a better violin than that. I couldn't let it go for less than five hundred."

"Two hundred," the waitress said.

"*Wait*," Iris said, with a glare at the waitress. She elbowed the pie aside. "Don't listen to her. There was a man here a few minutes ago who said your violin was really valuable. He said he'd pay two hundred *thousand* dollars for it, and you should call his office tomorrow, collect. He lives in New York City . . ." She dug in her own coat pocket and triumphantly produced Leo's business card. "Leo Franklin. Leo like the lion, Franklin like the President."

The waitress's glare could have soured whiskey; Iris averted her eyes, feeling a little guilty, but really, how unfair and *wrong*, not to tell a man what his property was worth if you *knew*. "I think you should wait and sell the violin tomorrow."

The man turned towards Iris, cocked his head to one side, and looked her up and down. It was a strange look—not the look of a poor man who'd just learned that his property was worth thousands of dollars. More the look of a fox that had approached the henhouse, and found it locked. But then he gave her a wistful smile and said, "I thank you, ma'am." His lips twitched as he turned to the waitress. "As kind as your offer was, I think I shall have to refuse it." He glanced down at the pie. "Since it seems I am about to come into some money, ma'am, let me thank you by paying for your meal." He counted out the money for sandwich, soup, coffee, and pie, and even included a generous tip. "Good night to both of you."

Iris ate her pie quickly; the waitress's stony glare made her nervous. She braced herself for the wind and rain and stepped out.

To her relief, the rain had stopped while she was eating, replaced with a thick fog. She crossed the street to wait for her bus, thinking over the evening, and stepped forward when she saw headlights coming towards her in the fog. But instead of a bus, a black Lincoln town car pulled up. The window rolled down, and Leo looked out at her from the passenger-side window. "Can I offer you a ride, ma'am?"

"Oh!" She stepped backwards, startled to see him. *He said he was catching a train—why is he in a car?* "I gave the man your card . . . The waitress wasn't going to tell him, can you believe it? She was going to buy it for a hundred dollars and sell it to you herself!"

"Let me show you something," Leo said, and climbed out of the car. He opened the trunk and Iris looked in to see a dozen identical violin cases. "We paid $25 each for them. The man you saw inside is an associate of mine—he's driving the car, in fact. We, ahem, test the honesty of waitresses, bartenders and restaurant owners all over this great country of ours." He closed the trunk.

Iris stared at him, speechless.

"They say you can't cheat an honest man. That's not true. It's easy to cheat an honest man, if he assumes that others are as honest as he is. But as a matter of principle, I *won't* cheat an honest man." He doffed his hat, held it to his chest, and bowed to Iris. "Would you like a souvenir, ma'am? A violin, perhaps? I hear there's a man in New York City who'll pay two hundred thousand dollars for violins."

"I don't need anything from you," she said.

"No, but I have a small gift for you, regardless." His hat still in his hand, he covered his face with it momentarily, then set it back on his head and said, "Your soldier will come home safe. You should marry him, because he will make an excellent husband to you. You will have many, many happy years together, and two children, a girl and a boy."

Iris shook her head. "You could say that to any girl in Washington and she'd think you had the second sight."

"You're right, of course. But your soldier is named Ben—Bennie, really, but he prefers Ben. And you will be very happy together." A final bow, and Leo got back into the car, and disappeared in the night.

"I can't believe you didn't tell anybody."

The Virginia farmhouse, two months later, was dark around them, their father long asleep; the lamp on the kitchen table guttered a little, and Iris's sister Reva adjusted the glow.

"Why?" Iris asked.

"Well, he was a con man. He as much told you so, he had a trunk full of violins! You could've called the police. Or just told your boss the next day, you work for the FBI."

"But if the waitress had given him the money, she would have deserved it, don't you think? *She* was trying to cheat *him*."

"For all you know, she has family at home who need that money to live on. What did they do to deserve being cheated?"

"Well, but she *didn't* buy that violin."

"Only because you stopped her!"

"I should go back there and tell her. Might make her more appreciative. Right now she's probably cursing my name every night."

"Probably . . ."

"How do you think he knew that my soldier's name is Ben?"

"You probably mentioned it and just forgot."

"No. I didn't. Besides, if I did, how did he know that Ben's given name is Bennie?"

"Maybe you had a letter, and dropped it . . ."

"I thought of that, but I checked. I keep all of Ben's letters in a box at home, and they're all there."

"Well, maybe he *does* have the second sight. It would be useful for a con man, don't you think?" Reva shook her head again. "I *can't believe* you didn't tell anyone . . ."

Ben will understand, Iris thought. She had already told him the story; she'd written to him about it the same night it happened, and sent the letter off to the base in England where he was stationed. It took months for his reply to reach her, but when it did, she could almost hear the chuckle in his Yankee voice as she read:

I'm glad to hear that your con man at least bought you some good peach pie. As for that waitress, if she had been cheated, it would've served her right for trying to cheat a man out of his violin. As for him knowing my name—well, my mother has the second sight, or so I was always told. I've never seen as it does her much use. Maybe she should go into violin sales. At any rate, I'm glad to hear the con man thinks I'll be coming home to you, because I'd like to introduce you to my mother one of these days. And I can hardly wait to see your beautiful smile again.

Fortune Teller
June 17th, 1952
Campbell County, Virginia

Nights were dark in the country. People kept saying that there'd be electricity at *all* the farms within three years, but no matter how many years passed, electricity to Iris and Ben's farm always seemed to be about two years away. Ben was in town, working the night shift at his new job at the gas company. Upstairs, Iris could hear her father coughing, and cringed a little inside, listening.

They said just a few months. Months, not years. It's not like the electricity: there will *be a spot in the Catawba sanatorium once he gets to the top of the list. We'll just keep all our windows open and hope for the best. I wouldn't worry so much if it weren't for Mitzi . . .*

No child should be exposed to tuberculosis, but Mitzi was already so small and weak. Born a little too early and a little too small, the doctor had told Iris she couldn't risk breastfeeding her; then the formula had made her sick, and for months she hadn't gained weight. Now at five she weighed less than thirty pounds. Eric, the baby, was almost twenty pounds already, grown fat and cheerful on his mother's milk. Iris did her best to keep her children away from her father, and boiled every sheet and pillowcase in the house daily, drawing the water up from the well on the porch and heating it on the stove.

Daddy has nowhere else to go. Nowhere. He went into debt for the first time in his life to send me to business school. It's not his fault he got sick . . .

I have to trust in God. God wouldn't punish me for doing the right thing by my Daddy, would He?

Then again, Daddy never did anything to deserve tuberculosis, either . . .

She heard the crunch of someone's footstep outside. "Ben?" she said, hopefully, though it was hours until he would usually get home.

"Ma'am?"

She opened the door and looked out onto the porch. A ragged-looking man stood on the porch, a bundle of something tucked under his arm. She felt a brief prickle of fear, but the bundle was just a ragged knapsack, and he didn't look dangerous, just poor. He did a slight double-take when he saw her, and she thought he must have expected her husband. "My husband is working in town, but my father is upstairs, if you need a man for something," she said. "It's a strange time for a visit. Do you need help?"

He was silent for a moment, then said, "I'm hungry, ma'am. I was just wondering if I could have some food in exchange for doing a few chores." He had a jumpy, rangy look, and his eyes were hollow.

"I'm not going to set a hungry man to working. Come on into the kitchen if you want something to eat. We can talk about chores once you're fed."

"Thank you, ma'am," he said, and followed her into the house.

Despite his hollow eyes, he was clean; inside, she saw that his clothes were mended, though he had holes in his shoes. There were fresh eggs, and bread, so she made him eggs on toast. There was plenty of bread left—Mitzi had picked at her supper, as usual. Iris made herself an egg as well, and then sat down at the kitchen table. Upstairs, she heard her father coughing again.

"What's your name?" she asked the stranger after he'd eaten half his eggs.

"Joe Truman. Joe like the ballplayer, Truman like the President of the United States of America."

"I am Mrs. Greene."

"It's a pleasure to meet you, ma'am. And your eggs are very fine. Thank you. I'd like to repay your kindness, now, if you've got any chores that need doing."

"I'd just love it if you'd sit here while I cut some wood for the stove, and come get me if my baby wakes up and cries, or if my father needs anything."

"Ma'am, please let me cut some wood for you."

"All right, then. Wood's out back. I'll get you a lantern to take with you."

Iris washed the dishes. She went upstairs, to check on her father—his eyes were closed, and if he wasn't asleep, he pretended to be. Downstairs again, she washed her hands, and then checked on Mitzi and Eric. Eric sometimes woke this time of night to nurse, but now he was asleep, sprawled dimpled and content on his sheets. Mitzi had kicked her sheet and blanket off; it was a warm night, but Iris smoothed the sheet back over her daughter anyway. *Truman, like the President of the United States of America.*

Iris stepped out the back door and watched as the man split a log into sticks of kindling. The kerosene lantern rested on top of the wood pile, casting a circle of yellow light. His sleeves were rolled up, and he'd already chopped a fair amount of wood. Iris watched him for several minutes, until he looked up and saw her. "What happened to the car?" she asked.

"Ma'am?"

"The big car with all the violins in the trunk. And your friend the violinist, what happened to him?"

"My partner decided to run off with my share of the money. That's the danger of working with a con man—sometimes you get conned. So I decided I didn't need a partner anymore, and I traded in for a different gig."

"Offering to work for food?"

"If you knock on a stranger's door and ask to come in for a friendly chat, sometimes they set the dog on you."

"Wash up and come back on in the house. I don't want to be gone for too long." *And I don't trust you out here without someone to keep an eye on you.*

"Yes, ma'am."

Back in the house, all was quiet and still. The man's knapsack was under the kitchen table; Iris wondered what she'd find in it if she looked. More violins? Patent snake oil guaranteed to cure baldness, madness, tuberculosis? Stock certificates for a silver mine?

"A crystal ball, actually," the stranger—Leo, she thought, that's what he called himself before—said from the doorway. "I tell fortunes these days." He settled himself back at the kitchen table, uninvited. "I did well by yours, didn't I? Ben came home. He's a good husband, not like your sister's truck driver, whose trips keep getting longer and longer. You have a daughter and a son, just like I said."

"You're an awful good guesser," Iris said.

"Do you want me to tell your fortune again?"

Tell me if we'll be safe from TB. Tell me if my daughter will grow up healthy. Tell me if we'll be able to stay in Virginia or if we'll lose our farm like Ben's family lost his when he was a young man . . . Iris bit her lip and turned her back on him. "No," she said. *Trust in God, not in charming violin salesmen who know things that are none of their business.*

Behind her, she heard the man sigh. "You're my worst nightmare and my fondest recollection, Miss At-least-they-didn't-name-me-Petunia," he said.

"I should get my Daddy and have him throw you out." *Or get that shotgun that Ben taught me how to use.*

"Let your Daddy sleep. I'll leave if you ask. Though it would warm my heart if you'd give me a cup of tea first."

The room was already too warm, but Iris added some wood to the stove and put the kettle on. "You can have your cup of tea, and then I think I'll need to say good night to you."

"Yes, ma'am."

The water was hot: she made him a cup of tea and set it down in front of him, not sitting down herself. He downed it meekly, in silence. The minutes ticked by.

"Just tell me if my daughter will grow up healthy," Iris said. "That's all I want to know. Eric's a big, strong boy, I don't worry about him, even with my father upstairs, but Mitzi . . ."

The stranger let out his breath in a sigh, and for a moment her blood went cold. But then he said, "Your daughter will grow up healthy. She'll have three children of her own someday." He straightened up in his chair, turning his cup around and around in his hands as if he were reading the leaves, even though she'd used a tea bag. "She's going to become a college professor. In fact, *both* of your children are going to become college professors."

Iris laughed out loud at that. Ben had tried to go to college before the war, but his family hadn't been able to afford it after the first year.

"You think that's funny? Your Ben's going to go back to college, and when he graduates he'll become a teacher. You, great lady, will have to settle for *working* at a college. You're going to have to move to Ohio, because after the Browns win their lawsuit, no Virginia school district is going to be willing to hire a Yankee schoolteacher . . . but you'll like Ohio."

I can't believe a word this man is saying, she thought.

The man set his empty cup down and picked up his bag. He put his hat on and turned to go. "When a con man tells fortunes, he doesn't usually tell the good parts. He tells the bad, and hints of dire fates that can be averted only by copious payment to the piper. But I do not cheat honest men, and I remember you, ma'am, even if that waitress has long since forgotten about the night she almost bought a Stradivarius violin. Let me tell you one more thing about Mitzi," he added, and her heart leapt to her throat. "I'll tell you that she won't much care for that nickname when she gets older. Amelia is going to want people to call her *Amy*." And with that, he stepped down off the porch and strode away into the night, leaving the house quiet and still.

Iris washed and dried the teacup and put it away. *I never told him Mitzi's real name,* she thought. *I really hope that means the rest of what he said was true. College for Ben and for both my children! But I'm not sure how we'd manage that for Ben, even with the government money . . . we'd need money to live on, we barely scrape by as it is.*

Well, maybe after my father goes to the sanatorium, we can move into Lynchburg and I can open a nursery school. Take care of some of the children in the neighborhood. Maybe Ben can keep working nights, go to classes during the day. Maybe . . .

If it's meant to be, then of course we'll be able to find a way.

*

Petunia Lucky
Springfield, Ohio
October 25th, 1999

The house was far too quiet with Ben gone. It was strange: he'd been in a nursing home for a few months before he died, not living at home, yet the house was far quieter now than it was then. There was the TV for noise, and Blossom, the old Airedale terrier, would pad around the house after Iris, but it didn't help much. *If only people lived closer . . .* but Amy lived in Wisconsin, Eric lived in Canada, even the grandchildren were scattered around the country.

Iris couldn't hear the mail arrive, but Blossom could; she pricked up her ears even half-asleep, and Iris got up to bring it in. Bills, charitable requests, sales pitches, and more bills. It was strange how expensive it was just to die. Ben had died in August, and it seemed like she was still getting bills related to his death. PAST DUE, one of them said in accusing red letters, though Iris was quite certain she'd paid every bill she'd seen. She sat down with a sigh and opened the envelope. ENVIRONMENTAL PERMIT FEES / INTERMENT, the bill said. It had the seal of the State of Ohio on it and some other gobbledygook, and the amount at the bottom was $824, plus a 10% fee for being late, so $906.40 in all. She groaned and reached for the checkbook again.

Something made her stop, though, and take a closer look. It looked like something from the state, but it was a plain post office box address on the self-addressed envelope inside. Was this even a real bill, or was it someone trying to take advantage of a grieving older woman by sending bills knowing she might not know how to tell a real bill from a fake?

A horrible suspicion struck her, and she went upstairs to her filing cabinet. She recognized the bills from the funeral home, the bills from the doctor and the nursing home, but there were six more bills that, on close examination, she realized had been sent from similarly suspicious post office boxes, though each had a different number. And she'd paid them. One for $64, one for $135, one for $214, one for $265, one for $412, and one for $524.13. *One thousand six hundred and fourteen dollars. And thirteen cents.* She felt sick. *How could I have been so gullible? Why didn't I look more closely at these? If only Ben were here . . .* And that made her cry again, alone in her little sewing room, until Blossom dragged her creaking self upstairs to lick her hand and wag her tail and ask for a walk, even though as old as Blossom was, she was happier staying home. *She knows* I *need a walk, though. She's a good dog.*

Out in the fresh air, Iris felt a little calmer. It was a beautiful October day: the sky was blue, the air was crisp, the leaves were changing colors. Her neighbors had pumpkins out on their front steps—it would be time to go buy candy soon, for the Trick-Or-Treaters. She'd get to see all the neighborhood kids dressed up in costumes; that was always so much fun. After she'd thought for a while about pleasant things, she felt a bit better.

But now *what do I do?* The gall of sending her a bill marked *overdue* when they had *already* bilked her out of over sixteen hundred dollars made Iris shake her head. *They say you can't cheat an honest man, but it was my honesty that they were taking advantage of. They knew I'm the sort of person who takes care of bills as quickly as I can. They knew that from the very first bill I paid.*

Maybe my son-in-law can help. Amy had married a thoroughly reliable man. Iris's son-in-law was able to straighten out all kinds of mix-ups. But the thought of explaining to him that she'd paid *six fake bills* without realizing it made her cheeks flush. *No, it's too embarrassing. I'll just live a little more frugally for a while. Make up the money. And forget about it.*

It could make a person angry, though.

For the first time in years, Iris found herself thinking about the violin man—Leo Franklin or Joe Truman or whatever his real name was. *He'd probably be calling himself Will Clinton these days.* It was a little absurd to think that the world needed more of *any* kind of con man, but . . . *If it's going to have con men, I think I like the sort of con men that take advantage of dishonesty rather than honesty.*

Back in her house, she was drinking a glass of iced tea when someone knocked at her door. For a moment, she imagined that it would be her long-ago visitor, back again for some reason, but when she opened the door it was a young man, not an old one. He started to say something about a truckload of meat that was going to spoil if he didn't find people to buy it, and she shook her head and said, "I really don't eat much meat anymore."

He looked into her face and then said, "My name is Leo Clinton. Leo like the boy who went down with the Titanic, Clinton like the President of the United States of America."

It's him. She hesitated for a moment, but . . . *Leo never did me any wrong. Why not ask him what he thinks. He might know if I have any chance of getting my money back.* "Come on in, Leo," she said. "I'll get you some iced tea."

The TV was on when he came in, blaring to the empty room; she shut it off. "You'll have to pardon me if I miss some of what you're saying. I'm a bit deaf these days, though I do wear a hearing aid." She poured two glasses of iced tea. Blossom came over to investigate the stranger, sniffed him a few times, then flopped back down by the door.

"Many years of happiness, yes?" Leo said when she sat down. "Just like I told you."

"Fifty-three," Iris said. "Fifty three years and six months."

"*All* of them happy?"

Iris thought about the Alzheimer's, the Parkinson's, the broken hip and pneumonia, the last weeks when Ben was so frail and helpless. "I wouldn't trade even one day of that time for anything," she said, knowing that her voice had faltered a bit. Leo didn't say anything, so she added, "He wrote poems for me—every birthday, every Valentine's Day, every anniversary, until the Alzheimer's made that too hard for him. My daughter typed up all his poems last year and had them bound into a book for us. My granddaughters read some of those poems at Ben's funeral."

"I never met your husband," Leo said. "But I know he must have been a fine man."

"He was so good to me," Iris said. "He was the best husband in the world."

"I'm very sorry for your loss, ma'am."

"Thank you."

Outside, a truck rumbled past.

"About those bills you were wondering about," Leo said. "Those weren't me."

"I know," Iris said. "You said you only cheat the dishonest." The unfairness of it welled up again for a moment and she sighed deeply and put her glass down. "Well, what's done is done, I guess. I don't suppose calling the police will make any difference."

"They'll take your report, if that's what matters to you. But if it were easy to catch con men then fewer people would be conned. Con men are a slippery bunch."

"You would know."

"They don't come more slippery than me." He gave her an amiable grin. *Was he always so young?* she wondered. *He looked old when I saw him the first time. Well, maybe not* old, *but older than me.*

"You think there isn't anything I can do."

"No, I'm saying that going to the police probably won't get you your money back. I have another option, if you're interested."

"What's that?"

"Cheat the cheater. I can help you figure out who got your money, and I can help you clean out his bank account. We'll have to work together, though. Some cons work best with two. Are you with me?"

Iris thought it over. *It could be dangerous,* she thought. *I wish Ben could advise me—what would Ben do?* Her responsible son-in-law would never countenance it, that was certain . . .

She smiled. "All right," she said. "I'll give it a try."

*

"The first step is to find out who our mark really is. His post office box is undoubtedly under a false name, but that's okay, we'll find out the real one." The box address had been in Xenia, so they'd driven there to stake out the post office. "It only takes a day for mail to get from here to there. You paid promptly every other time, so he'll no doubt be checking his box today."

On Leo's instructions, Iris had sent, not a check, but a written request to pay in installments. "You don't want to give the mark any more of your money, but you don't want him to know you're on to him, either. He'll have to write back and tell you it's fine, and then check back for your first payment in a couple of days, so if we somehow miss spotting him today, we'll have another chance. He's got box number 3536. Your job is to loiter in the lobby. I'll wait out front in the car. When you see the mark, don't talk to him, just make sure you follow him out so I see who he is, too. Then try to follow him to his car so that you can see the license plate number. Remember it, and then write it down as soon as you can. *Not while he can see you.*"

Iris had worried that someone would ask her what she was doing standing around in the entryway to the post office, but no one did.

The wait was boring. She had to watch box 3536 like a hawk, while not looking like she was watching it, since the man—*the mark*—might notice that. Leo had thought the mark would be there early, and sure enough, in the morning rush, Iris glimpsed him. He wasn't opening the mail, just shoving it into the pocket of his coat; she turned and followed him.

"Here, allow me."

"Thank you." She realized the mark had just held the door for her. She paused to let him get ahead of her, and then fell into step behind him, trailing after him to keep an eye on him in the parking lot. And there was the car: a red sedan. Iris didn't really know cars, but this one was shiny and very new-looking. Ripping off old ladies must pay well. *License plate. License plate.* She spotted it as he pulled away, and realized it was one of those plates with a word on it: MR LKY. *Mr. Lucky.*

"Do we follow his car?" Iris asked.

"No, that's much too easy to spot. No, our next stop is the police station. You're going to get us his name and address."

"I am?"

"They're not supposed to give that out, but you're not a suspicious character. You're a sweet older woman, and if you have a good story, you can get any information out of them that you ask for, I bet. Can you think up a good story?"

"I'll have to consider that," Iris said, and leaned back and closed her eyes. "Let me know when we get there."

"Excuse me, young lady. I was wondering if you could help me, please."

The receptionist looked up. She was about the age of Iris's daughter—fifty—and clearly a little startled to be addressed as "young lady," but she smiled kindly at Iris when she saw her white hair. "I'll do what I can, ma'am. What's the problem?"

"I was wondering if you could give me the name and address of the person with this license plate." Iris spread out the torn piece of notebook paper on which she'd written MR LKY.

"We're not supposed to just give those out. Did he sideswipe you or something?" The receptionist frowned.

"Oh, no, nothing like that. Oh, I'm so embarrassed about this." Iris sighed. "You see, I was in a parking lot and when I opened my car door I hit his car and made a dent. I knew I should leave a note for him with *my* name and address, but the pen in my purse didn't work. So I went into the grocery store to borrow a pen and while I was in there, he must have come back, because when I came out his car was gone. I feel just *terrible*. It was such a nice car. Shiny new paint. He must just hate me. Or what if his wife was driving it, if he has a wife? He'll probably blame her. If I just knew his address, I could send him a letter through the mail and offer to pay to fix it."

The receptionist was standing up, a kind smile on her face. "You wait right here, ma'am, I'll see what I can do."

To Iris's horror, the receptionist returned *with a police officer*. Was it illegal to ding someone's car and walk away without leaving a note? Iris felt faint with horror, but he just said, "I hear you want to make things right with some man with a red car?" There was nothing for it, so Iris swallowed hard and told the story again.

"Aw, let her have it," the police officer said, and the receptionist handed over a folded note. "Don't tell anyone we gave this to you, okay?"

"I won't. Thank you, I appreciate it so much," Iris said, and fled, clutching her purse hard enough that she thought her knuckles were probably bone white.

Back in the car, Leo laughed at the look on her face. "You got it! You did, I can tell. Let's see what Mr. Lucky's real name is. Or at least the name on his driver's license, which is probably also the name on his bank account." Iris unfolded the note and they looked at it. *Jason Beckett. 1 North Pine Circle, Xenia.* It had a phone number, too.

"Now what?" Iris said.

"Now we wait till the sun goes down the night before garbage day, and go dumpster-diving in Mr. Lucky's trash."

"This is why everyone should own a paper shredder."

Mr. Lucky lived in a gated community, as it turned out, but Iris was able to get them in by explaining to the security guard that she couldn't remember the house number or the phone number, but that Leo was taking her to her granddaughter's friend's house for her great-granddaughter's first birthday party. *Great-granddaughter. Well, if one of my grandchildren ever gets around to having children of their own, maybe I'll have one of those.* She couldn't remember the house number but she knew the street, it was Pine Circle, and her granddaughter had promised balloons out front, and maybe a banner . . . The guard waved her through. Once at Pine Circle, they found garbage cans sitting neatly out on the curb. Leo handled this part, popping the trunk open, then throwing the bags in and driving off before anyone saw them.

"Good party?" the security guard asked, seeing them again.

Iris shook her head, baffled. "I must have the address wrong . . ."

"She says she has it written down at home," Leo said. "We're going to go check." He squeezed her hand and the guard gave him an understanding nod.

They drove all the way back to Springfield, dumped the bags of actual garbage out by Iris's trash, and then hauled the sack of paper garbage inside to her dining room, where they could sort through it. To her chagrin, Iris found her own note, crumpled, mixed in with the rest of the paper. There were notes from others, as well—requests for itemized bills, pleas for more time to pay. "Quite the cottage industry," Leo murmured. Iris looked for envelopes with the addresses of other victims, but didn't find any.

"Bingo," Leo exclaimed, holding up a folded printout. It was a bank statement, complete with balances and account numbers. *High* balances: his checking account alone had $42,328.31 in it. Mr. Lucky's was the only name on the account. "We still need his signature," Leo said. They found it near the bottom of the pile: a faded carbon from a credit card charge.

Iris looked at the crumpled notes from the other "creditors." "Could we take this to the police?" she asked. "Would they do anything?"

"We *could* take it to the police," Leo said. "They'd probably be able to arrest him with this. Then the judge would let him out on bail, and off he'd go, and a week later he'd have a new name, and a new address, and a new post office box. He'd find a way to clean out his bank account on his way out of town. You'd never see your money again. Do you want to go to the police, or do you want to clean out Mr. Lucky?"

One thousand six hundred and fourteen dollars. Iris thought about it. "Clean him out," she said.

"Great. Next we're going to take advantage of the great institution of branch banking, where you can pick your geography and guarantee that the teller won't know your name. I'm going to be Mr. Lucky, and you're going to be my lovely bride, Petunia Smith."

"Aren't we going to have to sign something?"

"I'll handle all the forgery."

Iris looked at him dubiously. "You're younger than my son."

"I've been under a lot of stress lately, and I think that's aging me prematurely. Trust me. By tomorrow, I don't think anyone will raise an eyebrow when I say we're getting married."

The bank was heated much too warmly, Iris thought, sitting in the chair, clasping her purse. Leo's hair had gone snow-white overnight, and his face appeared drastically aged. They'd shaken hands with the banker. Leo had introduced himself as Jason Beckett and explained that he wanted to add Petunia to his account and make it joint. "We're getting married," he said with a conspiratorial smile. "This is my lovely bride, Petunia."

"Congratulations," the teller said warmly. "Petunia, you said?"

"I'm just so thankful my parents didn't name me Heliotrope," Iris said faintly.

"Well, we'll just need you to fill out some forms . . ." Out came the forms. Iris filled out the form as Petunia Smith, using a made-up address and Social Security number. *Surely they have Mr. Lucky's number on file; how is Leo planning to get that?*

"Ugh," Leo said as he was filling out his form, and put down his pen. "I'm having a senior moment here, I think. I can't remember my social."

The banker glanced at her computer screen. "I can give it to you if you can show me some photo ID," she said.

"No, that's okay, it's coming back to me now," he said with a broad smile, and filled out the rest of the form. Iris was perplexed for a moment, then remembered that he seemed to be able to read thoughts. *I wonder if he's reading my mind right now?* He glanced up with a raised brow for her, and then signed Mr. Lucky's signature with a flourish.

"I'll need to see some picture ID," the banker said when they were done. "It's just routine, you understand . . ."

Leo shook his head slowly, his eyes a little wide. "Neither of us drive," he said.

"Surely you have the state IDs for non-drivers . . ."

"I'm not in the habit of carrying it," Iris said.

"It's been a long time since I was carded," Leo said.

"Can't you just put it through anyway?" Iris said. "You know, we were really hoping to run off and get married *today.*" She leaned forward and in a whisper added, "Our children *don't approve.* We wanted to get this all taken care of before they could find out."

"Well, I . . ." The banker glanced at both of them. "Oh, all right. I'll just put down that you showed me State ID cards. You do *have* them, don't you? Okay."

Petunia's name added to the account, they left the bank and drove to a different branch, where Iris filled out another form to transfer nearly the entire balance of Mr. Lucky's account into yet another account. This time she went in by herself, but Leo gave her the account numbers and told her what to move where.

Finally, Leo dropped her off at home. "I'll be back tomorrow morning," he said. "We need to give the banks time to get the money actually moved over—right now it's just moved over on paper—and then we can withdraw the entire amount. We'll use cash, because that's untraceable. Can you be ready at around ten?"

"I surely can," she said.

The interior of her house was cool and a little dim; she fed Blossom and then turned on the TV. Thinking over the last couple of days, she alternated between nervous giggles and a rising sense of fear. *All that money.* Over forty-two thousand dollars. *Will they send me to jail, if they catch us? Will they let me tell the jury that he stole* my money first?

She could scarcely sleep that night. *My guilty conscience,* she thought. *I've been greedy. He only took sixteen hundred dollars from me. I stole . . .* She had to turn on the light to work out the exact sum. *Over twenty-six times what he stole from me. Well, if this works, maybe I'll try to figure out who else he stole from, and give the money to them.* She had no idea how she'd track down the other victims, but the thought comforted her enough to sleep.

She was ready for Leo by nine-thirty, and sat on her front porch, watching one of her neighbors setting out Halloween decorations: a plastic ghost, a witch crashing her broomstick into a tree, a giant grinning pumpkin that was inflated by a fan. The mail arrived, and the mailman gave her a wave. She looked at her watch: it was ten-thirty, and there was no sign of Leo. She picked up her mail to take it in the house, and saw an envelope with a hand-addressed label. It wasn't the handwriting of anyone in her family. She sat back down and opened it up.

My dear, dear Iris, the letter said. *Please accept my apologies for my failure to arrive this morning on schedule. I think I did warn you once that con men sometimes get conned by their partners, and that I only cheat the dishonest. And stealing a man's money is truly not an* honest *thing to do, even if he did steal from you first.*

A small sheaf of bills slipped out of the envelope and onto her lap, followed by a dime and three pennies. *I'm sure by now that you've started thinking about it, and don't really* want *most of that money, anyway. I have, however, enclosed one thousand six-hundred and fourteen dollars and thirteen cents. It is in unmarked bills and will get you in no trouble with your own bank.*

In case thinking this over starts to worry you at all, let me reassure you on a couple more points. The bank cameras were not working that day, and even if the banker who handled our account sees you at a later time, she will find you only faintly familiar—she won't remember you as the clever schemer who raided the account of one of their customers.

I do not think we'll meet again, but it has been a great pleasure knowing you, and an even greater pleasure working with you. By the way, this time next year, you will be a great-grandmother. Have a wonderful Halloween.

The letter was signed, *C.* She wondered if that was supposed to stand for Clinton, or if it stood for his real name.

Well. That was quite an adventure. She went to get Blossom's leash to take her out for a walk to the bank, to deposit her money. It was mostly in tens and twenties, but there was one crisp, new hundred-dollar bill. With a faint feeling of mischief—*someday, my ever-responsible daughter and son-in-law will have to go through these*—she attached the hundred dollar bill to the letter with a paper clip and then filed it away.

Won't this just make them wonder.

Author's Note

Iris is my real-life grandmother. In 2004, when she turned 80, I wrote this story as a birthday gift to her. The whole family went to Ohio to celebrate her birthday at Lake Hope State Park, and we read the story around the campfire one night, passing the manuscript around.

To my knowledge, Grammie never met an immortal con man, but much of the story is built from real details of her life, from her job at the FBI to the Airdale terrier Blossom. My Grampy doesn't appear as a character in the story, but he did in fact write her a love poem for each birthday and Valentine's Day, until the dementia stole his writing ability.

My Grammie moved to the Twin Cities a few years after I wrote this, and at the time of this writing is 92 years old and still living.

THE WALL

*I*t *was February of 1989, and I was a freshman in college. I* was sitting in the student center trying to do my Calculus homework and drink a cup of coffee, both of which were surprisingly hard, when someone pulled out the chair across from me and sat down. "Meghan," she said.

I looked up. She was *old*—not old like a senior, old like my mom. She actually looked kind of like my mom, and I bristled instinctively. "It's Maggie. Who are you?"

"I'd forgotten about the Maggie phase," she said, looking introspective. "I'm you. You, from the future."

I put down my pencil. ". . . Oh?" I said, wondering how this crazy person had found out my name. Maybe this was a non-traditional student doing a Psych class experiment. How do randomly chosen students respond to utterly implausible claims? "Uh. Why are you here?"

She leaned forward. "You should study abroad in the fall. In Germany. West Germany. In *Berlin*."

I blinked at her. "I don't speak German."

"All the more reason to go! You could *learn* German."

"But I already have my language requirement," I said. "In French."

"That is the sort of thing that Europeans mock Americans for. 'I already know one foreign language! That's practically *two* more than the average American!'"

That stung. I scowled at her. "Look. My mom didn't let me go to France last year. Even though we'd paid the *deposit*. And that was just a two-week trip with chaperones. And you think she's going to cheer-fully send me off on a study-abroad program?"

"You're eighteen now. How's she going to stop you?"

"She could *refuse to pay*," I said, incredulously.

"Dad would take your side," she said. "He feels guilty about not standing up to her about France."

I folded my arms, thinking about the fight with my mother and how my father wouldn't even *stay in the house* while we were arguing. It was sure nice to *think* he had a few regrets about that. "Mmm hmm. Why is it so important to you that I go to Berlin?"

"Because the Berlin Wall is going to fall this November. On the 9th."

Okay. This was clearly a joke. "The Berlin Wall is going to fall. This year. You even know the *day*. That's awesome. I can't wait. Now in the meantime, I should probably work on my Calculus homework."

She stood up to go, then turned back, her eyes narrowed in an expression that almost looked like something I'd seen in my own mir-ror. "You should just drop Calculus now," she said. "You're going to get a D."

She turned up again in May.

As weird as that first encounter was, I couldn't just put her out of my mind. Yes, she was probably a lunatic, but I did at least *think* about going to the study-abroad office to ask about studying in Ber-lin. The problem was when I imagined telling my parents I wanted to go abroad, it was the whole scene I found myself unspooling, com-plete with a migraine headache for my mother and a guilt trip from my father. It was usually my younger brother who defied Mom: I was the good girl. And I was *still* getting guilt trips for leaving Iowa for college, even though they'd gone along with it.

I finally stopped into the study-abroad office in April. It was too late to apply for a program in the *fall*, but I leafed through the bro-chures, filled with pictures of smiling students frolicking by the Eiffel

Tower, the Coliseum, giant golden Buddha statues, the Taj Mahal. I traced the Golden Buddha. Now, *that* would be something to see, if my mother ever chilled out.

I was more proactive with Calculus. When I couldn't get through the homework the crazy lady had interrupted, I concluded that *maybe* she was a Message from Somewhere that I ought to sign up for the free tutoring at the math skills center, and I headed there straight from the student center that afternoon.

The second time she came, she found me in the library. "Maggie?" she said, more hesitantly this time.

I looked up. "You, again? How'd you find me in here?"

"I remember my favorite library spots." She sat down next to me on the ugly orange couch.

I normally liked this spot because hardly anyone came to this section. Being pursued by a lunatic made me rethink the advantages of this strategy, but it seemed a bit premature to scream for Campus Security. "What do you want?"

"I want you to go to Germany. You didn't apply for a study-abroad program, did you?" I shook my head. "Well, that's okay. You can take a leave of absence in the fall, and just go."

"And tell Mom and Dad *what*, exactly?"

"Tell them you want to travel. Lots of students travel. You don't need their permission. There's actually a work visa program for American college students—you can get a work visa for six months in West Germany, so you wouldn't need their money."

"I'd go to West Germany and apply for a *job*?"

"Yeah, exactly."

"*I don't speak German.* What kind of job would I get, exactly?"

"You could teach English. Or—I don't know. You'd find something."

I gave her a look of disbelief. "Mom would have a nervous breakdown."

"At some point, you have to realize that her anxiety disorder is not *your* responsibility."

This was almost a word-for-word echo of something my high school best friend had said. I shot the woman a narrow-eyed look of my own. "Who are you, anyway? For real."

"I go by Meg. And I told you the truth. I'm you." She pulled something out of her pocket; it looked like a little like a calculator. "Here, I brought something to show you. This is my pocket computer."

I took it. It had a smooth, black surface. "It doesn't look very useful," I said.

"Put your thumb on the screen for a second. It's keyed to my fingerprints, which incidentally are the same as yours."

I did, and the black surface suddenly sprang to life, presenting me with rows of little pictures. "Does it have a mouse?"

"Your finger's the mouse. Tap on the icon you want."

I tapped on one randomly. It spit out a stream of music, and the orderly rows disappeared. The screen showed a cascade of images: a close-up of a snowy owl in flight, a wood landscape, and then the interior of a room with stone walls. Meg leaned over to look. "That's a game," she said. "It does useful stuff, too. When I'm in the future I can use it to get my e-mail—which everyone in the future has. I can use it to get on the Internet—almost all information is online in the future. It stores all my music, photos, and books. It's also a camera, a video camera, a credit card, a GPS—that's sort of like a talking atlas—and a phone."

I stared at it. The graphics were *amazing*. "When you took it out, I thought it was a calculator."

"It's a calculator, too."

"This is *really cool*," I said. "Can I keep this?"

"No. You have no way to recharge the battery, for one thing." She took it back. "*Now* can we have a serious conversation about getting you to Germany?"

"So does everyone in the future have a time machine, too?" I asked.

"No," she said, her gaze wavering a little. "No, mine is special."

I stared at the pocket computer and tried to imagine telling my parents that a woman from the future had told me to go to West Germany, and I *knew* she was from the future because she had *amazing futuristic technology* and even if I'd had the gadget with me I was pretty sure my mother would not be convinced.

"Okay," I said. "Here's the thing. I have to admit that you really might be from the future. If I'm going crazy, this is an awfully *detailed* hallucination. But."

"But?"

"I got a B+ in Calculus last term. You thought I was going to get a D!"

"You got a B?" she said incredulously. "A B *plus*? *How?*"

"Well, I went to the math skills center for extra help, and—"

"The *math skills center*," she said. "*Why* didn't I do that? I can't remember why I didn't even think to try that."

"Anyway," I said. "You've sort of undermined your credibility, you see. I think maybe you're from the future but we're actually from different time streams. Because I really can't believe the Berlin Wall is going to fall in less than six months. I mean, Gorbechev seems pretty cool and he's made some really amazing changes but Honecker—"

"Honecker's going to resign in October."

I stared at her skeptically. I'd started paying attention to the news after her first visit, and although there had been a lot of good news from the Soviet bloc, Honecker was really an asshole. And assholes with power rarely seemed to say "oh, hey, I've just realized something: *I'm an asshole.* Maybe I should resign!"

"He'll get sick," Meg said. "And Gorbechev can't stand him. He'll resign. *The Wall is going to fall and you can be there to see it.*"

"Here's the other thing: I have no money. 'Go to Germany,' you say, like I could just hitchhike there. I'd have to buy a plane ticket—"

"That's what credit cards are for."

"And I'd pay it off with *what*, exactly?"

"Your work-study earnings. It would be worth living with debt for a while if you could be there."

"I want to graduate in *four* years, not four and a quarter. Especially since I'm planning to do my student teaching the fall after I graduate. That's how it's set up. If I throw the schedule off I'll have to wait until the *following* fall."

"Oh, God," she said. "*Teaching*. Of course, you're planning around the *student teaching* calendar. Listen, you should just forget about it. You're going to *hate* teaching. I mean, you'll realize it during your student teaching year and then spend three or four years doing it anyway before you wise up and change careers. Really, if you pulled a B+ in Calc, just switch right now to an Econ major, it's going to be *so* much more useful to you later."

"Useful for what?" I said. "Am I destined to become an *investment banker* or something?"

"No, you're going to manage a non-profit focusing on public health. Econ would still be way more useful. At least take *statistics*. You can drop the Educational Studies stuff and take a bunch of Econ and Stats while you major in English."

"The only reason Mom isn't freaking out about the English major is that I'm doing the teaching concentration!"

"Maggie, *forget about what Mom wants*. You're a legal adult. You get to make your own choices!"

"Yeah? She's paying my tuition. What if she cuts me off?"

"She won't. She didn't cut my—she didn't cut *our* brother off for majoring in Theater, later."

"Robbie's going to major in *what?*"

"Yeah, and Mom threw a fit about it but she adjusted in the end. To everything." She sighed heavily and said, "At least *think* about it."

"Berlin, or my major?"

"Berlin," she said. "Your major, too. But mostly Berlin."

"Okay," I said, because it was clear this was the only way I would get rid of her. "I'll think about it."

She was crazy.

Or maybe I was crazy.

I didn't arrange for a leave of absence and I didn't buy any plane tickets. And I certainly didn't tell my parents about any of this. But when I packed to go back to college in August of 1989, I crept downstairs late one night and rooted through the filing cabinet with all the papers until I found my passport.

Meg knocked on my dorm room door in September. My roommate was out, which was actually a little disappointing, since it would have been nice to have some sort of external validation about the whole "I'm you from the future! Look at my futuristic technology!" routine.

I didn't invite her in, but she came in anyway and I sighed and closed the door behind her.

"Just go," she said. "Buy a ticket and go. Even if you fail your classes, it'll be worth it."

"I'm actually *taking statistics right now*," I said stonily. "So on one hand I should take statistics! It'll be so useful! When I'm a grownup! But never mind *that*, I should just fail all my classes and—"

"—*go to Berlin*, yes." She chewed her lip. "You could have taken the term off. I did *suggest* that."

"Yeah, well, I was actually looking forward to coming back in the fall, as it turned out."

She looked at me blankly and then recognition dawned in her eyes. "Peter. It's Peter, isn't it?"

"You know, for someone who claims to be me from the future, you don't seem to remember your own life very well."

She started pacing. "That's because I did my best to *forget* that I ever dated Peter. Oh my *God*, Maggie, he was the biggest mistake *ever*."

"Well, *you* might view him as a mistake, but *I* happen to like him!"

"He cheated on us. He gave us an *STD*, Maggie—oh, not that one," she said, when she saw me blanch. "Christ, if he'd given us AIDS I wouldn't be here because we'd probably have been dead before the better treatments started coming available. No, it was one of the curable-with-antibiotics kind. Thank God we didn't *marry* the son of a bitch. He's currently working part-time for cash to avoid paying his wife child support. In the future, I mean. He seems nice, sure, but he is an *ass*."

I sat down on my bed. "You know," I said. "When you were me, did you have some woman coming back from the future and giving you advice?"

"No," she said. "Or I never would have dated that stupid son of a bitch."

"Right," I said. "You got to *make your own goddamn mistakes* without some stranger from the future butting in. You know? If you'd had someone turning up and yelling 'oh, don't date that one! He'll give you an STD!' you might have wound up dating someone who was, oh, secretly gay—"

"Yeah, don't date Roger, either."

"I figured that one out for *myself*, thanks." I glared at her.

"Right. I should have remembered. Sorry."

"Look." I tried to calm myself down. "You seem like you'd really love to go to Berlin in 1989. You have a time machine so *why don't you just go there?*"

"Because," she said, through gritted teeth, "I can't go anywhere that's further than a quarter of a mile from *where you are*. Which in 1989 is *Northfield, Minnesota*."

"Why do you have to stay so close to me?"

"Because that is *how it works*. The time travel, I mean."

"Oh," I said. I felt bad, for a minute or two, and then I said, "Well, my point still stands. This is my life. I get to make my own mistakes. And I would like it if you'd stay out of them."

She stood up and walked to the door. Just before she left, she turned back. She looked like she was trying to hold back tears, but she smiled at me and said, "You're doing a good job of standing up for yourself. Try to use some of those assertiveness skills with Mom sometime. It would be good for both of you."

*

Erich Honecker was voted out of office by the Politburo on October 18th.

At that point, I started to think that maybe Crazy Meg was right.

You in the future, reading this, are probably thinking, *MAYBE she was right? MAYBE?* But you have to realize, it wasn't nearly as clear in October of 1989 what was about to happen. I'd signed up for German 1 on impulse (I hadn't said anything to Meg about that when she visited, because I was too pissed off about what she'd said about my boyfriend) and we spent some time in class discussing current events. On October 19th, one of my classmates said, "I can actually believe that the Berlin Wall is going to fall within my lifetime."

Within my lifetime. Not, you know, *early next month.*

Erich Honecker's resignation did not persuade me to run out and buy a ticket. I did go find out how much a ticket to Berlin would cost, but it was a lot more than I had in my bank account, and where the hell was I going to sleep once I got to Germany, anyway? The whole thing just seemed crazy once I was actually sitting in the travel agency office and I apologized for wasting the travel agent's time and left.

And then I went home and dumped Peter, because really, if Meg was right about Honecker, she was probably right about the STD.

On the first of November, I started watching for Meg, but she didn't come.

She didn't come on the second, either. I spent hours sitting around the student center, figuring that would make me easy to find. I tried the library. I tried the computer center, in case there was something about the time travel magic that meant she couldn't come the same place twice.

Meg hadn't told me what time on the 9th the Wall was going to fall (and really, what did she mean, *fall*? It was a huge, solidly-built, thoroughly reinforced wall; even an earthquake was unlikely to make much of a dent in it) but if I flew on the 7th, even with delays I ought to be there in time to see it. The 9th was going to be a Thursday, so I decided that it made sense to just stay until Sunday, the 12th, and fly back then.

I mean, that's what *would* make sense, if I went.

My parents expected me to call on Sundays. I could call them on the 4th and tell them that the 12th was going to be a really busy day for me and I might not call until late, or even Monday, and they wouldn't even have to know I'd been to West Germany until I'd come back.

The cheapest way to get to Berlin turned out to be convoluted: I had to fly from Minneapolis to Newark, Newark to Rome, and then Rome to Berlin. "I'm going to think about it," I said.

The travel agent looked at me, disappointed. "You should know that this is a really good fare and it won't last long. If you think for more than an hour or two it will probably be gone. That's how international fares work."

"Oh," I said, daunted.

"The fare if you fly KLM is more than twice as much."

It was $557.35 once you'd added the taxes and fees and so on. That didn't seem cheap to me, but when I considered how much the Paris program had cost . . . "Can you tell me where the cheapest place is to stay in West Berlin?"

"There are youth hostels that charge about $6 a night. In Deutsch Marks, of course. Have you ever traveled internationally before?"

"No."

"If you don't mind my asking, why are you so eager to go to West Berlin right now? There are many West German cities that are a lot more beautiful."

"I have a premonition that the Wall is going to fall next week," I said, wondering how crazy it would sound to say it out loud.

"Next *week*?" The travel agent raised her eyebrows and pursed her lips. "Well, if you're right, that should be really exciting. If you're wrong ... I don't think international travel is ever wasted." She smiled. "Do you want the ticket?"

Five hundred and fifty-seven dollars and thirty-five cents. I swallowed hard, but what was stopping me wasn't really putting that on my credit card, it was explaining it to my parents later. I knew someone who had five hundred dollars of debt on her credit card just from impulse purchases at the Renaissance Festival. Someone else who'd bought a computer. I'd asked around, you see, after that first abortive trip to the travel agency.

This is my life. Not my mother's.

I would have felt better if I could have gotten another pep talk from Meg. But I didn't see her outside the travel agency door, lurking. I was going to have to do this by myself.

I took a deep breath and put my credit card on the travel agent's desk. "Yes."

Meg turned up on the 5th.

"I brought money," she said. "You don't want to know what it took to get hold of a bunch of hundred-dollar bills that were printed in the 1980s, but I managed it."

"Awesome," I said. "I can deposit this in my bank account and use it to pay off my credit card bill when it comes."

She stood for a second like she hadn't quite heard me. "You're going to go?"

"I *bought my ticket.*" I'd been carrying it with me (out of fear I'd somehow misplace it), and I pulled it out and laid it on the table. "I'm flying on the 7th. Good enough?"

Meg stared down at my tickets in disbelief. "You are *awesome*, Maggie!"

"Are you allowed to say that? If I'm actually you?"

She shook her head. "You are so much more awesome than I ever was."

"How much money is this?"

"It's a thousand dollars even."

"I'll be able to stay somewhere nicer than a youth hostel, then!"

"I have a neighborhood in mind, once we get to Berlin. I'll have to meet you there." She grinned. "I managed money, but coming up with a passport with a current picture and an acceptable expiry date would have been a lot more tricky. Have you figured out what you're going to tell Mom?"

"I'm not going to tell her until I get back. I told all my teachers I have a premonition that the Berlin Wall's going to fall, and I want to see it happen. If I'm right they'll all let me make up what I miss."

She grinned at me wildly, and handed me the money. "I'll see you in Berlin."

Meg found me as I waited for the U-Bahn—the West Berlin subway train. "Do you have a plan?" she asked.

"I have a guidebook," I said, showing it to her. "Do you have a suggestion?"

"Forty years from here I'd know right where to go. In 1989 . . . Kreuzberg. That's the neighborhood near Checkpoint Charlie."

The streets of Kreuzberg didn't look like how I pictured West Germany. It was a poor neighborhood, with a huge population of immigrants. "Forty years from now, this is one of the trendiest neighborhoods in Berlin," she said.

I looked around. "Are you saying I should invest in real estate?"

She laughed. "Is it ethical to ask for investment advice from the future?"

"I don't know. It probably depends on how certain you are I'm heading to the same future you live in."

"Fair enough. Apple stock: buy in the early 1990s. It'll be cheap and everyone will tell you you're nuts. And then *stick with it.* It's not until the early 2000s it'll start bouncing back. Also, if you get a chance to invest in Google, do it. "

"Isn't Googol a one followed by a hundred zeros?"

"In 1989, yes." We stopped at a traffic light and I adjusted my backpack. "Of course, maybe I've stepped on a butterfly while I've been here and when you get to the future, everyone will use Amigas. I wouldn't count on it, though."

We found a clean, cheap hotel and checked in. "You can take a nap if you want," Meg said. "You'll be up all night on the 9th so if you don't switch to German time it's probably just as well."

"Are you *kidding me?*" I said. "I'm in *West Germany* and you want me to take a *nap?* You'd probably have suggested I spent my layover in Rome napping, too."

"You had a layover in Rome?" she said, surprised.

"Yes, and I went and saw the Coliseum." I opened the dresser drawer and emptied most of my backpack into it, changed into a clean shirt, and then put my much-lighter backpack back on. Now that I'd committed to the adventure, instead of feeling terrified—as I'd expected—I was feeling *utterly exhilarated.* "West Berlin has sights. Do you want to come?"

"I have to," she said. "If you get more than a quarter mile from me I go back to the future."

I'll spare you the catalog of places I went that day, except for one: the Wall. It was, Meg pointed out, our last chance to see it that way. There was a spot with an observation platform so we could look over, and Meg and I stared across the border.

The Wall was shocking to look at. On the western side, it was covered in graffiti. On the eastern side, the tall buildings near the Wall had their west-facing windows bricked over, to ensure no one tried to jump to freedom. There had been huge protests in East Berlin for days, but nothing we could see from where we stood. When we passed Checkpoint Charlie, Meg prodded me to take a picture of the sign that said YOU ARE NOW LEAVING THE AMERICAN SECTOR. I could have gone to East Berlin—they would issue a visa for a quick trip quite readily—but Meg had no passport, so we didn't.

The evening of the 9th, Meg was jumpy, and kept looking at her watch, like she thought the Wall might collapse while she wasn't paying attention. "They aren't actually going to tear it down for another week or two," she said. "Tonight's when the border opens."

Meg checked her watch while we were eating dinner. "The news conference is happening about now," she remarked.

"Is this something we can watch?"

"No. It'll be aired on West German TV in a bit. Gunther Schabowski—the Politburo spokesman—is giving a news conference. He's going to read a note he was handed earlier, which he didn't quite understand, that says revisions have been made to the travel laws that will make it possible for any citizen to exit at any border crossing. One of the journalists will ask him when this goes into effect and he will say 'immediately.'" She checked her watch again. "About an hour from now there will be wire stories saying that the Berlin Wall has been opened."

"Has it?"

"No. That will happen a little before midnight."

I looked out the window at the calm, chilly night, and wondered how dumb I'd feel about all this if she was wrong.

Back in our hotel room, we watched a soccer match. When it was done, the evening news came on. I couldn't follow it, but Meg translated: the lead story was about the news conference. They showed a clip of a man in a gray suit peering through glasses at a note, and then cut to images of the Wall, which still looked deserted. "This is how the East Berliners will hear about it," Meg said. "They're not supposed to watch the West German news, but everyone does anyway."

We put our coats back on and walked back to Checkpoint Charlie. West Berliners were gathering, though not many yet. From the east side, we could hear an announcement through a loudspeaker. The noise from the other side grew as the crowd swelled. There was chanting—*Open the gate, Open the gate.* No gunfire. Yet.

There was a sense of breathless anticipation among the West Germans, and more than a little fear, as the crowd on the other side grew. The East Berliners were packed in against the gate, and if the guards opened fire it would be a bloodbath—the first casualties would be to bullets, the next casualties would be to the stampede.

Open the gate. Open the gate.

Beside me, Meg gripped my hand.

At 10:45, the East German border guards at the Bornholmer Strasse checkpoint gave up: they opened the gate, and let the East Berliners flood through. The other checkpoints followed suit within minutes.

Where you are, in the future, this isn't a surprise. Because November 9th, 1989, is for you the night the Wall came down. If you're my age, you watched the TV footage. If you're younger than me, you probably still watched the TV footage but you watched it on some archive, maybe on your pocket computer, maybe for History class.

I was there.

The first people through looked utterly stunned with disbelief. They'd been some of the first to the border crossing: if the guards had panicked and opened fire, they'd have died in a hail of bullets, unable to retreat because of the crowds behind them. They'd spent hours not knowing what was going to happen, and now—now they were being grabbed in hugs and handshakes by West Germans who were crying with joy. They were being handed glasses of champagne and mugs of beer and bouquets of flowers and West German money so that they could go buy their *own* beer and champagne and flowers.

People were crying and singing (and drinking, of course) and taking pictures and cheering.

At some point a group of West Germans about my age climbed up on top of the Wall; this seemed like a good idea and both Meg and

I scrambled up with them. A group of East Germans climbed up to join us. Someone had music and we all danced together in an amazing dance party of joy and freedom, and I knew: even if I failed every class and my parents disowned me, *this moment was worth it.*

I looked at Meg, to tell her so, and I noticed that she was craning her neck to look for someone, her face dark with worry. Then the clouds cleared as she seized hold of a young man who'd been dancing a few feet away. "Come," she said to him in German clear enough that even I could understand. "Let's go somewhere in West Berlin, an all-night cafe, maybe. I'll buy us a midnight snack."

His name was Gregor, he was an East Berliner, and he spoke English, although it was halting and heavily accented. He was nineteen, like me, and he wanted to ask me questions about the U.S. and what I was doing in Germany, which would have been difficult to explain even without the language barrier.

Meg didn't talk much. Mostly, she stared at Gregor. I couldn't quite unpack the look on her face, but she was gripping her hands together very tightly as he ate. (He was ravenous, actually; he'd been about to eat a late dinner when the news came on, and he'd headed to the border crossing without food. And then been stuck there in the crowd for hours.)

"Gregor," Meg said abruptly, as he was finishing his sandwich. "I need you to make me a promise."

"Oh?"

"Promise me that you will never take up smoking."

It was such a random request that I started laughing, and Gregor looked at me and said, in English, "Who *is* this? Is she your mother?"

"She's from from the future," I said. "She makes predictions."

Gregor didn't seem to entirely understand this but he gave her a bemused look and said, "Can you make a prediction?"

"Yes," she said, sharply. "East and West Germany will unify on October 3rd, 1990. And if you start smoking, you will be dead before you're 45." She stood up abruptly. "Excuse me." She strode off toward the bathroom.

Gregor gave me a look of wide-eyed hilarity. "Thank you very much for the meal," he said. "If the border stays open and I can come again, I would like to see you again but I am not so sure about your friend!"

"I can't say I blame you," I said.

He scribbled down his address in East Berlin on a napkin and then asked, "Can I look for you here at this restaurant? Tomorrow night? How long are you staying in Germany?"

"I have a ticket to go home on Sunday. I'll come here tomorrow night," I said. "I'll wait for you."

"Yes," he said, an incandescent smile lighting his face. "You wait for me. Your friend, see if you can persuade her to see the sights!"

"That's a really good idea," I said, grinning.

Meg came back a few minutes later, red-eyed, and silently paid the bill. We walked back to our hotel in silence.

In our room, I said, "You know him."

"Yes."

"He's the person you really came back to find."

She was staring at the wall of the hotel room, her face fixed. "Yes."

"*All* of this—talking me into coming, paying for my ticket—was really about Gregor."

"Yes."

"*Why?*"

"Because I wanted to see him. One last time."

In the future, Meg and Gregor had met when they were forty. Too late for kids, she said, and when I made a face she laughed softly and didn't pursue it. They'd met at work, at the public health non-profit she'd mentioned; she'd been in policy, he'd been doing some sort of research. It had been a wild and intense romance, and they'd married just four months after they met. "Mom had a *conniption*, of course," she said, "but I did at some point learn to just ignore those."

But then Gregor died, at 44, of lung cancer. It was, Meg was *certain*, because of the cigarettes.

"So what if introducing us now was a mistake?" I said. "What if, by throwing us at each other here, now, today, we annoy the *piss* out of each other and we won't want anything to do with each other when we meet at 40, if we even do?"

"I thought about that," Meg said. "But I decided if I could talk him into not smoking, if he could have a long life . . . it would be worth it. Even if he had that life with someone else."

I thought about Gregor, and that brief glimpse we'd had of each other. I could certainly imagine *sleeping* with him. It was hard to imagine *marrying* anybody, but not any harder than it was to imagine myself as old as Meg.

"We used to fantasize about meeting . . . here," she said, waving her hand at West Berlin, out our window. "I mean, I really *did* have a premonition, actually, that the Wall was going to fall. Everyone else said 'maybe someday!' and I was thinking, *It's going to happen. It's going to happen really soon.* I thought about coming . . . but I didn't. Because of the money, because of Mom . . . anyway. He was here, of course, and he told me about it: waiting those dark hours at the gate, dancing on the wall, how *hungry* he was! I knew if I could find him, all I'd have to do was offer him some dinner and he'd follow me anywhere. I didn't really think . . . past that."

"And so that's what you did."

"It wasn't like I imagined," she said, her voice a little hollow. "It's him, and it's not him, and seeing him like this . . ."

"Especially since he looks at you, and sees someone the age of his mother."

"Well, yes and no. He looks at *you* and he sees . . ."

"Just stop," I said. "Don't mess with my head any more than you've already done."

She fell silent.

"Where did you get the time machine, anyway?" I said. "Meddling with the past can't possibly be legal."

"Well, it doesn't change anything for us, you know. My Calculus grade will always be a D."

"And Gregor will stay dead for you?"

"Yes. He's dead in my world."

"You came all this way . . ."

She shrugged. "It was Gregor who built it. His last project. It seemed fitting . . . to use it to go to him." She gave me a crooked smile. "This is my last visit. You won't see me again until, one day, you'll see me in your mirror."

"*There's* a terrifying thought."

She walked over to the door, but then turned back, her hand on the knob. "Your future is *yours*, you know. Whatever you make of it. With whomever you choose." She hoped I'd choose Gregor, and have him for longer; I could see it in her eyes, but she managed to keep from saying it out loud, and just gave me a final bright-eyed smile. She closed the door behind her.

I waited a few minutes—I wanted to give her time to get a quarter-mile away. Then I put my coat on, and went back out to party at the Wall.

<u>Author's Note</u>

Years ago, my mother mentioned that she'd seen the advertisements for the Woodstock Music Festival, and it wasn't all that far from where she was living—road-trip distance—so she'd briefly considered going. But she only liked a couple of the bands, so she concluded it wouldn't have been worth the trip.

"You missed the defining event of your generation because you didn't *like the bands?" I said, aghast.*

"Well, no one told me it was going to be the defining event of my generation," she said. "If I'd known that, of course I'd have gone!"

I told my children this story and at some point my older daughter asked me what the defining event of my *generation was. "The Fall of the Berlin Wall," I said.*

"Would you have gone to see that?" she asked.

I was actually in high school when the Berlin Wall fell. My husband and quite a few of my friends are a little older than I am, though . . . but none of them saw it coming, which isn't at all surprising. You really would need a time traveler to tip you off. A very very persuasive time traveler. "I can actually believe the Berlin Wall will fall within my lifetime," is something my husband remembers thinking less than two weeks before it actually happened.

SO MUCH COOKING

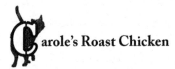arole's Roast Chicken

This is a food blog, not a disease blog, but of course the rumors all over about bird flu are making me nervous. I don't know about you, but I deal with anxiety by cooking. *So much cooking.* But, I'm trying to stick to that New Year's resolution to share four healthy recipes (entrées, salads, sides . . .) for every dessert recipe I post, and I *just* wrote about those lemon meringue bars last week. So even though I dealt with my anxiety yesterday by baking another batch of those bars, and possibly by eating half of them in one sitting, I am *not* going to bake that new recipe I found for pecan bars today. No! Instead, I'm going to make my friend Carole's amazing roast chicken. Because how better to deal with fears of bird flu than by eating a bird, am I right?

Here's how you can make it yourself. You'll need a chicken, first of all. Carole cuts it up herself but I'm lazy, so I buy a cut-up chicken at the store. You'll need *at least* two pounds of potatoes. You'll need a lemon and a garlic bulb. You'll need a big wide roasting pan. I use a Cuisinart heavy-duty lasagna pan, but you can get by with a 13x9 cake pan.

Cut up the potatoes into little cubes (use good potatoes! The yellow ones or maybe the red ones. In the summer I buy them at the Farmer's Market.) Spray your pan with some cooking spray and toss in the potatoes. Peel all the garlic (really, all of it!) and scatter the whole cloves all through with the potatoes. If you're thinking, "all that garlic?" just trust me on this. Roasted garlic gets all mild and melty and you can eat it like the potato chunks. Really. You'll thank me later. Finally, lay out the chicken on top, skin-down. You'll turn it halfway through cooking. Shake some oregano over all the meat and also some sea salt and a few twists of pepper.

Squeeze the lemon, or maybe even two lemons if you really like lemon, and mix it in with 1/4 cup of olive oil. Pour that over everything and use your hands to mix it in, make sure it's all over the chicken and the potatoes. Then pour just a tiny bit of water down the side of the pan—you don't want to get it on the chicken—so the potatoes don't burn and stick. Pop it into a 425-degree oven and roast for an hour. Flip your chicken a half hour in so the skin gets nice and crispy.

Guys, it is SO GOOD. Half the time I swear Dominic doesn't even notice what he's eating, but he always likes this dish, and so do I. If you make this much for two people, you'll have leftovers for lunch. But we're having guests over tonight, my brother and his wife and kids. So, I'm actually using two chickens and four pounds of potatoes, because teenagers eat a lot.

And chicken has magical healing properties if you make it into soup, so surely some of them stick around when you roast it? And so does garlic, so eat some and *stay healthy.*

xxoo, Natalie

Substitute Chip Cookies

So, we have some unexpected long-term house guests.

My sister-in-law Kathleen is a nurse at Regions Hospital. She's not in the ER or the infectious diseases floor but let's face it, it's not like you can corral a bunch of airborne viruses and tell them they're banned from OBGYN. Leo and Kat are worried that if this bird flu thing is the real deal, she could bring it home. Leo's willing to take his chances but when I said, "would you like to have the kids stay with me for a while," Kat said, "That would make us both feel so much better," so voila, here I am, hosting an 11-year-old and a 13-year-old. Monika is 13, Jo is 11.

We have a guest room and a sofa bed. Monika got the guest room, Jo's on the sofa bed, although we promised to renegotiate this in a few days if they're still here. (It's actually a double bed in the guest room but trust me, you don't want to make my nieces share a bed if you don't absolutely have to.)

I went to the store today to stock up just in case we want to minimize the "leaving the house" stuff for a while. Apparently I wasn't the only person who had that thought because (a) the lines were unbelievable and (b) I tried *four stores* and they were *all* completely out of milk and eggs. I did manage to get an enormous jumbo package of toilet paper plus a huge sack of rat food (did I mention that Jo has a pet rat named Jerry Springer? I didn't? Well, my younger niece Jo has a pet rat named Jerry Springer. The rat was not actually invited along for the family dinner, but Dominic ran over today to pick the rat up because he thought Jo would feel better about the whole situation if she had her pet staying here, too.)

The freezer section was also incredibly picked over but at the Asian grocery (store #4) I bought some enormous sacks of rice and also about fifteen pounds of frozen dumplings and you know what, I'm not going to try to list what I came home with as it would be too embarrassing. I'll just stick to the essentials, which is, *no milk and no eggs*. I did manage to get some butter, but it was the super-fancy organic kind that's $10 per pound so I was also a little worried about using up our butter reserve on one batch of cookies. And Jo really wanted chocolate chip cookies.

Okay, actually: *I* really wanted chocolate chip cookies. But Jo was very willing to agree that she wanted some, too.

You can substitute mayo for eggs, in cookies, and you can substitute oil for the butter. They'll be better cookies if you happen to have some sesame oil to put in for part of the oil (or any other nut-related oil) and we did, in fact, have sesame oil. And as it happens, those four grocery stores were *not* out of chocolate chips.

Here's the recipe in case you are also improvising today:

2 1/2 cups flour

1 tsp baking soda

1 tsp salt

1 cup of vegetable oils (preferable 2 T sesame oil + canola oil to equal 1 cup.)

3/4 cup white sugar

3/4 cup brown sugar

1 tsp vanilla extract

6 tablespoons of mayonnaise

12 ounces of whatever sort of chips you have in the house, or chopped up chocolate

Cream the sugar and the oil, then beat in the mayonnaise. I *promise* the cookies will turn out fine, no matter how gross the mayo smells and looks while you're beating it in. Mix the baking soda, salt, and flour together, then gradually beat in the mayo mixture, and stir in your chips.

Drop by rounded spoonfuls—oh, you know how to make cookies. You don't have to grease your cookie sheets. Bake at 375F for about ten minutes and if you want them to stay chewy and soft, put them away in an airtight container before they're all the way cool. If you like your cookies crunchy, well, what's wrong with you? But in that case cool them before you put them away, and in fact you'll probably be happier storing them in something that's not airtight, like a classic cookie jar.

I gave Dominic the first batch and he said, "you didn't use up all the butter on this, did you?" I told him we're not about to run out of butter. We are, however, about to run out of coffee. I may die. Even if I don't get bird flu. Excuse me, H5N1.

xxoo, Natalie

Homemade Pizza

So, how are things where *you* live?

Where *I* live (Minneapolis) there have been 83 confirmed cases of H5N1. The good news (!!!) is that it's apparently not as lethal in the human-to-human variant as it was back when it was just birds-to-human, but since it was 60% lethal in the old form that's not really what I think of as *good* good news. The bad news is that there's a four-day incubation period so those 83 people all infected others and this is only the tiny, tiny tip of a giant, lethal iceberg.

Probably wherever you live you're hearing about "social distancing," which in most places means "we're going to shut down the schools and movie theaters and other places where folks might gather, stagger work hours to minimize crowding, and instruct everyone to wear face masks and not stand too close to each other when they're waiting in lines." In Minneapolis, they're already worried enough that they're saying that anyone who can just stay home should go ahead and do that. Since Dominic works in IT and can telecommute, that's us. I'd planned to go to the store today again to maybe get milk and eggs. If it had been just me and Dominic . . . I still wouldn't have risked it. But I *definitely* wasn't going to risk it with Jo and Monika in the house.

I made homemade pizza for lunch. The same recipe I made last December right after I got the pizza stone for Christmas—but, no fresh mushrooms. We had a can of pineapple tidbits and some pepperoni so that's what we topped it with. I thought about trying some of the dried shitake mushrooms on the pizza but on thinking about it I didn't think the texture would work.

We are now completely out of milk, which makes breakfast kind of a problem, and we're also out of coffee, which makes *everything about my day* kind of a problem. Fortunately, we still have some Lipton tea bags (intended for iced tea in the summer) and that's what I used for my caffeine fix.

(Running out of coffee was pure stupidity on my part. I even remember seeing it on the shelf at the grocery store, but I'm picky about my coffee and I was planning to go to my coffee shop for fresh beans today. Ha ha ha! Folgers and Maxwell House sound pretty good to me now!)

xxoo, Natalie

Eggless Pancakes and Homemade Syrup

In the comments on my last post, someone wanted to know about grocery delivery. We *do* have grocery delivery in the Twin Cities, but every single store that offers it is currently saying that they are only providing it to current customers. I did register an account with all the places that do it, and I've put in an Amazon order for a bunch of items you can have delivered (like more TP) and I'm hoping they don't e-mail me back to say they ran out and cancelled my order... anyway, I don't know if I'll be able to order anything grocery-like anytime soon.

Some of the restaurants in town are still delivering food and I don't know how I feel about that. Dominic and I are very lucky in that we do have the option of staying home. That makes me feel a little guilty, but in fact, me going out would not make the people who still *have* to go out, for their jobs, even one tiny bit safer. Quite the opposite. If I got infected, I'd be one more person spreading the virus. (Including to my nieces.) Anyway, Kat has to go out because she's a labor and delivery nurse, and people are depending on her. But I don't know if a pizza delivery guy should really be considered essential personnel.

In any case, no one delivers breakfast (which was what I sat down to write about) and no one's going to bring me milk, so I made milk-less, egg-less, butter-less pancakes, and so can you. Here's what you need:

    2 cups of flour
    4 tsp baking powder
    1 tsp salt

Blend that together and then add:

1/2 cup of pureed banana OR pureed pumpkin OR apple
   sauce OR any other pureed fruit you've got around. I used
   banana because I have some bananas in my freezer.

1 1/2 cups of water

1 tsp vanilla extract

1/2 tsp cinnamon

1/2 cup sugar

Whisk it all together. You'll need to grease your skillet a little bit extra because this sticks more than pancakes that were made with butter or oil.

We're out of maple syrup, but it turned out we still had a bottle of blueberry syrup in the back of a cabinet and that's what we had with them. There are recipes online for homemade pancake syrup but I haven't tried them yet. Monika hated the blueberry syrup and just ate them with sugar and cinnamon. Jo thought the blueberry syrup was fine but agreed that maple (or even fake maple) would be better. (I'm with Monika, for the record.)

xxoo, Natalie

Miscellaneous Soup

So, before we get to the recipe today, I was wondering if people could do a favor for one of my friends. Melissa is a waitress, and so far *thank God* she is still healthy but her restaurant has shut down for the duration. So, it's good that she's not going to be fired for not coming in to work, and she's glad to stay home where she's safe, but she *really needs that job* to pay for things like her rent. Anyway, I talked her into setting up a GoFundMe and if you could throw in even a dollar, that would be a big help. Also, to sweeten the pot a little, if you donate anything (even just a dollar!) I'll throw your name into a hat and draw one reader and that lucky reader will get to have me make, and eat, and blog, *anything you want*, although if you want me to do that before the pandemic is over you'll be stuck choosing from the stuff I can make with the ingredients that are in my house. And, I just drove a carload of groceries over to Melissa because she and her daughter were basically out of food, and the food shelves are not running, either. (So, if you were thinking that blueberry-glazed carrots or something would be good, you're already too late, because she is now the proud owner of that bottle of blueberry syrup. Also, I'm out of carrots.)

Anyway, go donate! If you've ever wanted me to try again with the Baked Alaska, or experiment with dishwasher salmon, *now's your chance.*

Today, I made Miscellaneous Soup. That is the soup of all the miscellaneous things you have lying around. I actually make this quite often, but I've never blogged about it before, because I just don't think most people would be very impressed. Ordinarily, I make it with stock (boxed stock, if I don't want to waste my homemade stock on this sort of meal), and some leftover cooked meat if I've got it, and whatever vegetables are in the fridge, and either some canned beans or some noodles or both.

What I used today:

> 2 packets of ramen noodles, including their little flavoring satchet
>
> Wine (we are not even close to being out of wine. Too bad it's not very good poured over breakfast cereal.)
>
> 1/2 pound of frozen roast corn
>
> 1/4 pound of frozen mixed vegetables
>
> 2 cups dry lentils
>
> 1/2 pound of frozen turkey meatballs

I heated up 4 cups of water and added the flavoring packet, 1 cup of wine, and the lentils. From my spice drawer, I also added some cumin and coriander, because I thought they'd go reasonably well with the spice packet. I cooked the lentils in the broth. I thawed out the corn and the mixed veggies and threw that in and then cooked the turkey meatballs in the oven because that's what the bag wants you to do and then I broke up the ramen brick and threw that in and added the meatballs. And that's what we all had for dinner.

Jo hates lentils and Monika didn't like the frozen roast corn but after some complaining they ate it all anyway. And Andrea and Tom liked it fine.

Right, I guess I should fill you in about Andrea and Tom.

Andrea is a friend of Monika's from school; they're both in 8th grade. Monika found out (I guess from a text?) that Andrea was home alone with her brother, Tom, because their mother is so worried about bringing the flu home that she's been sleeping in the car instead of coming home. Tom is only three. Also, they were totally out of food, which is why Monika brought this up (after I did the grocery drop off for Melissa.)

I told her that *of course* we could bring some food over to her friend, but when I realized Andrea was taking care of a three-year-old full time I suggested they come over here, instead.

So now Monika and Jo *are* sharing the double bed in the guest room, because sorry, girls, sometimes "shared sacrifice" means a shared bed. Andrea is on the sofabed and Tom is on the loveseat. Well, he was on the loveseat last night. I think tonight he's going to be on the loveseat cushions and those cushions are going to be on the floor so he's got less far to fall if he rolls off again.

Can I just say, this is not exactly how I'd imagined my February. But at least we're all healthy and not out of food yet.

xxoo, Natalie

Ten Things I'm Going to Make When This Is Over

Dinner today was hamburger and rice. I kept looking at recipes and crying, and Dominic wound up cooking.

I kind of want to tell you all the things we're out of. Like, AA batteries. (I had to track down a corded mouse from the closet where we shove all the electronic stuff we don't use anymore, because my cordless mouse uses AA batteries.) Dishwasher detergent. (We still have dish soap, but you can't put that in a dishwasher. So we're washing everything by hand.) But you remember when we used to say, "first-world problems" about petty complaints? These are healthy-person problems.

We got a call today that Kat is sick. She's been working 16-hour shifts because some of the other nurses are sick and some of them were refusing to come in and they *needed* nurses because the babies have still been coming, because they're going to just keep doing that. Literally everyone is in masks and gloves all the time, but—today she's running a fever.

Leo says she's not going to go into the hospital because there isn't anything they can really do for you anyway, especially as overloaded as they are. She's just going to stay at home and drink fluids and try to be one of the 68% who've been making it through.

So yeah, I wasn't going to tell you about that when I sat down, I was going to tell you all about the things I've been craving that I'm going to make when all this is over but I guess what I really want to say is that the top ten things I want to make when all this is over are ten different flavors of cupcake for Kat, because Kat loves my cupcakes, and if you're into prayer or good thoughts or anything like that, please send some her way.

There's still time to donate to Melissa and choose something to have me make. But, seriously, you'll want to wait until this is over because there's just not much in the house.

Kale Juice Smoothies (Not Really)

Dear crazy people who read my blog,
I know—well, I'm pretty sure—that you're trying to be helpful.
But telling me that all my sister-in-law (the mother of my nieces!) needs to do to recover is drink kale juice smoothies with extra wheatgrass and whatever else was supposed to go in your Magic Im-

mune Tonic? *Not helpful.* First of all, she's sick with a disease with a 32% fatality rate. Second of all, *even if* kale or kelp or whatever it was was *magic,* have you actually been reading my blog? We are eating rice, with flavored olive oil, for fully half our meals now. Today we mixed in some dry Corn Flakes, partly for the textural variety but partly just because we could make less rice because we're starting to worry that we're going to run out of that, too.

I can produce a kale smoothie for Kat like I can pull a live, clucking chicken out of my ass and make her some chicken soup with it.

Also, this is a food blog, not a conspiracy theory blog. If you want to try to convince people that the government is infecting everyone on purpose toward some nefarious end, go do it somewhere else.

No love,
Natalie

Rabbit Stew

There are these rabbits that live in our yard. I swear we have like six. They're the reason I can't grow lettuce in my garden. (Well, that plus I'd rather use the space for tomatoes.)

I am pretty sure I could rig up a trap for it with items I have around the house and bunnies are delicious.

Pros:
- Fresh meat!

Cons:
- Dominic thinks it's possible we could get influenza from eating the bunny. (I think he's being paranoid and as long as we cook it really well we should be fine. I could braise it in wine.)
- I have no actual idea how to skin and gut a rabbit, but I have sharp knives and the Internet and I'm very resourceful.

- Jo is aghast at the idea of eating a bunny.
- We'd probably catch at most one rabbit, and one rabbit
  split between all these people isn't very much rabbit.

It's even more people now, because we've added another kid. (You can feel free to make a Pied Piper joke. Or a crazy cat lady joke. We are making *all the jokes* because it's the only stress release I've got remaining to me.) Arie is twelve, and came really close to being driven back to his cold, empty apartment after he suggested we eat Jo's rat. (If he were just out of food, we could send him home with food, but the heat's also gone out, the landlord's not answering the phone, and it's February and we live in Minnesota.)

Arie is Andrea's cousin. Or, hold on, I take it back. Maybe he's her cousin's friend? You know what, I just didn't ask that many questions when I heard "twelve" and "no heat."

xxoo, Natalie

This is no longer a food blog

This is a boredom and isolation blog.

Also a stress management blog. Normally, I manage stress by cooking. Except we're out of some key ingredient for like 85% of the recipes I can find, and also out of all the obvious substitutes (or nearly) and I'm starting to worry that we will actually run out of food altogether. I've pondered trying to reverse-engineer flour by crushing the flakes of the Raisin Bran in my food processor, like some very high-tech version of Laura Ingalls grinding up unprocessed wheat in a coffee mill in *The Long Winter*.

My cute little bungalow is very spacious for me and Dominic. For me, Dominic, and five kids ranging in age from three to thirteen, it's starting to feel a little cramped. Monika brought a laptop and she, Arie, and Andrea all want turns using it. (Jo doesn't ask very often, she just sighs a martyred sigh and says no it's *fine* she *understands* why the big kids are hogging the computer.) We are thoroughly expert on the streaming movies available on every online service but the problem is, if it's appropriate for Tom to watch, the big kids mostly aren't interested. We did find a few old-timey musicals that everyone could tolerate but now Tom wants to watch them over and over and Andrea says if she has to listen to "the hiiiiiiiiiills are aliiiiiiiiive with the sound of muuuuuuuuuuusic" one more time she might smash the TV with a brick.

We have a back yard and from an influenza infection standpoint it's reasonably safe to play back there, but it's February in Minnesota and we're having a cold snap, like yesterday morning it was -30 with the wind chill. (The good news: the cold temperatures might slow the spread of the virus.)

So here's what we did today: I had some craft paints in the basement, and brushes, so we pulled all the living room furniture away from the wall and I let them paint a mural. The good news: this kept them happily occupied all afternoon. The even better news: they're not done yet.

xxoo, Natalie

Birthday Pancake Cake

Today is Jo's birthday, and everyone almost forgot. In part because she clearly expected that everyone had more important things on their mind and wasn't going to bring it up. Monika, bless her cranky thirteen-year-old heart, remembered.

I thought at first we were not going to be able to bake her a cake. (Unless I really could figure out a way to turn cereal flakes into usable flour, and probably not even then.) But—when I went digging yesterday for the craft paint in the basement, I found this small box of just-add-water pancake mix with our camping equipment. If I'd remembered it before now, I totally would've turned it into breakfast at some point, so thank goodness for absent-mindedness. We also still had a package of instant butterscotch pudding mix, un-used since you really can't make instant pudding without milk.

The other kids took a break from painting the mural and instead made decorations out of printer paper, scissors, and pens. (They made a chain-link streamer.)

I think there's got to be a way to turn pancake mix into a proper cake, but all the methods I found online needed ingredients I didn't have. So I wound up making the pancake mix into pancakes, then turning the pancakes into a cake with butterscotch frosting in between layers (to make butterscotch frosting, I used some melted butter—we still had a little left—and some oil, and the butterscotch pudding mix.)

And we stuck two votive candles on it and sang.

Jo did get presents, despite my cluelessness. The mail is still coming—some days—and her father remembered. A big box full of presents ordered from online showed up late in the day, signed "with love from Mom and Dad," which made her cry.

We've been getting updates on Kat, which mostly I haven't been sharing because they haven't been very good. We're just trying to soldier on, I guess. And today that meant celebrating Jo's birthday.

It Feels Like Christmas

You guys, YOU GUYS. We're going to get a food delivery! Of something! Maybe I should back up and explain. The local Influenza Task Force arranged for the grocery stores with delivery services to hire on a whole lot more people, mostly people like Melissa whose jobs are shut down, and they're now staffed well enough to do deliveries nearly everywhere. Everyone was assigned to a grocer, and since we have eight people living here (oh, did I mention Arie *also* had a friend who needed somewhere quarantined to stay? We are *full up* now, seriously, the bathroom situation is beyond critical already and we've been rotating turns to sleep on the floor) we're allowed to buy up to $560 worth of stuff and it should arrive sometime in the next few days. They've instructed us not to go out to meet the delivery person: they'll leave it on our doorstep and go.

Of course, the problem is that they are out of practically everything. Minneapolis is such a hot spot, a lot of delivery drivers don't want to come here, plus things are such a mess in California that not much produce is going anywhere at all, so there was no fresh produce of any kind available. I was able to order frozen peaches—though who knows if they'll actually bring any. Of course there was no milk or eggs but they had almond milk in stock so I ordered almond milk because at least you can use it in baking. They also warned me that in the event that something went out of stock they'd just make a substitution so *who even knows*, see, it'll be totally like Christmas, where you give your Mom a wish list and maybe something you put on it shows up under the tree.

I did include a note saying to please, please, *please* make sure that we got either coffee or *something* with caffeine. If I have to drink Diet Mountain Dew for breakfast, I will. I mean, we had a two-liter of Coke and I've been rationing it out and it's going flat and I don't even care. Well, I do care. But I care more about the headaches I get when deprived of my morning caffeine fix.

Some of you were asking about Kat. She's hanging in there, and Leo has stayed healthy. Thanks for asking.

Someone also asked about the rabbits. So far I have not murdered any of the local wildlife, because maybe I'm slightly squeamish, and Dominic is definitely squeamish.

xxoo, Natalie

Rice Krispie Treats

So, here's what came in the box from the grocery store. In addition to a bunch of generally useful items like meat, oil, pancake mix, etc., we got:

12 cans of coconut milk

1 enormous can of off-brand vacuum-packed ground coffee

THANK YOU GOD

3 bags of miniature marshmallows

2 large cans of butter-flavored shortening

1 enormous pack of TP THANK YOU GOD. I am not
    going to tell you what we were substituting.

1 small pack of AA batteries

A sack of Hershey's Miniatures, you know, itty bitty candy
    bars like you give out on Halloween

14 little boxes of Jell-O gelatin

1 absolutely goliath-sized sack of knock-off Rice Krispie
    look-alikes

Most of this was not stuff we ordered. In a few cases, I could make a guess what the substitution was. I wanted flour, I got pancake mix. (That one's not bad.) I wanted chocolate chips, I got Hershey's Miniatures. (Again, not bad.) I ordered some grape juice concentrate because we've been out of anything fruit-like for days and days and although technically you can't get scurvy this quickly (I checked) I've been craving things like carrots and I thought maybe some fruit juice would help. I think the coconut milk was the substitute for the almond milk.

I have no idea why I got the Crispy Rice. I didn't ask for cereal. We still even have some cereal. But! They also gave us marshmallows and butter-flavored shortening (if not actual butter) so you know what it's time for, don't you? That's right. RICE KRISPIE TREATS.

I made these once when I was a kid without a microwave oven, and let me just tell you, they are a *lot* of *work* when you don't have a microwave oven. You have to stand over a stove, stirring marshmallows over low heat, for what felt like about two hours. They'll still give you stovetop directions but I highly recommend microwave cooking for these.

What you'll need:

3 tablespoons butter (or margarine or butter-flavored short
    ening. You can even use extra-virgin olive oil! But, I do not
    recommend using garlic-infused extra-virgin olive oil.)

1 10-oz bag of marshmallows (or 4 cups of mini marshmal-

lows or 1 jar of marshmallow fluff)

6 cups rice cereal (or corn flakes or Cheerios or whatever cereal you've got on hand but if you decide to use bran flakes or Grape Nuts I'm not responsible for the results.)

Put your butter and your marshmallows into a microwave-safe bowl. Heat on high for two minutes. Stir. Heat on high for another minute. Stir until smooth. Add the cereal. Stir until distributed.

Spray or oil a 13x9 inch pan and spread the marshmallow mixture out in the pan. Not surprisingly this is incredibly sticky and you'll want to use waxed paper folded over your hands, or a greased spatula, or possibly you could just butter your own hands but be careful not to burn yourself. Let it cool and then cut it into squares.

Dominic came in while I was spreading the stuff out in my pan and said, "What are you doing?"

I said, "I'm making Coq au Vin, asshole."

He said, "This is why I can't have nice things."

Maybe you had to be there.

For dinner tonight, we had minute steaks and Rice Krispie treats. *And there was great rejoicing.*

xxoo, Natalie

Katrina Jane, March 5, 1972 - February 20, 2018

I've got nothing today. I'm sorry.

My brother was coughing when he called to tell us the bad news, but said he wasn't sick, didn't have a fever, and definitely hadn't caught the flu from Kat.

Thanks for everyone's thoughts and prayers. I know I'm not the only person grieving here, so just know that I'm thinking of you, even as you're thinking of me.

You Still Have to Eat

Leo had Kat cremated but he's going to wait to have a memorial service until we can all come—including her kids. Monika was furious and insisted that she wants a proper funeral, and wants to go, and thinks it should be this week like funerals normally are, and of course that's just not possible. They can't actually stop us from having gatherings but there are no churches, no funeral homes, no nothing that's going to let you set up folding chairs and have a bunch of people sitting together and delivering eulogies.

We finally talked Monika down by holding our own memorial service, with as many of the trappings as we could possibly put together. We made floral arrangements by taking apart the floral wreath I had in the kitchen with dried lavender in it. We all dressed in black, even though that meant most of the kids had to borrow stuff out of my closet. Then we put out folding chairs in the living room and Dominic led us in a funeral service.

Monika had wanted to do a eulogy but she was crying too hard. She'd written it out, though, so Arie read it for her. I saved it, in case she wants to read it at the real memorial service. Well, maybe for her, this will always be the real memorial service. But there will be another one, a public one, when the epidemic is over.

In Minnesota after a funeral, there's usually lunch in a church basement and there's often this dish called ambrosia salad. (Maybe other states have this? I haven't been to very many funerals outside Minnesota.) I was missing some of the ingredients, but I did have lime Jell-O and mini-marshmallows and even a pack of frozen non-dairy topping, and I used canned mandarin oranges instead of the crushed pineapple, and mixed all together that worked pretty well. We had ambrosia salad and breakfast sausages for lunch. (I don't know why we got so many packs of breakfast sausages, but it's food, and everyone likes them, so we've been eating them almost every day, mostly not for breakfast.)

Monika asked if she could save her share of the ambrosia salad in the fridge until tomorrow, because she really likes it, and she didn't feel like eating, and didn't want anyone else to eat her share. (Which was a legitimate worry.) I put it in a container and wrote MONIKA'S, NO ONE ELSE TOUCH ON PAIN OF BEING FED TO THE RAT in S harpie on the lid. Which made her laugh, a little. I guess that's good.

Jo sat through the service and ate her lunch and didn't say a word. Mostly she looks like she doesn't really believe it.

Stone Soup

Arie informed me today that the thing I called "Miscellaneous Soup" is actually called "Stone Soup," after a folk story where three hungry strangers trick villagers into feeding them. In the story they announce that they're going to make soup for everyone out of a rock, and when curious villagers come to check out what they're doing, say that the soup would be better with a carrot or two . . . and an onion . . . and maybe some potatoes . . . and some beans . . . and one villager brings potatoes, and another one brings an onion, and in the end, there's a lovely pot of soup for everyone.

I started to point out that I wasn't tricking anybody, all this stuff was in my cabinet already, but then I realized that I didn't just have dinner but an *activity* and all the kids came into the kitchen and acted out the story with little Tom playing the hungry stranger trying to get everyone to chip in for the soup and then throwing each item into the pot.

Then they all made cookies, while I watched, using mayo for the eggs and dicing up mini candy bars for the chips.

It was a sunny day today—cold, but really sunny—and we spread out a picnic cloth and ate in the living room, Stone Soup and chocolate chip cookies and everyone went around in a circle and said the thing they were most looking forward to doing when this was over.

Monika said she wanted to be able to take an hour-long shower (everyone's limited to seven minutes or we run out of hot water). Dominic said he wanted to go to the library. I said I wanted to bake a chocolate soufflé. Everyone complained about that and said it couldn't be cooking or baking, so I said I wanted to go see a movie, in a theater, something funny, and eat popcorn.

Tomorrow is the first of March.

Hydration

Dominic is sick. It's not flu. I mean, it can't be; we haven't gone out. Literally the whole point of staying in like this has been to avoid exposure. It also can't be anything *else* you'd catch. We thought at first possibly it was food poisoning, but no one else is sick and we've all been eating the same food. According to Dr. Google, who admittedly is sort of a specialist in worst-case scenarios, it's either diverticulitis or appendicitis. Or a kidney stone.

Obviously, going in to a doctor's office is not on the table. We did a phone consultation. The guy we talked to said that yes, it could be any of those things and offered to call in a prescription for Augmentin if we could find a pharmacy that had it. The problem is, even though H5N1 is a virus and antibiotics won't do anything for it, there are a lot of people who didn't believe this and some of them had doctors willing to prescribe whatever they were asking for and the upshot is, all our pharmacies are out of almost everything. Oh, plus a bunch of pharmacies got robbed, though mostly that was for pain meds. Pharmacies are as much of a mess as anything else, is what I'm saying.

I'm not giving up, because in addition to the pharmacies that answered the phone and said they didn't have any, there were a ton where no one even picked up. I'm going to keep trying. In the meantime, we're keeping Dominic hydrated and hoping for the best. I always keep a couple of bottles of Pedialyte around, because the last thing you want to do when you're puking is drive to the store, and that book

SO MUCH COOKING

cooking

St. Paul Corner Drug

stuff's gross enough that no one's tried to get me to pop it open for dessert. So I've got it chilled and he's trying to drink sips.

If it's a kidney stone, Augmentin won't do anything, but eventually he'll pass the stone and recover, although it'll really suck in the meantime. (I wish we had some stronger pain medication than Tylenol. For real, *no one* has Vicodin right now. Not a single pharmacy.) If it's appendicitis, there's a 75% chance that the Augmentin will fix it. (This is new! Well, I mean, it's new information. There was a study on treating appendicitis with antibiotics and 75% of cases are a type of appendicitis that won't rupture and can be treated with antibiotics! And if you get a CT scan they can tell whether that's the kind you've got, but, well.) If it's diverticulitis, and he can keep down fluids, the antibiotics should help. If he's got the worse kind, and can't keep down fluids, they would normally hospitalize him for IV antibiotics and maybe do surgery. But again, not an option.

Oh, it could also be cancer. (Thanks, Dr. Google!) In which case there's no point worrying about it until the epidemic is over.

Cream of Augmentin

I got an e-mail from someone who has Augmentin they're willing to sell me. Or at least they say it's Augmentin. I guess I'd have to trust them, which is maybe a questionable decision. They want $1,000 for the bottle, cash only. Dominic was appalled that I'd even consider this. He thought it was a scam, and they were planning to just steal the cash.

Fortunately I also got through to a pharmacy that still had it, a little neighborhood place. Dominic's doctor called in the prescription, and I gave them my credit card number over the phone, and they actually delivered it. While I was on the phone with them they listed out some other things they have in stock and in addition to the Augmentin we got toothpaste and a big stack of last month's magazines. Shout out to St. Paul Corner Drug: we are going to get every prescription from you for the rest of our natural lives.

I was hoping that starting the Augmentin would make Dominic at least a little better right away, but instead he's getting worse.

Possibly this is just a reaction to the Augmentin. It's not as bad as some antibiotics, but it can definitely upset your stomach, which is pretty counterproductive when puking and stomach pain are your major symptoms.

I had appendicitis when I was a teenager. I spent a day throwing up, and when I got worse instead of better my mother took me to the emergency room. I wound up having surgery. Afterwards I was restricted to clear liquids for a while, just broth and Jell-O and tea, which I got really tired of before they let me back on solid food. My mother smuggled in homemade chicken stock for me in a Thermos— it was still a clear liquid, but at least it was the homemade kind, the healing kind.

If I could pull a live, clucking chicken out of my ass, like I joked about, I would wring its neck and turn it into stock right now for Dominic. Nothing's staying down, did I mention that? Nothing. But it's not like we have anything for him other than Pedialyte.

I'm going to try to catch a rabbit.

Rabbit Soup

You guys, you really can find instructions for just about anything online. Okay, I've never looked to see if there's a YouTube video on how to commit the perfect crime, but trapping an animal? Well, among other things, it turns out that the cartoon-style box-leaned-up-against-a-stick-with-bait-underneath is totally a thing you can actually do, but then you've got a live animal and if you're planning to eat it you'll still need to kill it. I wound up making a wire snare using instructions I found online in the hopes that the snare would do the dirty work for me. And it did. More or less. I'll spare you the details, other than to say, rabbits can scream.

You can also find instructions for gutting and skinning a rabbit online. I used my kitchen shears for some of this, and I worked outside so that Jo didn't have to watch. My back yard now looks like a murder scene, by the way, and my fingers were so cold by the end I couldn't feel them. I feel like I ought to use the fur for something but I don't think Home Taxidermy is the sort of craft that's going to keep the pack of pre-teens cheerfully occupied. (Right now they're reading through all the magazines we got from the pharmacy and I'm pretending not to notice that one of them is *Cosmo*.)

Back inside I browned the rabbit in the oven, since roasted chicken bones make for much tastier stock than just raw chicken, and then I covered it in just enough water to cover and simmered it for six hours. This would be better stock if I had an onion or some carrots or even some onion or carrot peelings, but we make do. The meat came off the bones, and I took out the meat and chopped it up and put it in the fridge for later, and I boiled the bones for a bit longer and then added a little bit of salt.

The secret to good stock, by the way, is to put in just enough water to cover the bones, and to cook it at a low temperature for a very long time. So there wasn't a whole lot of stock, in the end: just one big mug full.

The kids have been staying downstairs, trying to keep out of Dominic's way. Jo and Monika made dinner for the rest of us last night (rice and breakfast sausages) so I could take care of him. I saw Jo watching me while I carried up the mug of soup, though.

The bedroom doesn't smell very pleasant at the moment—sweat, vomit, and cucumber-scented cleaner from Target. It's too cold to open the windows, even just for a little while.

Dominic didn't want it. I'd been making him sip Pedialyte but mostly he was just throwing it up again, and he was dehydrated. I pulled up a stool and sat by the edge of his bed with a spoon and told him he had to have a spoonful. So he swallowed that, and I waited to see if it stayed down, or came back up. It stayed down.

Two minutes later I gave him another spoonful. That stayed down, too.

This is how you rehydrate a little kid, by the way: one teaspoonful every two minutes. It takes a long time to get a mug into someone if you're going a teaspoon at a time, but eventually the whole mug was gone. The Augmentin stayed down, too.

I went downstairs and set another snare in the back yard.

Something Decadent

So, thank you everyone who donated to Melissa's fundraiser. I put all the names in the hat and drew out Jessie from Boston, Massachusetts, and she says she doesn't want me to wait until everything is over, she wants a recipe now. And her request was, "Make something decadent. Whatever you've got that *can* be decadent." And Dominic is sufficiently recovered today that he can eat something decadent and not regret it horribly within ten minutes, so let's do this thing.

We still have no milk, no cream, no eggs. I used the frozen whipped topping for the ambrosia salad and the marshmallows for the rice krispie treats (which aren't exactly *decadent*, anyway).

But! Let's talk about coconut milk. If you open a can of coconut milk without shaking it up, you'll find this gloppy almost-solid stuff clinging to the sides of the can; that's coconut cream. You can chill it, and whip it, and it turns into something like whipped cream. We set aside the coconut cream from three of the cans and chilled it.

I had no baking cocoa, because we used it all up a while back on a not-terribly-successful attempt at making hot chocolate, but I *did* have some mini Hershey bars still, so I melted the dark chocolate ones and cooled it, and thinned that out with just a tiny bit of the reserved coconut milk. It wasn't a ton of chocolate, just so you know— it's been a bit of a fight to keep people from just scarfing that candy straight down. But we had a little.

Then I whipped the coconut cream until it was very thick and almost stiff, and then mixed in the dark chocolate and a little bit of extra sugar, and it turned into this coconut-chocolate mousse.

When eating decadent food, presentation counts for a *lot*. We used some beautiful china teacups that I got from my great-grandmother: I scooped coconut-chocolate mousse into eight of them, and then I took the last of the milk chocolate mini bars and grated them with a little hand grater to put chocolate shavings on top. We also had some sparkly purple sprinkles up with the cake decorations so I put just a tiny pinch of that onto each cup. And I opened one of the cans of mandarin oranges and each of the mousse cups got two little orange wedges.

And I tied a ribbon around the handles of each teacup.

And then we set the table with the tablecloth and the nice china and we ate our Stone Soup of the day by candlelight and then I brought out the mousse and everyone ate theirs and then licked out the cups.

Some days it's hard to imagine that this will ever be over, that we'll ever be able to get things back to normal at all. When everyone is sniping at each other it feels like you've always been trapped in the middle of a half-dozen bickering children and always will be. When you're in the midst of grief, it's hard to imagine spring ever coming.

But Dominic pulled through, and Leo didn't get sick. And tying the ribbons around the handles, I knew: this will all come to an end. We'll survive this, and everyone will go home. *I'm going to miss them*, I thought, this pack of other people's children I've crammed into my bungalow.

"Can I keep the ribbon?" Jo asked, when she was done with her mousse.

I told her, of course she could. And then she and Monika started arguing over whether she could have Monika's ribbon, too, because *of course they did*, and that was our day, I guess, in a nutshell.

xxoo, Natalie

ACKNOWLEDGEMENTS

Thanks to the Wyrdsmiths, past and present:

Eleanor Arnason
Kelly Barnhill
Rachel Gold
Bill Henry
Doug Hulick
Ralph Krantz
Harry LeBlanc
Kate Leith
Theo Lorenz
Kelly McCullough
Lyda Morehouse
Sean Michael Murphy
Rosalind Nelson
Adam Stemple

I joined the Wyrdsmiths writing group in 1997. For twenty years, I've met people at a coffee shop every two weeks (or so) to share story critiques, industry gossip, pep talks, and friendship. Every story in this collection was read by the Wyrdsmiths and rewritten based on their feedback before it was submitted anywhere. I would not be the writer I am without my fellow writers; I would not be the person I am without these friendships.

When I was feeling particularly dispirited about my writing career and chances of seeing publication again, Lyda suggested that I have her submit my short stories. Her faith in my stories kept me writing.

Thanks also to my patient editor, Patrick Swenson; my excellent agent, Martha Millard; and all the many editors who published these stories in their magazines. Finally, many many thanks to my husband, Ed Burke, and my daughters, Molly and Kiera Burke for their love and support.

PUBLICATION NOTES

ABOUT THE AUTHOR

Naomi Kritzer is a science fiction and fantasy writer living in St. Paul, Minnesota. Her 2015 short story "Cat Pictures Please" was a Locus Award and Hugo Award winner, and was nominated for a Nebula Award. Since 1999, Kritzer has published a number of short stories and several novels, including two trilogies.

OTHER TITLES FROM FAIRWOOD PRESS

CPSIA information can be obtained
at www.ICGtesting.com
Printed in the USA
LVOW03s2125270717
542404LV00002B/11/P